INTERFINITY

OTHER BOOKS BY BRYAN DAVIS

The Time Echoes Trilogy

Time Echoes
Interfinity
Fatal Convergence

The Reapers Trilogy

Reapers
Beyond the Gateway
Reaper Reborn

Dragons in our Midst

Raising Dragons
The Candlestone
Circles of Seven
Tears of a Dragon

Oracles of Fire

Eye of the Oracle
Enoch's Ghost
Last of the Nephilim
The Bones of Makaidos

Children of the Bard

Song of the Ovulum
From the Mouth of Elijah
The Seventh Door
Omega Dragon

Dragons of Starlight

Starlighter
Warrior
Diviner
Liberator

Tales of Starlight

Masters & Slayers
Third Starlighter
Exodus Rising

Standalone Books

I Know Why the Angels Dance
The Image of a Father
Spit & Polish for Husbands
Beelzebed

To learn more about Bryan's books, go to
www.daviscrossing.com

Facebook – facebook.com/BryanDavis.Fans

INTERFINITY

BOOK 2 OF
THE TIME ECHOES TRILOGY

BY BRYAN DAVIS

Copyright © 2017 by Bryan Davis

Published by Scrub Jay Journeys

P. O. Box 512

Middleton, TN 38052

www.scrubjayjourneys.com

email: info@scrubjayjourneys.com

Print ISBN: 978-1-946253-48-4

Epub ISBN: 978-1-946253-47-7

Mobi ISBN: 978-1-946253-46-0

First Printing – January 2017

Printed in the U.S.A.

Library of Congress Control Number: 2016918921

Cover Design by Rebekah Sather - selfpubbookcovers.com/ RLSather

Interfinity is a rewrite of *Eternity's Edge*, published in 2008.

CHAPTER ONE

MY GYM SHOES squeaked on the hospital hallway's sanitized tiles as I strode toward the sixth floor's waiting area. Anxiety tensed every muscle. I had to find my parents. Once mutilated and dead inside matching coffins, now they were alive. I had touched Dad's chain-bound arms through the cross-world mirror and felt his loving strength. I had heard Mom's voice and once again bathed in the majesty of her matchless violin.

Yet, the beautiful duet we had played at the funeral had once again become a solo. The portal collapsed, and there was no word from Earth Blue as to where my parents might be. After they disappeared from the bedroom where they had sought a way to return to Earth Red, no trace of them remained.

Mystery abounded. Who was that girl in red who kept appearing in the mirror to provide help in seemingly magical ways? Was she alive? I had only a photo showing Mictar carrying her limp body in a dark chamber. Patar had said she was in danger and that he'd try to help her, but that wasn't much to go on. Earlier in the evening, I had mentioned her to Dr. Gordon, but he had no clue about her identity.

When I reached the waiting area, I sat on a coffee-stained sofa and stared into the hall. I had to shake off these haunting thoughts. I mentally reentered Kelly's room and saw her lying on the bed, beaten and bruised from our ordeal, her shoulder lacerated and her eyes half blind. The words I said to her just moments ago returned. *We'll search for them together.* But how could she help? With all the dangers ahead, how could a blind, wounded girl help me find my parents?

A sharp, matronly voice cut in. "Ah, there you are."

I shot to my feet. Clara marched toward me, her heels clacking as she pushed back her windblown gray hair. Walking stride for stride next to her, Dr. Gordon stared at a phone, his face as grim as ever.

As they entered the waiting area, I nodded toward the hallway. "Tony's still with Kelly. Thought I'd let them have some daddy-daughter time."

While Dr. Gordon texted on his phone, Clara lowered her voice. "Dr. Gordon received a cryptic message from Simon Blue. Apparently something very unusual is happening on Earth Blue, and we're trying to get details."

"So that's our next destination."

"Yes. We have already alerted my counterpart on Earth Blue. She and Daryl Blue will be ready to pick you up at the observatory and take you to Kelly Blue's house."

"Good. That's the logical place to start looking for Mom and Dad."

"Are you going to break the news to Kelly?" Clara asked.

"I guess I'll have to, but convincing her she's in no shape to come won't be easy."

Dr. Gordon slid his phone into a pocket and spoke in his usual formal tone. "There are no further details available. We should get some rest and proceed to the observatory at dawn." He looked at his wristwatch. "Which is about six and a half hours from now."

"Okay," I said. "Let me talk to Kelly. I'll be right back."

As I walked down the hall, Jack came to mind. He had disappeared into the mirror riding on Mictar's back. What happened to him? Even if he escaped, he would be lost in a world not his own. Since Earth Yellow lagged behind Earth Red by about thirty years, he would feel like a time-traveling visitor from the past.

A man in scrubs caught up with and passed me, pushing a lab tray covered with glass bottles and tubes. With lanky pale arms protruding from short green sleeves, he kept his head down. He slowed in front of Kelly's door, but when it opened, he resumed his pace and turned into a side corridor, his head still low.

I could barely breathe. Was he Mictar? Why would he be so persistent in trying to get to Kelly? What value was she to him?

As I neared the room, Tony walked out. Bending his tall frame, he released the latch slowly and walked away on tiptoes. When he saw me, he jerked up and smiled, his booming voice contradicting his earlier attempts to be quiet. "Hey, what brings you back so soon?"

I kept my gaze on the side hallway. No sign of the technician. "Some news for Kelly. I have to head back to the scene of the crime."

Tony shook his head. "Better not go in right now. She fell asleep in mid-bite. And if she's too tired for pizza, she's too tired for company."

"No surprise. She's been going nonstop." I glanced between the door and the other hallway. "Okay if I sneak in and leave her a note?"

"Sure. Just don't wake her up."

"I'll be quiet." I reached for the knob and nodded toward the other hallway. "Mind checking something out for me? I saw someone suspicious head that way. A guy with pale arms wearing scrubs. It looked like he was going into Kelly's room, but when you opened the door to come out, he took off."

"Sounds suspicious." Tony crept toward the other hall, pointing. "That way?"

"Yeah. Just a few seconds ago."

"I'm on it." When he reached the corridor, he looked back, his muscular arms flexing. "Time to take out the trash."

I opened Kelly's door a crack, eased inside, and closed it. Walking slowly as my eyes adjusted to the dim room, lit only by city lights coming through the window on the far wall, I drew the bed's privacy curtain to the side and focused on Kelly resting on a pillow, her shoulder-length blonde hair splashed across the white linen. I stopped at her bedside, unable to draw my stare away from her wounded face.

Black scorch marks on her brow and cheeks and a thick bandage on her shoulder bore witness to her recent battle with Mictar. Her closed lids concealed injured eyes, maybe the worst of all her injuries, the result of Mictar's efforts to burn through to her brain and steal her life. Still, even in such a battle-torn condition, she was beautiful to behold, a true warrior wrapped in the sleeping shell of a petite, athletic young woman.

I searched her side table for a pen and paper. A portable radio next to a flower vase played soft music, a piano concerto—elegant, but unfamiliar. I spotted a pen and pad and pushed the radio out of the way, but it knocked against the vase, making a clinking noise. I cringed and swiveled toward Kelly.

Her chest heaved, and her hands clenched the side rails. She scanned the room with glassy eyes, panting as she cried out, "Who's there?"

I grasped her wrist. "It's just me. Nathan."

Her eyes locked on mine, wide and terrified. "Mictar is here!"

Making a shushing sound, I lowered the bed rail and pried her fingers loose. "You were just dreaming."

"No." She wagged her head hard. "I saw him. In the hospital."

"Do you know where?"

She turned her head slowly toward the door. As a shaft of light split the darkness, her voice lowered to a whisper. "He's here."

A shadowy form stretched into the room, its movement painstakingly deliberate. The intruder obviously didn't want anyone to hear him.

I grabbed the vase and dumped the flowers. Wielding it like a club, I crept toward the door, glancing between Kelly and the emerging figure. She yanked out her IV tube, swung her bare legs to the side of the bed, and dropped to the floor, blood dripping behind her.

The shadow, now fully in the room, halted. Kelly scooted to my side while tying her hospital gown in the back.

As the door swung shut, darkening the room, a low voice emanated from the black figure. "If it is a fight you seek, son of Solomon, I am more than capable of delivering it. In my current form, a glass vase will be a pitifully inadequate weapon. I suggest you give me what I want, and I will leave you in peace."

I tightened my grip on the vase. "Just get out, Mictar. It's two against one. It only took a violin upside your head to beat you before, and you couldn't even defeat Jack at the funeral."

"Alas! Poor Jack. He was a formidable foe. May he rest in peace." Mictar's tone lowered to a growl. "You can't take me by surprise this time. Your base use of that instrument proves that you have no respect for its power. And now you have neither a violin nor a Quattro mirror to provide a coward's escape."

I peered at Mictar's glowing eyes. The scarlet beacons seemed powerful and filled with malice. Yet, if he had as much power as he boasted, why hadn't he attacked? I set my feet and lifted the vase higher. "Why are you here?"

"To finish my meal. I have enough energy left to fight for what I want, but I would prefer not to expend it. If you turn the girl over to me freely, I will consume what I merely tasted at the funeral and be on my way. In exchange, I will leave you with two precious gifts. I will tell you how to find your parents, and I will relieve you of that handicapped little harlot."

I flinched. Kelly backed away a step.

"Ah, yes," Mictar continued as his dark shape slowly expanded. "That word is profane in your ears, yet I wager that it rings true in your mind. Kelly Clark is not the paragon of virtue your parents would want for your bride. She clings to you like a leech, because she is soiled by —"

"Shut up!" I shouted. "You don't know what you're talking about!"

The humanlike shadow swelled to twice its original size. "Oh, yes, I do. You want to know every lurid detail. She is your dark shadow, and you will never find your parents while you entertain a harlot at your side."

"No!" I slung the vase at Mictar. When it came within inches of his dark head, it stopped in midair. I tried to reach for Kelly, but my arm locked in place. My head wouldn't even swivel. Everything in the room had frozen, except for Mictar.

As his shadow continued to grow, his dark hands drew closer and closer. "I saved the last bit of my energy to perform one of my brother's favorite tricks, motor suspension of everything within my sight. Now I will take yours and the harlot's eyes, and I will need no more to fill Lucifer's engine."

My jaw locked, and my tongue cleaved to the roof of my mouth. A dark hand wrapped around my neck and clamped down, throttling my windpipe. Another hand draped my face. Sparks shot into my eyes, stinging them.

A knock sounded. The door opened, revealing Tony and a nurse.

Light flashed around Mictar's hand, but I still couldn't budge. Pain jolted my senses. My legs shook as if I had been lifted off the floor and rattled like a baby's toy.

The darkness flew away. Mictar's body, a black human form with no face or clothes, zoomed past the nurse and crashed against a wall. "Stay right there," Tony shouted, "or I'll introduce your face to another wall."

Like a streaking shadow, Mictar pounced on Tony, wrenched his arm behind him until it snapped, and slung him against the wall. Tony staggered, then slumped to the floor, dazed.

Mictar grabbed the nurse from behind. As she kicked and screamed, he laid a fingerless hand over her eyes and pressed down. Sparks flew. Mictar's body lightened to dark gray. Details traced across his pale face and bony hands. White hair materialized, slick and tied back in a ponytail.

I tried to lunge at him, but my feet wouldn't obey. I slid one ahead, then the other, too slow to do any good. Kelly hobbled toward the melee and helped Tony to his feet. While she cradled his broken arm, Mictar's body continued to clarify. The nurse sagged in his clutches, but he held on, light still pouring into his body from hers.

My muscles finally loosened. I stumbled ahead and rammed into Mictar, but, as if repelled by a force field, I bounced back and slammed against the floor. New jolts sizzled across my skin, painful, but short-lived. I looked up at his pulsing form, now complete and radiant.

Mictar dropped the nurse into a heap of limp arms and legs and kicked her body to the side. Tony picked up an IV stand and drew it back, ready to strike.

Tilting his head up, Mictar began singing. His voice, a brilliant tenor, grew in volume, crooning a single note that seemed to thicken the air.

Tony dropped the IV stand and fell to his knees. Kelly stumbled back and pressed her body against the wall. A vase exploded, sending sharp bits of glass flying. A long crack etched its way from one corner of the window to another.

Fighting the piercing agony, I rolled up to my knees and climbed to my feet, but the new shock stiffened my legs again, and the noise seemed to be cracking my bones in half. I could barely move.

Mictar took a breath and sang again. This time, he belted out what seemed to be a tune, but it carried no melody, just a hodgepodge of unrelated notes that further thickened the air. Red mist formed along the floor, an inch deep and swirling. As he sang on, the mist rose to my shins and churned like a cauldron of blood. With the door partially open, the dense mist poured out but not fast enough to keep the flood from rising.

A security guard shoved the door fully open. With a pistol drawn, he waded into the knee-high wall of red. Dr. Gordon and Clara followed, but when the sonic waves blasted across their bodies, the guard dropped his gun, and all three covered their ears.

The window shattered. Mist crawled up the wall and streamed through the jagged opening. Cracking sounds ripped through the air. The entire room seemed to spin in a slow rotation, like the beginning of a carousel ride.

"Nathan," Dr. Gordon shouted. "He's creating some kind of space-fabric vortex. The results could be disastrous."

The spin accelerated and drew me toward the window. "What can we do? I can't touch him."

Dr. Gordon staggered toward me, fighting the force, but he managed only two steps. "Neutralize his song!"

I leaned toward the center of the room but kept sliding away. "I don't have my violin!"

The outer wall collapsed. Fog rolled out and tumbled into the expanse six stories above the ground. The floor buckled and pitched, knocking us to our backs. While I fought to keep from being spun out of the room, the nurse's body slid across the tile and plunged over the edge with the river of red mist.

I grabbed the privacy curtain and held on. Mictar took a quick breath and continued singing. The bed's side table bumped against me. The pen fell, bounced off my shoulder, and disappeared in the fog. Holding the curtain with one hand, I looked up at the wobbling table where the radio still sat. With my free hand, I shook the supporting leg. When the radio fell, I caught it and turned the volume to maximum.

Now playing a Beethoven symphony, the radio blasted measure after measure of deep cellos and kettle drums. Trumpets blared. Cymbals crashed. Violins joined in and created a tsunami of music that swept through the room.

The mist swirled around Mictar. His song weakened. He coughed and gasped but managed to spew a string of obscenities before shouting, "You haven't seen the last of me, son of Solomon!"

The mist covered his head and continued to coil around him until he looked like a tightly wound scarlet cocoon. The room's spin slowed, and the cocoon seemed to absorb the momentum. Mictar transformed into a red tornado and shrank as if slurped into an invisible void.

Seconds later, he vanished, and the shaking ceased.

I turned off the radio and crawled up the sloping floor to where everyone else crouched. Dr. Gordon latched on to my wrist and hoisted me the rest of the way. His voice stayed calm and low. "Well done, Nathan."

Kelly threw her arms around me from one side, and Clara did the same from the other. "Don't ever leave me alone again," Kelly said, "not for a single minute."

Sirens wailed. An amplified voice barked from somewhere below, but I paid no attention to the words. I just pulled my friends closer. "Are you all right?"

Clara nodded. "My ears are ringing. Nothing painful."

"I'm fine," Kelly said. "But that poor nurse!"

Tony, sitting on his haunches in front of me, clenched a fist. "Now that's what I call taking out the trash!"

CHAPTER TWO

I SLID INTO THE backseat of Dr. Gordon's Town Car, collapsed my umbrella, and shook it before pulling it in and closing the door. "It's really pouring. Chicago on Earth Yellow must be having a monsoon."

"That would be my guess," Dr. Gordon said from the driver's seat. "I apologize for the lack of curb service. The police wouldn't let me drive under the portico."

"No wonder." I used my sleeve to clear the side window. From our perspective in the parking lot, the elephant-sized hole in the sixth floor made the hospital look like the victim of a missile attack.

"Did you get Kelly's new room number?" Clara asked from the front passenger's seat. She sat with a pencil poised over a notepad.

"Three fourteen. There's an armed guard at the door. And her father's staying. I hope they're enough."

Clara printed the number in neat block numerals. "How was she when you left?"

"Pretty upset. She didn't want to be alone. Like I said, her dad's there, but he's snoozing. After they put his arm in a cast and gave him some painkillers, he refused any more treatment and sacked out in her room."

Dr. Gordon started the engine and flipped on the windshield wipers. "Kelly is a valuable asset to our cause, but she would become a liability if she were to accompany you, and that's to say nothing about her crippled condition."

"He's right." Clara looked back at me. "Nathan, I know she's more to you than merely an asset, but we can't let her endanger her own life."

"Yeah. I know." My cheeks burned. I had to change the subject. "Did you bring Mom's violin?"

"Yes." Clara motioned toward the rear. "In the trunk. I have everything we need."

"Then we'll go." Dr. Gordon shifted the car into reverse and eased out of the parking space. Something slapped the trunk. Dr. Gordon slammed the brakes. "What was that?"

I spun in my seat. A girl hobbled to the door and pulled the handle, but the lock had engaged. I opened the door, revealing Kelly standing in the pouring rain, wearing her father's jacket over her hospital gown and clutching a small duffle bag.

"Slide over," she said.

I shifted to the other side. Kelly, soaked to the skin and her hair dripping, stepped in, plopped down on the seat, and slammed the door.

"Oh, my goodness!" Clara said. "Dear child!"

While I stared at Kelly's pain-streaked face, Dr. Gordon reached for the dashboard. "I will raise the temperature."

I swallowed past a lump in my throat. As Kelly hugged the wet jacket close, the deep furrow in her forehead told me I'd better stay quiet until she spoke her mind.

She let out a sigh and stared at me with her glazed-over eyes. "I told you never to leave me again, Nathan Shepherd, not for one minute."

I reached for her hand, now resting on the seat. She slid it away, but only a few inches. I reached farther and grasped her fingers. "I'm sorry. I didn't want you to get hurt any worse."

As Dr. Gordon drove out of the parking lot, Clara made a "tsk, tsk" sound and shook her head. "You poor, pitiful, hard-headed girl. I admire your spunk, but you can't simply waltz out of the hospital without telling anyone. At the very least, we will have to notify your father."

Her head drooping, she nodded. "I saw Mictar in my dreams again, and when I woke up, I was scared. I didn't want to bother Daddy, and Nathan was gone. I told the guard about my dream and asked him to check the other hallway. I assumed Daddy would be safer if I left, since Mictar's after me and not him, so I sneaked past the nurses. I knew no one would believe that Mictar was still around, so I had to find the only people who would." She looked at me, her wet eyebrows arching. "That is, I hope they still believe in me."

I opened my mouth to reply, but Dr. Gordon spoke up first. "My belief in you is actually enhanced by your tenacity. Virtue shines through our outer layers by means of our deeds."

"What he said." I grasped her hand. "I believe in you."

"Do you?" She gave me a hard stare for a moment before returning the grasp. "Look, Nathan, I know you're worried about me, but you said we'd do this together. If you really believed in me, you would keep your promises."

Her words stung. She was right. Dead right. And I deserved the rebuke. "I was wrong, Kelly. I'm sorry."

She blinked. "That's it? You're wrong and you're sorry?"

"Yeah. I'm not sure what else I can say."

"No, no. It's good. It's perfect. No excuses. I like it." Her frown melted into a smile. "I accept your apology."

I smiled in return. "Good. Thanks."

She rotated her shoulder, wincing. "My bandage is going to need changing. I brought some fresh ones in my bag."

Dr. Gordon nodded ahead. "My lodging is on the way. We can stop there."

After a few minutes of silent driving, we pulled into a Holiday Inn Express and parked under the motel's portico. Dr. Gordon held up a key card. "I suggest that Clara escort Kelly into my room to take care of her needs while Nathan and I stay here to go over our strategy."

Clara took the card and helped Kelly get out. A few seconds later, I sat alone in the backseat with Dr. Gordon staring at me from the front. I tried to relax, but my muscles tensed. The two dark eyes peering out from under two darker eyebrows made me feel like a diving eagle's next meal.

Dr. Gordon's stare eased, and he rested an arm on the top of the seat. "Daryl is staying with friends of mine outside of town. She will meet us at the observatory in order to assist me with the technological aspects, or, alternatively, she may accompany you on your journey to Earth Blue. Although Kelly's determination is admirable, and her interpretive skills are extremely important, her injuries are very real. I would never allow her to go unless her father approves and you are willing to shoulder the risk of taking on this extra burden. I heard your conversation with her, of course, but I wanted to give you the chance to speak your mind without her here."

Dr. Gordon's academic, gentle tone worked wonders on my nerves, as did his mention of Daryl. Her unique, movie-quoting humor was always able to break the tension. "Kelly's not a burden. I never wanted to go without her. Besides, won't Clara and Daryl Blue be there? They can help me with Kelly, too."

"Yes, of course. Daryl Blue is already waiting at the Earth Blue observatory to secure your arrival there, and Clara has the surviving camera and mirror piece. They also have Nathan Blue's mobile phone, which might come in handy."

I pulled out my phone and looked at the display. My old one sat at the bottom of the river in Chicago, and this new one's number wouldn't be activated on Earth Blue. Nathan Blue never had to experience that cold, dirty swim, so he kept his original phone.

I punched in Tony's number. "I'll see what Kelly's father has to say. I hope he doesn't mind me waking him up."

"I think not," Dr. Gordon said. "He would want to know where his daughter is."

The ringer sang out twice, then a roar blasted through the earpiece, the sound of a cheering crowd.

"Hello," Tony yelled over the racket. "What's up?"

"It's Nathan." I raised my voice to compete with the noise. "Kelly decided to leave the hospital early. Is that okay with you?"

"The leaves are hostile early? What are you talking about? Wait." As the roar grew deafening, Tony shouted, "Touchdown!" After a few seconds, the surrounding din silenced. "Say it again, buddy. I lowered the volume."

"You're watching a game on TV?"

"Yeah, I'm still in Kelly's room. She just called me a couple of minutes ago and told me she skipped out. Figured I'd watch the game while I'm gathering the stuff she left behind."

I took in a breath and let it out in one long sentence. "Kelly wants to go with me to Earth Blue to look for my parents, and I need her, because she's the music interpreter, and my parents might die if we don't work together to find them, so we're asking your permission to go, even though she hurt her shoulder and her eyes aren't working right, but since Clara is taking care of her, she should be fine, and I'll take good care of her, too, I promise."

I inhaled again and held it while waiting for Tony's reply. He'd say no at first, of course, but maybe he could be persuaded to—

"Yeah," Tony said. "That's fine. Just be careful."

I caught Dr. Gordon's inquisitive stare. "So it's okay?"

"That's what I said. She's a tough girl. Comes from good stock. Just let me know when you get back."

"Okay. Sure. We'll let you know." I slid the phone back into my pocket. "That was easy. He said it was fine."

"Very well. Now we can rest while we wait." Dr. Gordon withdrew his own phone and tapped on the screen. "I contacted Dr. Simon about what Mictar did at the hospital. We believe his destructive voice is a newly acquired ability. Otherwise he probably would have used it at the funeral."

"Could there be a connection between his singing and the girl in red?"

"Are you asking because Mictar employed the ability shortly after capturing the girl?"

"Right. Music opens the portals, and now Mictar seems to be able to sing one open. The girl in red might be the connection."

"A logical deduction. We'll have to explore it further." Dr. Gordon reached for the car stereo. "In the meantime, speaking of music, I have a CD in my player that you might find interesting—Haydn's String Quartet Opus Seventy-seven in G Major—performed by my own group."

"You play an instrument?"

"Viola. You are not the only accomplished musician in this car."

"Cool." I settled back again. "Let's hear it."

I closed my eyes and listened to the quartet, a highly skilled group, but the amateurish recording made them sound a bit distant. Still, it was a great rendition, enhanced by a lively style that the piece required.

Before it was over, the opening of the car door interrupted my reverie. Kelly hopped in, her hair clean and brushed and her clothes dry. She sported fresh blue jeans, blue Nikes, and a gray Newton High School sweatshirt. A thick white bandage protruded at the neckline and made a lump on her shoulder.

Kelly touched the cardinal logo on the front of her sweatshirt. "I thought a red bird would be good for traveling to Earth Blue, sort of like a passport saying where I'm from."

"Good idea. Maybe I should find something red." I touched my phone pocket. "I called your father a few minutes ago. He said you could go to Earth Blue."

"Must have been right after I called him. He said no at first, but I talked him into it."

"Great." I looked past her. "Where's Clara?"

"She's getting something for me at the coffee shop. I barfed the pizza Daddy brought yesterday, and I left before dinner came today. I'm famished."

When Clara arrived with a steaming cup of soup and reboarded the car, we headed for the observatory, an hour-long drive into a rural zone northwest of Chicago. After Kelly drank the soup, she leaned against my shoulder and closed her eyes.

While watching the countryside, I imagined the scene ahead — Interfinity Labs, the company that built the cross-world travel platforms. Since Gordon Blue was in jail, and his henchmen were either dead or no longer in the picture, the observatories in both worlds would probably be safe. The two Daryls had changed all the security codes, so only Gordon Red, and whomever else we trusted, could get in. Still, Mictar posed the most obvious threat. Who could tell when he might show up again?

Dr. Gordon parked next to the observatory's main door. I retrieved the violin case from the trunk, and the four of us entered the building, passed the security door

with the help of an updated code, and stopped at the hall's
elevator alcove. Since only two people could fit into the
car, Kelly and I rode up to the telescope level first. When
the doors opened, Daryl jumped from the computer desk
near the edge of the enormous domed room. "Well, if it
isn't beauty and the beast."

Laying a hand on Kelly's back, I guided her out to
the dimly lit tiled floor. "I guess those labels fit," I said.

Daryl jogged toward us, passing through the
shadow of the huge telescope that stood on a pedestal at
the center of the floor. Her red hair still bouncing when
she stopped, she spread out her arms, and a wide grin
stretched her freckled face. "But which one is the beast?"

"That would be me," Kelly said, raising her hand.
"I feel pretty beastly."

Daryl gave Kelly a gentle hug, then peeled back
her sweatshirt at the shoulder, cringing as the blood-
tinged bandage came into view. "Forget the beast. Are you
auditioning for a zombie movie?"

Kelly shrugged. "If they need a victim, I'm their
girl. I feel like I have a bull's-eye painted on my forehead."

"Not good, Kelly-kins, not good at all." Daryl's
grin contracted, giving her an uncharacteristically serious
aspect. "I was searching for signals on the radio telescope."
She nodded toward the computer desk. "And I picked up
some weird stuff."

Kelly pulled her sweatshirt back in place. "Define
weird. After what we've been through, I might not ever call
anything weird again."

Daryl spun and headed back to her station. "C'mon
and have a look."

I took Kelly's hand and walked with her to the desk where Daryl was already tapping at the keyboard. "With all the wounds in the cosmic fabric," Daryl said, "it's pretty easy to grab some inter-world traffic. I found one stream in particular that's really strong, and it has cadence and structure, sort of like a language. While the other signals kind of come and go, this one stays steady."

"Can you translate it and show it on the screen?" I asked.

Daryl looked up at the curved mirror that acted as the observatory's ceiling. "Not without the music, and Francesca's not here to decode it for us."

"Go ahead and put it on the speakers." I set the violin case down and popped the latches open. "Maybe Kelly and I can pick it out."

As Daryl slid her finger up a laptop's touchpad, random musical notes poured from unseen speakers. The mirrored ceiling flashed to life, displaying hundreds of irregular shapes—some red, some blue, some yellow—many with swirls of blended colors. They bounced against each other, excited globules beating in time with the noise.

The elevator door opened again, and Clara's booming voice interrupted my concentration. "I am his tutor, the executrix of his father's will, and the trustee of his estate." She stepped into the room and marched toward the desk. "I will make that decision, thank you very much."

Dr. Gordon trailed her, his face stern, apparently not intimidated by Clara's forceful ways. "You have no idea how dangerous travel is now," he said, holding his phone like a weapon. "We cannot ignore Dr. Simon's warnings."

She spun and pointed at the phone's display. "I am not going to rely on a message that has come quite literally out of the blue. Can you verify the message's sender or its accuracy?"

"No." Dr. Gordon thrust the phone into his pocket. "But it is a reasonable conclusion. I am familiar enough with Dr. Simon's normal communications to identify one of his messages."

I shook my head, unable to concentrate. The static coming from the verbal combatants was stronger than the static from the skies. "What's going on?"

Dr. Gordon straightened and focused on me. "I received a message from Dr. Simon. He says that recent cross-world activity has weakened the cosmic structure to the point that all transport is now extremely hazardous. There are holes within the holes, what we call embedded wounds. You could think you are going one place and end up in another, or, worse yet, fall into a timeless vortex."

"A vortex?" I repeated.

"Yes. It is only a theory, but data suggests the existence of places that are not physically within any of the three worlds. The signals match nothing else I have seen, and echoes I receive from the pulses I send have an intelligent cadence but lack consistency in a time framework. The only conclusion I can draw is that the inhabitants have enough intellect to recognize they are being called by an outside entity, yet their answers are inconsistent."

"Put it in English, please," Kelly said. "We're not all geniuses like Daryl."

Dr. Gordon spread out his hands. "The beings dwell in an environment that appears to be outside of normal reality. Accidentally traveling there is possible and potentially deadly."

"So," I said, "you don't want us to risk it. You want to cancel our trip."

"There is no sense in endangering your lives. As far as we know, your parents are now free. I have great confidence that your father will be able to devise a solution to the Interfinity collapse or signal us if he needs our help."

"Speaking of signals ..." I nodded toward the ceiling. "Daryl picked up something. We're trying to decipher it."

Dr. Gordon looked up at the dome and studied the display for a moment. "Interesting. Please continue."

I concentrated again on the random notes, glancing at Kelly from time to time. She closed her eyes, while Daryl, Clara, and Dr. Gordon looked on.

The noise eased for a few seconds, then started again, beginning a series of pulses that sounded familiar. What could be embedded in all that turmoil? How did Francesca figure it out when she listened to these impossibly mixed-up sounds? And if she and I were both gifted, shouldn't I be able to duplicate what she could do at the age of ten?

I pictured the young prodigy playing her violin in the midst of a shower of chaotic noise. Her eyes began to glow, reminding me of the shining light that seemed to emanate from her matchless spirit. Obviously listening with physical ears wasn't enough. I had to probe with invisible receptors, antennae of heart and mind that would piece together the scattered sounds.

Closing my eyes, I imagined a glowing musical staff floating in the middle of a black void, blank except for

the lines and clef mark. In my mind, I stood in front of the
sheet with my violin poised to play. As each note popped
into my ear, my image played it. A black spider flew from
my strings and formed itself into a musical quarter note
that landed on the middle of the staff and positioned itself
on the proper line.

A second note created another spider that flew
toward the page, transformed into an eighth note, and
stuck to the staff on the second line near the end. Spider
after spider glided to the page, and whenever they landed
near one another, they shot out black webbing that tied
them together until they created a perfectly arranged
musical piece.

I copied my imaginary stance and played the notes
on the visionary staff. After the first measure, the sounds
from the speakers seemed to arrange themselves, as if
the cosmos played the sheet I had created in my mind. I
opened my eyes and played along, copying each note I
heard.

Daryl pointed at me and whispered into Kelly's ear.
Kelly shushed her, while Clara gazed at the ceiling and Dr.
Gordon studied the computer screen.

Above, the colors blended and stretched into a
recognizable scene. A man and a woman sat in the midst
of darkness that held neither moon nor stars. Even their
resting place was nothing more than a shapeless black
lump.

After a few seconds, their faces clarified somewhat,
but they were still too fuzzy to recognize. I dug deep and
reached for the passion the composer intended. Every
stroke of my bow brought the couple more clearly into
focus. Soon I recognized Mom and Dad, but I said nothing.

I had to keep my concentration and hold this vision of the other world as long as I could.

On the dome's screen, Mom played a violin while Dad paced, staying within a short range, as if blocked by invisible walls on each side. With his hand to his chin, he seemed to be deep in thought.

Soon, Mom's violin music became audible, one of her own pieces, a soothing tune to which she had also composed lyrics, a ballad about a long-lost son who found his way home after many years of toil and torture at the hands of a wicked king in a faraway land.

Dad stopped and raised a finger. He spoke, but his words failed to come through. Mom lowered her violin and replied, but she, too, seemed like an actor in a silent movie. After a few seconds of conversation, she rose from her seat, and the two embraced. Then, tears flowing, she waved as he walked away. As if treading on thin ice, he stepped gingerly and disappeared from view. Mom reseated herself and raised her violin, ready to play again.

My arms weakened. How long could I go on? And why did this effort drain my energy so quickly? Would continuing do any good? I had already given it all I had, but I couldn't hear a word they said.

I sidestepped toward the center of the chamber. There really was only one option. Knowing I couldn't speak and play at the same time, I tried to signal Kelly with my eyes. But would she see me with her foggy vision? Had she been able to watch the scene in the mirror above? Maybe not, but she had perception beyond physical vision, so maybe she would know what to do.

"Get ready to flash the lights," Kelly said as she hurried to my side. "We're taking off."

Daryl jumped up and dashed to the switches. "On your signal."

"No!" Dr. Gordon raised a hand. "The data stream suggests exactly what I described. This is likely a view within a vortex. It's too dangerous."

Now breathing rapidly, I played with all my might. Of course I wanted to be with my parents, but falling into a vortex along the way would end our journey forever. Yet, this might be our only chance to find them. Didn't we have to try?

Kelly held the violin case in one hand and set her other hand on my back. "Clara, it's your call. What do you say?"

Clara stood next to Dr. Gordon, who typed madly at the keyboard. "Are you both willing to take the risk?" she asked.

"I am." Kelly compressed my shoulder. "You?"

I gave a quick nod and played on.

Clara pointed at Daryl. "Send them."

"No!" Dr. Gordon yelled, red-faced and still typing. "This is not your observatory, nor your equipment! I will not allow you to die on my watch!"

Daryl flipped the switch. The perimeter lights flashed on.

Dr. Gordon hit a final key with a commanding stroke. A chaotic array of colors splashed across the ceiling mirror, and the music shifted to Dvořák's *New World Symphony*.

White beams shot out from the trumpet-shaped lamps and collected at the apex of the dome. Dozens of shafts of light rebounded toward the floor and surrounded Kelly and me with a glowing picket-fence-like barrier.

The scene in the mirrored ceiling reshaped into a reflection of the observatory room floor that showed Clara and Daryl, but not Dr. Gordon, Kelly, or me. The image melted and slid down the picket fence's vertical shafts until everything outside of our laser cage vanished.

Within a few seconds, our surroundings reappeared—the same floor, the same telescope, though tilted at a different angle, and the same Clara and Daryl. Or were they the same?

I slowed my playing. My arms feeling like rags, I lowered the violin and let my shoulders droop. "We're on Earth Blue, aren't we?"

Daryl sashayed toward us, flipping her hair back in mock offense. "Don't act so disappointed."

I sat on the floor and buried my face in my hands. "We were close."

A voice drifted down from above. "No, you were not close."

I looked at the ceiling. Dr. Gordon, appearing upside-down in the reflection and standing near the telescope in the Earth Red observatory, stared down at me. "The signal emanating through the cosmic wound dissipated just as I was switching you over to Earth Blue. You and Kelly would have been thrown into a vacuum where you would have died instantly."

"He's right." Daryl Blue stooped and looked me in the eye. "I watched the whole thing from my computer. You and Kelly would be sparkling space dust by now, and I don't think anyone would name a star after you."

Above, Dr. Gordon walked toward the desk, shaking his head.

Daryl extended a hand. "Looks like you could use a lift."

"In more ways than one." I grasped her hand and rode her pull to my feet.

Kelly raised the violin case. "Want to pack up?"

While I put the violin away, Daryl Blue hugged Kelly, then pulled back. "Take a look, Kelly-kins," she said, tugging on her collar. "My shirt is blue, through and through. Daryl Red and I decided to be color coded."

"I can see that." Kelly squinted. "Barely."

"Oh, yeah. Forgot about your run-in with the evil eye snatcher."

"Daryl!" Clara Blue marched up behind her, wagging a finger. "Kelly's vision is not a joking matter."

"Don't worry about it, Clara," Kelly said. "I've put up with Daryl Red for years. One time I bloodied my nose while playing basketball, and she took a picture, posted it online, and asked our classmates to come up with captions. She's not exactly Miss Compassionate."

Daryl Blue laughed. "You have to admit some of the captions were hilarious, like *Most Likely to Bleed*."

Kelly frowned. "That's as funny as a toothache."

"So you had the same captions on Earth Blue and Earth Red?" I asked.

"Looks that way," Daryl Blue said. "I guess humor is universal."

Kelly huffed. "Universally corny."

While Daryl and Kelly walked toward the computer desk, Clara handed me a six-inch-by-six-inch square mirror, now protected by a rubberized frame. "Here's the Quattro mirror. I know you're disappointed about the strange turn of events, but can you get up enough gumption to go to Tony Blue's house?"

I took the mirror and gave her a nod. I had to get over my funk.

Daryl's voice piped up again, this time from the Earth Red observatory above. "We'll watch the fort from here. Keep Nathan Blue's cell phone on so we can text you if necessary."

"Oh, yeah." I leaned toward the desk and scanned its surface. "Where is it?"

Daryl Blue held up the phone and a Nikon on a strap. "Got you covered. Let's get moving."

CHAPTER THREE

CLARA BLUE DROVE Tony Blue's Camry off the
interstate ramp and into Newton, Iowa. A cold,
steady drizzle dampened the road, just enough to slicken
the pavement and make the tires swish.

As we passed by the local Walmart, an old man
with a cane hobbled toward a beat-up station wagon, one
of the few cars in the parking lot. A scarf wrapped his
neck, and gloves covered his hands, but his shivering body
proved that his winter garb was insufficient.

I shivered as well. The heater barely pumped
enough warm air to melt ice, forcing me to rub my hands
together in front of the vent to keep them from stiffening.
Since I might have to play the violin soon, I had to stay
limber.

In the backseat behind Clara, Kelly leaned against
the door, her eyes closed and her mouth partially open.
She hadn't uttered a word the entire trip, sleeping through
some of Daryl's effervescent stories about their antics in
elementary school.

As we passed between two browning cornfields
on the final road leading to Kelly's Earth Blue home, I
scanned the area for movement, watching for any sign of
Mictar. Sleet pellets mixed with the spattering raindrops

in the midst of thickening fog. No one in his right mind would be out, but this was Mictar we were talking about. He didn't qualify for the sanity club.

When we stopped in the driveway, I pulled the mirror from the glove box. "Everyone stay here while I check it out."

"Not on your life," Clara said as she whipped off her seat belt. "Safety in numbers."

Daryl leaned forward. "Yeah, Nathan. This house has ambush written all over it."

"I'll be careful. If everything checks out, I'll give the all-clear signal. No use risking anyone else's life."

"I'm going." Kelly yawned and shook her head as if casting off a fog. "You're stuck with me until this is over. Besides, you might need an interpreter."

"Okay. Just you." I looked at Clara. "If something happens and we don't come back, go to the observatory. If we're alive, we'll try to contact you there somehow."

Clara set her finger on the trunk release button. "Do you want your mother's violin?"

"Not yet." Still holding the mirror, I grabbed an umbrella from the floorboard, got out, and opened the umbrella over Kelly's head as she exited the car. Together we splashed through the driveway's puddles, puffing clouds of white on our way to the front door.

I turned the knob and pushed. Locked. Kelly dug into her jeans and withdrew a key ring. She chose a short silver key from a collection of four and unlocked the deadbolt.

After opening the door, I took a few skulking steps into the spacious foyer, which was not much warmer than outside. Obviously the furnace was off.

I flipped the light switch, but the room stayed dim, illuminated only by inadequate daylight coming from a nearby picture window behind a dusty grand piano. We had seen sagging power lines weighed down by ice. That explained the lack of electricity and the nearly empty roads along the way.

The bizarre October weather had probably frozen people's hearts in fear. It seemed that everyone had chosen to hibernate for a while, hoping they would wake up and find everything back to normal. But that wouldn't happen, at least not until we solved the Interfinity problem. *Normal* would have to wait.

I tucked the mirror under my arm and, with Kelly following, sneaked along the dim hallway, taking one slow step at a time. Something felt wrong—not just the chill, but a sense of danger that seemed to increase with every step.

Ahead on the right lay my bedroom, yet, not really mine. It had belonged to my Earth Blue twin, a victim of Mictar's fiery hand. I tried to shake away the memory of Nathan Blue's face and burned-out eye sockets, but the macabre images stayed put.

I shuddered. Since the celestial wounds were probably huge in this house, Mictar could easily be lurking nearby, our eyes his targets.

As I continued my furtive march, noise from outside faded. Kelly's rapid breaths became the only sound in the hallway. She clutched the back of my sweatshirt with a trembling hand that sent another shiver across my skin. Apparently she also felt the strange sensation, the stillness that portends a brewing storm.

"Are you going to try the Quattro mirror?" she whispered.

"In a second." When we came within a step of the bedroom, I stopped and reached the mirror across the doorway, angling it to see inside. So many times before, this mirror had provided a way to escape danger, either by showing a threat in advance or creating a scenario that saved us, but since the girl in red was probably unavailable, it might just be a normal mirror now.

The mirror reflected a thin white mist swirling at the center of the room, a slowly twisting eddy that stretched from the floor to near the ceiling. It looked like a skinny, stationary tornado, yet slower and less volatile. As it spun, tiny pinpoints of light pulsed on its perimeter, glowing and fading, as if powered by the misty turbine.

I eased toward the opening. Dr. Simon had said that something unusual was going on here, and a swirl of mist hovering over the floor wasn't exactly normal, but with all we had been through, it seemed no more than another oddity in a long string of oddities. Still, Mictar had disappeared in a spinning mist of red. Could this be something similar, a visible manifestation of one of the cosmic wounds?

Tucking the mirror again, I stepped into the room. The usual big mirror covered the opposite wall, reflecting my worried face and dampened, wind-tousled hair. This matrix of smaller mirror squares matched the one that had been in my Earth Red bedroom, including the empty space in the lower left-hand corner.

A queen-size poster bed abutted the wall opposite the mirror, its mattress torn by a long gash and its inner stuffing scattered across the carpet. The old trunk, the mysterious wooden box that had once hidden treasures in its impenetrable casing, sat against the wall — closed, as usual.

A frigid breeze blew in through the open window, flapping the drapes and blowing a clump of mattress padding over a toppled desk and lamp. Yet, the gusts seemed to have no effect on the funnel. It continued spinning unabated.

"Someone ransacked the room," I whispered.

Kelly tugged on my shirt. "Let's go in farther. I can't see much from here."

"Stay put till I shut off the draft." I crossed the room and closed the window. Two deep scratches marred the painted sash. Could Patar have dug these ruts with his pointed nails? Or Mictar?

I tried to twist the window lock into place, but the brass piece slipped and fell to the carpet, obviously already broken before I touched it. "Closed but not locked."

Kelly took a step in and blinked, the Nikon camera dangling over her sweatshirt's cardinal logo. "Something's moving."

I edged closer to the swirl but stayed a step away. "It's like a little dust devil made out of fog, and it has tiny sparks around it, like miniature fireflies. Seems harmless, but I'm not taking any chances."

"Better get Daryl in here. She can send a photo back to Earth Red and get Dr. Gordon's opinion."

"Good thought." I looked out the window at the Camry. Barely visible through the icy glass, Clara flexed her fingers in front of the air vents.

I pulled Nathan Blue's phone from my pocket and punched in Clara's number.

She raised the phone to her ear. "Yes, Nathan?"

"All clear so far. Can you send Daryl in? We need her to transmit a photo. You might as well stay out there. It's freezing in here."

"Will do. Be careful."

"Always." I terminated the call and pushed the phone back to my pocket. At the car, Daryl leaped out and hustled toward the front porch. While blowing fog whipped her hair, she puffed short bursts of white into the wind and rubbed her hands up and down her arms.

I turned back to Kelly. "She's on her way."

A door slammed. Light footsteps padded their way down the hall, then Daryl's smiling face appeared at the door. Her brow scrunched low. "What a mess. Either someone had the worst nightmare in history, or the mattress vomited."

Kelly grimaced. "Thanks for the lovely imagery."

"No problem." Daryl shuffled in and pointed at the swirl. "What's this all about?"

I shrugged. "No idea. Can you send a photo? Get Gordon's take?"

"Sure thing." Daryl lifted her phone, pointed it at the funnel, and took the shot. While her thumbs flew across the touch screen, she chattered rapid-fire. "I got a message from Daryl Red. She says Gordon Red got another message from Simon Blue. They finished analyzing the Earth Red Nikon. It has a Quattro lens, and when you pointed it at a Quattro mirror and took a flash picture, you did a *Ghost Busters* no-no."

I rolled my eyes. Daryl had dropped a cryptic movie reference on us again. "Okay. I give. What's a *Ghost Busters* no-no?"

Wearing a satisfied grin, Daryl acted out her explanation, using her phone as a gun as she rattled off her words. "Egon told Peter not to cross the energy streams with their ghost-capturing guns or all life as they knew it would end. It was sort of the same thing the two Gordons did when they sent a flash through their observatory mirrors at each other. It created a ginormous space-time hole that allowed Mictar and Patar to sneak out of who-knows-where and show up in our worlds."

When Daryl took a breath, I held up a hand. "Give me a minute to think." I studied the swirl. Was this some kind of cosmic hole? Could it be the path my parents took to that black vortex I had seen earlier? If so, how long would it last?

As Kelly drew closer, she kicked aside a pile of mattress padding. Something clinked near her feet. "What was that?"

I stooped and picked up a short piece of heavy chain with a broken manacle at the end. Where the band was broken, the metal seemed malformed, as if it had been melted. "Dad's chains came off. Maybe a blowtorch?"

Kelly touched one of the links. "I doubt it. I've watched my father use his torch. It would've broiled your dad's wrists."

I dropped the chain and peeked under the bed. A violin case lay on the carpet next to more of the mattress padding. I slid the case out and snapped it open. Inside lay Nathan Blue's violin. I smashed my world's version of this instrument against Mictar's face in the performance hall's prop room just a few days ago. Fortunately, this violin never suffered that fate.

Kelly took the Quattro mirror. "Let's see if we can get a cross-world view." She slid open the frame's fastener, pulled the glass free, and set the square near the wall mirror's empty space. It jumped from her fingers and snapped into place. A burst of energy swept across the reflection like a rippling wave of light, ending at the upper corner with a quiet pop.

Daryl's jaw dropped open. "Coolness!"

While staring at my reflection, I lifted the violin and bow. What should I play this time? Interfinity's mirrored observatory ceiling needed specific melodies to create portals, but this Quattro-enhanced mirror had responded to almost any kind of music. Yet, without the girl in red, maybe its power was gone, or at least crippled.

After tuning the violin, I pressed the bow against the strings. With the ridiculous weather outside, a Christmas song seemed appropriate, so I played Mendelssohn's tune for "Hark! The Herald Angels Sing."

Kelly closed her eyes. Her brow furrowed, accentuating the gash across her forehead the mirror's edge had gouged during our recent plunge toward the Mississippi River.

I tried to read her expression. Was she hearing words? Since she was the music interpreter, maybe she was getting another message that would help us.

As I continued the melody, the swirl in the reflection expanded. The tiny lights on the funnel's perimeter brightened, pulsing like miniature strobes. The misty edges drew closer to our reflected images. Although the real swirl stayed small, Daryl and I backed away from it, giving our mirror images some space between them and the mysterious funnel.

Her eyes still glassy, Kelly stared again at the mirror. Moving her feet in time with the music, she inched toward the reflection, lifted her hand, and eased her palm close to the glass. "There's something inside the mist."

I focused on the mirrored swirl —nothing but fog and lights, thicker and brighter than in reality, but no other differences.

Daryl touched the outer edge of the real funnel. "I don't see anything."

"It's a human figure." Kelly drew a picture in the air with her finger. "Like a ghost. Shapeless. Floating with the spin."

"Do you hear any words?" Daryl asked.

Kelly nodded. "A female voice. Singing. The words fit Nathan's music perfectly."

"Then belt it out, sister. What are you waiting for?"

"I'll try." Kelly cleared her throat and sang, weakly at first, but her strength grew as the verse poured out.

Called to courage, called to rescue,
Called to join the precious few;

Given strength to rise from earth,
Reach for light and give it birth.

Plucked from earth and rising sunward,
Plunge within and journey onward,

Never fear the cries of men,
Rise above their mortal ken.

Take the reigns of freedom's light;
Help the weak escape the night.

Kelly let out a long breath. "Now she's repeating the last phrases."

"Is the song familiar, Nathan?" Daryl asked. "Something your mother might sing?"

Unable to say much while playing, I replied with, "Not familiar, but it could be."

"Maybe we should try to go there," Kelly said. "We'll need a flash of light."

The funnel in the mirror expanded toward our images. With electricity out and no time to hunt for a battery-operated light, the only option we had was the flash on the camera from Earth Blue, but that would be, as Daryl had said, crossing the streams. And what about Dr. Gordon's warnings about cross-world travel? Did they apply here?

While Kelly kept her gaze locked on the mirror, Daryl turned to me. "So, Amadeus, what's the verdict?"

"Just wait," I said, lifting the bow to answer. "Maybe the mirror will tell us what to do."

Daryl backed away from the reflection and spoke in elongated sing-song. "We've got company."

In the mirror, the room's window slid open, forced upward by a hand with sharp fingernails. A white-haired man climbed through. Tall and lanky, he was dressed in black boots, loose trousers made out of some kind of shimmering white fabric with royal blue stripes running up each leg, and a darker blue shirt, silky, with three-quarter-length sleeves and a V-neck that revealed a snowy plume of chest hair.

I caught a glimpse of the back of his head. No ponytail. Unless Mictar had cut his off, this had to be Patar.

The newcomer approached the foreground of the mirror, though he was absent from the bedroom itself. Our three reflected images froze in place, staring at the now stationary funnel of mist.

I looked at the real Kelly and Daryl. They, too, stood petrified, their arms and legs stiff and their expressions locked as if time had stopped.

Patar set his hands on his hips. A frown dressed his face with scorn. "What are you doing here, son of Solomon?"

I spread out my hands. "I'm looking for my parents. What am I supposed to do?"

"Are you so dull of senses? You saw for yourself how your father was trying to help your mother play the great violin. Have you forgotten?"

I took a hard step toward the mirror. "Spit it out, Patar. Cut the questions and just tell it to me straight."

Patar's eyes flamed red, but his voice stayed calm. "I tell it straight, as you say, to those with enough wisdom to understand the mysteries of the cosmos. You, child that you are, must learn wisdom as you proceed through the maze of unknowns. Otherwise, you would never be able to choose the right path when no one with wisdom is there to guide you."

I let out an exasperated sigh. "Okay. So, I'm a child. Just give me something to go on."

"Very well." Patar's brow lifted. "Finding your parents is an act that most would declare noble, but it is the selfish vision of an unlearned boy."

"Selfish?" I slapped the mirror with a palm. "They're trapped in some kind of black vortex. Releasing them from their prison isn't selfish."

Patar thrust out his hands. As if blown by a hurricane gust, I staggered back and fell to my bottom.

He held up two fingers and roared. "Two humans! Only two! You search the universe for the ones you think you love, while the lives of more than fifteen billion others hang in the balance! You try to save two homo sapiens who give you comfort and status, while billions of souls you care nothing about teeter on the brink of destruction." He pointed a rigid finger at me. "That, young traveler, is selfish."

I scrambled to my feet and matched Patar's pointing finger with one of my own. "If you'd get off your high horse and tell me what to do, I wouldn't be searching for two needles in a galaxy-sized haystack. My father probably knows how to save the universe, so tell me where to find him so he and I can do it together."

A wry smile crossed Patar's face. "Your father is in no position to help, and even if you found him, you would become as incapacitated as he is. Just carry out what he began. Play the violin, and all will be made right." He backed away and set his hand near the misty funnel, still frozen within the reflection. "Use the camera. It will cut through to a place you have never been, the realm that houses Sarah's Womb. There you will find the violin, the healing instrument that I placed there for one who is gifted enough to play it. Once you find it, follow the wisdom you gain each step along the way."

"Sarah's Womb? What's that?"

"Allow words and places to define themselves, son of Solomon. All in good time."

When Patar touched the funnel, it jumped back into motion and spun as before. He vaporized, and his own misty form joined the slowly turning cyclone.

Kelly shook her head, blinking. "Did something weird just happen? I had a big-time déjà vu."

"Yeah," I said, "super weird." I nodded at the camera hanging at her chest. "Go ahead and use it. It'll be all right."

"Who was the creepy cotton-top character?" Daryl asked. "He disappeared."

"Patar. Don't worry about him. He's my problem."

The Nathan in the mirror packed the violin in its case while Kelly's reflected image lifted the camera to her eye and aimed it at the trio in the real bedroom.

"Uh-oh," Daryl said. "Your twins are way ahead of us."

I shoved the violin into its case. "It's showing what we're supposed to do. Let's just follow along."

As the real Kelly lifted the camera, turned on the flash, and pointed the lens at her duplicate, the funnel in the mirror enfolded our reflections in its cyclonic swirl.

I pulled the three of us into a huddle. "Now, Kelly."

She pushed the shutter button. The camera flashed. A jagged bolt of light bounced off the mirror, but it bent away from Kelly and knifed into the swirl. The lights on the perimeter brightened and absorbed the energy. As the vortex expanded toward us, I draped one arm around Kelly while my other hand clutched the violin. Daryl latched on to my elbow and squeezed until it hurt.

Within seconds, thick fog and sparkling lights drifted across our field of vision. A floating sensation—weightlessness, or maybe air pushing us upward—gave me an awkward, unbalanced feeling. Kelly and Daryl stayed quiet, their eyes wide and their bodies stiff.

Soon, the mist slowed and evaporated as if burned away by the sun. Yet, there was no sun. When the fog disappeared, only darkness met our eyes—complete, utter darkness.

I pressed my toes down. Whatever we were standing on seemed firm, but without even a hint of light, could we go anywhere?

Music filled the air, sweet and gentle. Was it a voice? The wind? It resembled no instrument I had ever heard. It was more like a thousand instruments blending their tones into a sound so perfectly balanced, they seemed to play as one.

I breathed a sigh. Such richness! Such clarity! I could listen for hours and still beg for more.

The sound of Daryl's wheezing breaths broke through the music. "You two sure know how to travel. That made the bus in *Speed* look like a kiddie ride!"

"Yeah, but the bus station needs better lighting. I can't see a thing."

"You can't?" Kelly said. "I see fine. Better than ever."

Two bright spots pierced the darkness—Kelly's eyes, shining in the midst of a black canopy. The glow spilled across her face and illuminated her cheeks and forehead.

"Check it out," Daryl said, laughing. "Kelly's got headlights."

Kelly blinked several times, casting our new world into blackness with each stroke of her eyelids. "Does this mean I have to lead you two around like a guide dog?"

"I guess so," I said. "At least for now."

"What does this place look like?" Daryl asked.

Kelly's radiant eyes drifted back and forth. "We're standing on an elevated walkway made out of something transparent, maybe glass. I can see through it, but nothing's holding it up, at least nothing I can see."

I ran my foot along the surface, smooth and slick. "What's down below, and how far?"

"Just a blanket of colorful mist moving parallel to the walkway underneath and on both sides, kind of slow, slower than a walking pace. Some swirls are caught up in the flow, like whirlpools of fog, sort of like that thing in your bedroom."

"Where does the walkway go?"

Kelly blinked, darkening her eyes for a moment. "Hard to tell. It's like we're out in the middle of a catwalk over a foggy swamp. We can go either way, but we'd just walk into a thick fog bank."

"Do you see any good reason to stay where we are?"

Her eyes swayed back and forth. "Nothing but rainbow-colored fog up, down, and all around."

I reached toward her. "Give me your sleeve, and we'll make a train."

"Here you go."

Her sleeve pushed into my palm. As soon as I tightened my grip on it, a tug pulled the back of my sweatshirt. "I'll be the caboose," Daryl said. "Lead the way, Kelly-kins."

"But which direction?" Again, Kelly's eyes moved from side to side. "There are two ways to walk."

"You said the mist is moving," Daryl said. "Let's just go with the flow."

I tucked the violin case against my side. "I'm ready."

Kelly turned her head forward, blocking the twin lights from view. The sleeve pulled. I hung on and shuffled my feet as I followed.

Daryl's body warmth and gentle breaths gave away her presence close behind. She whispered, "It feels like we should chant, 'Lions and tigers and bears, oh my.'"

"If you do," I said, "you're going over the side."

"That's a horse of a different color. No chanting."

"As I walk toward the fog bank," Kelly said, "it seems to pull farther away, but it doesn't expose anything except more walkway."

I tugged on her sleeve. "Maybe we should—"

"Wait." Kelly halted. "I hear something. Voices."

I held my breath. Daryl's breaths also fell to a barely perceptible buzz. Still, the ever-present symphony in the air played on, more beautiful than ever.

"The voices are coming from those swirls I told you about." Her sleeve jerked out of my hand. "Wait here," she said, her voice fading. "Don't move a muscle."

I set my feet. "Don't worry. We won't."

After a few seconds, Daryl grasped my hand and whispered, "Can you see her eyes?"

I scanned the darkness. "No sign of them."

Our surroundings felt heavy, as if the darkness weighed down my shoulders and seeped into my mind. Yet, the beautiful sounds eased any fear that tried to bubble up. This was a place of stark contrasts—a symphony of angels in the midst of a black void.

After almost a full minute, Daryl's hand began to tremble. "Okay, Captain Cool, I'm losing *my* cool. Say something to make me feel better."

"Well … this sure beats falling into a bottomless pit?"

"Wrong answer. Try again."

"How about—"

"I'm coming." Kelly's voice pierced the dark curtain. Seconds later, her bright eyes appeared. A strong tug pulled my hand. "I think I figured something out. Come on."

I followed, shuffling my feet more rapidly than my nerves would have allowed. Daryl stayed close, her breaths faster and heavier. As we walked, the music grew in volume, and the blended instruments broke into distinct tones.

When Kelly finally slowed down, she patted my hand. "We're walking alongside one of the swirls. I hear voices coming out of the top, like a bunch of people talking at the same time."

I tried to penetrate the blackness with my vision, but it was no use. "What are they saying?"

"It's too jumbled to tell. I just pick up some of the louder words." Kelly tightened her grip on my hand. "But get this. The swirls have different colors—some red, some blue, and some yellow. They kind of pop up out of rivers of color, like the colors are heading somewhere, and something boils from underneath, and words spew from the swirls."

Daryl released my shirt. "The three earths?"

Kelly stopped, and her bright eyes bobbed. "That's my guess."

A new sound merged into the musical air. A feminine voice? An alto? Maybe. But it was too perfect, too precise to be human. Yet, something was missing. The voice was like a question without an answer, an expression of love unrequited. It needed accompaniment, and maybe I could provide it and we could get some answers about this place.

I set the violin case down and fumbled with the fasteners until they snapped open. When I raised the violin and bow, I looked into Kelly's radiant eyes. "I'm going to try something."

Listening carefully to the simple aria, I waited for a phrase to end. Then, brushing my bow lightly across the strings, I answered in the same key, C Major, but altered the notes, composing an appropriate counterpoint on the fly.

Then we played together—a mesmerizing blend of melody and harmony that filled the air with a flowery scent. Roses, maybe? As I inhaled, something coated my throat and the back of my tongue with a sweet flavor, yet with a bitter aftertaste, like vanilla with a bite.

"Nathan," Kelly said, "what's happening?"

I opened my eyes. A stream of lively sparks flowed from my violin and through the darkness, eating away the black field and leaving light in its wake. When the stream swept past my ear, the music increased in volume, then faded again as the sparks painted the canopy with an ever-expanding brush of radiance.

When every spot of blackness had vanished, I lowered the violin. The surrounding fog retreated, as if blown by the musical breeze. We stood on a transparent walkway about two strides in width. A clear empty sky spanned the area over us, and rivers of multicolored mist flowed on each side of our path. The glassy trail extended into emptiness in both directions—a long walk into a wall of fog.

Kelly's eyes, as clear as crystals, twinkled like two drops of starlight. "You can see now, can't you?"

I nodded but said nothing. This new realm seemed to beg for silence, if only to allow for hearing that blessed voice again.

Daryl stuffed her hands into her sweatshirt's front pocket and inched toward the edge of the walkway, her knees shaking as she peered into the mist. Wide-eyed and mouth agape, she also seemed uncharacteristically mute.

Far in the distance, a solitary figure walked toward us. With his eyes focused on a book, he seemed to be in no hurry and unaware of our presence. Either that, or he simply didn't care.

Still feeling the need to stay quiet, I silently repacked the violin, left it on the walkway, and stepped between the man and the girls. As the man continued his approach, the material in his loose-fitting trousers swished together, the same blue-trimmed pants Patar had worn in the mirror. Muscles in his forearms, extending from his flowing navy blue shirt, flexed as he turned a page, and tufts of white hair blew across his forehead, staying just out of his eyes. His clean-shaven face seemed without wrinkle or blemish, a youthful contrast to his hoary head, and his pale complexion gave him a ghostly pallor, raising memories of Mictar and Patar, though this man was obviously neither of them.

I cleared my throat. The man looked up. His sparkling eyes widened as he slowed to a halt and scanned us. With white eyebrows lifting and mouth slowly opening, he seemed ready to speak, but he just kept staring. His expression gave away only surprise, no hint of pleasure or anger.

I took a step forward. Feeling a need to honor the sanctity of this place, I kept my voice low. "I'm Nathan Shepherd."

The man took in a deep breath and, scanning us one by one, began to sing, yet, not with words but with vowel sounds, long and short forms as well as diphthongs that rose and fell with the changing notes.

Kelly tapped my elbow. "He says, 'Greetings, young humans from the misty mire. It has been a long time since our land has been graced by the presence of new arrivals.'"

CHAPTER FOUR

THE MAN PAUSED his song, as if realizing Kelly was interpreting and needed him to slow down. After another moment, he continued at a more deliberate pace, and Kelly resumed.

"As you have likely been told by whoever sent for you, this is the land above the worlds. I am Tsayad, one of the guardians — the chosen priests who watch over this realm. Since your interpreter is here, I assume that you are ready to tell me what your purpose is."

He pressed his thumb into his book, marking his page, and gave us a gentle smile. His snowy eyebrows arched as though he expected a reply.

I looked at Kelly, then at Daryl. Daryl gave me an "I have no idea" kind of expression, while Kelly glanced between me and the camera dangling at her chest.

I squinted at her. What was she signaling? Was she asking if she should take a picture of this guy? I gave her a firm shake of my head. This was no time to guess what that camera might do.

Turning back to Tsayad, I opened my mouth to speak, then closed it. Should I try to talk? Everything about this place seemed geared toward communicating with music. The violin might work.

Keeping an eye on Tsayad, I stooped, pulled out the violin, and gave the empty case to Daryl. As I lifted the bow over the strings, Tsayad drew close, excited expectation in his eyes.

I paused. What should I play? Classical? Baroque? Modern? I shook my head. No, none of those seemed right. Would any piece created by someone else really work to communicate my thoughts? Wouldn't the music have to be something new, something I composed based on the passions and moods running within me?

Taking a deep breath, I concentrated on my thoughts and set my composing spirit in line with my emotions. Then, leading with a long A note and moving into a series of arpeggios, I recalled our story and poured out my feelings—anguish over my parents, fear during the flight from Dr. Gordon of Earth Blue, joy over finding a friend like Kelly—into a musical score. As I played, the story flowed from my hands more freely and fully than words could ever express. It seemed as though speech should always be this way — expressive, pure, pulsing with life.

When I finally reached the end, I let my arms dangle limply, exhausted by the effort.

Tsayad stared at me, his mouth agape. Ever so slowly, the white-haired man's lips spread out again into a wide smile. He clapped his hands twice, intertwining his fingers after the second clap. Then, swiveling toward Kelly, he sang again, this time in rapid bursts.

Kelly interpreted. "I am pleased to see that you are a virtuoso with my master's chosen instrument. This bodes well for your qualifications to help us. And I am saddened over your losses, but I cannot help you find your loved ones."

He raised one hand to his chin while the other held the book at his thigh with the pages facing out, his thumb still marking his place. I peeked at the black marks within—a complex musical score, too far away to read.

After a few more seconds, Tsayad's eyes flashed with light. He sang once more, this time with even greater enthusiasm.

Kelly's voice spiked with energy, as if echoing the man's emotion. "We should prepare you immediately. With the crisis brewing in the triad, it is fitting that the travelers sent you to us."

When he stopped singing again, he turned and gestured for us to follow, his smile warm and inviting.

I glanced at Kelly and Daryl in turn. "Any clue what he's talking about?"

Both girls shook their heads. "I guess we should follow," Kelly said. "No choice, right?"

"Right." I gave the man a nod, hoping that it would act as a universal signal of approval. He nodded in return, opened his book, and marched along the path, singing once again.

I followed with Kelly and Daryl close behind. Kelly whispered the song's meaning, her words barely audible as our shoes squeaked on the glassy path.

> To conquer wisdom's doom,
> We lift the holy tower
> With darkness fed by gloom
> Absorbed by torment's power.

I grimaced. So dark and dismal. And this man's voice certainly wasn't the one that had filled my mind with beauty so rich I could smell it in the air. Even the tune seemed warped, dissonant, twisted.

As we continued, the fog bank enveloped us, leaving only Tsayad's bare outline visible in front. The vapor muffled his song and Kelly's translation, yet not enough to make them inaudible.

> Travailing songs they raise
> In desperation's throes.
> Their sacrifice we praise
> In cantabile prose.

> O let the worlds below,
> Forever locked in dread,
> Send anguished cries of woe,
> Our sustenance, our bread.

A sense of cold filtered through the air. Every verse sounded more and more ominous, matching the foreboding gloom that weighed me down with each step into the thickening mist. Yet, what could we do but follow? I had no idea how to go home.

After another minute, Tsayad ended his song. A more textured walking surface silenced our shoes, leaving our uneasy breathing as the only discernible sounds. Kelly clutched my elbow from behind but said nothing. She didn't have to speak. Her fears came through her trembling fingers loud and clear.

After another minute or so, the mist thinned, allowing a vague white light to shine through from above. The path widened, the walkway now a terrazzo floor with sparkling flecks of copper and silver blended into polished stones.

When we finally broke into a clearing, I blinked at the brighter light. The floor had become a vast circle of glittering gemstones. Curved walls bordered the circle, sloping up to an apex that arched high overhead. Thousands of glass squares covered the surface, creating a huge dome of polished crystal.

About a hundred feet away, a group of perhaps twelve people dressed in garb similar to Tsayad's huddled around a glass dome, the apex of which rose a foot or so higher than their heads. Their bodies blocked whatever they were looking at within the dome.

At three locations on the surrounding wall, separated by equal distances, an image of an enormous rotating earth floated on the transparent mosaic—one with thin red mist swirling around it, another with blue mist, and the third with yellow. The mist that poured in from the walkway crept along the base of the boundary wall, making a surrounding river. When the multicolored stream passed one of the earth images, the mist of that earth's color crawled upward on the wall and joined the foggy portrait, as if feeding the planet's misty veil.

A loud crack sounded from one of the earth images. Tsayad spun toward it. A jagged line crawled along the wall. It stretched from the earth veiled in red toward the one in blue and struck its surface with a sizzling splash. Mist followed the crack from each side—red from one and blue from the other—and met in the middle, mixing together and turning purple. The purple mist bled into the crooked trail back toward each earth and began to spread slowly over the planets.

I scanned the rest of the wall. Other lines carved jagged paths between the earths, some arching over the ceiling to reach their targets. Orange, green, and purple mist traversed the crooked highways and created islands of blended colors that spread slowly across the respective earths.

Tsayad sang a few quick vowels toward the center of the circular floor, where the group of people stood.

Kelly whispered the translation. "Another breach. Widen it while it is fresh."

The twelve joined hands and sang toward the dome in their midst, a tune that carried a sharp cadence and a blend of tones — male and female; tenors, basses, sopranos, and altos; lovely, yet harsh; hypnotic, yet troubling.

Kelly's grip tightened. "Nathan, that song creeps me out."

I turned toward her. "What are they saying?"

"Awful things." Kelly let out a shushing sound and nodded ahead.

When I swung back around, Tsayad stood only a couple of feet away, reaching out a hand as he began a new song.

"Come and see," Kelly translated. "You are at the threshold of the altar where your abilities will be tested."

Tsayad strode toward the center of the room at a quicker pace. I glanced back at Kelly. "Maybe you'd better stay here."

She again tightened her grip on my elbow. "Not on your life. I'm not leaving you for a minute."

"Me neither," Daryl said. "This place makes *The Village* look friendly."

I gave them a nod and followed Tsayad, closing the gap as we neared the strange gathering. When he came within several paces of the group, he sang a short burst of vowels that sounded more like an "ahem" than words.

The group turned toward us. The seven men and five women, all with short white hair, flashed eerie smiles. Three of them shifted to the right, leaving a gap that provided a view of the glass dome. As they parted, they revealed the rest of the chamber's central area. Two other domes abutted this one, making a triangle of domes, each with white-haired people gazing into it.

I took a step toward the closest dome. Resembling the top half of a transparent sphere, the glass edges had been anchored to the floor with foot-long clasps and fist-sized bolts. Inside the dim chamber, a girl no more than fifteen years old sat at the center, shivering. Her head tucked between her knees, she pulled at the hem of her red dress, trying unsuccessfully to cover her legs.

Kelly whispered, "Nathan, is that her? The girl in the mirror?"

"I think so." My heart pounding, I crept closer to the dome. She looked so pitiful, so frightened. Why had Mictar put her in there?

The girl raised her head and swiped at her shoulder, as if swatting a bug away. Her face stretched into a terrified mask. She slid on her bottom toward the outer wall, pumping her legs furiously. When she reached the glass, she pressed a hand against her chest and panted while swinging her head back and forth as if searching for something on the floor.

Closing her eyes, the girl raised her head and moved her lips, apparently in song, but as I leaned toward her to listen, the men and women raised their hands and sang a warbling phrase that drowned out her voice.

Their song jolted my senses. This was nothing like the heavenly aria I heard when I first arrived. It was an operatic train wreck. Every note clashed with the others, battling to see which one could most effectively sabotage the choir. Still, it seemed that the individual singers hit each note perfectly, like twelve master artists painting a different portrait on the same canvas.

As the singing continued, clouds of black mist rose to the top of the room and disappeared into a purplish haze above, as if there were a chimney drawing out and dispersing the blended music.

A cracking sound returned. The purple breach stretching from the red planet to the blue widened. As the song continued, the girl inside the dome shook. Still singing, she wrapped her arms around herself, but she seemed unable to quell her shivers.

I rushed to the dome and laid my palms on the glass. "She's terrified! Let her out of there!" I looked at the other domes. They also enclosed human figures, but the interiors were too dim to discern any details.

I again gazed at the girl in red behind the crystal wall. Her features were all too clear — tear-streaked face, frazzled braids of red hair, and wringing hands. Her terror shook me to the bone. Then, she looked straight at me. With her eyes wide again, she mouthed two silent words. *Help me.*

Something grabbed my sweatshirt and slung me backwards. Holding the violin aloft, I fell on my side and slid across the polished floor. I jumped to my feet and whirled toward the dome. Tsayad scowled at me and sang a string of vowel sounds that resembled a strident scolding.

Kelly ran to my side. "He says it is forbidden to aid the supplicants. They must become accustomed to their new station so that we can monitor their activities without interference."

As Daryl backed toward us, she stretched out her words in singsong. "I think we should be going now."

I searched for an escape route. Two white-haired men guarded the sides of the narrow doorway we had entered.

Tsayad walked slowly toward us and extended a hand, his song now gentle and coaxing.

Kelly pressed close to me. "He says, 'Your fear is most exhilarating. Come, and we will prepare you for your station.'"

I swung the violin to my chin and played a frenzied series of dissonant notes. When I stopped, the guardian's scowl returned, only deeper and perplexed.

Leaning next to my ear, Kelly whispered, "Uh-oh."

"What?" I asked. "What did I say?"

Daryl hugged the violin case close to her chest. "I think you cursed in the language of the lyrically limited."

Kelly pulled me backwards. "You told him to release the supplicants or else."

"Or else, what?"

"You didn't say."

Tsayad stalked toward me. As he stretched out his arms, his eyes seemed to burst into flames.

A loud, shrieking note pierced the air. Tsayad halted and pivoted toward the source. From the gathering around the dome, a white-haired woman rushed toward us, shouting in a melodic trill.

Kelly translated. "Allow me to dispose of these dissemblers."

When the woman arrived, she pulled my sweatshirt's neckline down, exposing my chest, and sang two quick notes.

"You see?" Kelly echoed.

The woman released me and scowled. As she sang a mocking phrase, she seemed to laugh.

Kelly shuddered. "The grinding stone is too good for them."

Tsayad's eyes lit up again as he sang a note.

"The abyss?" Kelly said, giving words to his response.

The woman replied with a single low note. Kelly didn't bother to translate. Apparently the abyss would be our next stop.

"Take this," I said, pushing the violin into Kelly's hands. "You and Daryl get ready to run."

The woman snapped her fingers. The two men at the door marched toward us, each brandishing a transparent rod, like a policeman's nightstick made out of glass.

"Go!" I rushed toward the guards, dropped low, and swept a leg under one of them, toppling him to the ground. The other guard lunged. His glass rod pulsed with light and spewed a shrill noise that pierced my skull. I covered my ears to keep my brain from exploding.

With a quick roll, I dodged the guard, but just as I tried to jump to my feet, a burning pain stabbed my back. My limbs stiffened. My teeth clenched. A bone-rattling jolt surged up and down my spine and shot out to my fingers and toes. I tried to gasp for breath, but my lungs felt like stones.

Darkness seeped across my vision. Streams of black bled through a scene of Kelly and Daryl being led toward me by the white-haired woman. Then everything went dark. I sensed odors, pressure on my skin, and harsh ringing in my ears.

Strong arms lifted me into the air. Finally able to breathe without pain, I floated comfortably. The familiar feeling of approaching sleep crept in. I tried to shake it away. I had to get down and escape with Kelly and Daryl, but my limbs wouldn't respond. They hung limply, unable to move.

Something prodded my shoulder.

"Wake up, Nathan."

I opened my eyes. My vision returned, still dim, but clear enough to see my surroundings. Sitting next to me, the girl in the dome smoothed her skirt of crimson cloth over her crossed legs. "Are you hurt?" she asked.

From a supine position, I stretched my arms and propped myself on my elbows to get a better look at her. Her eyes, wide and worn by tears, reflected weariness, though the furrows in her brow expressed compassion. "No, I think I'm okay." I looked around at the dome. The inner glass reflected our bodies, shielding our view of the outside.

"You are okay now, my beloved." She laid a hand on my arm. Her face, though as youthful as her petite body, radiated wisdom far beyond her years. "But if you do not awaken soon, you will not be okay. Your rescuer will need your aid."

"Awaken? What do you mean?"

"You are dreaming, and you need to arouse yourself so that you may help your friends."

I sat up. "Dreaming? But this is so real."

With thin fingers, she twirled a tiny white button at the front of her dress that fastened a high neckline. "I am real, and this prison is real, but you are not really here. I saw what they did to you. Since we made eye contact, I was able to enter your dream as soon as you lost consciousness."

I scanned the mirrored walls. "How could you see me?"

"I am Scarlet. I see many things." She looked up at the low ceiling. "Behold, the tragedy of lost lives."

In the curved mirror, an airliner flying at a ninety-degree angle dropped slowly from the sky. The tip of its wing scraped the ground, sending it into a cartwheel tumble. Then it flipped, smashed into a field, and exploded in a huge fireball.

As memory of the searing heat raised prickles along my skin, I shuddered. "I was on that plane. At least for a while. I got off just in time."

She folded her hands and sighed. "I know. I helped you escape."

"I saw you in the mirror waving at me. I thought you might be trying to help." I shrugged. "I wasn't sure how you could, so I just trusted you."

"Trust is essential. I provided help whenever you had the faith to ask. I, in turn, took your supplications to your ultimate helper. My songs are the prayers you were unable to utter. The answers came in many ways—a gunman arrested on a bridge; your body shifted to another world as a bullet threatened to pierce your chest while your clothes miraculously changed into a hunter's raiment; you and your friends transported out of a falling car while at another time the entire car went with you; and any number of escapes in the midst of chases, unknown paths, and even violent winds. Such are the miracles of answered supplications."

I stared at her while my mind's eye took me on those impossible adventures again. "But how does it work? How can you know what's going on all the time?"

Scarlet slid closer and gazed into my eyes. "It is not wise to waste precious moments explaining the complexities of my ministration while you are dreaming. Soon after you awaken, you will not remember the details, only images — images of me, my prison, my sorrow. Just remember that you must come back and rescue us, the three imprisoned seers. You have only a little time. Interfinity is coming, and the guardians here care nothing for the life of any human."

"What will happen to the humans if Interfinity comes?"

"We call it Convergence, a tragedy of enormous magnitude beyond any that has ever occurred in history."

"Convergence? What kind of Convergence?"

"A fatal one." Her expression hardened. "Just stop Interfinity, Nathan, and you will prevent Convergence. Nothing else matters."

I tensed. Just stop Interfinity? She said it as if I could snap my fingers and make it happen. And her mood shift was troubling, frightening. I felt like we were in a narrow train tunnel with Interfinity barreling at us like a runaway locomotive. How could we escape, much less stop an unstoppable force? "Uh ... sure, Scarlet. I'll do my best."

"That is all I can ask, and you will have help." She took my hand and caressed my knuckles. "You, my love, are one of the gifted, and another is searching for you in her dreams. Perhaps we can guide her to a convenient place to meet you. If it is possible to heal the wounds through music rather than through sacrifice, the two of you will have to work together and play the violin in Sarah's Womb. On this possibility rests the future of all the supplicants."

"Patar mentioned Sarah's Womb. What—"

She pressed a finger to my lips. "No, Nathan. Save your questions." As she lifted her finger, her whispered voice took on a sense of urgency. "Arouse yourself now or you will perish, and the hope of the earth triad will perish with you. One truth you must remember as you make this journey—the stalkers feed on fear and the dissonance fear creates. If you run from the shadows that haunt your mind, all will be lost."

"But how will I remember all these things? Like you said, dreams just kind of fade away."

"I will do what I can to revive your memory." As she kissed me on the cheek, her lips trembled. "Someday I hope to anoint your cheek in person, but for now a dream will have to do."

Her vibrating voice tickled my skin, and the fragrance of roses washed in. This seemed far too real to be a dream, yet I had no choice but to believe her. Since she said I had to wake up, I needed to start trying.

Closing my eyes, I refocused my mind on reality and strained my senses to tune into my surroundings.

After a few seconds, Kelly's voice drizzled into my ears. "He's twitching."

Something poked me in the side. "Nathan, wake up."

I blinked. Scarlet and the domed prison had vanished, leaving only fog and the worried faces of Kelly and Daryl.

Kelly grasped my hand. "Can you get up?"

I surveyed my body. The pain returned, a hundred aches stabbing me from head to toe. I pulled her hand and rose, teetering for a moment while Kelly and Daryl kept me from falling.

Colored mist swirled on the glassy path at my feet. A musical note, friendly but firm, made me turn my head. The white-haired woman stood behind us. A serious aspect bent her face downward as she glanced nervously both ways along the path.

Kelly held the camera to keep it from swaying at her chest. "She says we have to hurry. She's on our side."

"Our side?"

"Yes, she —"

The woman sang again, rushing through her notes. Kelly translated with a rapid chatter. "My name is Abodah. If you are truly the healer, I have much to do."

I reached for the violin and bow tucked at Kelly's side. "I need to ask some questions, like, what is this place? How do I get to the violin in Sarah's Womb? When can I come back and rescue those three prisoners?"

The woman laid a hand on my arm. She sang again, this time more slowly.

"There is no need to play music to ask your questions," Kelly translated. "My mate and I have learned to understand your language, though I cannot speak it. He knows the ways of your people, so I suggest that you heed his counsel as he leads you to the places you must go. While you are gone, I will work with the suppliants to ensure that you have a clear path to the instrument, but if playing the healing music fails, rescuing them could well be impossible. Yet, I will see what I can do. Let us have no more questions. It is time for you to go."

Abodah knelt on the walkway and dipped her hands into the mist. Then, cupping a cloud of all three colors, she straightened and held out her hands. A stream of red mist drifted toward Kelly, while a blue one rose and floated Daryl's way. Finally, a second red stream lifted from her hands and caressed my cheek. Soon, all three streams evaporated, leaving only yellow mist in Abodah's cupped palms.

With a quizzical look in her eyes, she sang a brief tune.

"You are not from the same worlds," Kelly said. "To which one shall I send you?"

I laid a hand against my pounding head. Earth Blue seemed the obvious choice. That's where Clara was waiting for us. "Earth Blue. Is that all right?"

Abodah sang once more, and Kelly interpreted. "That is the easiest option. I will send you through the door by which you entered."

Abodah reached into the mist and scooped out a handful of blue vapor. Then, singing again, she anointed each of our foreheads with a moistened finger.

"I am marking you for travel," Kelly said. "It will lead you to your destination."

Abodah turned toward the opposite side of the walkway, spread out her arms, and sang a shrill note. The multicolored mist parted and piled up on each edge of the divide. In the gap, a deep gulf plunged into a black void.

Daryl gulped. "Holy Moses!"

Abodah extended a hand toward the chasm as if inviting us to enter. I stooped and peered into the darkness. "So is it safe to just jump right in?"

Kelly sang Abodah's reply. "It is a leap of faith, to be sure. My mate pursued Mictar through a similar rift in the cosmos, and one of the supplicants told me that he arrived safely. I assume that you, too, will land without harm."

"I guess we have no choice." I retrieved the case from Daryl, repacked the violin, and lined up my toes with the edge of the walkway. After what I had been through, leaping into a void seemed like no big deal.

Kelly took my hand, her eyes as bright as ever as she leaned close and whispered, "I rode on a doomed jet. I can do this."

Daryl wrung her hands against her chest and slid her feet away from the edge. "No way."

"Come on." I set the violin down and reached for her. "It'll be fine. Kelly and I have been through worse stuff than this."

She stopped, her eyes wide. "Ever see *Vertigo*?"

I took a step toward her. "Alfred Hitchcock, right?"

"Yep." Her voice trembled as she leaned away from my reach. "That's me. Crazy scared of heights."

With a quick lunge, I grabbed her wrist. "Then keep your eyes closed and hang on."

"No!" She jerked free. "I can't. I … I just can't."

I firmed my lips. Even though Scarlet's words were already fading, her warning about running from fear still echoed. "We can't leave you here, and there's no other way home." I reached for her again. "This is no time to lose your cool."

She leaped back and teetered on the opposite edge, her arms flailing. In a flash, Abodah lunged to her side and set her upright.

As Daryl lowered herself to a shivering crouch, Abodah sang.

"She must go with you," Kelly translated. "There is no time to lose." She then whispered to me, "What should we do?"

"We'll have to force her," I whispered back. "We can't stay. Her going phobic might get us all killed."

Kelly's voice sharpened. "Give her a break. Isn't there anything that scares you like that?"

"Not that I can think of." I frowned at my own words. They sounded merciless. Actually, lots of things scared me, but nothing made me lose my nerve like this. And, merciless or not, I had to be tough to get us out of this jam. I lowered my whisper further. "We can't stand around and wait. You get on one side of her, and I'll get on the other. We'll take her kicking and screaming if we have to."

"Are you sure?"

"Do you have another idea?"

She shrugged.

"Then, let's do it."

While Daryl kept her head tucked low, I crept to her side. As soon as Kelly stooped at her other side, I grasped Daryl's arm and pulled her to a standing position.

She tried to twist free, but Kelly held her in place. Tears streaming and her whole body shaking, Daryl looked back and forth at us. "Oh, please. Please don't make me go."

"We don't have any choice." As I pulled, Daryl hobbled along, though with her legs buckling, I practically dragged her across the path.

When we reached the edge, Kelly spoke in a soothing tone. "It's okay, Daryl. Trust us. Like Nathan said, we've been through scarier stuff than this, and he hasn't let me down yet."

"Yet?" Daryl squeaked.

I tried to hide a painful swallow. How could I be sure? Maybe Abodah was lying and thought it some kind of macabre joke to get us to jump in on our own. But I had to believe the best, and I had to give Daryl reason to believe. Softening my own tone, I loosened my grip. "Daryl, Kelly and I are going. You make your own choice. Are you with us?"

As her trembling eased, Daryl gazed into the void. "It's so dark."

Kelly looped her arm around Daryl's. "C'mon. We'll stay together no matter what happens."

Daryl squeezed Kelly's arm and closed her eyes. "Tell me when it's over."

Abodah swiveled her head to the side. Far along the pathway another white-haired figure approached. I snatched up the violin and whispered, "Now." We bent our knees and jumped into the void.

CHAPTER FIVE

THE MOMENT WE dropped into the chasm, a stream of blue rushed out from the surrounding walls of mist, wrapped around our bodies, and guided us down a dizzying corkscrew path into darkness. Above, the edges of the chasm merged, like a giant animal's jaws closing to trap its prey.

Utter helplessness took hold — falling without knowing when or if the plunge would end. Daryl screamed, but the rushing wind snuffed out her cry.

After what seemed like a full minute of free falling, a sense of wetness brushed my cheeks. The darkness began to fade, revealing a familiar swirling mist surrounding our bodies. Seconds later, our descent slowed. The mist spread out and thinned. The mirror, jagged and misshapen at first, materialized in front of us, slowly regaining its rectangular form and reflective clarity as the fog swept away.

I pried Daryl's fingers from my arm. "It's okay. We're back."

She crouched and laid her palms on the carpet. "Terra firma! Am I glad to see you!"

My legs a bit wobbly, I walked toward the mirror. "Now we have to find Abodah's mate if we want to know what to do next. I'm guessing she meant Patar, but how do we get him to come back?"

Kelly, her eyes glassy once again, lifted the camera. "In the meantime, do you want to develop the film? I took quite a few pictures while we were up there, especially of the girl in the dome."

"You did? That's great! I was trying to tell you not to."

"I know." She winked. "That's why I left the flash off."

"I'll call Walmart and see if they're open. The roads might be getting icy, but we should be able to make it."

"Only if you walk," Daryl said as she looked out the window.

I set the violin on the floor and joined her. "What do you mean?"

As she backed away, she pulled a curtain to the side. "The car's gone. No sign of Clara."

I pressed my nose against the glass. Although wind-blown fog still veiled the area, the entire yard lay in view. "She just left without us?"

"Or something made her leave." Kelly peeked over my shoulder. "Maybe she had to escape."

I checked my watch. Five till noon. Only about a half hour had passed. I searched the walls. "Is there a clock around here? Something that doesn't run on electricity?"

"I get your drift," Daryl said. "A time warp kind of thing. Maybe she got tired of waiting."

Kelly pointed toward the hall. "My father's den has a clock with a battery backup. Kelly Blue's father probably had one, too."

"I'll look." I jogged to Tony Clark's den at the opposite end of the house and halted at the doorway. A wide-screen plasma TV dangled on the wall by one of its corners. A half-size refrigerator lay open on its side with at least ten bottles of beer lying next to the door. Three long gashes marred a plush recliner, and clumps of padding lay scattered across the carpet. Jagged slices ripped through basketball posters that lined the perimeter. What was once a sports fan's paradise was now the victim of a malevolent vandal.

A digital clock sat on top of a trophy case. The numerals read 3:36. I checked my watch again. We had been gone for four hours. No wonder Clara left.

I walked in and pushed the trophy case's door closed. Shards of glass lay on the carpet and inside the case. Someone must have been desperate to find something.

A folded sheet of paper under one of the trophies caught my eye. I pulled it out and read a scribbled note on top — *Foundation's Key* written in my own hand. I unfolded the sheet and found musical notes hastily penned on a hand-drawn staff. The style — the way the quarter notes weren't completely filled in and how the numerals in the time signature didn't quite align — was again my own. Nathan Blue must have squirreled this music away in the trophy case for safekeeping.

After tucking the sheet into my back pocket, I hustled across the house. When I breezed into the bedroom, Daryl lifted her phone. "I had a signal for a minute, so I tried to call Clara. No answer, but I left a message."

Kelly cocked her head toward the garage side of the house. "If the motorcycles are here, we have wheels."

I laid a hand on my back pocket. Telling them about the music could wait. It might be nothing. "Getting the film developed isn't as important as finding Clara. Besides, riding a motorcycle in this weather is dangerous."

Daryl looked out the window again. "Maybe Clara will turn around and come back, you know, if she hits some icy spots. We could wait a little while. Talk about what happened in fog city."

"I suppose so." I touched Kelly's shoulder. "Do you need to change your bandage?"

"No. The bleeding's stopped. I'll be fine."

Using her foot, Daryl nudged the desk radio, now on the floor. "If this is battery powered, we can get some news." When she turned it on, a static-filled broadcast buzzed from the speaker. "Pretty fuzzy, but I can hear it. Maybe something important will come across while we talk."

We sat cross-legged on the floor facing each other. For the next several minutes, I told Kelly and Daryl about my visit into Scarlet's prison. We agreed that it was all probably just my imagination, even her name, though we would keep her words in mind just in case.

During our conversation, I picked up some tidbits from the broadcast. Apparently Jack, one of the passengers who survived the Earth Yellow plane crash, went to his old house in Earth Blue's Chicago, and his surprise return from the dead ignited a media frenzy. Later, a woman survivor showed up at her place of business, which only stoked the flames.

When the broadcast finished, Daryl whistled. "The whole world must be scared spitless. And now every freakazoid end-of-the-worlder is going to come out from under their respective rocks and announce the apocalypse. It's gonna get even worse."

"Which is why we have to do something about it." I withdrew the music sheet I found in the trophy case and spread it out close to Kelly. "Someone ransacked Tony's man cave. I wondered if they were looking for this. The only words say, Foundation's Key."

Kelly leaned to within a few inches of the sheet and squinted. "C Major?"

"Yeah. It's really simple. I could've played it when I was four."

Daryl poked my thigh. "Don't just sit there, Mozart. Play it and get the mirror stoked for action. Maybe we'll see something new that'll help."

"Might as well." After we rose from the floor, I picked up the violin and began tuning it while Kelly held the music sheet in front of me.

The radio's static spiked. A shadow darted across the wall—small, fast, fleeting — and disappeared behind the trunk. I jerked toward it but saw nothing. I whispered to Daryl, "Did you see that?"

"See what?"

"A shadow." Walking on tiptoes, I approached the trunk. A small human-shaped figure, as dark and shapeless as a shadow, rose from behind the trunk, climbed on top, and faced me.

Daryl gasped. "Tell me I'm watching *Poltergeist*!"

Hair flowed past her shoulders, and feminine contours lined her frame, revealing her gender. Yet, with vague blackness veiling any details, she seemed like a bodiless soul.

Kelly picked up the camera, took the violin, and pushed the camera into my hands. "Let's get a photo."

I raised the camera to my eye, turned on the flash, and focused on the diminutive ghost. As I reached for the shutter button, the radio noise heightened to a frenzy — buzzing, beating, sizzling in my ears and sending a tingle through my body. My finger trembled as it hovered over the button.

The ghost climbed off the trunk and walked slowly toward us, reaching out a dark hand.

"Nathan," Kelly said as she backed away, "I changed my mind. Maybe you'd better not."

"Don't you want to know what's going on?" I asked.

The noise grew so loud, Kelly had to raise her voice. "Yeah. Kind of. But …"

Another shadow stepped up behind the smaller one, taller and masculine. The static thumped in my ears like an audio jackhammer, threatening to break my eardrums. Now both shadows approached. In the camera's viewfinder, the girl's face grew clearer. A glimmer of light glowed in her eyes. Lips emerged, thin and delicate.

The noise fell silent. The girl's lips moved. "Nathan," she said. "I finally found you. I need your help to play the violin."

I hit the shutter button and staggered back. The camera flashed. Light shot out in a shimmering conic wave and spilled over the ghosts, illuminating every detail. Although the flash lasted only a split second, the light seemed to linger in the air, like glittering dust that spread the glow from one particle to the next.

As if blown by the wind, the girl's hair streamed behind her. Blues and reds painted her dress and smock. Her face blushed with pink, accenting her familiar high cheekbones. Although she was taller now, her identity was unmistakable.

I formed *Francesca* with my lips, but no sound came out.

Behind her, the man's face took shape—clearly Dr. Nikolai Malenkov, Francesca's adoptive father. His face carried a confused look, though not unpleasant. In his hands he cradled something long and thin, but with the flash still pulsing in my vision, I couldn't tell what it was.

Her voice floated in the air, warped but understandable. "Come to me, Nathan. We need to play the great violin."

Like embers in a dying campfire, the glitters faded, and the surrounding darkness swallowed their glow. Within seconds, the ghosts dimmed to black and disappeared.

I lowered the camera. All was now silent. Francesca and Nikolai were gone. Not a trace of moving shadows remained.

"Nathan," Daryl said, her eyes wide as she stared at the trunk, "tell me I really saw two shadow people who just vanished in the blink of an eye."

I could only nod. What had I done? Did I send Francesca off into another world? What were she and Dr. Malenkov doing here? Why were they ghostly shadows? And what was he carrying?

For the next few minutes, we bounced ideas back and forth but came up with no sensible explanation for Francesca's appearance, though we agreed that the vision was real. She was trying to contact us, and we had to go to her somehow.

After we settled our nerves, I retrieved my violin and lifted the bow to the strings. "Are you ready to try again?"

Kelly stood and faced the mirror while holding the music sheet in front of me. "I'm not sure what I'm ready for, but go ahead."

"Rarin' to go!" Daryl jumped up and hooked her arm around Kelly's. "That is if there aren't any bottomless pits to jump into."

"No guarantees." Concentrating on giving the simple tune the best rendering possible, I played it through. As soon as I finished and the final note faded, the upper-left square of the mirror flashed and emitted a faint popping sound. Less than a second later, the square to its right flashed and popped. One by one, moving horizontally to the end and beginning again on the next row, each mirrored square flashed with a burst of light.

Before the series of flashes reached the third row, the image in the first square transformed. Instead of reflecting the room, it displayed a snowy field dotted with small shrubs. The second square gave a side view of a gray-haired woman bending over the open hood of a car as if trying to do something to the engine. And on it went, square after square showing different scenes, popping up too fast to fully take in one before the next gave us something else to see.

Finally, four-hundred images—each showing a different, live-action scene—spanned the wall before us.

Daryl pointed at the second square. "Isn't that Clara?"

I scooted close and peered at the woman. Although black grease smeared her cheek, there was no mistaking my tutor. "She's stuck somewhere with engine problems."

Kelly touched one of the lower squares. "Do you think we can go to any of these places if we flash a light?"

"Maybe." I stepped back and tried to take in the hundreds of images. Could Mom and Dad be in one of them? That would be the first place I'd want to go.

I took a deep breath. It was time to concentrate, do this logically. "Daryl, you start in the lower-right corner and work your way to the left and up. I'll work from the top-left corner down. You know what my parents look like, right?"

"Yeah, you showed me their pictures. Well, not you. Nathan Blue did. I think I could spot them."

I raised three fingers, one at a time. "Try to find my parents, Francesca Yellow, or Scarlet, assuming that's really her name."

"What about Clara?" Daryl asked. "Won't she freeze?"

I gazed at my tutor's image as she stood next to the car's open hood, searching the snow-covered highway for help. No one was in sight. With bone-chilling wind whipping against her inadequate coat, she wouldn't last long out there. I had to help her right away. But what about Patar's warnings? Could I afford the time it would take to save one person?

After a few seconds, I nodded. Of course I had to go. Patar would just have to deal with it. "Okay. I'll go."

"Me, too." Kelly pressed her thumb against her chest. "I'm the mechanic. You and Clara can be my eyes."

"We should all go. But how? Should I pry Clara's square off and have one of you hold it while I flash a light?"

Daryl set a hand on her hip. "Good question, boss. Prying one loose might shut the rest of the mirror down."

"Not only that," Kelly said, "doesn't this mean that every square is really a Quattro mirror with the same power that the one in the corner has?"

"Which also means they're all dangerous in the wrong hands." I headed for the bedroom door. "Gotta get a flashlight and a screwdriver."

After a few minutes of fumbling around in the dark garage, I found the items. On my way back to the bedroom, I stopped at a hallway closet where three coats hung that seemed heavy enough for the cold weather we were about to encounter. I gathered them and hurried on. When I arrived, Daryl, now wearing the camera strap around her neck, nodded toward the hall. "We heard something out there, like a pounding on the floor."

"I didn't see anyone." After depositing the coats on the floor, I pushed the trunk in front of the mirror, stood on it, and pried Clara's square loose. As soon as it came off, the rest of the squares flashed brightly, then returned to normal.

I looked at the mirror in my hand. Clara was still there, now shivering in the car's driver seat with the door closed.

A creaking noise sounded from somewhere in the house, then another. I stiffened. Footsteps?

I whispered, "Everyone quiet," then jumped down from the trunk. After finding the detachable frame on the floor, I snapped it around Clara's mirror, grabbed the coats, and passed them around. As soon as everyone had pushed their arms through the sleeves, another floorboard creaked, much closer. I handed the Clara mirror to Kelly, lifted the violin, and played the key.

"Where's the flashlight?" Kelly asked.

"Right here." Daryl pointed the flashlight at the mirror and whispered, "On your command, Captain."

Just outside the doorway, the floor creaked again. Something thumped against the wall. I stared at the bedroom entrance, every limb stiff. Was it Mictar? Dr. Simon? Who would be stalking the house without announcing himself? Certainly not a friend.

I nodded at Daryl. "Let's do it."

CHAPTER SIX

JUST AS DARYL flashed the light, a series of thumps sounded inside the room, as if someone had repeatedly struck the floor with a rubber mallet, but no one was there.

Kelly gasped. "Nathan! Do you see him?"

"See who?" My voice stretched out and flew apart. The image of the bedroom pixelated and broke into a million pieces. A snowy highway scene took shape, and a blustery wind slapped my face, biting my cheeks with a frigid blast.

The Toyota sat at the side of the road only two paces away. Clara threw open the door and stumbled out, laughing. "Leave it to you to appear out of nowhere."

Daryl pushed the flashlight into her coat pocket and raised the camera to her eye. "We're multi-earth paparazzi. We show up when you least expect it."

I gave Clara a one-armed hug and looked at Kelly. "What did you see back there?"

Kelly's teeth chattered, "I … I saw a man. He looked like Jack. He had a beard, but his face was too bloodied and swollen to be sure. He just fell to his hands and knees on the floor."

"If I couldn't see him, how could you?"

"I've been seeing other things." She hugged the coat closer to her body. "If we can get someplace warm, I'll tell you about it."

I turned to Clara. "How far back to the house?"

"Under normal driving conditions, about four hours." Streams of white puffed from her nose. "With these conditions? Who can tell?"

"Four hours?" I kicked a snow drift, scattering crystals into the wind. Patar had warned me about getting sidetracked, and now here I was risking the entire universe to help Clara while precious minutes ticked away. "How long did you wait for us at the house?"

"About half an hour. I went in to check on you, but the house was empty." Clara gave me a scolding stare. "You literally left me out in the cold, so what else could I do? You said to meet you at the observatory, so I headed that way."

"Sorry. I couldn't help it." I looked at the mirror—back to normal. "Let's see if this thing will take us home."

While Kelly held the mirror, I tried to play the violin, but every note came out warped. Within seconds, the frigid wind stiffened my fingers to the point that I couldn't play at all.

Letting out a sigh, I nodded at the car. "Let's see if we can get this thing started."

"Not likely," Clara said. "I think it's just out of gas, and the service stations either have no power or they're shut down because no one's minding the store. No cell service, either."

I searched both ways on the four-lane interstate highway—nothing but snow-covered trees and grass along with a couple of farm houses dotting the white landscape, certainly no cars to flag down for help. A few vehicles sat stranded at the side of the road. About a hundred yards away, at the end of a trail in the snow, an old station wagon pointed in the wrong direction. "Have you seen anyone at all?"

Clara stuffed her hands into her coat pockets and nodded at a two-story house on a distant hill. Smoke poured through two brick chimneys, one on each end of the roof. "A woman who was driving that station wagon hiked up there. I was about to join her."

I touched Kelly's arm and nodded toward the abandoned car. "Ever siphoned?"

She shook her head. "But I've seen my dad do it."

"What did he use?"

"Just a hose and a gas can." As she replied, her ragged puffs of white matched her shivers. "We should ask for help at that house."

In the house's picture window, a yellow light moved from one side to the other—probably a candle or lantern. I handed Daryl the violin. "You guys try to stay warm in the car. I'll hoof it to the house."

Kelly looped her arm around mine. "Not a chance. You're stuck with me, remember?"

"Sure. Let's go."

While Daryl stayed with Clara, Kelly and I hiked to the house. Although the bitter wind continued to claw through our coats, and snow seeped through our shoes, the fast pace up the hill kept us warm enough. I wanted to ask Kelly more about the things she had seen, but with her teeth chattering as we huffed and puffed through the climb, I thought better of it.

Her cheeks, rosy red now, expanded and contracted as she blew through her mouth. Her eyes shifted toward me, still glassy, but she had caught me looking.

"Is everything okay?" she asked.

"Besides being stuck out in the middle of nowhere?" I shrugged. "I guess so. Why?"

She refocused on the slope ahead as we trudged on. "You were watching me, so I thought maybe you wanted to talk."

"I was wondering about what you saw in the bedroom, but I didn't want to ask. You looked too cold."

She clutched my arm closer to her side. "You're always looking out for my comfort. I like that."

"I like that you like it."

She smiled and said no more as we marched on to the house arm-in-arm.

The residents let us borrow an empty gas can and cut a piece from an old hose, but they had no gas to offer. The lady of the house, a mother of three young daughters who pranced around the living room in snowsuits while singing Christmas songs, filled a thermos with hot soup and sent it back with us.

It turned out that the mom was the driver of the station wagon, and after spinning out she was afraid to try to drive up the slope to their home. She gave us permission to siphon from her tank and told us to leave the thermos and can in the backseat. When I offered to pay for the gas, she refused and said, "Merry Christmas."

On the return trip, the wind slackened, and the sun grew warm, melting the snow. Kelly stayed quiet, her gaze far away as we scooted down the slope. By the time we returned, the temperature had climbed to at least eighty, and snow-melt rivulets created ankle-deep ponds at the roadside. We took off our coats and tossed them into the backseat along with Clara's and Daryl's.

With some coaching from Kelly, I siphoned enough gas to fill the two-gallon can, but a couple of mistakes along the way left me spitting, coughing, and gagging. The effort left a horrible film on my tongue and lips, and washing with the remaining snow did little to wipe it away.

After transferring the gas to the Toyota, we settled into the car with me driving and Kelly, at Clara's insistence, next to me, while she and Daryl sat in the back.

When I turned the key, the Camry roared to life. The fuel gauge now read about an eighth of a tank. "How far is it to the observatory?"

"Thirty-two miles." Clara leaned forward and looked at the gauge. "We should make it."

"Let's hope so."

"But what will we do when we arrive?" Clara asked. "What's the next step?"

"Go to Earth Yellow and find Francesca. I'll tell you about it on the way." I eased onto the road. After explaining to Clara everything that happened in the strange misty world and afterward, including Patar's strongly delivered advice that I play the big violin, we settled into silence. Daryl reached into a backpack and pulled out a Sudoku book while Clara leaned her head against the side window and closed her eyes.

As I drove, the image of Scarlet returned to mind along with her haunting words. Although I recalled only a few, something in the way she said them seemed unearthly, like ghostly lyrics of a lullaby, words lost in a dream world as if I were drifting in and out of sleep. *Remember that you must come back and rescue us ... You have only a little time ... Interfinity is coming ... You, my love, are one of the gifted, and another is searching for you in her dreams. Perhaps we can guide her to a convenient place to meet you ... The two of you will have to work together ... play the violin in Sarah's Womb."*

I clutched the steering wheel tightly. Francesca had made contact with me, maybe in a dream, but which option was the highest priority? I was being pulled in so many directions — Francesca and the big violin, my parents, Jack, Scarlet — too many missions to accomplish and not enough time to do them.

Kelly turned toward me. Something new sparkled in her eyes, something deep and searching. She seemed to want to say something but was unsure.

"What's up?" I asked, my voice low.

Kelly copied my tone. "You've been wondering how I'm seeing things you can't, right?"

I nodded.

She gave me a weak but friendly smile. "You know how I hear voices when you're playing music and when those people sang?"

"Uh-huh."

"It's sort of like that, but now it's also visual. It's like I haven't really lost my eyesight. It's more like it's been replaced by being able to see things that aren't there."

"Can you tell the difference? Do you know when other people can't see things you're seeing?"

She nodded. "They sort of flash over the background for a second, then they disappear. Normally, everything's blurry, but the stuff that flashes is super clear."

"What did you see besides Jack?"

"Before that, while we were in the bedroom, I saw Francesca pulling her music out of the trunk and packing it in a briefcase. Dr. Malenkov stood next to her, looking around kind of nervously. Then, they disappeared. I didn't want to tell you, because it was so crazy, but stuff like that keeps happening."

"Like what else?"

She gestured toward the windshield. "Cars on the road. The highway is deserted, but I see cars suddenly appearing and then vanishing. It feels like I'm dreaming while awake."

"That's even more bizarre." I refocused on the road. What could it all mean? Was she seeing glimpses of Earth Yellow? Was Francesca back at her home, collecting her things while her new father stood guard? Maybe these visions confirmed that we should go to Earth Yellow and find her.

Kelly stretched and yawned, then looked back at me with bleary eyes.

I reached for her hand and gave it a gentle squeeze. "Maybe you should try to get a short nap."

"I guess it couldn't hurt." She settled back in her seat and closed her eyes. Within seconds, her breathing altered to a rhythmic purr. Clara, too, seemed to be asleep.

Daryl closed her puzzle book. "Is it all right that I heard everything you said to Kelly?"

I shrugged. "I guess so. No secrets."

I caught a glimpse of her in the rearview mirror, biting her bottom lip. A few wisps of red hair had fallen across her freckled forehead. "Are you mad at me for being afraid to jump?" Her voice was thin and fragile.

"Not really mad. Frustrated, I guess. We had to escape, and we couldn't wait around for you to get over your phobia."

She lowered her head. "I know. I'm sorry."

I angled the mirror to get a better view. She wrung her hands, intertwining her fingers. "My fear of heights started just a few days ago. You ... I mean, Nathan Blue before he died ... and Kelly Blue came over to my house. They said something crazy about Dr. Simon wanting them to stop an airliner crash in another world, and they wanted to learn more about how the big jets work.

"You see, my dad's a pilot, so they thought maybe he could help, but he only flies the regional routes, you know, like propeller planes that hop a few hundred miles. Nathan said it didn't matter. He wanted to take a flight and see if he could get the mirror to transport them while in the air. So he told my dad all about the Quattro mirror and even gave him a demonstration. Well, Dad got really excited about the whole thing, so he took us up in his private plane.

"Anyway, the mirror didn't work at first, so Nathan decided maybe it would work if there was danger. Now, you have to understand that my dad is a real adventurer—you know, extreme sports, skydiving, whitewater kayaking—so he opened the back door and cut the engine. The plane kind of sailed for a while, and Nathan stood right next to the door playing his violin while Kelly held the mirror.

"Well, I didn't want to look like a coward, so I stood next to Kelly, but the plane took a sudden dip and

I stumbled toward the door. Nathan caught me by my shirt, and I was hanging over the edge with just my toes touching the plane. Let me tell you, I was so scared, I … well, never mind that. He pulled me back, Dad restarted the plane, and we went home. The mirror never did anything. Anyway, ever since then, I've been scared of heights. I have a hard time just walking up the stairs."

She looked at me in the rearview mirror, her eyes wide and wet.

"That must have been awful." While watching the road, I reached a hand back. She took it and wrapped it up with hers. For a moment, I stayed silent, feeling the anguish in her tight grip. "Since it just started a few days ago, maybe it's a temporary thing. You'll probably get over it soon."

She lowered her head again. "I hope so."

When we arrived at the observatory, I parked the car in front of the entrance and surveyed the grounds, now almost free of snow cover. Everything seemed quiet, not a soul in sight. Still, we had to be careful. Mictar was always a danger.

I turned off the engine and pulled out the keys. Kelly popped her head up, blinking. "Are we here?"

"Yep," Daryl said, looking at me hopefully. "Time to start a new adventure."

Clara roused herself and distributed our coats. "You never know when winter will start again."

After we put the coats on, I retrieved Mom's violin from the trunk. We strode through the front door and used the numeric codes to enter the facility's secure area and the elevator. Kelly and I rode first in case trouble lay waiting at the telescope level.

As we traveled upward, the mirror's reflection showed only our faces and the door behind us, no hint of any danger.

When the elevator opened, we entered the vacant main chamber. No one was around. The mirrored ceiling showed a duplicate of the observatory room. Two females sat at the reflected computer desk, upside down copies of Clara and Daryl. Dr. Gordon looked over their shoulders at the computer screens. Soft music emanated from speakers embedded in the curved wall, Strauss's Blue Danube.

Daryl Red stood and waved from the ceiling. Her voice broke through the waltz. "Welcome back. We've been wondering what's going on over there."

"We got sidetracked," I said.

Clara Red rose and stood next to Daryl. "Another jump through portals?"

"The weirdest yet." I glanced at the elevator's floor indicator. It had just arrived down below to collect the others. I looked up again and studied Daryl Red as she stood erect with shoulders squared, a pose of confidence. She seemed unfazed by all the danger. "Daryl? Are you afraid of heights?"

She walked closer to the center of the room. "Not especially. Why?"

"Daryl Blue is, so I was wondering."

Dr. Gordon raised his head. "Very interesting. A significant difference between parallel characters. The variance between my counterpart and myself was quite striking, as well."

"Anyway," I continued, "we have to go back to Earth Yellow, and it's your turn to portal jump. Want to come along?"

She pumped a fist. "Yes! Adventure time!"

"Super. But just don't mention the fear of heights subject to Daryl Blue, okay?"

"Sure thing, boss."

When the elevator door reopened, Daryl Blue bounced out and hustled to the laptop computers. She laid Nathan Blue's violin and camera on the desk and rubbed her hands together. With a big smile spreading across her face, her fingers flew between the keyboard and touch pad. "Setting course for Earth Yellow, Captain."

"No." I set Mom's violin next to the other one. "Wait."

She paused and looked up at me. "A new course?"

"Let's bring Daryl Red over. It's her turn to go with us."

The corners of Daryl Blue's lips quivered, and her eyes misted, making them sparkle in the dim light. She cleared her throat and turned back to the computer. "Sure. Right. It *is* her turn."

I looked at Kelly. She pursed her lips but said nothing. What was she thinking? She had seen Daryl Blue cower like a puppy. She had to know we couldn't afford to deal with that kind of phobia.

Holding back a sigh, I watched Daryl Blue set up the transfer. Even after rearguing the points in my mind, pushing her out of the journey felt like slapping a baby for spilling milk. She couldn't help it. But Mictar wouldn't care. He would exploit her fears.

I removed the film from the camera and set it on the computer desk. "Maybe you can develop the pictures and let us know if you find anything important."

"Sure." Daryl gave me a half-hearted nod. "I'll get them digital and shoot them over to Dr. Gordon. We'll analyze them together."

Kelly leaned close to Daryl and kissed her cheek. "You're a first-hand witness of that foggy world, so you can get Dr. Gordon up to speed while we're gone. No one else can do that."

"True. No argument from me." Daryl's smile returned, though not as bright as usual. "We're all set. Let's get that gorgeous redhead over here."

In the ceiling view, Daryl Red stood at the center of her chamber, her back within a foot of the observatory telescope. Lights flashed. Beams of radiance knifed into the floor and surrounded her body. Within seconds she dissolved and vanished. Then, in the center of the Earth Blue observatory, an indistinct human shape materialized, slowly transforming into the familiar redheaded girl.

She shook her head hard and turned toward us. "Wow! That was a blast!"

"Yeah," Kelly said. "You never quite get used to it."

Daryl Red ran to the desk and stretched out her arms. "Daryl Blue!"

As the two embraced, a tear tracked down Daryl Blue's cheek. She drew back, stripped off her new coat, and helped Daryl Red put it on. "I'll bet it's a perfect fit," Daryl Blue said, wiping the tear away.

After buttoning up the downy, knee-length coat, Daryl Red held Daryl Blue's hand. "Thanks for letting me go. I'll tell you all about it."

Daryl Blue pulled free and pivoted back to the computer. "I'll dial in Earth Yellow now."

She tapped in a few keystrokes. The Strauss waltz died away. The ceiling view warped and twisted, then broke into thousands of irregularly shaped globs of color. As she turned up the sound, a new melody swept into the chamber. Subtle violins hummed a few simple notes playing over a thrumming bass. Within seconds, the violins strengthened, blending with cellos and drums until they resounded in a brilliant crescendo.

I closed my eyes and drank in the unmatchable glory of Beethoven's Ninth Symphony. The colors above splashed together with every pulse of vibrant music, as if called to order by the master's guiding baton.

Seconds later, the colors painted a devastated forest scene. New saplings dotted the grassy landscape, vibrating wildly, like a video run at ten times its normal speed. The larger trees were gone, snapped or uprooted by the recent tornado, and someone had cleared the cones, leaves, and broken branches. Whoever did all the clearing work must have left the mirror standing. Otherwise, we wouldn't be able to see anything. Apparently, someone was expecting us, whether for good or bad.

I checked my inventory—the camera, Mom's violin on the computer desk, and the mirror in my hand. Everything was here.

"Nathan?"

Dr. Gordon's voice. I located the source—the laptop speaker. "Yes?"

"I have some advice. First, it is summer on Earth Yellow. I suggest that you shed your coats so you can travel light. Once you are there, the seasonal changes will commence at a normal rate, but since Earth Yellow's time passage compared to ours fluctuates wildly, you won't know how time passes in either Earth Red or Earth Blue. Keep that in mind.

"Second, remember that we have no idea where Mictar is. If he is on Earth Yellow, since he is a stalker in a world of prophetic dreams, he will likely learn where you are. Third, my guess is that the two Dr. Simons are still there trying to meddle with coming events. They might be able to help you locate your parents. Perhaps they will have thought ahead and provided transportation."

I nodded. "I hope so. It's a long walk from the observatory site to Kelly's house."

Kelly, Daryl Red, and I stripped off our coats, leaving us wearing sweatshirts and jeans. Daryl pulled her red shirt collar over her gray sweatshirt's neckline. "See?" she said, pointing at the collar. "I'm color coded."

Still seated at the desk, Daryl Blue did the same with her collar, revealing a sky-blue top. "Me too. A rhapsody in blue."

Kelly shook her head and picked up the camera. "Let's get out of here. One Daryl is quite enough for me."

I grabbed Mom's violin and guided Kelly to the transport point, Daryl Red following. When we gathered near the telescope, Daryl Blue called from the computer desk. "Say hi to Francesca for me."

As usual, lights flashed to life from trumpet-like fixtures around the base of the perimeter wall and shot toward the ceiling. Sizzling as they split apart, the beams zoomed toward the floor and created a cage of light around us.

The landscape in the mirror above seemed to reach down with a gaping maw and swallow us. The forest scene sharpened, and the frenzied saplings slowed to a normal waving motion, blown by a fresh, warm breeze from the south. The sun, low over the eastern horizon, peeked through a thin bank of clouds.

A tri-fold mirror stood before us. New supporting boards anchored it to the ground, and a wood-frame portico provided a roof about five feet over the top. Ropes tied a flapping canvas tarp to the portico's frame, giving the mirror shade—probably to keep the sun from flashing a light and accidentally transporting an unsuspecting raccoon that happened to be wandering by.

"I can see." Kelly grabbed my arm. "My vision is perfect."

I gazed into her eyes. The glassy fog had faded away, leaving behind crystal clear blue irises. "That's super. I wonder why."

"Let's get this show on the road." Daryl stripped off her sweatshirt, revealing a bright red polo, and tied the sleeves around her waist. "Um … where *is* the road?"

"Not far." Something behind the tarp caught my eye, a motorcycle tailpipe protruding beyond the mirror's support post.

I set the violin case down and hustled to the pipe. The two motorcycles Kelly and I had used were parked between the mirror and the back of the makeshift portico. A helmet sat on the ground near each kickstand, red and blue, matching the trim of our corresponding bikes. "Simon Yellow's been busy." I wheeled the red-trimmed bike into the open. "Want to bet they're gassed and ready to go?"

While I packed the camera, mirror, and violin in the saddlebags, Daryl scooped up the helmets and handed one to Kelly. "Where to first?"

"Either of you hungry?" Kelly laid a hand on her stomach. "All I've had lately is soup."

"Sure," I said. "But something fast."

Kelly put on her helmet, muffling her voice. "How are we going to find Francesca? Won't she and Dr. Malenkov be in hiding?"

"We don't have to find her." I mounted my bike, making room for Daryl behind me as she slid the other helmet on. "Just her guardian angel."

CHAPTER SEVEN

I CRUISED DOWN THE two-lane road, searching for a place to get a bite to eat while contemplating my guardian-angel comment. Gunther Stoneman surely fit that label. The young delivery-van driver had shown a true papa-bear spirit when we left him to watch over Francesca. If we could find Gunther, locating my Earth Yellow mother would be a snap.

After several miles, we spotted a Burger King near the entrance to the interstate. We dismounted and walked to the door, the two girls removing their helmets along the way.

While Kelly and Daryl scanned the menu, I kept an eye on the employees behind the service counter. They seemed slow, lethargic. The few customers seated at the tables were deathly quiet. Even the young children said nothing as they pushed ketchup-coated fries into their mouths and chewed without a sound. One pigtailed girl yawned and blinked weary eyes, barely able to hold her head up.

After Kelly and Daryl ordered and headed for the restroom, I fished the older dollar bills from my wallet, avoiding the higher denominations and the new designs that might draw attention to the inscribed dates. I handed them to the cashier, a female teenager — short, with black hair pulled back into a bun. As I stretched and yawned, I read her name tag. "Rough night, huh, Paula?"

She stuffed the bills into her drawer and scooped coins from the change slots. "No worse than other nights."

As she slid the coins and wallet to my pocket, I noted the bags under her eyes. She looked like she hadn't slept for days. But why? Why did everyone look so tired? And why so quiet? Could the nightmare epidemic have infected everyone? "So … what did you dream about?"

Paula looked up and blinked. "You."

I pointed at myself. "Me? Really?"

"Well, not you, exactly." She laid the change in my hand. "I'm a next-day dreamer, so I've already seen all of today's customers. I don't pay much attention, though. You've seen one, you've seen them all."

"Are you sure you saw me?"

She narrowed her eyes. "Maybe not. I think I'd remember a guy like you." Her face paled to an ashen gray.

"What's wrong?"

She took a half step back. "Are you a traveler?"

I cocked my head. Apparently I was supposed to know what a traveler was. "What do you think?"

She studied my face again. "You don't look tired, so you have to be." She added a sigh as she continued. "It must be nice to walk freely outside of the dreamscape and see places that no one else sees."

"I guess that's true. Travelers do have an advantage."

She leaned over the counter and whispered, "Then you'd better get out of here. You know the rules."

"Oh, yeah. The rules." I couldn't ask about the rules. Apparently everyone was already supposed to know them. I stared at the menu behind Paula, taking my time. Maybe stalling would cause her to give away more information.

She drummed her fingers on the counter. "The other customers are looking at you. They're going to know you're a traveler."

I reached for my wallet again. "If you get me a Whopper and a Coke, I'll get out of here as fast as I can."

She nodded. "Just don't tell anyone, okay? I mean, you won't report me, will you?"

Leaning close, I whispered, "I won't tell. Everything will be fine."

"As if I could trust a traveler." She whirled around, snatched our sacks of food, and set them on the counter. "The stalker won't make you suffer like I will tonight."

As I paid for my order, I hid a nervous swallow. "White ponytail and ghoulish eyes, right?"

"So you *have* seen him." She tilted her head. "Are you sure you're a traveler?"

"I'm not sure of anything." I put my wallet away, gathered the food sacks, and strode to the dining area where Kelly and Daryl waited at a booth. "Come on," I said. "We can't stay."

Daryl flicked her thumb toward the booth behind her. "Something weird's going on. Those people are talking about a murder that'll happen tonight. They say the police know about it, but they're not going to—"

"There you are!" Gunther strode through the door wearing jeans and a Chicago Bears T-shirt.

I smiled. "I was just about to try to call you. How'd you know we'd be here?"

"Too risky to explain in public." Gunther leaned toward the door. "Let's get out of here."

We followed him out to where we had parked the bikes. His Stoneman Enterprises van and a flatbed trailer sat across several spaces at the back of the lot. A metal ramp spanned the gap between the trailer bed and the pavement.

"Load up your bikes," Gunther said, "and let's get moving."

I pushed up my kickstand. "But how did you know we'd be riding—"

"Never mind that." Gunther grabbed Kelly's motorcycle handles. "Let's go."

After securing the bikes on the trailer, Gunther hustled to the driver's seat. Daryl sat up front with him while Kelly and I climbed into the back. A comfortable new bench seat had been installed, much better than the hard floor we had used the last time.

Gunther slapped the van into drive and jerked the load into motion. He hurried through the parking lot and into traffic with barely a glance at the other cars. I bit into my hamburger and looked at Daryl, then Kelly. While they munched, their eyes seemed to ask the same questions I had. When would Gunther explain what was going on? What was he so worried about?

As the van accelerated on the interstate, the dashboard's stereo system played soft music, a cellist performing a sacred hymn, combining with the mellow violins of an accompanying orchestra. The soothing music seemed to calm everyone down.

When the van reached highway speed, Gunther let out a deep breath. "Have you figured out what's going on around here?"

After swallowing my mouthful, I nodded. "Sort of." I glanced at a newspaper on the seat. The headline read, "New Dream Rules Now in Effect." I handed it to Kelly and leaned toward the front. "It looks like the nightmare epidemic we heard about has spread to almost everyone. Some people are dreaming about their own future, and then it comes true. Even if it's a bad dream, they're afraid to do anything that might change it. If they try, they'll have a terrible nightmare the next night, usually about dying, and they can't stop it from happening."

"That's true for next-day dreamers." Gunther pointed at himself. "I'm a traveler, and I saw you in my dream, even your motorcycles, so I knew to bring a trailer. It took me a while to figure out which Burger King it was. That's why I'm a little late."

Kelly passed the newspaper to the front seat. "Did you see yourself coming here?"

"No. Travelers don't always see the future. We see things that might happen anywhere in the world."

"Might happen?"

"Yeah, it's sort of an expectation, like what people want to happen. Sometimes it comes true, and sometimes it doesn't. Francesca's a traveler, and she saw you at the Burger King, too, so with both of us dreaming the same thing, I had to check it out."

"Have you been in contact with her a lot?" I asked.

"Just about every day. She's been looking for you. She says the only way to stop this mess is for you to join her."

"I suspected that. We saw her on Earth Blue while she was in my bedroom in her dream." I shook my head. That sounded too strange to be true. But what wasn't strange in this dawning of Interfinity?

"Francesca didn't mention your bedroom," Gunther said, "but you can ask her about it yourself. If you can't put a stop to this dreaming business, the whole world is going to crack. The financial system almost collapsed when people started investing based on their dreams. That's the main reason the rules went into effect."

"But how can the government enforce them?" I asked. "They can't control dreams."

Gunther looked back at me and wiggled his fingers as if casting a spell. He stretched out his reply, altering his voice to a creepy bass. "No, but the Enforcer can."

"Who's the Enforcer?"

Gunther refocused on the road. "This freak shows up on TV every so often. At first, he predicted major events perfectly and claimed he could control the nightmare epidemic. When the dreams spread to almost half the population, he set down rules. We're not allowed to try to change the future. When people tried to take advantage anyway, he haunted their next nightmare. Lots of people died, either during the dream itself or because of a terrible accident the next day."

"Mictar's the Enforcer," I said, "but I can't see how it fits in with his agenda to merge the three earths."

Daryl raised a finger. "It's the fear factor. If you scare people enough, you can get them to do anything."

Gunther nodded. "It's working. Everyone's scared. Except Francesca. Nothing fazes her."

"Is she thirteen now?" Kelly asked.

"Yes, and a beautiful young lady. She has a great handle on what's going on, but her father is just confused by the whole thing. Fortunately, he trusts me completely, so I get to come over whenever I want."

During the rest of the journey, I explained to Gunther everything that had happened in the other worlds, including Mictar's plunge into the mirror at the funeral, our recent encounter with Francesca and Nikolai, and our experience with the stalkers and the supplicants in the misty world.

Since I filled in as many details as possible, and since Kelly added her color commentary in dozens of places, by the time I finished, we had passed Iowa City and were closing in on Newton.

Gunther pulled off the highway at the Newton exit. "We're meeting at Francesca's old house. It was sold at auction to a guy named Vernon Clark, but no one's moved in yet."

Kelly whispered to me, "Vernon Clark is my grandfather."

"About a month ago," Gunther continued, "Dr. Malenkov asked Vernon for permission to come to the house to get the trunk Francesca left behind. Once he got a key, they started going there regularly. You'll see why in a few minutes."

After passing between the familiar cornfields, tall and fully tasseled, we pulled into the driveway next to the cottonwood tree, which was now dressed in late summer greenery. Gunther got out and stretched as he looked up at the sky. "Cloudy. Maybe Iowa will sleep easy tonight."

I joined him and gazed at the gray skies. Thick clouds streamed in from the west and covered the descending sun. "Do clouds keep Mictar from stalking dreams?"

"Not sure. The blanket effect might be psychological, but it seems to help. Maybe people feel kind of vulnerable when the weather's clear, like the ghosts can reach down from wherever they are and pierce our minds."

As we walked toward the front door, the sound of the garage opening made us halt. Dr. Malenkov, the younger Earth Yellow version, stepped out, his eyes darting. "Please park the van inside without delay."

While Gunther hustled back to his van, Kelly, Daryl, and I quick-marched into the garage. Dr. Malenkov ushered us toward the inner doorway. "Welcome, friends. Francesca will be so glad to see you." He added a soft laugh. "And, of course, I am glad to see you, as well."

After Gunther drove the van into the garage, I helped him detach the trailer and roll it next to the van. While the motorized door closed, I withdrew the mirror and violin from the saddlebag. "Where is your car, Dr. Malenkov?"

"Hidden. I wanted to be sure we had enough room for you here." He waved a hand toward the open inner door. "Come, come. The time is approaching."

Gunther and I joined the girls and followed Dr. Malenkov through the laundry room, kitchen, and hallway. Violin music filled the air, growing louder as we walked. When we reached the bedroom door, Dr. Malenkov paused and peered inside. A white glow emanating from the room bathed his face as he turned to me, smiling. "She is ready."

The music stopped. As the glow faded, we filed in. Francesca sat on a solitary wooden chair with a music stand in front, a violin and bow on her lap. With her shoulders back and her head straight, her hair fell in ringlets of black down the sleeves of her flowing white dress. Although she was now a young lady, a familiar child-like mirth sparkled in her eyes.

She smiled as she rose to her feet. "I'm glad you finally came." Her soft voice carried across the empty room in lilting echoes. "I have been praying for your arrival for three years."

I took a step closer. My throat narrowed painfully. She was more woman than girl now — too young to be my mother and too old for the playful banter we once shared. I gave her a nod. "I'm glad I could make it."

Kelly hugged Francesca. "It's good to see you again."

Francesca returned the embrace, her eyes staying focused on me, as if probing my mind. She angled her bow toward me. "You figured out the gift."

"I think so." I lowered my head. Just looking at her scalded my soul. Somewhere in the cosmos my real mother needed help, and here I was, probably a billion miles away. Being here was important, incredibly important, but my heart ached to find her.

Francesca extended a hand and touched my cheek with her fingertips. As her smile weakened, a tear dressed her eye, and her voice returned to that of a little girl. "The gift is scary, Nathan. I'm not sure what to do with it."

Her touch felt cool and soft, just like Mom's. Trying to keep my voice from cracking, I reached for a low tone. "I got your message. Are you still on a mission to play the huge violin?"

She nodded. "But it's probably more complicated than you think. When your mother described the violin, she saw it in a vision. She wasn't really there. She and your father were trying to break through to another world, the Quattro world, I suppose, but they failed."

I looked at the sheets of music on her stand, a variety of compositions from the classical and romantic periods. "I see you've been experimenting."

"Different pieces have different effects, but …" She pulled out a music book from behind the stack. "This one works better than any. And it's the only baroque piece that works at all." She nodded at Dr. Malenkov, who stood next to Gunther near the door. "My father and I arranged it as a duet."

When I saw the title—Vivaldi's *Four Seasons* — I smiled. My mother's Earth Yellow twin came up with the same duet. "So you figured out how to get through to the Quattro world?"

"Only in one sense. I can walk through it like I'm in a dream."

I nodded. "Something like that happened to me, too."

"Because you have the gift." Her bright smile widened. "But I learned something very important. I can take my father with me in the dream if we sleep while touching."

"Now that's really strange," Kelly said. "Touching can make people share a dream?"

"If one of the sleepers is gifted. My father never remembers the dream when he wakes up, so I'm not sure if he's dreaming it, too, but it feels like he's really there, because he talks to me and gives me advice. I wish I could show you, but what we're about to create is a waking vision, not a sleeping dream." Francesca lifted the violin and set the bow over the strings. "Are you ready to join me? It's always faster with two playing."

I held up my mirror. "Do we need this?"

She shook her head. "The cosmic wound is deep at this spot. We can pierce it visually with music. We'll use the mirror for when we actually travel there. I want you to see what's going on while it's relatively safe."

"Sounds reasonable." I handed the mirror to Kelly and lifted my violin. "Let's have a look."

"What do *we* do?" Daryl asked, nodding at Kelly. "Do the ungifted just stand here and play Old Maid?"

"You can stand with us," Francesca said. "But you won't be able to see what we see. Just listen carefully and you'll hear what's going on. You might pick up on something important."

"That's fine," Daryl said. "Kelly has radar ears. Like a bat."

Kelly smirked. "Better than the mouth of a howling monkey."

"I love you, too, Kelly-kins." Daryl blew a kiss. "Now get those bat ears ready."

Turning to me, Francesca bowed her head. "Here we go. From the top." She played a long note, crisp and clear. Yet, it rang like a death knell, raising haunting memories of the recent funeral, the last place I had attempted this piece. It would take all my strength to play without trembling.

I joined in, at first with an echo of her introduction, then with a fast run along the fingerboard, pausing at the high end with a series of eerily beautiful half notes. With each stroke of our bows, white mist erupted, as if we were brushing up thin dust from the strings of violins long abandoned in an attic.

The streams of mist flowed together. Like two serpents slithering up a pole, they wrapped around each other and grew thicker with every note. Soon, they created a funnel-like swirl, the same kind of cyclonic fog that had sent Kelly, Daryl Blue, and me to the misty world. The lower tip of the funnel hovered over the carpet next to my shoes, and the outer edges brushed against my bow arm as I continued playing.

Francesca's eyes began to glow. Rays of white poured forth, like twin searchlights scanning the room. As the mist spread, two other spotlights intersected the first ones, creating a crisscross set of wandering headlamps. It seemed as though two cars were trying to find their way in a foggy parking lot.

I blinked. Were those two other lights coming from me? I turned my head. The lights followed. I aimed them at the swirl. As my glowing vision penetrated the cyclone, images flowed in—a long, glassy path, a dark chasm on one side and a foggy swamp on the other. It looked exactly like the misty world I had visited.

"I think it's big enough." Francesca stopped playing and nodded toward the funnel, now at least five feet wide. "Everyone step in and huddle close."

I lowered my violin and followed her into the funnel — a cool mist, not as wet as the funnel I had traveled in before, more like dry ice vapor than fog. Kelly and Daryl Red joined us, but Dr. Malenkov stayed on the outside. "We will keep watch," he said, patting Gunther on the shoulder. "You will be unaware of your physical surroundings while you are in there, so we will be your eyes in this world."

Francesca set her feet and raised her bow again. "We have to keep playing, or the viewing portal will collapse." She began the duet from the first measure. I joined her again, trying to pour in the passion the piece deserved, but the overwhelmingly strange surroundings kept tugging at my concentration.

As we stood within the swirl, the mist absorbed the eyebeams and spread light throughout. Particle after particle of mist reflected the light with pinpoint flashes of various colors. As the number of flashing points grew, the reflections created a tapestry of tiny strobes that slowly eased their frantic pulses until they stayed lit in their chosen colors.

Soon, the picture completed itself, now the living image of the misty world. Francesca and I stood upon the glassy walk, safely away from the edges. This time, no darkness shrouded our initial view. The long walkway, easily visible within the first fifty yards or so, led away in both directions, vanishing in cloudy curtains in the distance.

I slid a shoe along the glass. It felt real — hard and smooth. As before, music filled the air, a combination of perfectly blended, yet unidentifiable instruments.

Gesturing with a curled finger, Francesca walked alongside the flowing mist. "This way."

I hustled to stay at her side. "This leads to the stalkers. I've been here before."

"But you're not here now." She flashed a grin, that little grin I loved so much on her ten-year-old version. "The stalkers won't give us any trouble as long as we stay quiet. They can't see us, so we will be able to go wherever we wish."

She marched along the path, her violin and bow swinging with her gait. I followed with my own violin tucked at my side, yet somehow I was still playing the Vivaldi duet in the Earth Yellow bedroom. I felt the passion of the melody as I subconsciously stroked the vibrating strings, yet that same violin was now within a virtual reality world I had recently visited in concrete reality. Which reality was the *real* reality?

I shook my head. I had to push the weirdness out of my mind and concentrate on Francesca's instructions. She was a girl on a mission, and I had to figure out what this was all about.

After walking through the bank of fog, we emerged into the enclosed mirrored circle with the images of earth emblazoned on the wall. A new jagged trail marred the crystal surface, a path of green that stretched between Earth Blue and Earth Yellow.

The room seemed darker this time, as though the lights had been turned down for the evening. A gentle song played in the air, the now familiar nondescript vowel sounds, creating a soothing, repetitive chant that resembled a lullaby. Maybe it was nighttime here, and most of the people had gone to bed, or whatever they did to rest.

Even in the dimness, most of the room's features were still visible. As before, the triangle of supplicant domes sat at the center of the gem-laden terrazzo floor, but no white-haired stalkers crowded the glass enclosures. One stalker strode around the periphery, keeping a steady pace as he passed the domes.

Francesca took my hand and let out a quiet "Shhh." The stalker slowed for a moment and angled his head as if listening. Then, with a shrug, he continued his march until he reached an open door in the mirrored wall and disappeared inside.

Francesca whispered, "Remember, they can hear us."

"Have you seen the supplicants?" I asked, pointing at the domes.

"Yes. I'm not sure if they're dangerous, so I didn't try to contact them."

"They're not dangerous." I strode to the closest dome and gazed inside. Scarlet sat with her legs crossed and her head bowed. Her chest expanded and contracted in a steady rhythm. In her sleeping posture, eyes closed without a hint of tension or wrinkle, she seemed peaceful, angelic.

Just as I poised my knuckles on the glass to knock, Francesca tugged on my sleeve. "No time. I have to show you the violin."

I pulled back my hand. She was right. I would have to visit Scarlet later.

Francesca crept noiselessly around Scarlet's crystal prison until she reached the place where it abutted the next dome. She stepped over the point of intersection and into the space separating the three prisons.

I followed while peering into the other domes. In the one to my left, another female sat in Scarlet's posture, a girl with blonde hair that draped her pale yellow dress. To my right, a male teenager also slept, copying the pose of the other two. The boy, about my own age and with dark hair in wild disarray, cringed every few seconds, as if suffering through a nightmare.

I turned back toward Scarlet and let my gaze wander to the wall beyond her dome. The image of Earth Red towered above, blemished with shapeless clouds of orange and purple hovering over the points of injury inflicted by the other worlds. As I turned to take in the entire vision, Earth Blue came into view behind the boy's dome, and Earth Yellow behind the other girl's.

Francesca knelt and set a finger on a glass-panel inset in the terrazzo beneath our feet. The same size and shape of a door, the panel reflected the ceiling as well as the top edges of the surrounding domes.

Tucking my violin and bow again, I swept my fingers over the mirror-like glass, but they didn't appear in the reflection, nor did our bodies. We were like ghosts in this place, able to haunt but unable to cast a shadow.

She moved her finger along a row of seven nickel-sized lights set in the glass, evenly spaced across the center. Looking up at me, she whispered, "Watch and listen."

As the misty world's background lullaby played, the lights on the panel alternated between white and red, as if responding to each note of the song. I knelt with her and concentrated on the tones' pattern, a definite code. When the third light from the left flashed red, I pointed at it. "Middle C." I then moved my finger to the first light. "That's an A, one octave down from middle A."

She grinned. "That's my son. I knew you'd figure it out."

"I figured out that it's a code, but that's about it."

"It's a musical combination to get through this door." Francesca touched each light in turn. "You have to produce a perfect A–B–C, and so on for each light, but the octaves change every time I come. I have to listen until I pick them all out."

"Not very secure, is it?"

"It's not as easy as it sounds." She lifted her violin and bow. "I have to be fast and accurate."

"What happens if you get it wrong?"

"You don't want to know. Let's just say you'd hear enough dissonance to make Shostakovich proud."

I frowned. "I *like* Shostakovich."

"And some people like the sound of squealing tires." She smiled and winked. "Just watch for approaching stalkers. When I play, anyone around will be able to hear me. We'll have to hurry, because the glass stays open for just a few seconds."

I scanned the room. No one was coming. "Let's do it."

She looked at the floor panel and played A through G at various octaves, so fast that her fingers seemed to blur. From left to right the lights flashed to red, then back to white. She played the string of notes again, and the lights flashed blue in the same order. Finally, on the third run, the lights flashed yellow, then faded to black.

The panel's reflective surface melted away. Only a section of transparent glass remained, revealing a stairwell descending into darkness. Francesca rose and set her foot over the highest stair. Her gym shoe sank into the glass. "Let's go," she said as she descended into what now appeared to be clear gel. "We don't want to get stuck."

A movement in the distance caught my eye. The stalker we had seen earlier was heading our way. As I pushed my foot into the goop, I tapped her shoulder. "Someone's coming."

Francesca quickened her pace, holding her nose as her face sank through. By the time I had descended to waist level, she had submerged completely. As soon as I dropped below the surface and broke into the clear, I looked up through the still-transparent door. The stalker climbed into the triangle area and stared quizzically at the glass panel. He laid a hand on the surface. As he pressed down, his fingers splayed, but nothing passed through.

Walking on tiptoes to silence my shoes, I held my breath. If the stalker couldn't see or hear us, maybe he would just go away.

The four-foot-wide staircase twisted in a steep spiral, eventually descending into complete darkness. After about thirty steps, Francesca whispered, "We're almost there. You still with me?"

"Right at your heels ... I think."

"Okay. Here it is." Her hand touched my chest, halting my progress. "It's another door, but it's upright and not transparent, and it uses the same code as the other one. When it opens, just look. Don't step through or it'll be the longest step you ever took."

"Got it."

She played the seven notes again three times, pausing about a second between each run. A glow appeared around a rectangular shape, making the outline of the doorway easy to see. The glow ate away at the edges as it approached the center of the door . Light filtered into the stairway, illuminating Francesca as she kept her violin poised in playing position.

"Take a look," she said, nodding at the doorway. "They call this place Sarah's Womb, but I haven't figured out why."

Touching the side of the opening to keep my balance, I leaned out. An enormous chasm with a rocky surrounding wall yawned below, interrupted about a hundred feet down by a wide ledge that encircled the cylindrical chamber. The ledge seemed to be the remains of a floor that had collapsed in the center, leaving a circular pit. A single step from our precipice would send us plunging through its jaws and into a black void.

Above, a jigsaw pattern of hazy glass — the floor of the misty world — provided filtered light. A shadow crossed the glass, drifting slowly from one side of our ceiling to the other, a stalker patrolling on the other side of the ceiling.

I grabbed a rocky protrusion at my side and held on. Danger lay below and above, and both directions looked like dead ends. Literally.

CHAPTER EIGHT

F RANCESCA POINTED INTO the chasm with her bow.
"The violin your mother mentioned in her vision is
down there. The strings are stretched across this chasm.
The only way down is a basket tied to a rope." She reached
out with her bow and touched one of two ropes dangling
in front of us. She then pointed at a pulley protruding from
the rocky foundation above the outside of the doorway.
The rope looped over it, and a large knot kept it in place. "I
pull the basket up, get inside, and lower myself, but there's
room for only one of us."

I stared into the void. When my eyes adjusted, four
lines of light came into view — the violin strings. "We're
right over the chasm. What do you do, swing until you can
get to the side where the ledge is?"

"Exactly. It sounds dangerous, but it's safe."

"Safe?" I peered again into the seemingly
bottomless pit. "You're kidding, right?"

She laughed. "I'm not kidding. I slipped once and
fell out of the basket. I kept falling for a long time but
never hit bottom. I just snapped out of the vision. Since
we're not really here, I don't think we can be harmed
physically."

"Then why are we worried about the stalkers hearing us?"

"I said we can't be hurt *physically*. I meant in reality. They can make sounds that will make your head feel like it's going to explode. But it goes away when you leave the vision."

"When does the vision end? When we stop playing?"

She nodded. "But time passes a lot faster here. We're not even to your solo yet."

"Yeah. It's kind of weird, but I knew that. I still feel myself playing the piece." I gazed into the chasm again. The violin strings looked like four shimmering golden ropes tied at each end to span the hole below, the ends anchored to the surrounding ledge. The basket swung lazily over the strings, as if pushed by a gentle draft. "I'll go first. Then I'll lower you."

After setting my violin and bow down, I grabbed the rope just below the knot and pulled the rope through the pulley, making the basket rise to the top. Rectangular and made of dense wicker, it looked like a gondola from a hot air balloon, only smaller, barely enough room for one rider. The rope led into the basket's passenger compartment and through a hole in its floor, apparently secured underneath with a knot big enough to keep it from popping out.

I gave the basket's base a nudge with my foot, making it sway. It seemed sturdy enough, but riding in it could prove to be a wobbly adventure.

"Bring my violin when you come." Still hanging on to the rope, I climbed in and descended by letting the rough, intertwined fiber slide bit by bit through my hands.

Knowing I couldn't get hurt made the job easier. Still, friction warmed my skin, then burned, but not enough to make me let go.

The pulley knot passed through my hands, indicating that I was about halfway down. It wouldn't be long now.

Finally, the basket stopped. I pulled on the rope and gave the basket a shove with my body, then repeated the process until I began swinging back and forth in wider and wider arcs. As the rope bit into my palms, pain again burned my hands. Maybe Francesca was wrong. Maybe we could get hurt here. The mysteries of these visions had to be deeper than what appeared to the eye.

When the basket landed on the ledge, I jumped out and pulled the rope again to lift the basket back to Francesca. I let the excess rope add to a coil that already rested on the ledge near my feet. Coming out from the bottom of the coil, the rope led to the wall where it was tied to a thick iron hook. The whole system was primitive, but it worked.

After Francesca climbed into the basket, I lowered her, feeding the rope hand over hand. When the knot lodged at the pulley level, I pulled on the rope and, letting it run through my hands, I made the basket swing. When it came close enough, I grabbed the side and hauled the basket to safe ground. As soon as Francesca disembarked with both violins and bows in hand, I noticed a long pole lying on the ledge. A shepherd's crook on the end could easily grab the basket, probably the tool the stalkers used.

Francesca handed me my violin and bow. "Follow me."

Just as she took a step, I grabbed her elbow and pulled her back. "Wait a minute. Let me check this place out."

I looked in the direction she was about to go. Just as it had appeared from above, the ledge curved into the dimness, creating a full ring around the void. The entire chamber was really a circular pit, with a rock-encapsulated stairway dangling over the middle like a stony finger, our path downward from the stalkers' abode.

A glow emanated from narrow gaps at the edges of the ceiling where it didn't quite meet the surrounding cylindrical wall. The gaps revealed the lower arcs of the three earths displayed in the upper chamber. From this angle, the fissures between the planets seemed deeper, making the entire wall appear fragile.

A faint cracking sound echoed from above. A few shards of glass tumbled through the gap and down to the ledge where we stood. As soon as the shards struck the stony surface, they melted into crystal-clear rivulets that coursed in meandering paths toward the dark pit. When the liquid spilled into the void, the entire chamber rumbled.

The ground quaked hard, making Francesca fall into my arms. As the quake rumbled on, I pulled her into a crouch and hugged her close. The basket tipped off the ledge and plunged. Rope reeled from the coil until it tightened against the wall hook with a dull twang.

Soon, the last crystalline drop disappeared into the pit, and the trembling eased. I rose to my feet and helped Francesca to hers. She ran a hand up and down my arm, her eyes wide. Her expression said it all. The danger was greater than she had thought, and the more wounds inflicted on the cosmic fabric, the worse the danger would get.

"Okay," I said, setting my violin and bow down. "Show me the rest."

With the pit to her left, she walked along the ledge and halted where the first golden string crossed our path at knee level. The other three strings lay beyond it, each separated by a gap of about six feet. Well to our right, the strings coiled around broomstick-sized dowels anchored to the stone floor within an alcove carved into the wall. Under the strings, a polished black layer of wood acted as the fingerboard for this enormous violin.

Francesca set her violin and bow down, stepped over the first string, and sat on the second. It carried her weight without a problem.

I ran a finger along the string of gold. As thick as rope, it pushed a tingling sensation through my still-burning skin. This was the place Mom described. During her visions, she tried to play a tune, obviously pizzicato since she didn't have a bow, but the strings were too far apart. She would have had to lunge from one string to the other, probably leaping over one or more strings between each plucked note while still maintaining perfect rhythm.

No wonder Francesca needed my help. With two people it would be a lot easier, each person manning two strings, and no leaping required. But what was the point? She had said the strings spanned the celestial wound. Would playing music repair it?

Gripping the string, I pulled it up an inch or so. Plucking it would be no problem, but would the sound alert the stalkers? "Have you tried playing it?"

She nodded. "But I have no idea what I'm supposed to play." She bounced on the string. "And I can play only four notes, because I can't press a string down. Even if I were heavy enough, I couldn't pluck it while I'm pushing on it. And every time I play a note, the ground shakes like it did a minute ago. It's impossible to keep your balance."

I pushed all my weight on the string and pressed it against the fingerboard. I was heavy enough, so Francesca could play while I pushed, but we would still have to jump around from string to string like maniacs. Still, maybe only four notes were necessary. Mom didn't mention having to push the strings down during her vision.

I felt for the music sheet in my back pocket. Foundation's Key was a simple tune, but it had more than four notes. If that was the right piece to play, we could never manage it with only the two of us. I let out a sigh. "We'll need help."

"I know. I think if we come here for real with Kelly, Daryl, and my father, we could play almost anything."

"True." Kelly knew music, so she could help, and so could Dr. Malenkov, but what about Daryl Red? At least she wouldn't freeze when she saw the pit, like Daryl Blue would, and she could pluck a string when told. "Okay, so if we use a flash from the camera to come here, how do we avoid being seen?"

"That's the tricky part, which is why I showed it to you first so you could see all the obstacles."

I mentally ran through the path, from the glassy walkway to the domes to the panel in the floor. Being invisible had made everything much easier, but we still had almost been caught. "It's impossible. Once we're visible, we're dead meat."

"We have to try, don't we?" Francesca looked toward the void. "If we don't heal the wound, we'll all die anyway."

"I know that ..." I closed my mouth. I had almost added "Mom" in response to the feminine voice that had nailed me with a good argument so many times before.

While looking at the stairway above, I stooped low. From this angle, more of the upper chamber came into view through the gap near the wall. "Maybe I should go back upstairs and see if Scarlet can help somehow."

"Scarlet?"

"The girl in the dome. The one in the red dress. She seems to know a lot about everything."

Francesca rose from the string, careful to keep it from sounding a note. "Well, it's time for your solo anyway. When I stop playing, I'll be pulled back into my bedroom. I'll tell everyone what's going on."

I straightened. "So I guess I have to climb back up the rope to get to Scarlet."

"If you want to go that way. Like I said, if you fall, you'll just appear in the bedroom. Then you could start over and come in through the foggy path."

"I'll climb. I want to test something."

She picked up her violin and bow. "Do you remember the notes to open the floor panel?"

"I think so."

"The door by the pulley stays open for a long time, but you'll have to play the key again if you want to go through the upper door." She angled her head as if listening to something in the air. "Okay. It's time for your solo. Play well, my son." Still clutching her violin, she blew a kiss and faded away.

I rubbed my eyes. Would I ever get used to all this appearing and disappearing?

After jogging around the pit's perimeter to where I had left my violin, I grabbed the rope and reeled the basket up to my level. Apparently the knot had slipped through the pulley, and I had to jerk it back over the wheel to pull the basket higher. With a firm tug, I popped the knot through. Now the basket hung over a point near the center, swaying across the violin strings in a rhythmic motion.

As if ringing a huge church bell in a tower, I pulled on the rope and released it, timing the pulls to increase the basket's sway, as if it were a violin bow stroking the strings.

A bow? Might that be the best way to play the gargantuan instrument? But no one made a bow the size of a vaulting pole.

When the basket swung close enough, I grabbed the shepherd's crook and snagged the side, giving the rope slack as I fished it in. The knot, now tighter and smaller, moved freely through the pulley. It would no longer lodge itself in the pulley wheel to prevent a plunge.

After setting the violin and bow in the basket and climbing aboard, I swung myself over the center. As I passed, I again imagined a bow stroking the golden strings and playing Foundation's Key. With another slight pull, I adjusted the gap between the basket and the strings and pictured myself leaning over with a bow to reach them. Although the process would be difficult, it just might work.

I pulled hand over hand and hoisted myself up. My raw skin burned, and my muscles ached, but I didn't want to test Francesca's claim that falling into a bottomless pit was nothing more than waking up from a nightmare. Even without Daryl Blue's phobia, that seemed like a scary way to snap out of this vision.

Soon, perspiration drenched my back and sleeves, but after another minute, I reached the doorway and leaped through.

After retrieving the violin and bow, I released the basket and hurried up the stairs. Again, my muscles ached. Even though I wasn't really here, the effort was grueling. No wonder Mom was exhausted after she explored this place in her own vision.

When I reached the glass panel, I peeked out. No one was around. I lifted the violin and bow, picturing Francesca doing the same when she unlocked this door from above. The notes flowed to mind, and I played them through in a rapid echo. The lights in the panel, barely visible from below, flashed red. I played the notes again, making the lights turn blue, and then a third time. The lights blinked yellow once and turned off.

I climbed the remaining stairs, pushing my body through the liquid glass, and emerged in the midst of the domes. Glancing around for any sign of a stalker, I crept toward Scarlet's dome and peered through the transparent barrier. She still appeared to be asleep, sitting cross-legged, her head bowed low. With a sudden gasp, she jerked her head up and stared straight at me. For a moment, she seemed ready to smile, but the sadness in her eyes crept to her lips, weighing the corners down.

As she spread her red dress over her legs as far as she could, her voice sounded through the glass loud and clear. "I am lonely. Come in and talk with me for a while."

When I set my hand on the dome, my fingers passed into the prison, followed by my hand and arm. As I leaned forward, my head and torso entered as well.

Scarlet's smile broke through. "Fear not, Nathan. Wandering in the land of visions will bring you no lasting harm, unless, of course, you awaken the stalkers."

I pushed the rest of the way in and sat in front of her. Crossing my own legs to match hers, I laid the violin in my lap. "If I'm seeing a vision, how can you talk to me?"

She touched her chest. "I am your supplicant. Entering visions is what I do. I entered your dream while you were unconscious, and now I have drawn you to myself in this new vision."

"But why? What is a supplicant?"

She smiled, though her brow furrowed. "I see that you have forgotten what I told you earlier."

"I remember some of it, but it's kind of foggy."

"A supplicant is the office of a Sancta, which is Latin for a sacred place. We are a specialized order of angelic beings who are called to come to the aid of chosen humans." She spread out her hands, gesturing toward the wall lining her enclosure. "The fools thought this cage would prevent me from helping you. They crippled me for a time, but I have learned to use these mirrors to see the outside worlds. Yet, I can see only the world you happen to be in, for I am assigned to protect you."

"Why me?"

Her smile brightened. "You are the gifted one from Earth Red who carries the window to my perceptions.

When you were in danger, you asked for my help, and I sang for you. A supplicant makes petitions on behalf of his or her gifted one."

I gazed into her reddish brown eyes, beautiful and haunting. "So are you Quattro?"

She laughed gently. "Your father's name for me. It is pleasant, but I prefer Scarlet, for I am the Earth Red supplicant. At least I was until Mictar dragged me to this awful place."

"Do you know why he did?"

"Not yet. I have suspicions, but I want to be certain before I speculate verbally." She took my hand and enfolded it in both of hers. "Although we are together only in a vision, you are the first gifted assignment I have been able to meet. I am lonely and I have longed for your presence ever since I learned you were a gifted one. Let us talk of more pleasant things than my imprisonment."

Her touch sparked a surge of warmth, scrambling my thoughts. Not a single idea came to mind. "What do you want to talk about?"

Her voice perked up. "Your friend, Kelly. Tell me about her."

"Well ..." I gazed again at Scarlet's lovely face. Not a hint of jealousy spoiled the sincerity in her probing eyes. "She's really kind of amazing. I've never met anyone who is so ..." I searched for the right word, but it seemed out of reach. "So cool, I guess. I mean, she's brave, loyal, strong—"

"And lovely," Scarlet added, compressing my hand. "Don't tell me you haven't noticed."

I lowered my head, trying to hide my uneasy smile. "She is."

Scarlet laid a hand on my cheek. "Nathan, do not be embarrassed. God gave her beauty, just as he gave her strength, courage, and loyalty." As she stroked my skin, she lowered her voice to a whisper. "And she has given you her most precious gift. Her heart."

I raised my head. Scarlet had scooted so close, our noses nearly touched. With breath like roses, she whispered, "I have also given you my heart, my beloved, but in a very different way. When you return in physical form, will you come for me? You have the power. Will you set me free before it's too late?"

I stared at her wide orbs. Everything felt so real—the warmth of her skin, the beat of her rapid pulse, the tingle from her thumb as it caressed my knuckles. How could this be a vision? Her eyes pleaded for an answer. Pure entreaty, intermingled with fear and love, poured forth.

I swallowed through my tightening throat. "I'll figure out a way to rescue you. I won't let you down."

Her head drooped until it nearly rested on her chest. "I am thankful for your promise, though it is one you cannot keep without my help. When you return, I will—" She lifted her head suddenly, her eyes widening. "Go!" She slid away on her knees. "You must leave now!"

A loud wail pierced the silence, like a panther squealing a high-pitched growl. I grabbed the violin, jumped up, and pressed my hand against the glass, but my fingers wouldn't pass through.

Scarlet leaped to her bare feet. "His song is binding the glass. It is now impenetrable, even for a vision walker like you."

"Is there another way out? Can't I just stop playing my violin back where I really am?"

She shook her head. "The song cuts off your subconscious mind, so you can't communicate with your awake mind to tell it to stop playing."

The song's pitch shot up in frequency. Excruciating pain tore across my skull, like an earthquake rolling inside my head. Still clutching the violin, I covered one ear and paced around the dome. "It's about to make my brain explode!"

Scarlet spread out her arms, her palms pointing upward. Raising her voice above the screeching din, she sang in a beautiful, fast-paced melody.

> O guiding hand of songs within the stars,
> You hear my cries from Red's accursed dome.
> O let the one who listens from afar
> Awake the gifted child and bring him home.

An invisible force snaked around my abdomen and squeezed my breath away. I could barely choke out my words. "What are they doing now?"

Scarlet smiled. "It is not a stalker who embraces you." Rising on tiptoes, she kissed my cheek. "Hurry back, my beloved. I will be waiting."

I toppled and fell. Something dropped on top of me, a body, but there was no red dress, only blue jeans and a sweatshirt. Feminine arms wrapped tightly around my waist. I wriggled to loosen the strong grip, but my muscles were spent. Finally, my captor sat up on my thighs and pushed her hair back.

I blinked. "Kelly?"

She rubbed her palms across the cardinal logo on her sweatshirt. "You're drenched."

I raised an arm along with its perspiration-soaked sleeve and stared at the violin in my hand. As the misty funnel faded behind Kelly, Francesca and Daryl shuffled out from it and looked on. Gunther and Dr. Malenkov stood near the bedroom door.

"What happened?" I asked.

Still on her knees, Kelly slid to my side, keeping her stare fixed on me. "I heard what was going on—you and Francesca with the big violin, you and Scarlet talking, that screeching noise, Scarlet's song, everything. I yelled at you to stop playing, but you wouldn't, so I tackled you."

As I stared back at her, some of the more personal parts of my conversation with Scarlet replayed in my mind. "You heard everything?"

A hint of a smile bent her lips, but it quickly vanished. "Sure. What's the big deal?"

"Nothing, I guess." I pushed against the carpet with weary arms, too tired to string my words together in a coherent sentence. "We have to go there. Play the violin. Rescue Scarlet. And the others."

Bracing my back as I rose, Kelly nodded. "And save the world. I heard that."

"We have to make sure we're ready," Francesca said. "We need to get it right the first time. If we keep breaking through cosmic walls, the celestial wound will swallow the very instrument that's supposed to heal it."

Still wobbly as I straightened, I held out my violin bow. "We need a bow. A big one, maybe ten feet long. But it has to be light enough to carry."

"Balsa wood?" Kelly asked. "And hollow it out?"

"Maybe. But who could make it?" I turned to Gunther. "Could you?"

He shrugged. "I don't know about woodworking, much less about making a violin bow. Maybe Nikolai could help me."

Dr. Malenkov shook his head. "To make it so big while maintaining a light weight and proper balance would take an extraordinary craftsman. Perhaps we could employ a local instrument maker I know."

"If you mean Mr. Hancock," Gunther said, "no way. He'd be too scared to do anything besides what he sees in his dreams."

"My father could do it." Kelly touched Francesca's bow. "Just give him a normal-sized one and the proportions you want, and he'd make it work."

I pressed my hands against the sides of my head. "Okay. Information overload. My brain's about to explode again." Closing my eyes, I ran through the confusing tangle of options. Since we were on Earth Yellow, we couldn't contact Kelly's father — no network connection to Earth Red. Back on Earth Blue, we still had hundreds of mirrors to look through, any one of which might lead to Mom and Dad. Daryl Blue had had time to develop the photographs, but going back to see what she had learned from them would risk putting another wound in the cosmic fabric. And, finally, what could we do about the stranglehold Mictar held on the people of Earth Yellow?

Lowering my hands, I looked at Kelly. "How old would your father be on Earth Yellow now?"

Kelly glanced at the ceiling. "Let's see ... maybe sixteen or seventeen?"

"How young did he start woodworking?"

"Well, he used to brag about making a crossbow from a tree that lightning knocked down. He swore that the electric jolt made it the most accurate crossbow in the world." She raised a finger to her chin. "I think he was twelve, but I'm not sure."

I looked at the wall mural, a musical staff with notes climbing up the lines. "So it's pretty likely that he's good at it now."

"I guess so, but how are you going to contact him? He won't have any idea who you are."

I touched one of the notes and traced its outline. "When did he move into this house?"

"Not sure. I could find out when we get back to Earth Red."

I thumped the wall with the heel of my hand. "We can't wait that long. Once we get back there, time will zoom by here."

Dr. Malenkov withdrew an envelope from his jacket and pulled out a letter. "I keep Vernon Clark's note of permission with me if by happenstance someone should ask why I spend so much time here." As he read, his eyes darted back and forth. "Here it is. My family and I will be moving into our new home by the end of the summer." He folded the letter and put it away. "That would be next week."

Looking again at Kelly, I pointed at the floor. "Was this your dad's bedroom?"

She nodded. "Until Grandpa moved into a nursing home. Why?"

"I'm betting a young Tony Clark won't be able to resist solving a mystery." I reached for the letter. "May I see it, Dr. Malenkov?"

"Certainly." He unfolded it and gave it to me. "It is handwritten and difficult to read."

I peered at the messy script. "I can make it out." After reading it for a few seconds, a shell of an idea came to mind. If I could convince young Tony that I was from the future, maybe I could get him to make the bow.

Gunther looked over my shoulder. "I can hear the wheels spinning. What are you plotting?"

"I'm trying to figure out a way to entice Tony to make the bow, like giving him a glimpse of the future."

"You're right about Daddy loving a mystery," Kelly said. "He'll move heaven and earth to solve one."

I pulled my wallet from my back pocket, fished out a twenty-dollar bill, and showed it to everyone. "How about strange-looking money from the future?"

She took the bill and looked it over. "That might work. Put mystery and money together, and he'll do anything."

"Very interesting," Dr. Malenkov said, "but how will you incorporate constructing the bow?"

"I'm not sure." I looked at Kelly. "Got any ideas?"

"Yep. We'll need pen and paper." She winked. "And duct tape."

CHAPTER NINE

WITH A DRAMATIC swirl of my pen, I signed the bottom of a wrinkled sheet of paper in red ink. I lifted the page and read it out loud. "Tony Clark, I implore you to heed my words. I am from a future time, and I must return there before the window to my world closes. I have heard of your woodworking prowess, and I need a trustworthy young man like you to perform an unusual task. Yet, knowing also of your intelligence, I realize that it will take much persuasion to convince you of my tale.

"I need a special violin bow. It must be ten feet long, proportional to the dimensions of a normal bow, and light enough for a person to carry without trouble. I realize that this is an odd request, but I cannot reveal its use except for the fact that I need it to save my world.

"I know you must be doubting. That is why I left proof of my incredible story. You will find attached a twenty-dollar bill. Notice the date and the unusual design. Put it under a magnifying glass and study the details. You will undoubtedly agree that no counterfeiter in the world could create it.

"If you, Mr. Clark, will construct this bow, a friend of mine in your world will contact me, and I will come back and give you a bill that matches the one I enclosed.

With two such bills in your possession, displaying differing serial numbers, dates, and Federal Reserve banks, you will be able to prove that the one you now hold is genuine, for why would a counterfeiter create two different plates if it would be so difficult to make even one? Such a bill could make you rich and famous.

"If, however, fame and fortune are not your desire, I implore you, for the sake of my world, and perhaps yours as well, do me this favor. The task is small, yet the rewards are great. I remain, respectfully yours, Nathan of the Red World."

Gunther clapped his hands. "That is amazing!"

"Sounds like some spam emails I've been getting," Daryl said. "This one is even wilder."

"But every word is true." Kelly grinned as she jerked the page out of my hand. "You're a sly one, you are."

"Thanks, but the note was your idea." I held up a roll of duct tape. "The perfect way to attach a twenty-dollar bill."

"I'll take care of that part," Gunther said. "When they move in, I'll make sure he gets it."

Kelly handed him the letter. "Just remember, even though he has a big head about his talents, he's not stupid, so try to come up with a clever way to deliver it."

"Trust me. I'm already dreaming up something. And I'll get a regular bow for him, too."

I tossed the roll of tape to Gunther. "I guess that's all we can do for now. We'd better get back to Earth Blue."

Francesca took Dr. Malenkov's arm and leaned against his shoulder. "Hurry back, Son. If Tony gets to work right away, it will probably be only a few days from your perspective, or maybe less."

"Right. We'll try to figure out a way to stay in touch. Maybe Dr. Gordon's got a handle on those pictures by now. He might have an idea about how to stay safe when we go to the misty world for real."

"It's going to take more than Dr. Gordon to get us past those stalkers," Francesca said.

Kelly leaned close to Francesca and kissed her on the cheek. "I'll miss you."

"And I'll miss you, as well." Francesca averted her eyes. "Good-byes are always painful."

"They are." Kelly backed away. She seemed withdrawn, sad, upset. She swiveled toward me, her eyes glistening. "Can we go now?"

I took her hand. "Yeah. Sure."

Kelly, Daryl, Gunther, and I returned to the van and drove toward the observatory site. Along the way, we discussed plans for delivering the letter and twenty-dollar bill to Tony. The radio played in the background, filling in periods of silence. News reports described the latest nightmare-related deaths and gave rules updates straight from the Enforcer. During the five hours of travel, we took turns catching naps. Since Kelly's eyesight stayed clear, she had no trouble driving while the rest of us snoozed.

When we reached the forest and unloaded the motorcycles, Kelly wheeled one of them under the shelter while Gunther held the other upright in front of the mirror and aimed its headlight toward the glass.

Kelly pulled the tarp down and hid her motorcycle. "I think we're ready."

"Good." I handed the camera to Kelly and the mirror to Daryl, then began tuning the violin, making ready to play the *Carmen* piece that would restore the image of Earth Blue to the tri-fold mirror. For some reason, it had blacked out and returned to a normal reflection, probably because Daryl Blue had changed the channel to Earth Red to consult with Dr. Gordon.

When Kelly and Daryl joined me in front of the mirror, Gunther gave us a nod. "I guess I'm a guardian angel for Tony Clark now, too, the angel on his shoulder who'll keep prodding him to make that bow."

"Let us know when it's done." I pointed at the ground. "Maybe you could plant a sign here where we can read it."

Daryl snapped her fingers. "That's it." She pushed the mirror square into Kelly's hand and backed away from me. "Forget posting a sign. I'll stay here and set up communications."

I lowered the violin. "How? They don't have the Internet, and even if they did, how would you hook up? Interfinity's radio telescope hasn't been constructed."

"It's what, the early eighties?" Daryl spread out her hands. "The rudiments of the Internet are already in place. I know how to construct a radio transmitter and receiver, and I know all the protocols. It shouldn't take long."

"But wouldn't it mess up your life?" I asked. "I mean, you'll age twice as fast here compared to Earth Red, maybe faster."

"Hey, we're talking about saving the universe." Daryl smiled and slid her arm around Gunther's waist. "We'll figure it all out. He's got the muscles and wheels, and I've got the brains."

"And a whole thimbleful of humility," Kelly added.

Daryl nodded. "At least that much. Maybe more."

I raised the violin again and eyed Daryl with new admiration. She was willing to make a huge sacrifice—leave home and family to embark on a mind-bending project with someone she barely knew. "I'll tell Daryl Blue to watch for your call."

After taking a deep breath, I began the *Carmen* piece. Kelly pressed closer and crouched to stay out of my way as I stroked the strings. Soon, the mirror darkened, and our images warped into ribbons of color. I pushed through the demanding piece, my arms weakened by the strenuous climb over the void, even though it was nothing but a vision.

Soon, the observatory floor came into focus. Daryl Blue rose slowly from her chair. Since Earth Yellow's time passage compared to the other earths fluctuated, her motion appeared jerky, almost at a standstill for a moment and up to half her normal speed at other times.

Gunther pushed the motorcycle closer. "Be thinking about us. The nightmare situation here is really a ..." Flashing a grin, he shrugged. "A nightmare."

"We will." I nodded at Gunther. "Hit the light."

The headlamp's beam bounced off the three mirror faces and intersected a few feet in front to create an elliptical halo, flat and standing upright, with a rainbow-like perimeter—seven layered stripes that surrounded a glowing yellowish-white oval.

I repacked the violin in its case, took Kelly's hand, and walked into the ellipse. The scene around us shattered into millions of pieces. As if taken by a fresh breeze, the pieces flew apart and disappeared, revealing the telescope room. At first, the room was distorted in a twisting coil, but it slowly straightened and clarified. Within a few seconds, we were back.

Daryl Blue hurried to us. "Where's Red?"

I gestured behind us with a thumb. "She stayed to set up a network so we can communicate with Earth Yellow. Since time's moving a lot faster there, she might try to call you soon."

Jogging toward the desk, Daryl shouted back, "I'll bet I know what frequency she'll use. I'll see if I can find it and lock it."

Kelly tightened her grip on my hand. "Keep close. My eyesight's messed up again."

I tried to get a look at her eyes, but she kept her head low. The sudden changes were probably getting to her. After several hours of normal eyesight, now she had to once again view the world through a dirty filter.

As I led her to the computer desk, I glanced at the ceiling. Daryl Red and Gunther were no longer there, nor was the motorcycle. The grass waved furiously, rain beat against the ground, and a man ran by, far faster than humanly possible.

I caught a glimpse of his circular glasses. He had to be Dr. Simon, but was he the Blue or Yellow version? It was impossible to tell.

The ceiling faded to black and then to the familiar chaotic blobs of color. Daryl, staring at the laptop, slid her finger across the touch pad. As a line of numbers ran along the bottom of the screen, she shook her head. "No trace of Red's signal yet. She'll probably need a couple of Earth Yellow days to get it done. In the meantime, I'll tune Dr. Gordon back in."

I led Kelly to a chair at an adjacent desk and scanned the dim chamber. The telescope cast a long shadow across the tiles, the entry for guided tours stood slightly ajar, and the elevator door was closed. The floor indicator displayed a red numeral one. "Where's Clara?"

Keeping her gaze locked on the computer screen, Daryl flicked her thumb toward the ceiling. "Clara Red is with Dr. Gordon up there. Clara Blue went to get some munchies."

I looked up. My faithful tutor stared back at me, her arms crossed over her open trench coat. Dr. Gordon sat next to her, studying an image on his laptop screen.

Clara's voice boomed through the wall speakers. "You weren't gone very long. Did you accomplish anything significant?"

I eased closer to the center of the room. "Quite a bit. We spent at least twelve hours on Earth Yellow."

"Only two and a half hours here," Clara said. "Tell us what happened, and we'll report on the photos."

As I began the story, Clara Blue returned with enough sub sandwiches for everyone. Daryl only nibbled at hers, while Kelly ate more heartily. I took a big bite at every convenient pause in my tale. My stomach clock said I hadn't eaten in half a day, and all the rope climbing in the misty world, real or not, had left me famished.

After I told about Daryl Red's commitment to stay on Earth Yellow, I settled back in a desk chair. "That's about it."

"Very interesting," Dr. Gordon said. "I trust that you will find our discoveries equally interesting." He swung around in his chair and looked up at us, though it seemed downward from my viewpoint.

"Daryl," Dr. Gordon continued, "the photographs I selected for examination should now be in your folder. Please display number one on your screen."

"Will do." Daryl pecked at her keyboard for a second, then pointed at her monitor. "Got it."

I rolled my chair closer and studied the photo. Facing the camera, Tsayad appeared to be speaking in song, probably a minute or so after he greeted us on the glassy path. Carrying his songbook, his head tilted slightly upward, he seemed normal, at least as normal as a stalker could look.

"Do you see anything unusual?" Dr. Gordon asked.

"Besides the white hair, the pale face, and the mist all around?" I shrugged. "Not really."

"Daryl, focus on his hands and enlarge the area."

"No problem." Within a couple of seconds, the stalker's hands filled the screen, both grasping the songbook.

"Nathan," Dr. Gordon said, "I want to see if you notice this feature on your own in order to be sure that I am not just imagining it."

As I studied the photo, I rolled closer and closer to the screen. The stalker's right index finger pointed at a note on the right-hand page, and his left thumb on the opposite page held the book open. Nothing unusual. Yet.

"Daryl," I said, "can you blow up that line of music, the one his finger's on?"

"Sure thing."

I rose to my feet and drew within inches of the monitor. "It's C Major, but it's kind of strange. There are lots of sharps and flats, no sense of following the key."

"Exactly," Dr. Gordon said. "Did your experience in that world provide any reason for such dissonance?"

My mind latched on to that word—dissonance. It had cropped up, something Scarlet had said. The stalkers feed on fear and the dissonance fear creates. It wasn't much, but it was something. "I'll think about it. Go on to the next one."

"Very well. Daryl, display number two."

A new image replaced the first, a photo of the three domes, including the twelve stalkers surrounding Scarlet's dome. Barely visible between the legs of two stalkers, Scarlet sat in her trembling crouch, appearing small and frail.

"This discovery is subtler," Dr. Gordon said. "Concentrate on the positioning of the people surrounding the dome."

I again leaned as close as possible. Kelly and I had heard this ungodly choir singing their dissonant notes while they faced Scarlet, but the notes had come too quickly to catch a musical pattern, and we weren't there long enough to study the way stalkers stood. Now I could focus on their positions.

Able to see through the dome to the other side, I counted by gender—seven men and five women. Something else was like this, something in my musical training that echoed this seven-versus-five circular pattern.

A phrase popped to mind—a chromatic circle. If the males stood for the natural notes, and the females the sharps or flats, they could easily represent the complete scale. I lifted a finger toward the closest choir member. "They're musical notes. Each stalker stands for a note in the chromatic circle."

Dr. Gordon nodded. "Good. I was wondering if I was just imagining things."

"So what do we do now?" I asked.

He rose and walked toward the telescope, one hand in his pocket as he assumed a thoughtful pacing mode. "I suggest going back to the four hundred mirrors to search for your parents. Risking unnecessary cross-world jumps isn't wise, but if you locate Solomon, acquiring his aid would be worth the risk. In the meantime, Daryl Blue will try to communicate with Daryl Red. When the bow is finished, we will summon you for another journey to Earth Yellow to get it."

"What effect is Interfinity having on Earth Red?"

Dr. Gordon stopped and looked up. "Confusion and wide-spread panic, not only from the appearance of long-dead airline crash survivors, but the rift in the cosmos is now visible in the heavens. At night, a black chasm obliterates our view of at least a tenth of the stars. They are simply gone."

"Gone?" Kelly asked as she cast her wandering gaze upward. "How could stars disappear?"

Dr. Gordon shrugged. "That's what the top astronomers on the planet are trying to figure out. But while they're scratching their heads, the world is suffering a sanity meltdown."

"It's kind of like that here on Blue," I said. "People are confused, especially older folks who feel like they're living in the past."

Dr. Gordon resumed his slow pacing. "And the weather phenomenon continues to puzzle me. It's as though Earth Yellow's atmosphere has encroached on the other two without a reciprocating effect. Maybe our two universes are materializing within each other somehow, one overlapping the other so that the worlds will merge physically. If so, the danger level has become literally astronomical. The gravitational collapse alone could annihilate both planets. Our peril cannot be overestimated."

"That's not exactly comforting." I withdrew the Earth Blue phone from my pocket and checked the battery indicator. Still plenty of power. "I'm off to see the mirrors again. Give me a call if you hear anything from Daryl Red. If you can't get me on the mobile phone, try the landline. If it's out, try smoke signals. I'll get back in touch somehow."

Clara Blue tapped my shoulder. "Shall I go with you?"

"Better not. Daryl might need your help, and if we have to jump to another world, we want to punch as few holes as possible."

"Well, I'm coming," Kelly said, rising from her chair. "You need my ears."

"And your tackling skills. You never know when I'll need someone to pull me out of a dream."

Clara Blue crossed her arms over her chest. "Okay, Mr. Practical, have you thought about where to get fuel, or did you forget that the Toyota is almost empty and operating gas stations are likely to be few and far between?"

I licked my lips and cringed at the hint of gasoline still coating the surface. Siphoning my way to Iowa wouldn't work. "Knowing you, you already have an idea."

"You're right." She pointed in the general direction of the observatory's rear exit. "I checked the outbuilding. If you look behind the lawn mower, you will find two small gas cans. It won't be enough to get all the way to central Iowa, but it's a start."

"Great. Thanks."

Daryl Blue gave Kelly a peck on the cheek. "Take care of yourself." Her voice cracked. "I don't want to lose another Kelly-kins."

Blinking, Kelly took her hand. She opened her mouth to speak, but, after pausing a moment, she closed it and returned the kiss.

Silence descended on the telescope room. The gravity of countless dangers likely weighed on everyone's mind. With Interfinity at hand and Mictar lurking in every dark corner, the shadow of death seemed to hover overhead.

Offering only a wave, Kelly and I left, hand in hand.

After gassing up the Toyota and packing the violin, camera, and mirror, we began the long drive back to Kelly Blue's house in Iowa. The skies, now gray and darkening, spattered cold rain across the windshield and slickened the pavement.

I flipped on the radio and pressed the scan button, searching for a good signal. The digital readout sped through the FM frequencies, topping at 107.9 and starting over again. Obviously, no stations were nearby. When I pressed the button again to end the search, mild static buzzed through the speakers, and a rhythmic bump sounded every second or so, as if a percussionist struck a drum in time with an inaudible melody.

I reached to turn the radio off, but Kelly grabbed my wrist. "Leave it there. I hear something."

I pulled my hand back. "What?"

"I'm not sure. Just let me listen."

As we passed close to the Burger King we had visited while on Earth Yellow, the static increased in volume and pitch. I decelerated and pulled into the parking lot. "Let's change the frequency one notch at a time." I pressed the tuning button. The static altered, pitching higher again. "Anything interesting?"

"Try going up a few more."

I hit the button twice. The static separated into several scratchy voices, some bass singers, some sopranos, and a couple in between. As I continued climbing the frequency range, the jumbled sounds clarified until the chorus of voices sang without distortion. Although each singer performed with professional polish, they sang oddly blended notes, without melody, without purpose. The voices seemed to compete with each other, some in one key and some in another, until the combination sounded more like an operatic war than a choir performance.

Kelly winced. "That's awful! It sounds like Pavarotti is having a temper tantrum."

"Can you interpret?" I asked, turning the volume down a notch.

"They're all saying different things, but I'll try to pick up something." She opened the glove box and withdrew a pen. "Got any paper?"

I pulled Foundation's Key from my pocket. "You can use the back of this."

She retrieved Daryl's puzzle book, lifted her feet to her seat, and set the paper and book on her knees, drawing them close to her eyes. While she jotted down some words, I drove slowly out of the parking lot. "Let's see if we can keep moving and still pick it up." As I accelerated, the signal faded but not enough to squelch the voices.

Kelly turned up the volume and continued transcribing lyrics. "I count at least eight voices, and they're all saying something different. I'm piecing them together the best I can."

I glanced at her as she worked. At times, she just listened intently, then, with tiny, precise letters, she slowly formed a word, pursing her lips to mouth the syllables as they appeared on her paper.

I squeezed the steering wheel and looked at the darkening sky. It was a good thing we had four hours of driving ahead. With so many voices, her transcription could take every minute.

Although no other cars competed for road space, I took my time. Every few miles, as the signal wavered, I adjusted the volume. Soon, a pattern developed. Whenever the thickness of the clouds overhead decreased, the strength of the signal increased.

Was the music, if it could be called that, coming through the wounds in space? Could the singers be the twelve white-haired freaks torturing Scarlet from their stance in the chromatic circle?

I pressed the gas pedal. Scarlet needed help. I had to rescue her from their clutches, even if it meant wounding the cosmic fabric again.

After writing a few more words, Kelly settled back in her seat. "It's really strange. Most of the voices are singing about morbid things like death, fear, and war, but one female inserts other words out of the blue. So I concentrated on her voice. She sings in what sounds like F-sharp Major, and every time she sings an A-sharp, I hear a word that doesn't fit what she's saying overall. That's when I write the A-sharp words that my mind translates."

"That's amazing. With all that noise, you gotta have perfect pitch to pull out those notes."

She doodled on the page, making a warped quarter note. "It has to be more than that. I've always been good at identifying notes, but ever since you showed up at my house, I've been hearing things I've never heard before. All the sounds separate neatly from each other, almost like I can see them in my mind."

"You picked up a sixth sense of some kind."

"I guess so." She tapped the pen on the paper. "Anyway, here's what I have so far. Solomon location square music."

"She mentioned my father. I wonder how she knows him."

"No idea. I'll keep listening. Maybe there's more." She angled her ear toward the radio and squinted at the paper again as she painstakingly transcribed from the midst of the turmoil. Sometimes the voices stopped for a while, as if giving the singers a few minutes to rest, but they always started back up again, beginning with a ten-second-long burst in which everyone belted out a C-natural at various octaves before crashing into the usual cacophony of horrible dissonance.

After an hour or so, the music halted — another rest. Kelly slid her feet back to the floorboard and held the paper close to her eyes. "There might be more, but here's what I have so far. Solomon location square music key circle sleep interpreter dream bedroom Patar."

I echoed the words in a whisper. "Solomon … location … square … music …" I looked at Kelly. "Then what?"

She read from her notes. "Key circle sleep interpreter dream bedroom Patar."

"A string of nouns. It needs verbs."

"I noticed."

I turned the radio volume up one notch. "Can you catch any verbs when she sings a different note, maybe stray verbs that don't fit in with the rest of the stuff she's singing?"

Kelly lifted her feet again. "I'll try, but the music is so obnoxious, it's giving me a headache."

"Let's make a pit stop while they're resting. We need gas anyway." I exited the Interstate at Walcott, a few miles west of Davenport. An Iowa 80 truck stop and a Pilot Travel Center faced each other on the secondary highway, but darkness covered every opening except for a faint glow from the window in the Pilot's doorway.

Driving slowly, I pulled up to one of the Pilot's service islands. There was no sign of electrical power—no prices on the pumps or words on the instruction screens. It felt like a disaster scene — a war zone or the aftermath of a plague.

I opened the door and stepped out. "Come on. Might as well see if we can use the restroom." As I approached the entry, I scanned the late evening sky. The clouds had raced away, replaced by a purple canvas speckled with hundreds of shimmering lights, much bigger and brighter than stars, probably more evidence of Interfinity's approach.

The air had grown hot. Did that mean it was still summer on Earth Yellow? Or maybe Indian summer? Or could it have already cycled to the next year's summer?

I pushed my sleeves up past my elbows. Although I had long ago shed my sweatshirt and thrown it in the backseat, I had to keep the overly hot shirt. I had nothing but skin underneath.

Kelly walked next to me, her poorly focused eyes meandering from side to side. She had also stripped down to her shirt, a cooler short-sleeved white tunic, loose and flowing.

Something crashed behind us. I pivoted and scanned the highway. At the truck stop across the road, a man in a business suit had just broken a door window with the butt of a rifle. He reached through the jagged hole and opened the door from the inside before disappearing into the darkness.

"What's going on?" Kelly asked, blinking.

"Armed robbery," I pointed toward the truck stop. "The upper class has sunk to looting."

She squinted that way. "What are we going to do?"

"The thief has a rifle. I don't think it's a good idea to get shot stopping a beer-and-pretzel heist."

Kelly let out a weak sigh. "I guess not."

Still looking back, I pushed the door open and walked inside. When I turned, the twin barrels of a shotgun pressed against my forehead.

CHAPTER TEN

"STORE'S CLOSED," A woman on the trigger side of the gun said. "Got a problem with that?"

I backed away a step and pushed Kelly behind me. Swallowing, I tried to keep my voice steady. "Uh ... no problem. I just needed gas, and the door was open, so I—"

"Thought you'd see what you could take." The woman lowered the gun to her hip, the barrel still pointed toward us. With only an oil lamp on the counter casting light on her stocky body, her features blended in with the dim interior of the store. Yet, her wide eyes communicated more fear than bravado.

"I wasn't going to take anything." I drew in a deep breath, keeping an eye on the shotgun. That lady could pull the trigger at any moment. The memory of Tony Clark getting his guts blown out sent chills across my body. "I know how to stop what's causing all these weird events, but if I don't get gas, I can't get where I'm going."

Wrinkles in her brow slowly eased. "You got money?"

I flicked my thumb toward the pumps. "Does the credit card thing work?"

She shook her head. "Cash only, but if I can't get the generator running, nothing will work."

I dug out my wallet and rifled through the bills. "What's the price per gallon?"

Now, instead of fear, her eyes revealed confusion. She set the gun butt on the floor and glanced back and forth as if lost. "I ... I don't know."

A gust pulled the door open and slammed it shut again, knocking over a stack of newspapers. The room grew cold, and the smell of burning firewood drifted by. An overhead fluorescent light flickered on, and a hum sounded from the cash register.

She leaned the shotgun against the counter and ran her fingers through her short graying hair. "What happened? My hair is gone."

Kelly blinked at her. "Was it long and as black as a raven?"

"Yes." Her whole body quaked as she continued to comb her fingers through her hair. "What's going on? Why aren't more cars out there?" She backed to the counter and stared wide-eyed. "Is the world coming to an end?"

Kelly stepped forward, her hand extended to guide her way. When she reached the woman, she set her hand on her shoulder. "Turn on the pumps, and I'll tell you all about it."

The woman nodded stiffly. "Okay. I can do that."

I strode toward the door and picked up one of the spilled newspapers, the most recent edition of the *Chicago Tribune*. With only one section, it seemed lightweight, void of anything nonessential. I thumbed through the few pages. No advertisements appeared anywhere, just long articles and a few black-and-white photos.

As I made my way to the car, I pushed my sleeves back down and read the front headline. In big, bold letters

it spelled out "PANIC!" A smaller sub-headline read,
"Midwest and Southeast Hardest Hit by Cosmic Terror."

When I shifted my eyes to read the article, a thump
and a loud hum jerked my attention toward the gas
pumps. The island lights flashed on, and zeroes appeared
on the digital meters. I set the paper on the trunk, pushed
the nozzle into the tank, and squeezed the trigger. The
gallons meter began counting, but the dollars and cents
meter ticked up at a slow rate. It would easily stay under a
dollar by the time the tank filled.

While the gas flowed, I read the newspaper's
lead article. The world's governments had guessed that
the cosmic abnormalities were the result of some kind of
imminent alien invasion. The long-dead airline-disaster
victims had to be imposters, brought to earth to create
havoc and gain influence. The United States would
lead the effort to battle against the encroaching power,
apparently another realm invading through some kind of
wormhole in space. Details about how they would carry
out this battle were sketchy at best. The entire country now
operated under a state of emergency. With widespread
blackouts and very little fuel available, law enforcement
had been relegated to foot patrols in many areas. The
National Guard kept order in the cities, but little if any
help was available in rural areas. Crime was rampant.

I folded the paper in half. Saving the airline
passengers had brought more trouble, validating Patar's
warning. The stalker's words, spoken while everyone else
on board sat frozen, returned to mind as if whispered in
my ear. *If these souls are cheated out of death, their escape might
create more darkness than light. Take care not to stir darkened*

pools when you know neither the depth of the water nor the creatures that lurk beneath the surface.

I shivered. Patar was right again. Maybe it was about time I put away my emotional attachments and listened to him. Without Dad around to steer me away from a dumb step, I needed a word of wisdom, or maybe a kick in the pants, which Patar seemed more than willing to deliver.

After topping off the tank and grabbing the newspaper, I hurried toward the store's entry. As soon as I opened the door, the clerk, sitting on a stool behind the counter, greeted me with a big smile. Kelly leaned against the front of the counter, munching on a stick of beef jerky.

"Welcome back, Nathan," the clerk said. "Kelly and I are having a very nice talk."

I laid the paper on the counter. "It looks like you're feeling better."

"I am. This lovely young lady explained everything to me."

I gave Kelly a quizzical look. "Oh. That's good. I guess." Nodding at the paper, I added, "How much for this and the gas? The pump registered only fifty cents."

The clerk waved a hand. "On the house. And more to boot."

"Drinks and snacks," Kelly said, holding up a bulging plastic bag. "We're all set."

After getting back on the road, I reached into the bag and pulled out a bottle of Dr Pepper. "What went on back there?"

Kelly swallowed the last bite of jerky before answering. "It was so weird. For a minute, she was all blurry, then I could see her clearly, but she was younger, with long jet-black hair. Then, she went blurry again. The whole time we were talking, everything seemed to fade in and out, even the store itself, like I was seeing two different worlds. But the other world was always clearer."

"Dr. Gordon must be right. The two universes are melding. You're seeing into Earth Yellow, and it's clear to you, just like it is when you're there."

"I guess so. Anyway, I just got her talking about her past, and she perked up right away. We were close friends in no time. A listening ear can calm almost anyone down."

"Good job."

"Speaking of listening ears, I'd better get back to work." Kelly flipped the radio on. The choir had restarted their ghastly song. She assumed her translating position and planted her pen on the paper. She squinted more than usual, cocking her head from time to time as if making sure she heard something right.

After about a half hour, my phone rang. While Kelly stayed glued to her task, I answered with a whispered, "Hello."

"Nathan. It's Daryl. Daryl Blue. I can barely hear you. What's wrong?"

"Nothing. I just have to stay quiet. What's up?"

"Daryl Red's got something cooking in the communications pot. No voice yet, but she's going to try to send a text message to you."

"That was fast."

"Seems like it to us, but it's been months on Earth Yellow. She said she had trouble getting the parts she needed. With the whole world in a nightmare turmoil, it was tough getting anything done."

"Yeah." I glanced at the newspaper in the backseat. "Trouble's popping on this world, too."

"All three worlds are ready to crack. Dr. Gordon's been monitoring the news on Earth Red. Every nuclear-equipped nation has an itchy finger poised over the doomsday button. If we don't fix this thing soon, it's going to make *Independence Day* look like a friendly picnic with our alien friends."

I heaved a sigh. "We're working on it."

"I know, but there's a new problem. I can't tune in the mirror at the Earth Yellow Interfinity Labs site. Dr. Gordon thinks someone might have moved it to make ready for the construction of the laboratory's first building back when they were called StarCast. That means we can't go there unless one of the magic mirror squares does the trick. Plus, the time difference between us and Earth Yellow makes communicating with Daryl Red a real chore. Basically she has to wait for hours to get a response from me that takes only a few minutes. So, as soon as you get the text message, try to answer her. When she finally gets your message, she'll have been waiting a long time."

"Got it. Talk to you soon."

I set the phone down. After I gave Kelly a quick summary of the call, she returned to her painstaking chore, straining to listen while squinting at her paper.

A few seconds later, the phone chimed its message alert. I pulled the car to the shoulder, stopped, and read the phone's notification — three new messages. I read them out loud, three parts of a single note.

"Nathan. News update. Tony Clark moved into Francesca's old house, and Gunther delivered the letter. Tony's making the bow and should have it done in a couple of weeks. That might be only a few days for you. Maybe hours. Who can tell? Anyway, I had to modify one of the original IBM PCs and use an asynchronous cable to hook it to my radio transmitter. What a pain! But at least it works. Daryl Blue picks it up and modulates it to a cell signal. Just reply to let me know you received it. She'll pick it up again and send it my way. I'll be waiting."

"Poor Daryl," Kelly said. "She probably feels trapped."

"Most likely." I typed a reply with my thumbs, speaking the words out loud. "Good work. Will try to get there soon." I sent the message, set the phone down, and pulled back onto the highway.

My fingers tightened around the steering wheel. The fate of the entire world—no, three worlds—waited for me to get a ten-foot-long bow that was being constructed by a teenager in another realm; take it to a ridiculously dangerous fourth world; and play an impossibly huge violin, all while saving my parents and three color-coded supplicants from death at the hands, or the voices, of the choir from hell. Could it get any more complicated?

When we reached the final exit, just a few miles from the Earth Blue home, Kelly turned off the radio. "Okay, I think I have all the verbs, and I heard a few other words, too. I had to mix them in with the nouns we had before, but there were a lot of possible combinations. Here is one that makes some sense." She licked her lips and held the paper close to her eyes again. "Solomon lives. Location is square where music harmonizes. Key is circle of fifths. Sleep with interpreter. Follow dream in bedroom where Patar stalks."

"The new words help a lot. At least it makes some sense now."

"Could Abodah be the singer who's helping us?" Kelly asked. "Is she secretly giving us instructions?"

"Probably, since she's hiding her words from the others. But it's so cryptic."

"I could try shuffling the verbs around to see if I can come up with something better."

"You might as well. As soon as we get back to the mirror, we'll check out all the squares again. Maybe one of them will give us a clue."

When we arrived at the house, I pushed the garage opener, but the door stayed closed. The power outage continued. I parked in the driveway, helped Kelly out, and skulked with her toward the door.

I carried the Quattro mirror and my violin, while Kelly kept the camera on a strap around her neck. Clouds once again blanketed the sky, bringing a new chill to the air. As Daryl had indicated, summer on Earth Yellow had long ago flown by, and winter was at the doorstep. Could another snowfall be far away?

Once inside the bedroom, I removed the mirror's frame and placed the reflective square in the larger mirror's gap. The mosaic was again complete. No longer needing the frame, I tossed it to the floor.

While Kelly held the Foundation's Key music, I played it through. Within seconds, the squares flashed with light, and over the next minute or so the reflection morphed into four hundred unique scenes.

I lowered the bow. "Okay, read the message again."

Kelly squinted at the back of the page. "Solomon lives. Location is square where music harmonizes. Key is circle of fifths. Sleep with interpreter. Follow dream in bedroom where Patar stalks."

I walked closer to the mirrored wall. "Maybe we need to figure out which squares make a circle of fifths."

"I was supposed to learn about that stuff in music theory," Kelly said as she joined me. "But I guess I purged my memory when my mother left."

"Foundation's Key is in C Major. The circle of fifths for that key will start with C-natural." I pointed at one of the squares and shifted my finger from square to square in a circular pattern. "Then it moves by fifths through twelve notes, G–D–A–E–B–F-sharp, and so on. This is just a guess, but maybe we have to figure out which square represents C-natural and find the circle in the mirror."

"How can a mirror represent a note?" She angled her ear toward the wall. "I don't hear any music."

I lifted the bow again and played a long middle C. "Did that change anything?"

"Not that I can tell, but I'm half blind. And I didn't hear anything but the violin."

I played every C possible, pausing after each one, but nothing changed. Some of the images showed country landscapes and deserted highways, others provided views of city skylines, and a few gave us glimpses of rooms inside homes with families huddling around fireplaces or storm lanterns. In one sparse living room, four wide-eyed children locked their stares on a father as he read to them in the glow of a single candle.

Kelly moved a finger gently across the family's image. "They're so scared."

"Is your vision improving?"

"No, but I don't really need to see them. It's like I can feel what they're feeling."

"Your interpretive skills must be getting stronger."

"I know, but sometimes it's a curse. I don't want to feel other people's fear."

I laid my hand over hers. "If we want to help them, we have to figure out what following the dream means."

She drew back and lowered her head. "It'll have to be your dream. I don't think mine will ever come true."

"Why not?"

She shook her head. "Never mind. Let's concentrate on yours."

I tried to catch her gaze, but she kept her eyes low. What could be getting her down? What dream could be so lofty that it could never come true? Her mother coming home? Maybe. But it was probably better not to ask. If she really wanted me to know, she'd tell me.

I injected a bit more energy into my voice. "My dream is to get my parents back, but it seems like it won't ever come true, either."

"Maybe Abodah meant a literal dream." Kelly looked at me again. "Maybe you have to go to sleep here, and Patar will stalk your dream. Then he'll tell you what to do."

I gave her a reluctant nod. "I've been fighting sleep. When the universe is about to collapse, it's kind of hard to take a nap break."

"I know, but you've been awake for what? Thirty hours?"

"I got a short nap while you drove on Earth Yellow a while back."

"Not enough. You're exhausted. If you don't rest, *you'll* collapse."

I took a deep breath and let it out slowly. "You're right."

"There's still enough mattress left." She pulled the ripped mattress away from the wall and laid it flat on the floor. "Just lie down and see what happens. I've had more sleep than you, so I'll stand guard."

I looked at the mattress. In spite of its condition, it seemed inviting. I probably could fall asleep, and maybe Patar would come and pay my dreams a visit. He had done it before. But what if an interpretation was needed? The message said to sleep with the interpreter. Could I do that with Kelly? Sure, our touching would be innocent — merely holding hands just to get the job done. But what would she think? I couldn't just ask her to sleep with me, could I?

I took her hand and drew her closer. "My thoughts are really jumbled. Can you—"

"Read your mind again?" She gave me a sly smile. "While you were staring at the mattress like a zombie, I was trying, but I hit a brick wall."

I nodded at the violin, still in my hand. "Would it help if I played some music?"

"Maybe. Something from your heart. Like you did for Tsayad."

"Will do." I raised the bow and brushed it softly across the strings. My mood called for something gentle. As I played, she smiled. Her glassy eyes cleared and focused on me, raising a reminder of the first time we met, the moment she opened the door to her house and I saw her face — pretty but dirty, welcoming but irritated.

The contradictions shuffled my own feelings. Fondness for her blended with an odd annoyance, and the confusion radiated to my hands. I pushed deeper into the strings. As if driven by an uncontrollable inner passion, I made the bow rocket back and forth. A thousand thoughts raced through my mind, too fast to focus on a single one. They streamed from my frazzled brain directly into the violin, flying into the air as a string of music, melodic at first, then tortured and dissonant.

Kelly's smile faded. After several seconds, she blinked and turned her head.

I stopped playing. My chest heaved through labored breaths as I coughed out my words. "What's wrong?"

She swiveled back. A tear moistened her cheek as she looked me in the eye. "I'm not a harlot."

I stiffened, but I managed to keep my face calm. "I know you're not. I've never thought that."

"Then your music tells lies."

I let the violin droop at my side. "Mictar said that, not me. Maybe I'm just mad at him."

Kelly shook her head. "You believed him. You think I'm not good enough for you." She sniffed, and her voice cracked. "And maybe … maybe you're right. You need a sweet little princess who's as white as snow."

"Look." I raised the bow but resisted the urge to point it at her. "I'm not going to lie to you. The stuff I heard bothered me, but it's in the past."

"You'd like to think so, but in your eyes I'm damaged goods."

"Damaged goods? Did you hear that in my music?"

She nodded. "And now … now you want us to sleep together." Biting her bottom lip, she crossed her arms and turned away. "I promised myself I wasn't ever going to make the same mistakes again. Not for you. Not for anyone."

I touched her arm but thought better of pulling her around. "But it's just so we can dream together. Nothing else is going to happen."

She turned back, her eyes ablaze. "Nathan Shepherd, don't pretend you know what it's like. You were raised in a cocoon. I'll bet you've never even kissed a girl. Right? Am I right?"

Heat roared into my cheeks. Avoiding her question was impossible. "You're right."

"Then you have no idea how it feels when you're with someone you care a lot about. Then the lights go out. And you're close. And you hear each other's soft breathing and feel their warmth. And … and …" She looked away. "Never mind. You wouldn't understand unless you've been there."

I set a finger on her chin, turned her face toward me, and looked her in the eye. "You're right. I don't understand. But this much I do know." I paused, hoping the words would come out with all the strength and resolve I felt inside. "You can trust me. No matter what happens, you can trust me."

"I do trust you." As tears welled in her eyes, her lower lip quivered. "I just don't trust myself."

As I gazed at her, her words echoed — *someone you care a lot about*. She had essentially admitted that she cared about me enough to be nervous about sharing a mattress.

The idea sent a new shot of warmth from head to toe, a combination of delight and anxiety.

Why? Because she cared for me. She wanted me. And her past haunted both of us.

"We'll stay separate." I sat on the floor and patted the mattress. "You get the comfy spot, and I'll sleep down here. We can hold hands and be apart at the same time."

Wearing a doubtful expression, she lowered herself to the mattress and lay down, then curled up and faced me. "Now what?"

"This." I lay on the floor and touched her fingers. The light in the room faded, leaving only her body's silhouette, the bare outline of her facial features, and her shining eyes in view.

After a minute or so, her lips puckered slightly as she spoke again. "Have you ever had the opportunity to kiss a girl, Nathan? I mean, have you ever been on a date? Been alone with a girl who liked you?"

"Not really. I've been on group outings with girls. I've never been anywhere long enough to get to know anyone, so dating hasn't been an option."

Kelly's eyes closed. After nearly a minute of silence, she whispered, "Would you kiss a girl you like if you had the chance?"

"I would love to."

Her eyes opened. "Really?"

"Definitely. But only after I hear, 'You may now kiss your bride.'"

She let out a low humming sound. "A first kiss on your wedding day." Her voice emanated from near total darkness, except for a weak glow in her eyes. "That's really romantic."

The glow seemed to penetrate my mind. Once again her piercing gift invaded my thoughts and cast away any idea of evading the issue. "I want my wife to be the only girl I ever kiss, and the only way I can be sure of it is to wait until our wedding day."

"Is that like ... a commandment? I mean, something you have to obey?"

"No. Not a commandment. More like a preference. It's a gift for my future wife."

As a whispered sigh drifted toward me, Kelly's glowing orbs blinked out. "I hope I'm there to see it." Her grip on my hand tightened for a brief second, then loosened, but our index fingers remained curled together.

I lay back and closed my eyes, but Kelly's anguished face stayed in mind. Her voice replayed. *I'm not a harlot. ... In your eyes, I'm damaged goods. ... I promised myself I wasn't ever going to make the same mistakes again. Not for you. Not for anyone.*

The words echoed again and again. Did I really think she was damaged goods? She made a promise never to do again whatever she had done. Could I treat her as though she were the untouched princess she had talked about? Could I ever stop wondering what she had done? Maybe Mictar was right when he said, *"You want to know every lurid detail. She is your dark shadow, and you will never find your parents while you entertain a harlot at your side."*

I winced at the spiteful words. But were they true? Would the darkness of her past act as a blinding shield?

Yet, one truth never failed. Light always overcomes darkness. Dad once told me, *Sacrificial love is a light that shines in the darkest places.*

If I could shine that light for Kelly and for myself, maybe her past wouldn't matter.

I opened my eyes. The two glowing orbs had returned. Kelly was looking right at me, close enough for her injured eyes to focus clearly. "What are you doing?" I asked.

"Reading your mind again."

"But I wasn't playing music. I—"

She set two fingers on my lips and let out a quiet, "Shhh." Then, interlocking her index finger with mine again, she closed her eyes. "Sweet dreams, Nathan."

I released a long breath and let my eyelids droop. Kelly's cool, soft touch sent prickles across my skin. Her closeness felt good.

After what seemed like a few minutes, I opened my eyes and checked my surroundings. I lay on the floor, one finger curled around Kelly's. The room was dark, illuminated only by a glow from a yard lantern outside. Had I awakened in the middle of the night, or was I dreaming?

I sat up and looked at the floor. My body still lay there, breathing rhythmically. Smiling at my own awkward fetal pose, I gave my sleeping body a light pat on the shoulder. This was a dream, a strikingly realistic one, but definitely a dream.

Something new lay on the floor near the mirror. A body? I jumped up, leaving my sleeping form behind, and rushed to the mirror. The body appeared to be a rather hefty man lying on his stomach.

Craning my neck, I listened. The man was breathing.

With careful hands, I rolled him over. In the dimness, I could barely make out the man's bearded face. Yet, even with dark bruises blotching his skin around his closed eyes, his identity was clear—Jack, my friend from the airplane crash.

CHAPTER ELEVEN

I SHOOK JACK'S SHOULDER. "Jack, can you hear me?"

"Who's there?" he whispered.

"It's Nathan. Remember me?"

A weak smile shifted Jack's beard. "Remember you? I've been searching for you. But in my condition that has been a lost cause."

I leaned closer and looked at his eyes. The sockets were empty. A sick feeling boiled in my stomach as I tried to keep my voice steady. "I assume Mictar did that to you."

"He did." Jack reached out a hand. "Help me up, and I'll tell you about it."

I pulled him to a sitting position and glanced at Kelly. She continued sleeping soundly. The sight of my own snoozing body near hers seemed too strange to be true. "This is really a weird dream. I've never had one so vivid."

"As well you might expect." Jack sniffed the air. "Ah! Kelly is nearby. I'll never forget her scent, a lovely vanilla mixed with strawberry."

"Yeah, she's here. She's sleeping. I guess she's not dreaming, or maybe she couldn't join my dream."

"Then she will have to hear my story another time." Jack pulled a crumpled fedora from underneath his jacket. As he passed the brim through his nervous fingers, his vacant sockets aimed toward Kelly. "When I rode on Mictar's back into the mirror, there was a sudden burst of light."

As if cued by Jack's words, the mirror on the wall flashed. The reflection transformed into a movie screen, showing Jack riding the evil stalker's back. Mictar staggered under the weight in the same bedroom we sat in now, while a funnel-like swirl of mist spun at the center of the room. Behind them, my parents looked on, horrified.

Although no sound came from the mirror, Jack filled the air with a vibrant storytelling voice. "A window opened, and a man who looked just like Mictar began to climb in. At the same time, your father tackled the real Mictar and sent us both toppling over a desk. I leaped to my feet and tried to crawl over the bed, but Mictar kicked your father away, pounced on me, and covered my face with his hand. Light as bright as the sun scorched my eyes, too painful to describe. From that point on, I couldn't see, so I can only tell you what I heard."

Noises erupted from the mirror. The movie's sound kicked in. Dad lay on the floor, holding the side of his head with bloody fingers. Jack, still on the bed, groaned under Mictar's scalding hand. Patar burst through the open window and lunged at Mictar.

The two stalkers wrestled on top of Jack, clawing at each other and ripping the mattress.

Mom leaped to Dad's side. "Solomon! Are you all right?"

He shook his head. If he said anything, the grunts and strange sounds coming from the combatants drowned him out.

Jack pulled free and rolled off the bed. The weight release sent one end of the mattress into the air. Mictar and Patar crashed to the floor, still wrestling savagely. They sang in bursts of harsh notes that sounded more like musical profanity than song.

Mom helped Jack crawl to safety next to Dad, just a few inches away from the expanding swirl of mist.

Jack blinked. "I can't see! My eyes are on fire!"

Smoke poured from his eye sockets, creating twin black plumes that drifted toward the ceiling. Mom shifted over to him and swabbed his forehead with her sleeve, but her desperate expression reflected the futility of her efforts.

Patar kicked Mictar in the groin, leaped up, and rushed to Jack. He laid his hand over the bearded man's eyes. "You will lose your sight," Patar crooned, "but you will not die."

Mictar climbed to his feet and pointed at Jack. "I tasted his life force! I must have the rest!"

Scowling, Patar barked a reply. "A taste that leads to slavish lust should never be taken. You have struck the match, but you will not bask in these flames."

Mictar hurled another musical obscenity. "… your trite moralisms! His life energy seal is broken. He cannot survive."

"Not in this realm." Using his free hand, Patar scooped mist from the swirl. He sniffed it, then, after letting some of the mist filter through his fingers, he sniffed it again and applied it to Jack's forehead as he talked to my parents. "I am sending him to a place where he can survive—the realm of dreams. His only hope will be to find the healer of the broken womb. When the crack is sealed, perhaps he, too, will be restored."

Patar lifted Jack to his feet and guided him into the swirl.

Mictar pointed a stiff finger. "Your healer is a fool! A chicken with no head! He is too enamored with selfish infatuations to ever find his parents or this eyeless rescuer!"

As the mist enveloped Jack, Patar stayed outside the swirl and looked at Mictar. "Perhaps you are right. The road ahead of the healer is cruel and heartbreaking, far more difficult than he is now able to endure, but I will never give up hope. He is the only one remaining who can heal the wounds."

The mist dissolved Jack's body. Within seconds, he was gone.

"I must have more!" Mictar lunged at my parents and grabbed each by an arm. A scream shot from Patar's mouth, a visible lightning bolt of sound, black and jagged. The bolt slammed into Mictar and covered him with darkness.

Patar dove headfirst and clutched Mictar's ankle. "Go into the mist!" Patar yelled. "I will keep my brother here!"

Mom and Dad jerked away from Mictar's grasp and hobbled toward the swirl. Splotches of black on their arms dripped like sticky tar down their fingertips.

Another musical note sounded from Patar. He followed it with a shout. "Solomon, I set you free from your manacles."

A sizzling crack broke the metal bracelets on Dad's wrists, and the chains fell to the floor. He and Mom walked into the swirl, and, in a few seconds, they, too, disappeared.

Patar released Mictar, jumped back, and brushed his hands against each other, sending crumbs of black to the floor.

Slowly rising to his feet, Mictar coughed and wheezed. When he straightened, he let out a spiteful laugh. "They have been anointed with dark energy."

"Not enough to harm them," Patar said in a matter-of-fact tone. "They will resist it."

"Perhaps, but they cannot escape from where you have sent them."

Patar laid a hand on the outer perimeter of the swirl. White mist brushed against his fingers. "Yet you cannot accost them there. In fact, you are transforming into material dissonance yourself, so you will be a living specter until you find a way to revive."

Mictar, his face now a mass of black, looked down at his equally black, formless body. "I am able to refuel, and I know just the place to restore myself. There is a certain girl who does not yet know how gifted she is. I tasted her, and now I must have her."

"She is of no concern to me," Patar said, waving a hand. "I will keep this portal open long enough for the healer to find it, but by the time you are reenergized, the path Solomon and Francesca have taken will no longer be available."

"I will find another path."

"Not unless there is substantial healing." Patar picked up a clump of mattress padding and squeezed it tightly, letting the pieces fall to the floor. "The paths are fragile. The catalyst you desire for your machine is out of your reach."

Mictar laughed again. "This is a delicious irony, indeed. If your healer does his work, he will be the reason I am able to capture his parents."

"True, but there is another way, a way that will make your Lucifer engine impotent." A frown sank the lines on Patar's face. "You know what that is."

Mictar spat a wad of black goo onto the floor. "The boy would never do it. He is a romantic, too dependent on emotions." He gazed at the dark club that was once his hand. "If I could, I would do it myself. Such a source of energy would make me invincible. Lucifer would no longer be necessary."

For a moment it seemed as though a smile was about to break through on Patar's face, but he suppressed it. "Is it not strange that a mere wisp of a girl dressed in red has chilled your heart and painted a stripe of yellow down your back?"

"Laugh on, my brother. Since you enjoy the human euphemisms, I will counter with, 'he who laughs last, laughs best.'"

Patar nodded. "We shall see. Perhaps the healer's journey will provide the wisdom he needs to accomplish what you and I cannot bear to do ourselves."

"You overestimate his character." Mictar set a dark foot on the windowsill. "He is human, and he will die with all the other rodents that populate the planets."

As soon as Mictar jumped out, the mirror dimmed, and the image transformed into a normal reflection of the room.

Now in near darkness once again, I let out my breath. How long had I been holding it? The scene in the mirror had kept me transfixed. I had lost all grip on reality.

I looked back at my sleeping body. Of course, not sensing reality should be no surprise. After all, this was only a dream.

I turned to Jack. He seemed real — frumpy clothes stained with blood, thinning hair with a bald spot in back, and skin reeking of body odor and cologne.

"Were you able to hear all that?" I asked.

Jack continued threading his hat through his fingers. "I did. Much of it for the second time, though the discussion between those … whatever they were … was new to me."

"Stalkers." I held my hands against my temples. "My brain is officially overloaded. If I'm dreaming, then maybe nothing I saw really happened. But if it did happen, then you were sent to the realm of dreams. Does that mean that the Jack I knew is really here? I mean, you're not just dreaming this?"

A smile brightened Jack's blackened face. "I'm not dreaming, but if you are, how can you be sure that I'm telling the truth?"

I lowered my hands. "That's the problem. Dreams aren't real, so I can't count on anything I see or hear."

"And I can't prove I'm real, at least not until you wake up."

"Why when I wake up?"

Jack blinked his vacant eye sockets. "I could tell you something you don't know. Then you could check on it later."

"Okay," I said, nodding. "I'm with you on that. What do you have in mind?"

Jack stroked his beard. "When you passed by me while I was kneeling at a cemetery plot, did you see me?"

"Yes. I was in a hurry to get to the funeral, but I saw you there."

"If you get a chance to look at the tombstone, you can read my name inscribed there: John Alton Flowers. Or it might be easier to call someone and search the death records. Then you'll know that I'm really here, because you couldn't have dreamed my name."

I nodded again. "Fair enough. If I can remember. I'm not too good at remembering dreams."

"All I can do is pray that you will." Jack pushed up to his knees. "And pray that you can help me leave this place."

I pulled Jack the rest of the way up. "I'm guessing I'm the healer they talked about, and I have to seal a crack to get you out of here safely."

After straightening his fedora, Jack set it gingerly on his head. "I can't help you with what it all means, but it sounds like you'll be learning a lot as you go."

"Too much, I think. Maybe I should get Kelly's help. She's always been able to interpret—"

Music played from somewhere nearby, interrupting my thought. The thrumming beat of a bass drum accompanied a sweet composition of strings, the same piece that had bridged the gap between Earths Blue and Yellow at the observatory—Beethoven's Ninth Symphony. This time the fourth movement played on invisible instruments, and a host of voices trilled the German lyrics of *Ode to Joy*.

I let the mesmerizing beauty wash over me. The last time something like this happened in a dream, Mozart's *Requiem* had painted the air with a Latin hymn of sadness and comfort, words I could easily translate. But these lyrics were unfamiliar. I had never learned German or studied the poem that had inspired Beethoven to pen this masterpiece.

I glanced at Kelly, still asleep on the mattress. "Excuse me a minute."

"Certainly," Jack said, touching the brim of his hat.

I walked over and gave Kelly a gentle nudge. She yawned, sat up, and stretched her arms, but a copy of her body still lay in bed, unmoved and clutching my hand.

"Is this a dream?" she asked.

"Pretty sure." I pointed at her other body. "Unless you have a clone."

She grinned. "That's cool. I can talk to you while I'm sleeping."

"It looks that way, but …" I paused, not quite sure how to express my doubts.

"But what?"

"I'll buy that a stalker can enter someone's thoughts while he's sleeping. But two people dreaming the same dream? It doesn't make sense."

She spoke while stretching into another yawn. "You don't believe Francesca?"

"Her father never remembered the dreams. She was the gifted one, so maybe the dreams were just hers."

"Maybe." She blinked several times. "I like this dream. I can see clearly."

I nodded toward Jack. "Recognize him?"

"Uh-huh." She waved at Jack.

"He can't see you. Mictar took his eyes."

She squinted. "Poor guy. Good thing he's only part of a dream."

"I'm not so sure." I took her hand, and we walked toward the mirror where Jack stood, worrying his hat again with his fingers.

"I hear the young lady," Jack said.

"Yes, I'm here." Kelly touched one of the scorch marks on Jack's brow and grimaced. "The pain must be horrific."

"I could tell you the story," I said, "but if this is all a stupid dream of mine, it would be a waste of time."

Kelly frowned. "It's not just your—"

The mirror flashed again. The reflection transformed into a furnished bedroom, brighter than this one and void of the broken scatterings left behind by the battle between the stalkers. A fully dressed bed sat on the far side, and a desk and chair abutted the adjacent wall. Several posters hung on the painted surface, featuring basketball players in graceful stop-action poses. One was Michael Jordan flying through the air in a North Carolina uniform, but the others were unfamiliar.

Kelly rattled off the players' names. "Magic Johnson, Michael Jordan, Kareem Abdul-Jabbar, James Worthy—"

"Okay, okay. I get the picture. You know your sports teams."

"I'm just proving something. If this were your dream, you wouldn't know the players, so I couldn't tell you who they were."

"Maybe I know them in my subconscious mind. I've heard all those names before."

"True, but—" With a sudden thrust, she pointed at the mirror. "Nathan, look at the wall next to the stack of soda cans."

I searched the image. A violin bow hung from hooks on the wall, stretching across the room from one end to the other. The bedroom door opened, and a young man stepped in. After adding a Pepsi can to the top of his pyramid, he turned on a television atop a dresser and flopped on the bed.

Kelly gasped. "My father!"

"Are you sure?"

"He's younger, but that's him."

"But why would we be seeing him? What's the point?"

Kelly hovered her hand over the glass. "If this is Earth Yellow, and he's already made the bow, maybe we should flash a light and go there."

"But it won't work if I'm just dreaming this."

Kelly set her hands on her hips. "What's it going to take to convince you that I'm dreaming this with you?"

"I didn't mean that. I was just saying if it's only a dream, then how can we physically go—"

Jack tugged on my sleeve. "If I may offer an opinion?"

"Sure."

"Instead of merely arguing about whose dream this is, perhaps you could do as I have done and offer more compelling evidence. When you awaken, you can compare what you have dreamed to what you find in reality."

I rolled my eyes. "My own dream is giving me advice. What next?"

The mirror darkened. Kelly's father disappeared, along with the bed, cans, and bow. A familiar face and form took shape. With eyes glowing reddish brown and a simple calf-length dress coating her body in red, Scarlet set her hands on the inside barrier. "I have been waiting for you, Nathan."

My throat clamped shut. Her startling beauty and haunting voice sent a jolt through my body, stiffening my limbs.

Kelly let her arms fall to her side and stared.

Scarlet turned and cast her gaze on Kelly. "Nathan, I am glad you have brought the interpreter. There is a brightness in her spirit that will serve you well."

I suppressed a wince. Kelly might not like the *serve you* part. Then again, if she wasn't dreaming with me, she wouldn't care. Yet, since Scarlet was able to penetrate dreams, she was probably really with me. Why would she mention Kelly if Kelly weren't real?

Scarlet turned back to me. "Ah! I hear the great ode. Do you know the words? They speak now of your oneness with your friend."

I cocked my head to listen again. "It's in German. I never learned German."

"I hear English," Kelly said. "It's beautiful."

Scarlet's smile seemed to light up the room. "Then speak the ode, interpreter. Let your beloved hear the words of truth."

Kelly nodded with the music's rhythm and translated the German phrases.

> Whoever succeeds in the great attempt
> To be a friend of a friend,
> Whoever has won a lovely woman,
> Let him add his jubilation!

"Yes." Scarlet laid a hand over her chest. "It is jubilation to win the heart of a faithful woman. And now I will sing another truth to you, Nathan Paul Shepherd, for you have won my heart, and I will be faithful to you as long as I live." Moving her hand in a wide circle over the mirror, she sang in a lovely alto.

> The circle of music, eternal and blessed,
> The key to salvation where mortals find rest;
> To find the right portal to seek what was lost
> And journey to danger, you must count the cost.

> For hearts will be humbled and lives will be spent.
> A brave one will fall in the endless descent,
> And sight will be lost while perception is gained.
> The free will be bound and all captives unchained.

> The stalker appearing will show you the square,
> Then take care to follow, yet heed my sad prayer.
> The journey will force you to choose whom you love;
> The bright one, the sad one, the creed, or the dove.

As the tune faded, Scarlet faded with it, her melancholy eyes leaving a residual glow. A wisp of a voice trailed away like a distant echo. "Come for me, Nathan. I will be waiting."

Seconds later, a new form replaced her lovely visage. A tall, pallid stalker approached the mirror from a distance, his ankles surrounded by a white cloud, as if he had just marched out from the misty world.

Kelly grabbed my arm and pulled me close. "Is that Mictar or Patar?"

"Patar," I replied. Then, lowering my voice, I added, "I hope."

As the white-haired man drew near, he slowed, dragging something behind him. His load resembled a human body, but shadows covered the corpse's face. He turned his head, perhaps intentionally, just enough to show that he lacked a ponytail.

He stopped and stared at me, his eyes pulsing red. "Son of Solomon!" His voice echoed throughout the room. "When will you learn not to trifle with the power of Quattro?"

I gulped. "What do you mean?"

As the dead body swayed under his tight fist, Patar's voice deepened and rolled into a prophetic cadence. "While worlds hang in the balance, you are toying with emotions. While terrified children seek rescue from death, you are playing house with those fair of face and capturing their fragile hearts."

"But I'm not. I'm just—"

With a lightning fast thrust, Patar jerked the body forward and shoved it close to the mirror.

Kelly covered her eyes with her hands. "Oh, dear God!"

I stared at the macabre sight — a face stretched out and hanging by the hair from Patar's powerful grip. With blackened, vacant eye sockets, a warped reflection of my own face stared back at me—Nathan Blue, his mouth agape in a silent scream.

Nausea boiled in my stomach, and my mouth dried out. I couldn't say a word.

Patar lowered Nathan Blue but kept a grip on his hair. With his other hand, he pointed directly at me. "If you continue to attend to the trivial and neglect the essential, you will join your counterpart in the agony of the endless void. Your lack of wisdom will not only allow Interfinity to come, it will accelerate its arrival."

Fighting back fear, I squared my shoulders. "Why didn't you just give it to me straight before? Maybe I wouldn't have wasted so much time."

"I told you to play the great violin. Was my command unclear? You have your own mother's testimony to its existence. The bow is ready, yet you are sleeping with your girlfriend in a world not your own."

My face grew hot. I felt caught, naked, ashamed. What could I have been thinking? Was Patar right? Should I have waited on Earth Yellow until the bow was ready?

Balling my fists, I tried to rally my defenses, but they seemed weak, even in my own mind. "I had to come back and study the photos, then we came here to look for—"

"Your parents." Patar nodded, and his voice took on a sarcastic tone. "I know your reasoning all too well. Saving relatives and friends at the expense of the entire world seems perfectly logical to you."

I kicked the wall. It hurt, but I hid the pain. "I wanted to find my parents so I could get some straightforward advice, not the runaround you always give me!"

"Finding and playing the violin was straightforward enough," Patar said. "A thorough explanation would seem foolish to you, and if I were to provide you with the simplest solution, you would ignore my counsel."

I shouted, "Try me!"

Patar laughed. "Your arrogance dresses you in a clown's garb, son of Solomon, if you think you know the crisis or its solution better than I. Trust me. You will despise my counsel."

"Then prove it. Show me that I'm a fool. Better that than for me to run around color-coded worlds like a chicken with its head cut off ..." I bit my lip. That was exactly what Mictar had called me. After taking a deep breath, I pointed at the body hanging from Patar's grip. "Better than ending up like the other Nathan."

A smile widened the stalker's pale face. "Very well. I will prove it. Here is the simplest solution." He drew closer to the mirror, so close, his eyes took up most of a square. His voice dropped to a low bass. "To heal the wounds and bring the crisis to an end, return to the place you call the misty world and ..." He paused, his smile vanishing. "And slay the supplicants."

Patar's words sucked the air from my lungs. I could only gasp through my reply. "What? You can't be serious!"

"You heard me. Cast their bodies into Sarah's Womb, and harmony will be restored. Although we pity their wretched estate, we cannot allow emotions to cloud our thinking. They must die."

I took two steps back. "But I can't ... I can't *kill* them!"

Patar's smile returned. "I have done as you requested and given you a straightforward command. You despised it and played the fool, exactly as I predicted. If you wish to disbelieve me, there is nothing more I can tell you. You are free to follow the other option, to find the violin and play it, but that path is far more treacherous."

My legs now weak, I shuffled back to the mirror. "What about the circle of fifths? Scarlet said you'd show us the square."

"As I said earlier, you are unwise to trifle with the power of Quattro. I am aware of the song of that doomed supplicant. Her plaintive cries will not avail her." Patar stroked his narrow chin for a moment. "Yet, I will again do what you ask and give you enough information to locate what you are seeking, if you have enough wisdom to find it. You will see the square, but I will not tell you where the key is."

Patar sang a low C for a few seconds, switched to a short E so high the window pane vibrated, then, touching mirror squares in turn, he sang various notes in rapid succession. Each square flashed with a unique color as he touched it, and the note continued to play from the glass, carrying a vibrato that made it shimmer. When he finished, the entire room blazed with colors that danced on the walls as if celebrating the pulsing music.

Shifting his gaze back to me, Patar bobbed his head, apparently listening to the song he had created. It was captivating and beautiful, yet, even with the extraordinary flood of musical notes, Beethoven's ode still broke through.

"Interpreter," Patar said, pointing at Kelly. "Interpret the great song. The son of Solomon must hear the brilliance of the poet's message, the one that enchanted Beethoven himself."

Trembling, Kelly cleared her throat and spoke.

Be embraced, you millions!
This kiss for the whole world!
Brothers, beyond the star canopy
Must a loving Father dwell.

Do you bow down, you millions?
Do you sense the Creator, world?

Seek Him beyond the star canopy!
Beyond the stars must He dwell.

When the words ended, Patar's frown deepened. "Heed what you have heard, son of Solomon. You will find what you seek beyond the stars, but if you wish to save the cosmos that bears them on its shoulders, you must carry out the task I have set before you. Throw the supplicants into the womb, and all will be healed. Yet, if you choose the alternative path and reach the fabric beyond the star canopy, I can no longer give you advice. It is fraught with danger, and even I cannot tell what you must do to avoid a fatal step."

I spread out my hands. "But why all the puzzles? Why can't you just tell me where the key is?"

"To protect your life. If you lack the wisdom to find the key, you will surely lack the wisdom to safely follow the alternative path. The wisest of all decisions would be to sacrifice the supplicants, but since you have allowed someone to romance your heart during this hour of crisis, I doubt that you are clear minded enough to make the wisest choice."

Patar vanished, and the mirror darkened, leaving only a reflection of the room — no song, no colors, no music.

I raised a hand and searched for my fingers in the mirror but found no sign of my reflection or Kelly's or Jack's.

Looking deeper into the image, I found two bodies, my own on the floor and Kelly's on the mattress. The sleeping Kelly trembled, clutching my hand tightly.

I compressed Jack's shoulder. "I'll try to figure out how to save you, but I'll have to wake up to do it."

Jack fumbled for my hand and shook it heartily. "I will be waiting."

I guided Kelly back to the bed. "I think I've had enough of this dream."

"You don't know German," she said.

We each sat, our legs melding with the legs of our sleeping bodies. "Right. What's that got to do with anything?"

"This is my dream. You couldn't have translated the song."

"And I never told you my middle name before."

"Paul?"

"Right." I lowered my head. "Okay. I was being stubborn, but it will help me believe it for sure if we test the theory. When we wake up, you tell me my middle name, and I'll know you were really in my dream, and I'll tell you the names of the basketball players."

She nodded. "Fair enough."

I lay down, blending my two bodies into one. Kelly did the same, and we joined hands to mimic our physical forms.

CHAPTER TWELVE

WHEN THE DREAM ended, my mind fell into blackness until a ringing sound stirred my senses. I awoke and sat up. Angled rays of sunshine flowed in from the window. Was it morning?

The ringing sounded again — a telephone. I patted my pocket. My phone was still there, but that wasn't making the noise. I jumped up and bounded out of the room, following the rings until I found a wall-mounted phone in the kitchen and snatched up the receiver.

"Hello?"

"Nathan, it's Daryl Blue. I couldn't get you on the cell, and it took us forever to find this phone number. It's not in the book, and they must've changed it when Kelly died."

"Sorry. Glad you found it."

"Listen. Daryl Red's fit to be tied. Time is flying there, and she sent me about a thousand messages. I can't keep up. I told her to cool her jets, but she says she's only sending a couple a day. So when you get back into cell range, you might want to put your phone on silent. It'll chirp like a coffee-addicted canary if you don't. She's probably sent you, like, a hundred text messages."

The mention of coffee perked my nose. A coffee canister sat on the kitchen counter with a small purple envelope on top. "So what's happening on Earth Yellow?"

"That Mictar freak tracked Francesca down, so Gunther took her and her father and mother into hiding. Daryl Red's living with Vernon and Tony Clark, posing as an exchange student from England. It works out great, because Tony is handy with tools, so he helped her get her network stuff up and running. They have a pretty cool setup now."

"Can we find Francesca? We'll probably need her."

"Daryl Red hasn't heard from her in a while. Gunther knows how to make contact, but I guess the heat's been on, so he doesn't want to risk it. The last time Daryl Red talked to him, he said that wherever he goes, people report him to Mictar—something about Gunther not being in their dreams. Any idea what he's talking about?"

"Yeah, but it would take too long to explain."

"Anyway," Daryl continued, "the bow is ready. Daryl Red wants to come home before she graduates from high school."

"Let me think a minute." I picked up the envelope from the canister and read the front. The script said, "Daddy" in Kelly's handwriting.

I glanced down the hall at the bedroom door. Kelly and I could go back to Earth Yellow. Maybe Gunther and Francesca would see us in their dreams and come out of hiding. But we couldn't go until we solved the mirror puzzle and found the key to locating my parents, regardless of what Patar said. This might be our only chance.

"I'll have to call you later. Tell Daryl Red to hang tough. We'll get her back home before she's an old lady."

"She's going to be ticked, but I'll tell her."

"Thanks. You hang in there, too." I ended the call and ran down the hallway with the envelope in hand. When I careened into the bedroom, Kelly stood close to the mirror, her gaze fixed on the reflection.

"Paul," she whispered. "Your middle name is Paul."

I eased close to her side and watched her eyes in the mirror. "Michael Jordan, Magic Johnson, Kareem Abdul-Jabbar, and … James something."

"Close enough." She slid her foot over the spot where Jack had stood. "Do you think he was real?"

"Hard to tell. He gave me something to check, though. I'll do it as soon as we get a chance."

She pointed at the mirror. "The colors faded."

"What colors?"

"The ones that showed up on the squares when Patar sang."

I shook my head. "I didn't see any colors."

"Do you hear the notes?"

"No. Nothing."

"I still hear them, but they're a lot softer now." She squinted at the mirror. "How does the circle of fifths work?"

I drew a circle in the air and pointed at the top. "In C Major, we need to find a C-natural and work around from there. Since you have perfect pitch, you should be able to pick it up."

"But I hear more than one C-natural."

I forked three fingers. "The C-natural we need," I said, using my other hand to point at my middle finger as I wiggled the other two fingers in turn, "must have G-natural on one side and F-natural on the other."

"Okay. I get it." She took the envelope from me. "What's this?"

"Something I found in the kitchen on top of the coffee."

"The coffee?" She opened the envelope and slid out a folded card. "It's my handwriting."

"I noticed." I leaned over to get a look, but she kept the card folded, reading the Hallmark poem on the front. "Is it to your father?"

She nodded. "When I was little I used to write notes to him and put them with the coffee. I knew he'd see them first thing in the morning."

"Are you going to read it?"

"I'm not sure. I didn't write it. Kelly Blue did."

"Must have been right before she died. Her father never got a chance to read it before he got murdered."

"I guess it will be all right." She flipped open the card and held it close to her eyes, blinking as she tried to focus. I drew back while she read out loud.

Dear Daddy,

This is very hard for me to write for a lot of reasons, but I have to say this in case something happens to me. You see, Nathan and I are about to do something very dangerous, and if I don't come back, I want to make sure you know what's on my mind.

I always knew that Mom was the one who broke up your marriage, but when she left I treated you like dirt. For some stupid reason, I punished you for what she did. I know you're not perfect, and you drove her crazy with all the sports you were into, but you didn't deserve how either one of us treated you. Mom broke your heart, and I should have been there to mend it. Instead, I stomped on it and smashed it to bits. I'm so sorry.

Without Mom around, you had such a hard time. You always wanted a son, but you were stuck with a daughter, and you didn't know how to raise me, so you did it the only way you knew how. So, instead of being an expert in makeup and girly gossip, I know how to do a pick and roll, clean spark plugs, and shoot a can off the top of a fencepost.

Kelly's fingers trembled as she turned the card over and read the back, her voice rattling.

I love you, Daddy. I take back all the terrible things I said about hating basketball, fixing cars, and hunting. In fact, I'm even wearing that safari outfit you bought for me, and I let Nathan use the one you bought for Uncle Bill so we would match. I'm sorry for saying it was ugly and didn't fit. It feels really good right now, like you're giving me a warm hug. If this is my last day on earth, I will die wearing your gift of love.

Remember what Nathan told us about forgiveness. If I don't see you again on earth, I hope I see you in heaven.

Kelly pressed the card against her chest. Her face twisted. Tears streamed down her cheeks as she lowered her head and wept.

I laid a hand behind her head and pulled her close. As she cried on my shoulder, the room seemed to grow cold as if haunted by the father and daughter who once lived here. It was a sad home, indeed. I could almost feel the aching hearts. After years of turmoil—a broken marriage, misplaced expectations, and too many unspoken words of love—Kelly Blue's father died without knowing what his daughter wanted to tell him. Yet, he died a hero. He blocked a shotgun blast to save a life. My life.

I gave the imaginary ghost of Tony Clark a nod. *Thank you.*

One of the note's sentences repeated in my mind. *Remember what Nathan told us about forgiveness.* Apparently Nathan Blue had been bold enough to tell Kelly and Tony about what mattered most. I would do the same. As soon as the time was right.

After a minute or so, Kelly drew back, sniffing. "I can't … can't dwell on this. We have to … to move on." She stuffed the envelope and card into her back pocket and shuffled to the mirror. Leaning close to the squares, she slid sideways along the carpet, listening to each one. As she eyed the mirrors above her head, her voice strengthened. "I'm too short to reach the higher squares."

I pushed the trunk close. "How's that?"

"Perfect." After stooping to listen to the lower squares, she straightened as she moved from row to row. When she reached the third row from the top, she climbed onto the trunk and continued listening.

She paused to the left of the center of the mirror and pointed at one of the squares. "I think I got it. This orange square is the C note we want."

"I still don't see any colors." I stood on tiptoes and touched the square to the left and just below the one she indicated. "Is this the F?"

"Yes." She pointed at the square to the right of the C and one row down. "And this one is the G."

I picked up the violin and bow. "Okay, listen for these notes. They should make a circle that goes down from the G and then around to meet the F. Since they're squares, it won't be a perfect circle, but it should be close."

She nodded. "Go ahead."

I played a note. "That's a D-natural."

She pointed at the square one row down and to the right of the G. "Got it."

I played another note. "A-natural."

"Right here." Again she moved down a row and one to the right. "Just play the note. You don't have to tell me what it is."

As I played through E–B–F-sharp–D-flat–A-flat–E-flat–B-flat, Kelly moved her finger from square to square, making as perfect a circle as the squares would allow. When I finished, I set the violin down and studied the mirror, mentally drawing the circle Kelly had outlined.

The twelve squares enclosed thirteen others, but one lay in the geometric center. I pointed at it. "What note is coming from that one?"

Still on the trunk, Kelly bent to set her ear close. "Another C-natural. Middle C."

"That's gotta be the right one."

When Kelly dismounted the trunk, I slid it to the side and picked up the violin and bow again.

"Foundation's Key?" she asked.

"Yep. Let's see what's there." I played it through. Within seconds, the squares again showed four-hundred different destinations.

Kelly and I moved close to the mirror and studied the chosen square. It held a night scene, a cemetery with dozens of tombstones of various shapes and sizes dotting a hillside and casting long shadows in the light of a rising moon. In the midst of the purplish canopy above, a dark gash of emptiness stretched from one horizon to the other, taking up about a fifth of the sky.

I touched the glass where a tombstone stood, the very same marker Jack had knelt beside, but the inscription was far too small to make out.

As if summoned by my desire to read the letters, the scene rocketed toward us, like a camera zooming in on a target. When it stopped, the tombstone spanned the entire mirror.

I moved my finger away from the name and read it out loud. "John Alton Flowers." As I stepped back, my hand trembled. "It's Jack. He's really alive in the dream world."

"How do we get him out?"

"I'm not sure, but I can't worry about that right now." I touched the image of the tombstone again. The view eased back until the dark gash in the heavens draped the square reflection. "It must be Earth Red. Gordon mentioned a rift in the sky."

"So, do we go there?" Kelly asked. "Flash a light and take off?"

"I don't think so." I nodded toward the hallway. "I got a call from Daryl Blue. It's already been a couple of years on Earth Yellow, and the bow's finished, so Daryl Red wants us to come and get her before she dies of old age."

"I don't blame her. So long away from home. I can't imagine."

"But do we try to bring her home, or follow what we learned in the dream?"

"Learned from the dream? You mean to kill the supplicants?"

I shook my head. "Not that part. I could never kill Scarlet or anyone else."

"Of course you wouldn't want to kill her, but your father said Patar would guide you in the right way, and Patar didn't exactly mince words."

I stared at her. She was dead right. The other Nathan's empty eye sockets were a pretty good clue that Patar wasn't messing around. But if I could find my parents, I could explain to Dad what was going on. Maybe he didn't know everything about Patar. He'd never condone killing the supplicants, even if it meant saving the universe.

Or would he?

"I meant the part about the key mirror," I said. "We know where it is now."

Kelly pointed at the square in the lower left corner. "Look. It's Daryl Red. And she's with my father. Tony Yellow, I mean."

I crouched to get a good view. Daryl sat at a desk in front of a green-screen computer monitor, typing while Kelly's father stood next to her holding an umbrella over her head. A strange gadget was poised at the edge of the desk's surface. It looked like an old radio with a miniature satellite dish spinning slowly. A drizzle of rain clouded the background of trees and shrubs, and droplets fell from the sides of the umbrella. Two orange extension cords trailed away beyond the mirror's edge.

Kelly touched the glass. "She does look older. But what did she do to her hair?"

"So Earth Yellow is still clear for you." I took a closer look. Daryl's red hair had been pulled back and fastened tightly by a banana clip that left the rest of it in a mess of glitter-sprinkled ringlets blown about by the moist breeze. Her serious stare at the monitor gave her the aspect of a college student conducting research for a major project.

"We should go there," Kelly said. "We need the bow, and we can rescue Daryl. Two birds with one stone."

"True, but ..." I touched the middle-C square we had singled out. "This is the key. We can't ignore everything we learned in the dream, especially since Scarlet said we needed to use it."

Kelly nodded. "Then let's take both. Maybe the mirrors will give us a clue about where to go."

"I suppose you're right." After finding the screwdriver and a flashlight, I pried the key square loose and pulled it free. The other squares dimmed and slowly reconstructed the normal reflection, but the image of the dark cemetery in the square in my hands remained steady. Using the screwdriver again, I removed the square that had shown Daryl on Earth Yellow and placed it on top of the other one.

I draped the camera strap around Kelly's neck and held up the flashlight. "We'll use this for our flash. The area in the key square looked dark, so it'll come in handy if we go there."

"Speaking of handy …" She picked up the violin and headed for the bedroom door. "Let's pack everything we might need and flash the mirror from inside the car. If Scarlet doesn't mind transporting everything, a stocked vehicle would come in even handier."

After stuffing the car's backseat with pillows, blankets, boxes of nutrition bars, and bottles of water, as well as the violin, the camera, and the two mirrors, I tossed my empty backpack into the rear and slid behind the steering wheel.

Kelly sat in the passenger's seat and propped the key mirror on the dashboard. Since the car sat on the driveway in the same cold drizzle that apparently plagued Daryl Red on Earth Yellow, the air within carried a moist chill.

"Let's drive into cell range," Kelly said. "We can get an update from the two Daryls."

I started the engine. "Gotta hurry, though. No telling how long the mirror will keep showing that cemetery."

While I drove, the rain eased, allowing sunshine to peek around the fast-moving clouds. The holes in the dark blue sky seemed closer, bigger, brighter.

I kept glancing at the phone. When the signal bars rose, the phone trilled. I read the screen. "Text messages. A bunch of them."

Kelly blinked at the display. "You'd better pull over. I don't think I can see them."

I stopped on the shoulder, cut the engine, and read the messages in order, starting with the first one this morning.

"Nathan, if you don't get your butt back to Earth Yellow pronto, I'm going to strangle you with a violin string. Love and kisses, Daryl."

"Nathan, I can't wait until doomsday. Then again, maybe doomsday is almost here. Signed, A Candle in the Wind."

"Nathan, Kelly's dad keeps asking me out, and he's getting more aggressive. I told him to buzz off and get interested in Kelly's mom. Signed, The Other Woman."

"Nathan, if I don't hear from you today, I'll strangle Tony with a violin string, then myself. Well, I would if I wasn't so yellow. Signed, Daryl Red Singing the Blues."

I turned to Kelly. "That's the latest."

"How long ago did it come in?"

I checked the time stamp. "Just a few seconds."

"Then maybe you can send her a message before her day is over."

"It'll be faster if I just tell Daryl Blue what to say." I turned on the phone's speaker and pressed a speed dial. "You can listen in."

After half a ring, Daryl Blue answered. "Nathan! Finally!"

"Is something wrong?"

"Everything's wrong. Your land line doesn't work anymore, so I couldn't call you. Daryl Red's ready to kill Tony, and—"

"Yeah, I picked up on that."

"But that's not the worst of it. We lost power at the observatory, and we're almost out of generator power. Soon we won't be able to communicate with Daryl Red at all. She knows about it, and she's ready to jump off a cliff, if she could find a cliff in Iowa. And who knows how long cell service will hold out?"

"Can you send one message for me?"

"I'll try. We might only have a few seconds left."

I glanced at the mirror in the backseat, the square that would open a portal to Earth Yellow. What would be the best option? Go to the nightscape scene in the circle of fifths square and hope that Daryl Red somehow survives her ordeal without us? But even if she could cope, what if Tony kept his eye on her and not on Kelly's mother? That would mean no Kelly Yellow.

Not only that, if Kelly and I traveled to the place Patar indicated, what might happen? If I succeeded in healing the cosmic wounds and repelled Interfinity, how could I risk allowing travel again? Daryl Red would never be able to get home. I would save the universe but ruin her life and maybe a lot of other lives on Earth Yellow. That might be a rational trade-off, but who was I to make a decision like that?

"Nathan?"

The voice from the cell phone shook me from my thoughts. "Yeah. Sorry. I was just thinking. Where was I?"

Her voice faded to a whisper. "What do you want me to tell Daryl Red?"

"Tell her I'm on my way." I set the phone down and banged the steering wheel with a fist. "I can't believe this!"

"It'll be okay." Kelly touched my elbow. "We'll go to the other place as soon as we get Daryl out of her jam. Don't forget, what we do there only takes a little while here and on Earth Red. And like I said before, we need the bow Tony Yellow made."

"I know, but I keep getting the feeling that I'm putting on the clown suit Patar talked about."

"Don't worry about that freak. Just keep telling yourself that he wanted you to kill Scarlet. You're not the clown." Kelly retrieved the other mirror from the backseat and propped it on the dashboard. "He is."

The mirror no longer showed the Earth Yellow world, just a reflection of my tense face. "Let's see if I can fire it up." I grabbed the violin and played Foundation's Key. Within seconds, the mirror's image showed Daryl still sitting at the desk, now with her head resting on her folded arms.

The rain had stopped, eliminating the need for a doting, younger Tony to shelter her with an umbrella. Her head moved up and down in a spasmodic rhythm.

"I think she's crying." Kelly pointed the flashlight at the mirror. "Can we go?"

I nodded. "Let's do it."

She flashed the light. The world surrounding the car melted like candle wax and dripped away, revealing the familiar house. We still sat in the car, now parked between Daryl's table and the cottonwood tree in the front yard.

I pressed a finger to my lips and opened the door quietly. Kelly slid out through the driver's side, and we skulked toward Daryl on tiptoes.

The old-fashioned radio hummed, and the tiny satellite dish rotated, making a slight squeak with every turn. Daryl's head bobbed, and her quiet weeping blended with the other sounds.

I gritted my teeth. I wanted to say the right thing, something funny to break the tension, like, "Don't shoot me, I'm only the violin player," but her pitiful cries squelched any thought of using her as the butt of a joke.

I laid a gentle hand on her shoulder. "I'm here, Daryl. I'm sorry it took so long."

CHAPTER THIRTEEN

DARYL'S HEAD POPPED up. She stared at me with red eyes, tears following well-marked tracks down her cheeks. At first, a hint of a smile turned her lips upward, but a furrowed brow took over and twisted her face into a ferocious scowl. She rose from her chair, her shoulders high. As she rounded the corner of the desk, she lifted her hand and pushed a finger into my chest. "Do you have any idea how long I've been waiting for you, Mister Nathan Shepherd?"

As she pressed hard with her finger, I backpedaled, but she closed the gap. "I'll tell you how long! Two years, eight months, fourteen days, three hours, seven minutes, and …" She glanced at a watch on her wrist. "And forty-five seconds!"

I halted. Daryl kept poking my chest, her cheeks flaming. "I finished high school, started college, rejected three marriage proposals, started my own computer consulting business, and moved into an apartment to get away from Romeo, a.k.a. Tony Clark, who is ignoring Kelly's mom in order to deliver a single red rose to me every day. I've been trying to push him away, but I still have to come to his house to use the transmitter, because I can't get a signal from inside my apartment, and I can't run an extension cord from my kitchen to the park across the street. So he says I'm coming here because I can't stay away from him."

Daryl drew in a long breath. As she raised her finger to make another point, she stared at Kelly and me in turn. Her brow loosened, and her bottom lip trembled. She slid her arms around me and leaned her head against my chest. "Oh, Nathan! I'm so glad you came to get me! I waited and waited and sent so many messages, and I got only one answer over all that time. I thought I'd never get out of this place! Never!"

Kelly rubbed Daryl's back. "I'm sorry it took so long. It was only overnight and part of a day for us."

I added my own hand to Kelly's comforting rub. "Didn't you get another message? I just sent it telling you I was on my way."

Daryl shook her head. Her tears seeped through my shirt, but I didn't dare pull away.

"That must mean power's out at the Earth Blue observatory," I said. "Daryl Blue couldn't relay it."

Squeaking hinges sounded from the front door, followed by a booming male voice. "Hey! What's going on here? Who are you two?" A gangly young man, at least six foot three, ambled from the house, his eyes bugging out as he approached. "Why is Daryl crying?"

I gently pushed Daryl away and cleared my throat. "We're old friends. Daryl's really glad to see us." I extended a hand. "I'm Nathan."

As Tony took my hand with a crushing grip, he leaned over and peered at my face. "You look just like Flash, a friend of mine. You're a little younger, but I swear you're his twin. You wouldn't happen to be related to Solomon Shepherd, would you?"

"My father's name is Solomon, but he's a lot older." With a nod, I gestured toward the computer and transmitter. "That's quite a setup you've got there."

"You bet it is." Tony released me and took three long strides toward the desk. "We're getting signals from outer space, and Daryl's trying to translate them. Maybe we can 'phone home,' like in *E.T.*" He slapped his thigh and let out a roaring belly laugh. "Pretty funny, huh?"

Kelly clutched my arm and whispered, barely moving her lips. "My father was a real comic, wasn't he?"

Daryl wiped her eyes. "Tony, why don't you go inside and get them something to drink? They came a long way to get here."

"Will do." Tony glanced at the car in the middle of the yard. "Must've been too tired to stay on the road." He grinned. "Get it? Too tired? The car has tires?" Now chuckling, he strode back into the house, repeating the joke to himself.

Daryl grabbed my shirt and jerked me close. "I've been listening to those lame jokes for almost three years. Get me outta here right this minute."

"Wait." Kelly raised a hand. "Shouldn't we make sure he switches his affections to my future mother? If he's heartbroken over you, maybe they won't get together."

Daryl set a fist on her hip. "Don't worry, Kelly-kins. Your mother will make sure she catches the rebound. She's chasing Tony like a hound hunting a fox. She's not likely to lose his trail."

"We can't just leave," I said. "We have to get the bow."

Daryl sighed. "Right. The bow. I forgot."

Tony pushed the door open with his foot while holding four long-necked bottles. "Got a game tonight," he said as he passed two of the cold, wet bottles of Pepsi to Kelly and me. "Coach would kill me if I had a beer."

He handed one of the bottles to Daryl and winked. "It's nice and cool, but not as cool as you."

Daryl's cheeks reddened. "Thanks, Tony. You're … um … pretty cool yourself."

I sipped the drink and nodded at Tony. "So Daryl tells me you constructed a big violin bow."

"Yeah. I found this letter that promised me a rare twenty-dollar bill if I followed all the instructions. But when I finished the bow, no one showed up to give me the money. So I just hung it up on my wall." He took a long drink and let out a quiet belch. "It looks pretty good there, actually. I decided to—"

Tony's jaw dropped open. "What did you say your name is?"

"Nathan. The same guy who signed the letter." I pulled out my wallet and withdrew a twenty. "Sorry it took me so long to bring it."

Tony snatched the bill and examined it. "It's just like the other one. Andrew Jackson's head is a lot bigger."

"Yeah. Check out the date. It's from the future, too."

Tony blinked. "That's like the new movie!" He looked at Daryl. "What's it called?"

Daryl rolled her eyes. "*Back to the Future*, Tony."

"That's it." He shifted his wild stare back to the twenty. "I have to see that again."

After taking another drink, I eased toward the front door. "All right if I get the bow?"

"Sure." Tony strode ahead and held the door. "You paid for it. Besides, what am I going to do with a ten-foot-long bow?"

I walked inside and headed straight for the bedroom. Tony followed, as did his loud voice. "You know where to go?"

"Yep." I entered the bedroom and reached for the bow, suspended by metal hooks, but it hung too high on the wall.

Just as I leaned toward the desk chair, Tony marched in and pulled the bow from its perch. "Here you go."

I took it and gestured for him to sit. "Let's talk for a minute."

Tony set his drink on the desk and pulled up the chair while I settled on the bed with the bow at my side. "Listen. I can tell that you like Daryl. Am I right?"

"Yeah." Tony grinned. "She's amazing. Smart, cute, funny, and she loves movies."

"But she hasn't been responsive, has she?"

"No. Playing hard to get, I think." Tony took a quick swig from his bottle. "She keeps coming around here, though. Almost every day, so she must like me a little. I've been sending her roses, but I'm not sure it's working. You got any ideas?"

I gazed at Tony's earnest expression. His sincerity and frankness were refreshing. Maybe it wasn't right to keep the truth from this poor guy. "You ever wonder why Daryl knows so much? I mean, she's not just smart, she probably upgraded that computer like she knew every bit of technology that was ready to hit the market."

"Yeah. She's on top of things all right. Kind of spooky sometimes."

I pulled the twenty-dollar bill from Tony's fingers and showed it to him. "This isn't the only thing from the future."

Tony's eyes seemed to pop from his skull. "Daryl is?"

I nodded. "And so is the girl who came with me. We have to take Daryl back to the future."

As Tony stared at me, his smile slowly weakened, and a deep line traced across his brow. He shook his head and chuckled under his breath. "You had me going for a while. Who put you up to this? Flash? You're really his brother, right?" He looked around the room. "That old camera hound's probably already got a hundred shots of me acting like a fool. He'll probably show them to the whole team, and they'll get a kick—"

"It's not a joke." I laid the twenty back in Tony's hand. "You saw the car in the yard. Did you see any tire tracks?"

"I already figured that out. If everyone on the team chipped in, they could carry it. They couldn't afford a Delorean, so they brought a Toyota. I've never seen that model, though. I guess it's new."

"You could say that." I leaned closer to Tony. "Listen. I'll prove we're from a future world, but you gotta help us out. First, did Daryl teach you how to use that computer and transmitter?"

Tony shook his head. "She wouldn't let me touch it, but I watched her enough times to figure it out."

"Good enough. When we get back, I'll try to contact you through it. Second, when you go to see *Back to the Future* again, I think you should invite that other girl who's been trying to get your attention."

"Molly? The law student?"

"Yeah. I think …" I bit my lip. I was about to say, "you'll have a wonderful life together," but that would be a lie. Taking a breath, I finished with, "you and she should get married."

Tony's brow bent down a notch. "Molly's cool most of the time, but she's got a hot temper if you cross her, you know, typical Irish. But if you can prove what you say, I'll keep her in mind. I mean, if you know the future, I'm not going to argue with you."

"One more thing. Can I get Flash's phone number? I have a message from the future for him, too."

"Sure." Tony grabbed a pad and pen from the desk, jotted down the number, and ripped off the top sheet. "Here you go."

I stuffed the sheet into my pocket. Considering all the information I had just spilled, would Tony be able to keep it to himself? He was probably a prime target for Mictar's dream-stalking, so he might not be able to hide what he knew.

As I rose from the bed, I looked Tony in the eye. "Are you a next-day dreamer or a traveler?"

"Neither. I don't dream at all. Makes life easier. I pity those folks who are getting harassed even when they're trying to sleep."

"Yeah. It's like the Gestapo." Cradling the huge bow in both hands, I headed for the door. "Let's go."

By the time we reached the car, Kelly was already in the front seat with the mirror in her lap, and Daryl sat in the back among the snacks and bedding.

I eyed the bow. It would never fit inside the car. I laid it on the roof and looked at it doubtfully. Could we take the chance that it might not come along for the cross-dimensional ride?

"I'll get some duct tape," Tony said. "That ought to—"

Tires squealed as a van sped toward us along the narrow road, whipping the dying brown corn stalks as it passed between the fields. The familiar "Stoneman Enterprises" lettering and the slender feminine arm waving through the passenger-side window meant that my celestial duet partner had arrived.

"Friends of yours?" Tony asked.

"Yeah. I'll introduce you in a minute."

When Gunther pulled to a stop in the driveway, Francesca jumped out and ran to me. Wearing jeans and a long-sleeved gray T-shirt, she seemed dressed for manual labor. Her raven curls bounced in a bushy ponytail behind a baseball cap as she sidled up to me. "I'm ready to go."

I gazed at her sparkling eyes, now at the same level as my own. Based on Daryl's account of time passage, Francesca had to be around sixteen now. "Tracked us down in a dream?"

She gave me a sly wink. "Gunther and I are better than a pair of bloodhounds."

Gunther, his bulging flannel shirt showing more muscle as well as a few extra pounds around the waist, lumbered up the driveway. Dangling a set of keys, he gestured with his head toward the van. "I'll trade you. That bow will fit in the back."

I traded keys. "Help me move all our stuff?"

"No problem." Gunther headed straight for the Toyota.

Dr. Malenkov stepped out of the van and walked toward me, his face solemn under his slightly grayer head. "My wife is too grief stricken to join us. She said her good-byes at home."

"I can understand that." I reached for his hand. "Please tell her we'll take good care of Francesca."

"Yes, we know," Dr. Malenkov replied, accepting the handshake. "Your mission's purpose cannot be delayed by our concerns for one precious life. What is one life, or two or three for that matter, if billions are saved?"

I felt my smile shrivel. As usual, Dr. Malenkov's words were saturated with wisdom. He wore the sad countenance of a father sending a daughter to the front lines of war, not knowing if she would ever return to his arms.

After I introduced Tony to the newcomers, we moved the food, drinks, bedding, and other items from the Toyota to the van. Soon, with me behind the wheel, Kelly in the front passenger's seat, and Daryl and Francesca in the back, we were ready to go.

Kelly held the key mirror in front of the radio while Francesca studied my copy of Foundation's Key. After a few seconds, she lifted my violin. "Let's get this show on the road, Son."

I set an elbow on the window frame and leaned my head out. "Here comes your proof, Tony. Don't blink."

While Tony backed away from the van, his eyes as large as ever, Francesca played Foundation's Key, giving the simple melody an exquisite rendering. The mirror darkened and again showed the field and sky, but now, with one horizon brightening to soft purple and orange, it seemed as though morning was about to break.

Holding the flashlight with both hands, Daryl pointed it at the mirror. "Fasten your seat belts! We're getting out of here!" She clicked the switch. The beam shot toward the mirror. The reflected glow filled the van's interior and shimmered across the surrounding glass.

I shielded my eyes from the blinding light. A heavy, static-filled bass rhythm pounded from the radio speakers. It banged against my eardrums and pulsed through my heart—throbbing, aching, pressing in from all sides.

As the glow dimmed, the static eased. Music blended in, a violin playing a lovely, yet depressing piece. The windows cleared. A dark sky surrounded us, as if we were wrapped in a blanket of black. Not a single star interrupted the inky canopy.

I lowered my window. The music grew louder. With low tones that sang of loneliness and sorrow, it seeped into my mind and weighed down my heart. It was the music of the melancholy, a mournful dirge that swept away every joyful thought.

"The words are so sad," Kelly said. "Someone's in a lot of pain."

"You hear words? Can you tell us?"

"Let's see if I can find a good place to start." After a few seconds, she sang softly, keeping her melody close to the violinist's tune.

Weep, O my soul. Weep and lament.
Weep for the loss of my heart.
Weep for the solitude, weep for the past,
Weep as my soul tears apart.

I have lost my beloved, my shelter, my rock.
I have lost the fruit of my womb.
I have lost the light that shines in the night.
I have lost my heart in this tomb.

Kelly let out a long breath. "Now it's repeating the first part."

A surge of heat pulsed into my cheeks. The music seemed familiar, but I couldn't quite place it. I leaned around the seat and eyed Francesca. "Recognize the music?"

She nodded, speaking with a faint tremor in her voice. "I wrote it as something to play when I'm thinking about my parents. It helps me grieve, sort of like a musical way to cry."

"Did you ever record it?"

"Never. It's not even finished, and the part that's playing now is new to me."

"Someone else finished your work?" Kelly asked. "Who could do that?"

I flung open the door. "My mother could." I pushed my foot down on something firm, allowing me to get out and scan the area, but neither streetlamp, nor headlight, nor star shone through the murky blackness.

From somewhere close by, the music played on. I drank in its beauty. Only one person could play with such perfection, such passion. Only one. Mom had to be around somewhere.

I spun to the van. "Daryl, hand me the flashlight."

As she reached it through the open door, the glow spilled over her trembling hands. "What … what's out there?"

"Don't know yet." When I took the flashlight, I laid my hand over hers. "What's wrong?"

"I'm terrified of the dark." She gulped and took a deep breath. "But it's okay. Just leave that on, and I'll be fine."

I aimed the light toward the apparent source of the music, but the beam disappeared only a foot or so away from the bulb, as if swallowed by the darkness. "Mom?" I shouted. "Are you out there?"

My voice sounded like it struck a barrier that absorbed every syllable.

The music continued unabated. If anything, it seemed louder, even sadder than before. As I took a step toward it, the floor under my leading foot crumbled. I jumped back to solid ground just in time.

Breathing in short gasps, I leaned into the van. "Francesca, can you come out and play an echo?"

"Sure." She exited the van and joined me near the driver's door. Kelly, too, got out and leaned against the panel on the same side, while Daryl stayed put in the backseat.

"Okay," I said. "It sounds like she's starting over. Play right behind her and echo each measure. Fortissimo."

Francesca played the first measure. Her own notes carried into the black air, pure and true.

The other violin halted in mid-measure. Francesca played the notes and stopped at the same place.

After a few seconds, the music began again, this time playing another piece, fast and furious.

Kelly jerked on my elbow. "She's yelling. She's calling your name and asking where you are."

I tossed the flashlight to the seat, took the violin from Francesca, and played a reply, pouring my thoughts into the music, just as I had in the misty world. I hoped to shout, "I'm here. How can I find you?"

When I finished, I lowered the violin and waited in silence. My legs trembled, aching to dash ahead as I strained to hear the slightest noise.

The music hummed again, this time calmer, long strokes that caressed my mind with gentle hands.

"Nathan," Kelly interpreted. "My son. My love. I am enraptured to hear your song. God has granted you passage to my prison, but the path to where I sit is fraught with danger."

I played a quick response. "What is this place?"

Her music deepened to the violin's lower registers. "Your father believes this is a cosmic storage warehouse for dark energy," Kelly said. "It has a fabric network that erodes as energy is added, paralleling the erosion of the worlds' barriers. Falling through the fabric could take you to one of many worlds, perhaps to one that has not yet even been discovered. The danger is great, for the fabric of space crumbles even as we speak. After nearly falling into the void several times, we found a sturdy place. Yet, I sense that the foundational cracks are closing in."

I pressed my toes down. The ground was still solid enough to support my body as well as a van, yet a plunge into the void lay only two steps away. I played again. "So we're not in outer space? Is that why we can breathe here?"

"That's our guess. It seems that we are in a web structure that has trapped an oxygen-rich gaseous pocket within. Perhaps it was created artificially for the purpose of holding prisoners, but who can solve such mysteries when trapped within a realm of darkness?"

Now stroking the strings more slowly, I said, "Speaking of mysteries, if Mictar killed your Earth Blue duplicate, why didn't he burn out her eyes?"

As Mom's violin replied, Kelly again gave the strings a voice. "He did. Dr. Simon of our world replaced them with eyes from a cadaver and applied makeup to hide the scorch marks. He was unsure if the deception would work, but it was the only idea we could come up with."

A cadaver's eyes? Did Patar show me one of those eyes in the vision while Mozart's Requiem Mass played? Since he had withdrawn it from one of the coffins, maybe so. "Where did Dad go?" I asked with a quick series of bow strokes.

"He ventured out to seek an escape, or at least food and water, but he never returned. I fear that he has fallen into the depths below."

I poised the bow above the strings but hesitated. Dad would never intentionally leave Mom alone for very long. Like she said, something must have happened to him. I lowered the bow and looked at Kelly and Francesca in turn. "What do you think?"

"What are our options?" Kelly asked. "Will the mirror take us anywhere?"

From the backseat, the flashlight in hand, Daryl leaned over the front and extended the mirror toward the open driver's door. The glass showed only darkness, not even a reflection. "Give it a whirl," she said.

I played Foundation's Key through, but the mirror stayed dark. After trying three more times, I shook my head. "Quattro must not work here."

Mom's violin replied with Kelly interpreting. "Son, I heard you play the song that calls for Quattro's aid. Although it opens a window to a sacrificial supplicant, the mirror is little more than a polished piece of glass. It was given as a tool for times of trouble when you are unable to escape on your own or when you need to find your way on a journey. It will not serve you well when it is time to turn and face the danger head-on or when you have already found your destination."

I stared at the blank mirror. She was right. Whenever I used Quattro to get out of danger, I turned my back and let someone else do the work. That was great when I was getting shot at in the river and about to crash in a doomed airplane, but what about now? Maybe it was time I stepped up and took charge.

I played one more question. "Mom, are you hungry and thirsty?"

"Yes, Son," Kelly said as the music replied. "It has been quite some time since I have had food or water."

"Keep playing, Mom. I'm coming."

After a few seconds, Mom's initial lament began again, though with a noticeable change in tone, just a shade more lively. I set the violin on the front seat and touched the flashlight in Daryl's hand. "Put the mirror away, and fill my backpack with a few bottles of water and some of those snack bars." I leaned farther into the van and smiled. "Please?"

She aimed the light at her own wide smile. "Sure thing, boss." Within seconds, she had filled the pack and passed it forward.

Kelly tapped me on the back. "What are you going to do?"

As I withdrew from the van, I slid my arms through the straps. "I'm going to rescue my mother."

She hooked her fingers around my elbow. "I'm coming with you, and don't try to talk me out of it."

"And me," Francesca chimed in.

Daryl groaned. "I guess I'm supposed to make it a brave and cheery foursome, aren't I?" She let out a huff, opened the back door, and slammed it, then circled the van, holding the flashlight and propping Tony's bow against her shoulder. "You were going to forget this, weren't you?" she said, tipping the bow toward me.

I caught it at the center point and balanced it. "You sure you're okay?"

"As long as I have this," she said, aiming the flashlight downward, "I'm fine."

After passing the bow to Francesca, I studied the spot where the beam spread across the ground. Weak and failing, the glow spilled from the bulb as if it were shimmering water. It fell and disappeared into tiny cracks in the black floor.

I stooped and traced one of the cracks with a fingernail. As I tried to scratch through it, I couldn't make a dent. The light had somehow liquefied. It must have gone somewhere. But where?

Our voices had also changed. The vocal sound waves traveled a few feet, enough for us to converse, but they either dispersed or became absorbed. Yet, somehow, music pierced every obstacle.

I straightened and pointed toward the sound. "The music's coming from that way, but the ground's too brittle straight ahead. We'll have to make a wide circle and go single file."

Daryl pushed the flashlight into my hand. "Want to lead the way?"

"Sure." I swept the beam slowly from side to side and crept forward. As before, the light splashed, spread out, and filtered into the fabric below, leaving a residual glow that painted a shimmering path.

When the beam reached the point where the floor fell out from under me, I stopped the sweep. The light poured straight down and disappeared. I found a safer route to the right and, with the others following, traced a meandering path toward the sounds of the sad violin.

After a few moments, it seemed that we had to be within a few yards of the goal. Ahead, the floor dropped away into nothingness with no obvious path to the left or right. I halted and pointed the beam forward. The light spread out and fell downward, like water shooting from a hose, but the faint glow carried far enough to paint a portrait of a dark female form standing with a violin raised to her chin. Her eyes reflected the failing light, two brownish-orange circles only fifteen feet away.

I took in a deep breath and shouted as loud as I could. "Mom!"

The music stopped. A voice, as quiet as gentle rain, replied. "Nathan?"

I shouted again. "I can't see how to get to you!"

The shadow's arm pointed. "There is one brittle path to your right, perhaps eight to ten feet away. Your father took it when he left on his journey, but I fear it could be far weaker than before."

"I'm probably the lightest," Kelly said. "I'll take the backpack to her."

"She's my older double," Francesca countered. "And I probably weigh only a couple of pounds more than you do."

Daryl raised a finger. "I volunteer to stay. Someone has to survive to tell about your untimely deaths."

"If anyone goes, it'll be me." I slid the backpack off. "Mom, put down the violin."

The shadow crouched for a moment, then rose again. "It's down."

"Get ready to catch a backpack."

Mom braced her feet and extended her arms. "Ready."

I slung the pack toward her. Although it smacked against her chest, she managed to hang on and stay upright.

"It's food and water. I hope it's enough."

Her shadowed arms lowered the pack, then drooped at her side. "You are a blessed young man, Nathan, a true son of your father."

The words draped across my mind—*a true son of your father*. Was I really? Would Dad have made the same choices I had made? With all of Patar's stinging accusations, I felt more like a bumbling fool than a chip off the old block.

I inched my way to the right. "I'm coming over there."

As I searched for the path, a slight tug on the back of my shirt told me Kelly was close behind, as usual. And that meant the other two girls were probably tagging along as well.

When I found a spot where the beam stopped pouring unhindered into the void, I held the flashlight steady and set a foot lightly on the path. It seemed firm. I pressed my weight down. So far so good. Only about four more steps. I pushed my other foot forward. Again, no problem.

Kelly let go of my shirt. "I'll stay two steps behind you so we don't put too much pressure on one spot."

"Crawl on your hands and knees," Daryl said. "You'll distribute your weight."

"Good thinking." I pointed the flashlight ahead. Mom's shadowy form reached out, now only about ten feet away. The glow washed over her face, revealing her anguished expression—a deeply furrowed brow above eyes filled with alarm. I tossed the light to Daryl and eased my body down to hands and knees.

Now blind, I inched forward, sliding over the tactile blackness. I felt like a trapped miner trying to escape from a deep tunnel—no light, no map, and no idea if I was about to tumble into an air shaft.

"You can do it, Nathan," Kelly said. "You're almost there."

"Maybe. If I could see."

"I'll try to blaze the trail." Daryl said. The beam appeared on the floor where my hand would slide next. "Is that better?"

The light poured through wide cracks, revealing more danger. "Only if seeing impending doom is better."

I glared at the fragile floor. Should I chance it? Maybe I could jump and latch onto Mom's arm. But would she be able to hold on?

I rose to a crouch and lunged, but the floor crumbled beneath me. I flailed for Mom's hand but swiped through empty air. Yet, for some reason, I stayed suspended over the blackness. Another force pressed against my throat, choking me.

"I've got you," Kelly grunted.

I looked up. Kelly's fists clutched my shirt, and my collar was strangling me, but if I lifted my chin to loosen the choke, I would probably slip right out of the very thing that kept me from a one-way ticket to nowhere.

Her knees bending, she pulled, but her arms quaked. "Swing your leg up!" she yelled. "Francesca will catch it."

The younger Francesca dropped to her knees and reached down. "Aim for my hand!"

I couldn't answer. I couldn't even breathe. When I tried to swing, a faint ripping sound jolted my senses. My shirt was tearing. I had only seconds before I would plummet.

Grunting again, Kelly swung my body from side to side to add to my momentum. Each swing caused a new tearing sound. She cried out with a guttural scream.

I grimaced. The pain in Kelly's wounded shoulder had to be ripping through her body. How long could she hold on?

Finally, I thrust my leg up as high as I could. Francesca grabbed my ankle. "I've got him! Pull!"

With the pressure on my throat loosening, I sucked in precious air. As they slowly eased me upward, a new sound grated in my ears, a faint cracking from beneath my rescuers' shoes. "It's collapsing!" I shouted. "Let me go, and run for it!"

"Never!" Pushing with her legs, Kelly lunged backwards. I shot up over the edge and sprawled on top of her with a heavy thump. More cracking sounded from beneath our bodies. The moment we scrambled to our feet, the floor gave way.

CHAPTER FOURTEEN

WE PLUNGED INTO darkness. Kelly and Francesca screamed. I held my breath. As we dropped, I grabbed Kelly's arm, then Francesca's, and looked up. Daryl stood at the rim, gazing down at us, the flashlight still in hand. The glow illuminated her terrified face as she shrank in my view. A stream of liquid light followed us into the depths like dripping, phosphorescent wax. Seconds later, she disappeared in the upper reaches, and blackness swallowed her puny torch.

After a moment, the two girls quieted, and I exhaled. With complete darkness and silence surrounding us, there seemed to be no sensation of falling, not even a rush of air. Yet, since we could breathe, air had to be whooshing by, unless the air pocket was falling with us, or the ceiling had zoomed upward, or …

I shook my head. Every option seemed impossible. This place didn't follow any rules—physics, gravity, or logic.

Francesca whispered, "Is everyone okay?"

"I'm fine, except I can't see anything." I blinked at the darkness. "Did we stop falling?"

"We stopped," Kelly said. "My vision is working again, so I guess we moved to another world. We're standing on solid ground, but I don't feel pressure under my feet."

I turned toward her. As in the misty world, radiance illuminated her eyes, now appearing as beams sweeping the area like car headlights. The beams passed over vertical stone slabs near my feet, too quickly to give me an idea of what they were. I ran a finger along the top of one—smooth marble, about three feet wide and four feet tall. "Where's the violin? Maybe it'll get rid of the darkness."

"I put it down," Francesca said. "I needed both hands to haul you up."

Kelly tugged on my sleeve. "I hear something. Like a horn. And it's getting louder."

A blaring howl grew in volume, coming from somewhere above. A pair of lights shone from a large, rectangular object falling through the darkness.

I shouted, "Everyone out of the way!"

We scattered. Gunther's van landed with a rattling, squeaking thump. The van's horn silenced, and its headlights flicked off. A new light flashed on at the driver's window, and Daryl leaned out in the midst of the glow, her hair frazzled. "Wow! What a trip!"

I squinted at her. "Did more of the floor collapse?"

"No. I figured, do I want to be stuck in a cosmic web for all eternity chatting with your mom? I mean, she's really nice and all, but I came here for adventure. I said, 'What the heck? Might as well go out in style.' So instead of just jumping after you, I turned the headlights on, leaned on the horn, and drove the van into the hole, hoping you'd notice and get out of the way."

Kelly's eyebeams shifted back and forth as she shook her head. "Crazy as ever."

"Did you pick up my violin?" I asked. "We need some light."

"Yep." Daryl extended the violin and bow through the window. "I'm all for fiddling away the darkness."

I set the violin under my chin and raised the bow. Just as I was about to play, Kelly grabbed my wrist.

"No," she whispered. "Wait."

I lowered my voice to match hers. "What's up?"

"I hear singing. It's getting closer."

I ducked behind the stone slab and pulled Kelly and Francesca down. Daryl jumped out of the driver's door and joined us.

"Is the van in plain sight?" I asked. "I can't see it."

Daryl aimed the flashlight at the letters on the side panel. "As plain as a zit on the Mona Lisa."

I pushed the light toward the ground. "Douse it."

Daryl flicked it off. "As if that's going to help."

"The singing's getting closer," Kelly said. "It's a male voice."

"I hear it now." I passed a hand in front of Kelly's face. "Won't he see your eyes?"

"If it's daylight to him like it is to me, he probably won't." Kelly aimed her eyes at a winding path. With the beams steady now, the residual glow washed over the surrounding slabs, clarifying them.

"Tombstones," I whispered.

"Shhh. I see him now."

A youthful male shuffled into the light, his head down and shoulders sloped. As he drew closer, Kelly's beams followed, painting twin circles on his torso, but he didn't seem to notice.

Appearing to be about fifteen and dressed in a dark, form-fitting shirt and loose, equally dark trousers, he sang a mournful tune, using the vowel sounds we had heard from the stalkers.

Kelly translated in soft whispers.

To wander home,
To rest, to roam,
'Tis peace entombed
And mortal gloom.
Awaiting dark,
Forlorn and stark,
I weep for days gone by.

The young man lifted his head and gazed above, tears streaming as he lamented.

To see my Scarlet's rosy face,
To hear my Amber's golden song,
To feel again our hued embrace,
Apart we're weak, together strong.

He stopped and stared straight ahead. After blinking for a moment, he strode to the van and touched the side panel. He pivoted on his heels. Kelly's beams struck his eyes, raising a splash of blue.

The boy sang a short burst of notes.

"I see you." Kelly translated. "Stand and show yourselves."

She stood and stepped toward the boy. I shot to my feet and marched past her with a hand extended. "I'm Nathan Shepherd. Who are you?"

The boy stared at my hand. "I am Cerulean."

I stepped back. "You speak English. I thought you would answer in song."

"If you thought this, then why did you address me in English? I merely responded in kind."

"I … I'm not sure. Habit, I guess."

A sympathetic smile bent Cerulean's lips. "I am familiar with your facial expression, Nathan of the Red World. You are flustered and confused."

"How do you know me?"

"I have seen Nathan of the Blue World many times through his mirror. I learned to love him dearly, though I am no longer his supplicant. He has gone to be with the Everlasting One."

As Kelly's beams moved across Cerulean from his torso to the top of his head, I studied his boyish features—smooth skin, bright sapphire eyes, and blue hair, spiked at the center. With his top shirt button unfastened, the upper portion of his chest was exposed, revealing darkness just under his neckline, a stark contrast to his pale skin.

"How did you get out of your prison?" I asked.

"I am still there. This is the realm of dreams, and I am doing what I can to prevent a stalker from frightening someone you know quite well. Daryl of the Blue World is dozing under a travel mirror, making her vulnerable to a dream attack. Since she is terrified of great heights and graveyards, a stalker has manipulated her night vision and created this cemetery. I entered her dream to cancel the stalker's efforts and bring her peace."

"That wasn't a song of peace you were singing a few minutes ago."

"That was my own lament, for I have been separated from my sisters." Cerulean gave me a weak smile. "Daryl would not be able to understand it. In fact, she likely did not hear it at all." He nodded in the direction he entered the graveyard. "She is just now phasing into her dream world, believing herself to be in the eighth grade and reliving a night when she was lost in the woods and came out in a church cemetery."

Daryl Red spoke up. "I remember that night." Kelly's eyebeams locked on her as she rose from behind the tombstone. "I'll talk to her."

Cerulean grasped her wrist. "You will only add to her confusion. Watch quietly. Perhaps you will learn something useful."

In the distance, a glow appeared, revealing Daryl wearing a blue nightgown. With her hair tied into pigtails, she seemed much younger. As she drew closer, the glow spread, illuminating the graveyard. A bat fluttered up from behind a tombstone and dove at Daryl's tear-streaked face. With a pitiful cry, she flailed her arms. When the bat angled away, she hunched over and walked on, still sobbing, but instead of tears, a black mist emanated from her eyes and rose into the air.

"What's that black stuff?" Daryl Red asked.

Cerulean touched his face near his eye. "Dark energy, a product of her fear. The stalker who created this vision will collect it for the Interfinity engine."

"Interfinity?" I repeated. "That's what my father called the merging of the worlds."

"Because your father learned it from us. Mictar's engine is also called Lucifer, but the reason would take too long to explain."

"That means my father must have gone to the misty world before—"

"Shhh." Cerulean set a finger on my lips. "It is time to supplicate for this dear child. I feel the stalker is ready to harvest this garden of terror."

A ghostly apparition rose from one of the graves, a semi-transparent man in a torn pilot's uniform. Pus oozed from open facial sores and dripped to the ground, raising sizzling splashes. As he limped toward Daryl Blue, a putrid stench permeated the graveyard. He reached out with long, gnarled fingers and moaned through his words, stretching out the syllables in a lamenting tone. "Soon you will join me. You will fall from the heavens and perish."

"My uncle," Daryl Red whispered. "He was a pilot, like my father. He died in a plane crash before I was born."

Daryl Blue turned to run, but the ground collapsed into a deep chasm. Flailing her arms, she stood on tiptoes to keep from falling. A rush of black mist flowed from somewhere, nearly veiling her head.

His trembling hands still reaching, the man continued his slow approach, repeating his ghostly mantra as he drew closer and closer. "Soon you will join me. You will fall from the heavens and perish."

Cerulean leaped into the open and sang with a powerful, vibrant voice.

> Begone thou ghost of fear and gloom
> And hearken now to Daryl's choir.
> They cast aside thy phantom hands
> And rescue her with freedom's fire.

As he sang, a stream of sparkling light flowed through the air, pulsating with the rise and fall of the tune.

The stream wrapped around young Daryl's torso and pulled her away from the precipice.

Now more perplexed than frightened, she stared at her uncle's apparition. As the stream released her, the black mist around her head thinned, and the sparkling light flowed into the air, seemingly taking the angelic voices with it.

Cerulean continued his song.

Go back to shadows all ye ghosts;
Restore the ground from whence it came.
Begone ye graves and stones of death;
Restore the light to Daryl's flame.

The ghostly man faded away. With a loud rumble, the floor of the chasm behind young Daryl rose back to the surface and snapped into place as if it had never collapsed. The glow around her body brightened. As it flowed across the graveyard, the tombstones sank into the ground and lush grass sprouted over the patches of bare earth that had marked the resting places of the departed.

Soon, the cemetery looked like a pristine meadow. Orange and blue wildflowers sprouted at Daryl's feet. She plucked three, twisted the stems together, and pushed the bouquet into her hair. Now smiling, she skipped away in the direction she had come. The brightness faded, leaving us in a slowly dimming world.

"She will awaken soon," Cerulean said. "This place will dissolve. You will have to find an escape."

A new sound emanated from somewhere above, a cacophonous mixture of notes, sung in an array of vowel sounds.

I covered my ears. The music, if the horrible noise could be called that, sounded familiar. "The stalkers?"

Cerulean aimed his blue eyes toward the dimness above. "They are standing around my dome and capturing the energy of supplication. They use their foul song to transform my prayers and Daryl's deliverance into dark energy." He dipped his head and sighed. "Even my rescues are being used for evil purposes."

"Is there anything we can do?" Kelly asked.

"Nothing. You must go. When her dream ends, this dreamscape will collapse, and you will fall into another sphere. I cannot predict where you will go."

I showed him the mirror. "Should I use this?"

Cerulean caressed the glass with a gentle finger. "Yes. Return to your vehicle. Scarlet will guide you to safety."

As the light continued fading, we hurried to the van. While I settled into the driver's seat with the violin, Kelly mounted the mirror on the dashboard. Daryl and Francesca watched from the back, leaning forward between the headrests.

I played Foundation's Key again, hurrying through the notes. The mirror darkened. A faint image of a face appeared in the midst of the black reflection, a feminine face with shining red eyes. Scarlet's voice, soft and gentle, emanated from the glass. "I heard you calling for me earlier, my beloved, but I could not find you."

"I was in a place of blackness, where my mother is."

Her auburn eyebrows dipped. "It seems that my vision cannot penetrate there, but since you are in the realm of dreams now, I can speak to you."

I lowered the violin. "Where should we go?"

"The mirror can return you only to one of the earthly realms. Yet, I can send you to someone who can give you help."

"My father?"

Scarlet's eyes dimmed. "I have been unable to locate him. Even his dreams are out of my reach."

"Then, who?"

"I do not know his name, but I will illuminate your path. You will see him soon." The face in the mirror clarified. Scarlet, her lips trembling, spoke in a lamenting tone. "Do not forget to come for me, Nathan. I cannot escape, and the stalkers will never let me go. You are my only hope."

"But how? How can I get back to you?"

Her voice faded. "Play my song. I know not the title, but it strums the sorrows of my heart and eases my pain." Seconds later, she vanished. In her place, a construction site appeared, a building with no roof and a man on a ladder adding bricks to the top of a wall.

As the light in the surrounding dreamscape dimmed to blackness, a loud crack sounded from underneath the van. The left rear wheel sank, angling our bodies toward the depression. More cracks erupted. The van sank again, and the entire world faded to black.

I grabbed the steering wheel. "Daryl Blue's waking up."

Daryl Red aimed the flashlight. "Say the word, Captain."

"Hit it!"

The beam shot out and bounced off the mirror. The surrounding blackness sizzled. By the thousands, dark pinpoints sparkled with colorful light until the image in the mirror materialized around us.

With the entire landscape now in view, I scanned the area. The van sat on a slab foundation, facing a tri-fold mirror that had been bolted to the concrete surface. A curved, plaster wall stood behind the mirror, making a semi-circle and leaving the area behind us open to the trees. Only a few stacked cinder blocks marked where the rest of the observatory's domed wall would be built.

I leaned my head out the window. A cold breeze brushed back my hair. "They're building Interfinity Labs here."

"You mean StarCast," a man with a British accent said. "It is not Interfinity yet."

I looked at the outside rearview mirror. A short, bald man with owl-like glasses walked toward me on the driver's side. "Dr. Simon? Simon Blue?"

"You guessed correctly." Dr. Simon opened the van door and motioned for me to get out. "We have much to do and little time to do it."

I hopped down to the foundation and hugged myself to fight the breeze. "Interfinity's almost here. We have to figure out how to get back to the misty world and play the violin."

"Yes, yes," Dr. Simon said, waving a hand. "I know all about that. But first we have another disaster to try to avert."

"But we'll create more holes in the cosmic fabric."

Dr. Simon pointed at the sky. "There are many holes, and the wounds we inflict on the fabric are minuscule compared to the greater danger the stalkers are creating."

"Exactly. We have to stop them. That's why we can't afford to get distracted. I have to find the violin as soon as possible."

"Nathan Shepherd," Dr. Simon said, giving me a fatherly glare, "are you a true son of Solomon? If you are, then where is your compassion? If you knew someone was about to die, would you try to save his life? Or would you skip away to do what you perceived to be your duty, saying 'Have a nice day,' while he dies in flames and his widow and children are doomed to suffer for years to come?"

I stepped back. Dr. Simon's words shot through my heart. I took a deep breath and looked him in the eye. "What do you have in mind?"

He pulled a small three-ring notebook from his pocket, leafed through the pages, and stopped somewhere near the middle. "The space shuttle Challenger will launch tomorrow, and it will explode moments later because of a flaw in the O-ring seal in one of its solid rocket boosters. Extreme cold will exploit the flaw and create a disastrous chain reaction."

"So now you want me to be an astronaut?" Shaking my head, I stepped back again. "You're out of your mind. They would never let me on board to—"

"Don't take me for a fool," Dr. Simon snapped. "I know you can't buy a ticket and stroll aboard a space shuttle. But you can use the Quattro mirror to send the seven astronauts elsewhere before they ever set foot in the craft. That should give us time to convince them to inspect the O-rings. At the very least, we could delay the launch and hope for warmer weather."

"But won't the astronauts dream about the explosion? And the launch workers? At least some of them have to be next-day dreamers, right?"

"If only it were that simple. It seems that many major disasters are hidden from dreamers. Just a few months ago, a Midwest Airlines flight crashed after taking off from Milwaukee. In order to test a theory I have, I went to the gate shortly before takeoff and interviewed some of the passengers about their most recent dreams, and they all reported that they slept without dreaming the previous night."

"No dreams at all?"

Dr. Simon shook his head. "My theory is that Mictar has access to disaster lists, and his stalkers suppress the dreams of the victims of coming major catastrophes."

"But don't the people notice that no one dreams about the disasters? They dream about everything else, so it's obvious."

"Of course. But the entire world lives in fear. Everyone must sleep eventually, and sudden death has come to many who have questioned the status quo. Self-preservation is a strong motivator. Apathy becomes a life-saving choice." Dr. Simon's voice deepened. "The question for you, Nathan Shepherd, is whether or not you will join in their apathy."

While my traveling companions exited the van, I lowered my gaze and mentally replayed the video footage of the Challenger disaster. How many times had I wished I could travel to the past and stop the tragedy? Now I had the chance to do it, an impossible dream come true. But what about the billions of others on the three earths?

As if reading my mind, Dr. Simon spoke in a soothing tone. "Who can tell when the worlds will merge or how much time we have? The hours you spend on this assignment will take only moments in the other worlds. I have been traveling back and forth between Earths Blue and Yellow for several Yellow years now, and the ultimate collision still has not arrived."

I stared at the sincere eyes behind the circular lenses. Dr. Simon had a good point. Interfinity seemed like a doomsday prophecy that would never arrive—lots of ominous signs but nothing that proved it would result in the end of the cosmos. Maybe it was a big, barking Doberman without any teeth.

I looked at my companions. Kelly leaned against the van's side panel, rubbing her arms in the cold breeze as she seemed to search my mind with her gaze. Daryl stood next to her, shifting uneasily from foot to foot. Francesca crossed her arms and glanced between me and the other girls. With her lips parted, she seemed ready to offer advice, but she stayed silent.

Kelly pushed away from the van and shuffled toward me, shivering. Splotches of red marred the shoulder of her sweatshirt, evidence that some of her stitches had broken loose. "Don't go, Nathan." She stopped and grimaced before looking me in the eye. "We can't afford to get sidetracked for a whole day. Besides, we couldn't stop the jet disaster."

"Right," Daryl said. "Crashing the government's space party and convincing the Feds to postpone the flight would make your airliner mission look like a game of Pin the Tail on the Donkey."

I shifted my gaze to Francesca. She walked toward me, her eyes sorrowful, yet piercing. Leaning close, she whispered, "You must do what you believe to be right. Not what Solomon Shepherd would do; what Nathan Shepherd would do. Your father has been your guide, your rock, but the wisdom he instilled in you is not a spreadsheet of formulas that yields an unmistakable result in the bottom cell." She kissed me on the cheek and backed away. "Wisdom provides a glimpse of the face of God, but not always his whole counsel."

Barely able to breathe, I watched the lovely young lady rejoin the other girls. With her long dark locks flowing in the breeze, she looked more like Mom than ever, and her breathtaking words proved that Mom's heart beat within her breast.

I turned toward Dr. Simon and tried to show in my expression the pain of my decision. "I can't go. I have to save the cosmos."

Dr. Simon firmed his chin, but he seemed more resigned than angry. "Very well. I will not beg you to have pity, but I can offer another option that will take far less time and effort." He glanced at his wristwatch, then returned his gaze to me. "In just over two hours a pilot will take off from a Chicago area airport and crash due to mechanical failure. Saving his life should be a simple task."

I shook my head. "I can't do it. Regardless of what you think, Interfinity is almost here. I saw how everything is crumbling. You know how the nightmares are enslaving everyone. We need to—"

"What's the pilot's name?" Daryl asked.

Dr. Simon raised his eyebrows, then flipped to another page in his notebook and pointed at a line near the top. "Harold. Harold Markey. Twenty-eight years old, father of two."

Daryl gasped. "My uncle!"

"I see," Dr. Simon said. "Your father's brother, I assume."

Her eyes wide and pleading, she lunged to me and grabbed my arm. "We have to rescue him!"

"We?" I pointed at Dr. Simon. "If it's so easy, why not him? And where's Simon Yellow? Can't he help?"

Dr. Simon adjusted his glasses and looked at his watch again. "My Earth Yellow counterpart is already at Cape Canaveral, but Scarlet seems to serve you and not us, so we need you to summon her aid. Since she desires to be rescued, and since we know how to open the portal to the misty world, we assumed she would send you to find one of us."

I balled my fist. "How do we get to her? Tell me!"

"I have the appropriate musical piece right here." Dr. Simon withdrew an iPod from his pocket. "I will give it to you if you acquiesce."

I glared at the white rectangular iPod. "You mean I have to go to Florida and save the shuttle before you'll give me the tune?"

"Or to the local airport to save the pilot." Dr. Simon took yet another look at his watch. "Make your choice, one pilot or seven astronauts. Either option presents you with a noble task. Our primary goal is to save lives, of course, but we also want to learn how to harness the power of Quattro. As long as Scarlet and the other supplicants are imprisoned, they might as well be useful, and perhaps we can learn how to use their power of deliverance on a wider scale at a later time."

I glared at him. Would this self-proclaimed deliverer really hold back information that could save the universe? I shook my head. "I have to stick to my mission."

Daryl spun and slammed her palm against the van but said nothing.

"Don't be a fool," Dr. Simon growled. "You won't be able to accomplish your mission without passage to the stalkers' world. You can dream your way to the violin, but you can't play it as a ghost."

Kelly edged closer, slid her hand into mine, and gave it a gentle squeeze. Apparently she knew something but didn't want to give it away to Dr. Simon.

I drew in a long breath. "If you want to save them, then go for it. I'll find another way to get to the violin."

"Very well." Dr. Simon pushed the iPod back into his pocket. "I will work with my counterpart to try to prevent the space shuttle disaster. Then we will get another musician to play the violin in the stalkers' world. I doubt that such a stubborn, insensitive boy would be able to play the piece properly anyway."

I tightened my fist again. "Stubborn? Insensitive? Just because I won't—"

Daryl jumped in front of me. "Let *me* try to save my uncle."

CHAPTER FIFTEEN

D R. SIMON BLINKED at Daryl. "You? Why?"

"Because I'm here. Because I can. And because I can't help anyone play a violin. I can sing pretty well, but I stink on every instrument known to mankind." She looked at me. "I'm sorry. I understand why you can't save him, but I have to try. My father has been depressed ever since his brother died. That's why he got fired by two big airline companies. Maybe I can save Daryl Yellow from going through what I had to suffer."

She turned back to Dr. Simon. "Will you take me to that airport?"

Dr. Simon glared at me. "Of course I will. If you rescue him, I won't be able to experiment with Quattro, but I'm glad to see that someone has a heart."

My cheeks flamed. I was ready to shout one of a dozen protests that boiled in my mind, but when Kelly's thumb caressed my knuckles, the rage settled to a simmer. I set my jaw and nodded at Daryl. "I understand. Do what you have to do. We'll figure out how to get to the misty world somehow."

His scowl deepening, Dr. Simon waved toward a car sitting in a field beyond the unfinished wall. "We should go now. I will try to reunite you with the others after you save your uncle." He marched away without looking back.

Daryl followed, her anguished gaze locked on me. With her red tresses billowing across her sad eyes, she blew me a kiss, then turned and ran to catch up with Dr. Simon.

As soon as they were out of earshot, I motioned for Kelly and Francesca to huddle with me. "Any ideas?"

"Not from me," Francesca said. "Even if we could drive back to Iowa and use the portal in my old bedroom, it would take too long. And Vivaldi's Four Seasons just took us to that world in a dream realm, not in reality."

I nodded. "We have two mirrors here. We should be able to use at least one of them."

"Let's dial up Daryl Blue," Kelly said. "You know that tune, and we can ask Gordon Red about the iPod."

"Do you think he would know the right music to get to the misty world?"

"Maybe he won't have to know. Remember Scarlet said to use *her* song. It might be labeled in the iPod's directory in a way we can recognize."

I pointed at her. "Brilliant."

Francesca hurried to the van and returned with the violin. "What do you play to summon Earth Blue?"

"Waxman's Carmen Fantasy."

I reached for the violin, but she held it back. "Really?" she asked. "I love that piece."

"I know. You taught it to me."

She raised the violin. "Shall I?"

"Mother," I said with a formal nod, "I would be honored."

Furrowing her brow, Francesca played the opening notes, keeping her eyes on the mirror. As her hand danced across the fingerboard, beautiful music flowed through the snow-laden saplings and drifted toward the unfinished wall to our right. The man on the ladder, maybe a couple of hundred feet away, looked our way, his trowel frozen in place as he paused to listen.

I watched myself, Francesca, and Kelly in the reflection. The image faded, first as if a cloudbank had drifted in front of the sun, then as if late evening had spread a blanket of darkness across the field. Soon, a hint of light shone through—the lamp on the computer desk in the observatory. The glow strengthened, revealing Daryl Blue tilting her head toward us, but her movements seemed painfully slow. A smile emerged, but it took several seconds for it to spread across her face.

Francesca lowered the violin. "She's in slow motion."

"Earth Yellow is still speeding along," I said. "To her, we probably look like we drank a gallon of coffee."

Kelly stepped closer to the mirror. "How do we tell her to ask Dr. Gordon what's on the iPod?"

Daryl Blue raised her hand to wave, but she looked like a movie advancing one frame every five seconds. It would take a miracle to communicate this way. But Tony Clark could send her a message. We needed a phone, but were mobile phones widely used in this time period?

"The Challenger disaster is tomorrow," I said. "Do you know what year that happened?"

Kelly shook her head. "That was before I was born."

Francesca counted on her fingers. "It's nineteen eighty-six. I've missed some time here, but I've been keeping track of the years since you first showed up at my house."

"Do you have mobile phones yet?" I asked.

She nodded. "I've seen them for a while, but my father says they're too expensive."

I looked at the bricklayer. As the muscular man went back to work on the wall, a bulky device swung at his waist. "Want to bet he's got one?"

"Looks like it," Kelly said. "Who're you going to call?"

"Tony Yellow. He can use the computer and transmitter to send a note to Daryl Blue telling her exactly what we need. Then she can send back a list of the songs on the iPod."

"How long will that take?"

"A lot less time than driving back to Iowa." I took a step toward the bricklayer, but Kelly pulled me back.

"Let me do it," she said.

"Okay. But why?"

"Trust me on this, Nathan. He'll respond better to me." Kelly jogged toward the office part of the StarCast building. Even with loose-fitting jeans and a baggy sweatshirt, her feminine form was obvious.

I let out a sigh. No doubt she was right. Once Kelly turned on the charm, what guy could resist helping her? Especially with blood oozing from her shoulder.

Within a minute, Kelly was talking on the worker's mobile phone, the bricklayer standing at her side … too close to her side in my estimation. Soon, she jogged back, huffing white vapor.

I stepped between her and the bricklayer. "Get it done?"

She nodded. "Tony Yellow's sending the message now, and Eddie will tell us when he calls back with the list of songs."

"Eddie?"

She cast a glance toward the worker. "I had to give him my phone number to get him to agree to help."

"Your phone number? But that'll just get him your father here on Earth Yellow."

"I know." She shrugged. "I told the truth. It's my real phone number."

"Look," Francesca said, pointing at the mirror. "Something changed."

Kelly and I turned. Daryl was now reading the computer screen, but the text was too small to decipher. Her hand inched toward the touch pad, traveling at a fraction of normal speed.

"She's probably going to send a note to Gordon Red," Kelly said.

I crossed my arms. "This is like a marathon race between two snails."

As I watched the unbearably tedious action in the mirror, Kelly picked out a spot a foot or so away from me and leaned against the van, crossing her arms and adding a shiver. From time to time she looked at the bricklayer, but her lips stayed tight, showing no signs of emotion.

Warm prickles crawled along my skin. Her glances at him made my heart sink. But why? Just because she showed casual interest in him? Maybe simple curiosity? My annoyance was stupid, groundless. Yet, I couldn't shake it. I would be a fool to think I hadn't grown attached to her. Any hint that her heart might search for another guy made me feel lonely and cold inside.

Heaving a sigh, I looked again at the mirror. Daryl was now eyeing a new message on the screen, a list of some kind, maybe the songs we were waiting for.

I leaned close to Kelly, almost brushing her cheek as I whispered. "Cold?"

Shivering harder, she nodded. "Very."

I draped an arm over her shoulders, careful to avoid her wound, and pulled her close. As she snuggled into my embrace, a smile trembled on her lips, but she said nothing. Still nearly cheek to cheek, I whispered again. "Keep me in mind, okay?"

She turned her head and met my gaze, a look of confusion in her eyes at first, but her face slowly relaxed. Tears welled, and her lips trembled harder. "You're already there, Nathan. I thought you knew that."

New warmth flashed across my skin. I wanted to break the eye-lock, but I didn't dare. Not now. Not when her heart was so vulnerable.

I cleared my throat and tried to speak with enough passion to truly express the fire kindling inside. "I did know it. I just want to stay there."

As she turned back toward the mirror, a tear crawled down her cheek. "I'll never ask you to leave."

Daryl slowly tapped her keyboard, her movements jerky now as the speed changed sporadically. A few seconds later, a masculine voice sounded from beyond the curved wall.

"Kelly, your phone call."

She pushed upright and looked at me. "Want to come?"

I winked. "You can handle it."

"Back in a minute." She brushed away the tear and jogged toward the building.

Francesca pushed her hands into her sweatshirt pockets and walked across a thin layer of snow on the foundation. She stopped at my side, blowing vapor as she watched Kelly. After a few seconds, she looked at me. "She's a lovely girl, you know. In so many ways."

Once again it seemed like my real mother had spoken. I had to answer truthfully. Mom would never settle for anything else. "Yeah. Trust me. I know."

Francesca took Kelly's place at my side. She snuggled even closer than Kelly had. "It's so strange to have a son close to my age. I can be affectionate without fear of misunderstanding."

I looked into her eyes, soft and walnut brown. There was no doubt about it. The spirit of my mother lived inside this beautiful teenager. And I loved her — completely, devotedly, with pure passion. New warmth yet again flooded my body, and I let it flow. I loved this girl in a way I couldn't comprehend. But it felt good all the same.

Soon, Kelly jogged back and hopped up to the foundation, a sheet of paper in her grip. Smiling, she showed it to me while Francesca looked on. "Eddie wrote them down while I called them out."

I scanned the list. "Looks like about forty pieces. We can't try them all. I don't even recognize some of the titles."

Francesca shook her head. "Same here. You probably learned the ones I taught you … or will teach you, I suppose."

"But what would be Scarlet's song?" Kelly asked. "Is there anything you recognize that relates to her?"

Francesca ran her finger down the page. "Something with *red* in the title or something *close* to red?"

"Not likely," I said. "Scarlet mentioned that it strums the sorrows of her heart. The clue would be in the content, not the title. It would probably be emotive, something that makes you feel lonely or lost."

Francesca pointed at each title in turn. "Brahms' Lullaby? No. Rhapsody in Blue? No. The Hallelujah Chorus? No. Never heard of this one. Never heard of this one, either."

Kelly set her finger on a line near the bottom. "Here it is. I'm sure of it."

I read the title. "Moonlight Sonata?"

"I used to play it on our piano whenever my parents …" She bit her lip, then blinked as her voice pitched higher. "Whenever they weren't getting along. It always made me feel kind of lonely, but after a while, I always felt better."

"It's worth a try." I looked at Francesca. "Do you know it?"

"Not memorized, but I can hear some of it in my head. Maybe I could improvise. It might come back to me while I play."

"Yeah, I've heard the first movement enough times. We could work it out together."

"But it's a piano piece," Kelly said. "A violin could never get the sound right. It needs to be melancholy, with lots of forlorn echoing."

"Maybe that won't matter." I nodded at Francesca. "Let's give it a try."

Francesca raised the violin once more and played the first notes of the sonata, soft and solemn. As she played, I shook my head in wonder. She was so good, so very, very good. Even though she was still quite young, her playing carried a sweet perfection I had never been able to reach. Try as I might, something was missing, something elusive, a heart and passion that resonated with every stroke of her bow.

Why, then, had she, as my mother on Earth Red, told me otherwise? At least once a month for the last three years she had looked me in the eye and said, *"You are an heir, the recipient of a musical inheritance. You have more talent than I could ever hope for. You just have to learn to reach into your heart and let it bleed through your fingers."*

Sighing, I turned to the mirror. It seemed to darken at times, but the slow-motion scene of Daryl in the observatory always came back. She typed something on the screen, but, again, it was too far away to read. Could she have figured out the tune? Maybe she was telling Dr. Gordon which one we had selected.

Kelly leaned close and whispered, "I don't think it's working. She's playing the notes perfectly, but it's just not the same."

"I don't think there's any chance of finding a piano around here."

"I have an idea." She opened the van door. "See if you can find a classical station."

I hopped into the driver's seat and flipped on the radio. "What are the chances they'll play the Moonlight Sonata?"

"Probably zero, unless we exert some influence." Kelly leaned in through the door. "If you find one, try to catch the station's call letters."

I twirled the tuning dial, mumbling as I paused at each strong signal. "Country ... commercial ... sounds like jazz ... classic rock ... country again ... another commercial ..." I halted at a station. A woman read a series of orchestral concert announcements, each one enunciated perfectly and with a formal air. "This could be classical, and it's a clear signal."

After a few moments, the woman gave the station's call letters, WNIU, then a Liszt concerto began.

"WNIU," Kelly repeated. "I can get the number from directory assistance."

"Eddie's phone again?"

"Yep. I just have to dream up a request they can't resist." Kelly headed toward Eddie's ladder, calling back as she ran, "Crank up the volume."

I turned the radio's volume to max, stepped around to the rear of the van, and opened the door. I pulled out the mammoth violin bow and stood in front of the mirror at the point where the light beams had created a cross-world window before. With the van's headlights aimed at the mirror, creating another one shouldn't be a problem.

As the Liszt concerto reached its ending crescendo, I set the bow down and nodded toward Francesca. "You and Kelly should stand here while I turn on the headlights."

Still holding the violin, Francesca took her place. "Assuming her efforts are successful."

"Trust me. She'll come through. She always has before."

When the final note faded, the female announcer's voice returned. "I received a most unusual request."

I winked at Francesca. "Here it comes."

"A girl named Kelly wishes to dedicate a special piece to the astronauts of the space shuttle Challenger who are scheduled to launch tomorrow morning. She claimed that she had a terrible vision about the shuttle exploding shortly after takeoff. I know what you're thinking. Travelers are forbidden to speak about their long-distance prophecies, and reliance on dreams that forecast disasters is dangerous, but I cannot ignore her courage. My own cousin will be aboard that shuttle, and I will pass along the technical information Kelly has given me. In the meantime, to express my gratitude, I will interrupt our scheduled programming and play her request, Beethoven's magnificent Moonlight Sonata."

Vibrant piano notes played from the radio speakers and reverberated in the semicircular structure. Wearing a broad smile, Kelly hopped back onto the observatory foundation and bowed dramatically. While I clapped, she straightened. "You should be proud of me. I did it all without a single lie."

"I am proud," I said, reaching for her hand. "You're the best." I pulled her and Francesca together, positioned them in front of the mirror, and dashed back to the van. With a hand on the headlight switch, I waited for the mirror to do its magic. It darkened, and the Earth Blue observatory floor vanished. Seconds later, the now-familiar crystal walkway appeared, swirling mist still bordering each side.

I searched the scene for any sign of stalkers — clear for now, but would it be clear when we arrived? I tightened my grip on the headlight's knob. There was only one way to find out. With a quick pull, the headlamps flashed on. The beams bounced off the reflective glass and created the familiar rainbow halo in front of the mirror. Multi-colored light bathed Kelly and Francesca.

"Hurry," Kelly yelled as she cradled the huge bow in her arms. "I can feel it taking us."

I reached across to the passenger seat and felt for the Quattro mirror. It was gone. But where? I couldn't go without it. And what about the second one? It was probably in the back somewhere, hidden under the bags of food we had transferred from the car.

"Nathan! Now!"

I jerked out the keys, silencing the radio, then slapped the lights off and grabbed the camera. Just as the two girls began to fade, I leaped into the halo. Color splashed everywhere, and the construction scene crumbled away, leaving us in darkness.

A hint of moisture brushed across my face. "Kelly. Do you see anything?"

"Not yet."

"Nor I," Francesca said. "But I know I've been here in my dreams. It feels the same."

I draped the camera's strap over my head and set it against my chest. A glow appeared in the distance. Then, second by second, the darkness faded, revealing the seemingly endless walkway of the misty world. As before, the same sweet melody infused the air, and the harmony I had played to brighten the world was still intact.

"That's better," I said. "Time to find the biggest violin in the universe."

"Wait." Francesca pulled on my arm. "I can't see anything except your eyes. Kelly's eyes, too."

I peered at Francesca's pupils. They dilated and contracted as my gaze crossed hers. "Do you hear anything?"

"Yes. A voice singing a simple melody. Just notes. No words."

"Do you hear a harmony blending in? A second voice?"

She shook her head. "Only one voice."

"What key?"

She closed her eyes for a moment. "C Major."

I grasped her wrist and pushed the violin toward her chin. "The song asks a question. You have to play an answer."

She set the bow over the strings. "I think I understand."

Closing her eyes again, Francesca played. At first her notes seemed out of key, certainly nothing close to C Major, but as she continued, her tune blended in, duplicating the harmonizing voice I could already hear.

She opened her eyes, blinking, but said nothing as she increased to forte. Her eyes shifted back and forth as if following the path of a butterfly. Finally, she lowered the violin and winked. "I can see now. You're a good teacher, Son."

I reached for the bow in Kelly's arms. "I'll lead the way, but you two stay close."

As I strode on the smooth walkway toward the fogbank in the distance, mist from the bordering rivers rose in columns and swirled at my side. Carrying the long bow made for an awkward march, but concentrating on keeping the two ends balanced helped distract me from the dangers that lay ahead.

Questions lurked. Would the guards be at the doorway? What would I do when I arrived? The guards carried those sound-generating rods that really packed a wallop. Might there be a way to neutralize them?

Soon, we plunged into the fogbank. Now blinded by the soupy veil, I slowed the pace. The entry door to the chamber of domes would be too narrow for the bow, so I pointed it straight ahead and pressed on.

As the path widened and the floor transformed to the rougher terrazzo, I slowed further. Only the anxious breathing from the girls reached my ears. Although my shoes stayed in sight, little else crossed my field of vision, only mist rising in silent clouds of white. Under my shoes, the gemstones now seemed dull, unable to sparkle in the haze.

I stopped and stared in the direction the supplicants had been before. As Francesca and I had witnessed in our vision, the stalkers were gone. Still, we had to watch for guards. This time, we weren't invisible.

Creeping forward, I looked for the triad of domes. The outline of the closest one slowly came into view as well as the back of a lone male stalker who stood facing the glass, holding a sonic stun rod.

The stalker sang a series of low vowel sounds that alternated between a long *A* and a long *O*. It sounded more like a chant than a song, a report that weakened as it drifted into the soupy air.

Kelly whispered the translation. "The second hour ends. The third begins. All is well. All is well."

Another voice rang out, echoing the song of the first. Then a third crier repeated the call, but he added a different ending, and Kelly again provided the words. "The supplicants have opened the dream gates. Let us follow and discern their purpose."

"There are three," I said. "If they report every hour, maybe I can disable the closest guy without a sound, and we'll have an hour to get to the violin and play it. With all the mist, the other two might never know what happened."

Francesca shook her head. "It won't work. You have to play the violin to open the stairway door. They'll hear you."

"Good point." I looked past the guard. Barely visible inside the dome, Scarlet sat upright with her head low and her arms wrapped around her knees.

I crept a few steps closer. If I could get her attention, maybe she could help. I waved a hand over my head, but she stayed perfectly still. The guard mentioned that the supplicants had "opened the dream gates," so she was probably asleep, shutting out the surrounding prison.

After passing the bow to Kelly, I rose to tiptoes and eased forward. It was time to act, now or never. When I came within reach of the guard, I paused. He emitted a slight wheeze accompanied by slow, rhythmic breaths. Was he asleep, too?

The final words of the third guard reentered my mind. *Let us follow and discern their purpose.*

I pumped a fist. Scarlet was helping after all. She and the other two supplicants were distracting the guards in the world of dreams.

Gesturing for the others to follow, I sneaked past the stalker and gazed into the dome. Scarlet, now easily visible, kept her face buried between her knees, her reddish locks draped over her arms. She trembled. Her head twitched. Yet, she stayed asleep.

I waited for the girls to catch up, Kelly carrying the oversized bow and Francesca holding the violin. Together, we skirted the dome and stepped into the enclosed area.

As before, the floor panel's glass displayed a row of seven lights. With a misty cloud hovering over us, it reflected only our tired, anxious faces. "We don't have a tune playing in the air," I said. "How are we going to figure out the code?"

Francesca readied the violin. "We'll just have to try every octave. Maybe we can figure out the code without waking them up."

She leaned close to the glass and played A through G, watching for a flashing light. When she hit the lowest D, the fourth light flashed red. With every rise in octave, a different light gave an identical signal.

I glanced at the stalkers in turn. With eyes closed, they seemed mesmerized, as if lost in deep thought. The other two supplicants copied Scarlet's pose. They, too, displayed noticeable twitches, shaking off an occasional shiver as they dreamed on.

After playing the highest notes, Francesca ran through the pattern she had learned, using the proper octave for A, then for B, and so on. When the lights returned to their white state, she played the notes again, turning the lights blue, then a third time to complete the unlocking procedure. As soon as the lights faded, the panel's reflection disappeared, revealing the dim stairwell.

Francesca stepped into the liquid glass and waved at Kelly. "Let Nathan take one end of the bow while you follow with the other end. We'll have to hurry to get the whole thing in before the door closes." She descended into the darkness.

I grabbed one end of the bow and backed down the stairs, keeping an eye on our surroundings. As Kelly shuffled forward, I pushed my way down. The glass seemed thicker with every step. When my head sank below the surface, I broke into the clear, but as soon as Kelly's feet pushed through, she slowed to a trudge as if she were wading through tar.

I pulled, threading the bow through my hands as Kelly descended. When she submerged up to her neck, she halted, apparently unable to go another inch. I laid the bow down, grabbed her around the waist, and kicked her feet out from under her. Then, pulling myself up, I hung on and dangled, hoping my weight would be enough to draw her through.

Slowly, very slowly, she descended. Her chest heaved, then froze as her face lowered into thickening glass, cutting off her air supply.

Francesca joined in and pulled. Kelly popped through, and all three of us tumbled down the stony staircase. I grabbed both girls and braced my feet and back against the sides of the corridor, stopping our fall.

Suppressing a groan, I struggled to my feet and helped Francesca up, then Kelly. Since we had fallen only a few steps, the chamber above still gave us enough light to see each other.

I rubbed a scraped elbow through the sleeve. "Are you two okay?"

Kelly nodded without a word, though she grimaced as she held a hand over her shoulder.

Francesca extended the violin. One of the strings dangled, a curl of wire bouncing at the end. She pulled it out and tossed it away. "The key will be tougher to play without that string."

"You'll adjust." I picked up one end of the bow. "At least this isn't broken."

"Thank God for that," Francesca said.

I looked up through the glass door. No sign of stalkers. "We'd better get moving."

Francesca led the way, padding softly on the uneven steps as the stairwell grew darker. When she reached the dead end, she applied the key again, adjusting her fingers to play each note on the three remaining strings.

As before, a glow ate away the door. A light from the other side cast a dim wash over our bodies, allowing me to see more clearly. I set a hand on Kelly's good shoulder and whispered, "Watch your step. The next one's a real doozy."

CHAPTER SIXTEEN

KELLY PEERED INTO the dark chasm. "Good thing Daryl Blue isn't here to see this."

"Exactly why I wanted her to stay at the observatory." I bit my lip. "Sorry. Too harsh."

Francesca used the smaller bow to draw the pulley rope into the corridor. "We have to be extra careful. No waking up if we fall."

The thought of plunging helplessly into the void raised a shudder. "Let's get going. We'll leave the big bow and camera here for now." I pulled the camera off and set it on a stair. After hauling the basket to the top, I got inside and copied the lowering procedure I had used in the vision.

It seemed odd that every sensation felt the same, the heavy weight of the loaded basket and the warming friction as the rope slid through my hands. After reaching the strings' level, swinging over to the ledge, and climbing to solid ground, I pulled the rope and sent the basket back to the top.

Francesca's voice filtered down to my level. "I'll go first," she said to Kelly. "Watch what I do." She climbed into the basket, waited for me to lower her, and then worked with me to swing her toward the side. I glanced back at where the rope attached to the iron hook in the wall, an anchor in case I couldn't hold the weight. If the rope slipped, at least she wouldn't fall forever.

After using the hooked rod to haul her in, I reeled the basket up again. Moving stiffly, Kelly copied Francesca's actions, and when all three of us stood safely on the ledge, I let out a long breath and pointed at the violin strings spanning the chasm. "Now to get the bow."

I climbed into the basket and, with the girls' help, hauled myself up. When I reached the stairwell, I found the bow protruding through the doorway and grabbed it. After I balanced it on the top edge of the basket, the girls reeled me down.

When the basket drew near the strings, I called, "Stop."

The descent halted. The basket dangled just above the strings. "Perfect. As soon as I tie myself in place, you two go to the fingerboard."

"Foundation's Key?" Francesca asked.

I nodded. "Do you remember it?"

"Sure. Not a problem."

"Then let's do it."

While Kelly and Francesca reeled out a bit of slack, I looped the rope around my chest and fastened it with a double knot, securing me in place above the strings and allowing the girls to release the rope. As if a child again on a playground swing set, I pushed against the basket and forced it into a slow swing, making the arc bigger and bigger as I continued to rock back and forth. Once I started playing the strings, I wouldn't be able to keep the momentum going, so I had to gain as much amplitude as possible.

As the basket swayed, I looked at the oversized fingerboard. Kelly sat in Francesca's lap. Their combined weights held down the string in the proper place to play the first note.

After taking a deep breath, I grasped the bow with both hands and leaned against the side of the basket, making it tip. Pressing my feet against the sides to keep the basket in place, I lowered the bow toward the string.

I let the bow hairs rub gently and played the first note of Foundation's Key. A loud tone erupted from the string and reverberated through the chasm. The chamber's faint light strengthened. The walls shook. Rocks broke away and tumbled into the void.

As I swung back for the next note, I glanced at the girls. Fighting the quakes, they staggered to the proper string and pounced on it.

When I reached the string, I pushed the bow down and stroked it smoothly. As before, the note echoed through the chamber and shook the walls, and the girls again rocked where they sat. With the chamber still brightening, the fear in their faces clarified. Francesca barked out their next position as they hurried to the third string.

The torturous process continued through the fourth, fifth, and sixth notes, until a shrill voice sang from above. The camera dropped past and plummeted into the void. At the stairway, a stalker glared at me, apparently cursing in his strange musical tongue.

"No time to sing with you," I mumbled. "I'm kind of busy."

As I swung back for a seventh note, a tug on the rope pulled me out of line, but I managed to adjust the bow's position enough to play the note.

Above, two stalkers jerked the rope while a third looked on from behind. The basket slipped away from my feet and shot toward the ceiling.

Still clutching the bow, I plunged feet first into the void. When the basket snagged on the pulley, the rope tightened with a twang, and the knot I had fashioned punched me in the solar plexus, knocking my breath away. The loop slid up my sides, ripping my skin before stopping at my underarms, making me dangle under the strings.

The girls shouted, "Nathan!" in unison.

Unable to answer, I tried to catch my breath. At the stairway, the stalkers worked feverishly to shake the basket loose and send me plummeting again. Below, the dark reaches seemed a bit brighter, a vague grayness.

Up at the ledge, Kelly held the loose rope that led to the anchor hook in one direction and down to me in the other. She leaned over the chasm as far as she could. "Hang on! We'll pull you up somehow!"

Still clutching the bow, I grabbed the line with my free hand. The knot unraveled. Just before the loop around my body slipped away, I dropped the bow and wrapped both hands in the rope. As the stalkers jostled my lifeline, I began to swing again. With every pass through the arc, the rope slid through my fingers.

Above, Kelly kept her grip on the line that led from me to the loose coil on the ledge and then to the anchor. She could never haul me up, and, if the basket ripped away, I didn't want to jerk her down with me. "Kelly! Let go! The hook should hold me if I fall."

Kelly let go and stood next to Francesca. The stalkers tore at the basket's wicker until it looked like shredded wheat.

A grunt sounded from above. One of the stalkers tumbled into the void, then the other two followed, flailing their arms as they plunged. As I swung to the side, a white-haired man zoomed past, then a woman. The third stalker thrust out his hand and clawed my back, digging sharp nails into my skin before snagging my belt. The rope slid at least a foot in my grip. Blood seeped between my fingers, but the loop around my knuckles drew tight, halting my fall.

The stalker, now hanging on to me by one hand, reached for the rope with his other. I planted a foot on his shoulder. As we struggled, I caught a glimpse of his face—Tsayad, the same stalker who had greeted us as a friendly host. But now he was the grim reaper.

I shoved my heel into Tsayad's neck and pushed with all my might. He slipped away, screaming a cacophonous song as he vanished into the depths below.

"You're all clear, kid," someone yelled from above. "Now let's blow this thing and go home."

I regripped the rope and looked up. Daryl stood at the edge of the doorway, trying to pull the basket down as it continued to rip against the pulley. "Daryl! How did you—"

"Never mind that," she shouted. "Can Kelly and Francesca pull you up? I won't be heavy enough to counter your weight."

Kelly called out, "Swing him toward me!"

Daryl grasped the rope and worked it back and forth parallel to the strings. I timed her efforts and helped from my end. Blood streamed from my torn hands down my forearms, but giving up was not an option.

Soon, I swung within reach of the sheer walls on each side, still far below Kelly's level. She picked up the hooking pole and fished for the rope but couldn't quite reach it. She dropped to her stomach and extended the pole as far as she could.

When I swung to the opposite side, Francesca came into view, sitting between Kelly's legs, gripping one with each arm. As she pushed Kelly farther out, she yelled. "Don't worry! I've got you!"

Finally, Kelly snagged the rope. "Pull me back!"

I tried to watch their efforts, but as Kelly eased onto the ledge, I could see only the rope hooked in the pole and Kelly's and Francesca's fingers wrapped around the end. As they pulled, I tried to push my feet against the wall and climb, but my toes couldn't catch hold of any crevices. Rivulets of blood poured into my sleeves. I couldn't hang on much longer.

With Francesca still holding on to the rope, Kelly leaped out, grabbed it, and began to climb toward the top. Gripping with hands and crossed legs, she slowly inched upward. The sounds of stifled grunts made their way down to my level as she huffed and puffed.

I held my breath. With her shoulder so badly wounded, how could she possibly make that climb? The pain had to be pure torture.

Daryl, now on her knees, reached out a hand, but Kelly was still far below, struggling, grunting, gaining a foot or two, then sliding down a few inches before battling again to regain lost ground.

"Come on, Kelly-kins!" Daryl yelled. "You can do it!"

The mystery of Daryl's presence rushed back to mind. Had she already rescued her uncle? With time racing so quickly on Earth Yellow, it was possible.

The moment Kelly neared the top, Daryl thrust a hand down and jerked her to safety in the stairwell. Kelly struggled to her feet, whirled toward the rope, and, with Daryl hanging on to her waist, leaned back over the void.

She grabbed the remnants of the basket, and the two girls jumped out over the chasm. Their combined weights lifted me. At the ledge, Francesca reeled the line through her hands, guiding me toward her, while Kelly and Daryl sank toward the violin strings.

As I rose, Daryl's eyes flashed with terror, but she managed to keep her body calm except for a few weak kicks as she struggled to hold on to Kelly's waist.

When I came within reach, Francesca clutched my shirt with one hand and hoisted me to safe footing. Still holding to the rope, I spun and helped Francesca halt Kelly and Daryl's descent.

The two girls hung over the void, their bodies twisting as they swung. With each pass, their feet swept inches over the violin strings. The basket, now torn to shreds, fell away piece by piece until it was gone.

With Francesca standing in front of me, I pulled the rope, but it slid through my bloody hands.

Francesca kept a firm grip. "We can do this." Inch by inch we managed to haul Daryl and Kelly a foot higher.

"Hang on," Kelly yelled. "We'll swing toward you."

I tried to ignore the blood dripping from my throbbing hands. "When they get close to this side, we'll have to let out line to lower them to the ledge."

Sweat streamed down Francesca's cheeks and dampened her collar. As she and I pulled and released, Kelly and Daryl swung precariously, coming closer and closer to the ledge with each cycle. Twenty feet away. Fifteen feet. Ten.

"Almost here," Francesca grunted. "A couple more times ought to do it."

I glanced at the hooked pole. That would help, but I couldn't grab it without releasing the rope.

As the two girls swung away again, Daryl stared wild-eyed at the void below. When they passed over the center, her dangling feet brushed one of the strings, playing a loud, vibrating note. Again, the echoes bounced off the walls. The ledge shook beneath our feet.

Francesca dropped to her knees and lost her hold on the rope. I tightened my grip and looped my legs around Francesca's torso, anchoring us in place.

Flexing my muscles, I pulled with all my might. Pain shot through my shredded hands. Once again, the rope slipped through the blood. Daryl smacked into the strings, tearing her loose from Kelly. As Kelly continued on her arc toward the ledge, Daryl clutched a violin string with one hand, her legs kicking frantically over the void. "Kelly! Help me!"

Francesca climbed to her feet and held the rope again. With the pressure lessened, I snatched the hook and reached for Kelly. She batted it away, slid down to a knot, and held on with one hand while swinging back toward Daryl. Kelly reached down and grabbed a string. It stretched for a second, then pulled her back to the center. Still holding to the rope, Kelly released the string and snagged a fistful of Daryl's shirt.

"I've got you!" Kelly yelled. "Let go!"

"I can't! I'll fall!"

"You won't fall! I won't let you fall!"

"You can't hold my weight with one hand! Your shoulder's hurt!"

Kelly's voice seemed to shake the floor. "You just … have to … trust me!"

"I can't!" Daryl stared down at the void again and shook her head. "I just can't!"

Kelly looked at me with frantic eyes. "Pull us up! I'll have to jerk her loose!"

I strained against the rope. "How about if we set you down on the strings?"

"I don't think it will hold both of us."

Francesca and I pulled. Kelly rose, still clutching Daryl's shirt. For a moment, the shirt slipped up over her head, exposing a thin camisole and her bare waist, but when it caught under her arms, she began to rise. As she elevated past the string's level, she kept a tight grip on it, halting her progress and stretching the string upward.

"Let go!" Kelly screamed. "You're slipping!"

Daryl said nothing. Her face as taut as the string, she just hung on.

Kelly turned again to me. "Give us a hard pull!"

"No," Daryl shouted. "I'll let go of it." She closed her eyes, then, after taking a deep breath, released the string. Kelly shot up, Daryl still in her grip. The string let out a thunderous twang. The walls and floor responded with a jolt that rocked the entire foundation.

Francesca and I fell on our bottoms. The rope reeled through our fingers. I caught the line and twisted it around my hand, jerking the girls to a stop.

Daryl's shirt slipped over her head, leaving it flapping in Kelly's hand. Daryl fell at an angle, crashed into the wall, and plummeted until her limp body dropped out of sight.

"Oh my God!" Kelly's call stretched out, loud and wailing. "Daryl!"

Francesca struggled to her feet and buried her face in her hands. "Oh, Lord! Have mercy!"

Now holding Kelly's weight by myself, I called out, my voice shaking as the ground settled. "Swing back, before you fall, too."

Sobbing, Kelly began swinging the rope, her gaze fixed on the void. As she neared the ledge, I pulled her into a final swing. She let go of the rope and landed next to me. She fell to her knees and banged her fists on the ground, one hand still clutching Daryl's shirt. "Why did this happen?" she screamed. "Why?"

Francesca stooped and rubbed Kelly's back, saying nothing.

I looped the rope around the pole and dropped to the ground next to Kelly. I reached to touch her head, but as blood dripped to the rocky floor, I drew my hand back. She, too, dripped blood from one hand. A path of dark red dampened her sweatshirt at the shoulder and extended down her arm.

I tightened my jaw. We couldn't wait. No matter how terrible it was to lose Daryl, we had to go on. As I tried to spit out my thoughts, my voice squeaked. "We have to get back. There's no telling when more stalkers might show up."

Francesca laid a hand on my knee. "Give her a minute. She just lost her best friend."

"She wasn't my friend." Kelly threw the shirt at me. "That was Daryl Blue."

I picked up the shirt — sky blue and spattered with Kelly's blood. Acidic bile burned my throat. How could this be? When she stood on the stairwell and tried to pull the rope, she must have been out of her mind with fear. She grabbed Kelly's waist, jumped over the pit, and helped pull me to safety. It must have been like a thousand nightmares at once.

A tear spilled to my cheek as I whispered, "But she did it anyway."

Spasms rocked Kelly's voice. "She knew … the Moonlight Sonata … would bring her … to this place. She must have … followed the stalkers … through the door."

Francesca looked at me. "Maybe she found out Daryl Red had to leave, so she decided to take her place."

I nodded, a grim heaviness weighing down my shoulders. I wanted to kick myself in the teeth. I had brushed Daryl Blue away because of her phobia, and now she was gone. She had battled her fears, only to fall prey to the very phantom that had stalked her. And was she still falling? Was this a bottomless chasm that would keep her plunging, trapping her in a nightmare that would never, ever end? Then again, maybe she was no longer suffering. Her impact against the wall must have knocked her out, or worse.

I bit my lip hard. I had been such a jerk! Daryl lost her life saving an insensitive moron.

After taking a deep breath, I shook my head hard. No time for this. Jerk or no jerk, we had to move. I pulled on Kelly's arm. "I'm sorry. We have to go. I don't know why we don't already have a bunch of stalkers screaming their fool heads off from those stairs."

Kelly rose and looked up at the stairwell, her eyes red as she wiped tears from her cheeks. "Who goes first?"

Francesca grasped my forearms and turned my palms up. "You can't pull anyone with these."

My throat still burning, I whispered, "We'll loop the rope around my wrists, and you can tie it around your waist. I can walk into the alcove where the strings are anchored and haul you up one at a time. While the first one goes up, the other can help me while down here, then the first one can pull from the top to help with the other one."

Kelly sniffed and wiped her nose. "And then we'll pull you up together."

The tedious process took almost half an hour, but we successfully completed our plan. We tiptoed up the stairs with me leading the way, followed by Kelly, then Francesca, the violin once again in her grasp. When I reached the transparent door, I peered out. With heavy mist still draping the world above, the outer walls of the domes were barely visible, and no one was in sight.

Francesca replayed the key, again adjusting to omit the broken string. I climbed the remaining steps and pushed through the glass until I emerged at the surface. While Kelly and Francesca exited, I looked around. Everything seemed exactly the same except that the three guards were no longer there. Scarlet and her supplicant counterparts slept, still twitching from time to time.

I touched Scarlet's dome with a fingertip. Could the supplicants be keeping the entire population asleep somehow? Should I try to wake her to ask, or would that ruin everything?

Kelly tugged on my shirt and pointed at the wall. "Check it out."

I glanced up. Earth Red, now barely visible through the mist, had changed. Fewer orange and purple stains blemished the surface. Many of the cracks between it and Earths Blue and Yellow had thinned, and only fine streams of mixed colors ran through the channels.

"I guess we did some good," Francesca said. "But was it worth it?"

"And that choir from hell will just undo what we did." I crouched and tried to push my fingers under the dome but couldn't find a gap. Kelly knelt at my side. "Let's just ask Scarlet what to do. The safe way."

"The safe way?"

She lay on the hard floor. "Let's enter the dream world and see if she'll talk to us there."

I spread out my hands. "Sleep? Here?"

"Aren't you exhausted? You can probably go to sleep if you try."

"Go ahead, Nathan," Francesca said. "I'll keep watch. If anything happens, I'll wake you."

As I lay next to Kelly, she took my hand. Her grip hurt my wounded palm, but I kept my hand in place. "My mind's racing so fast, I don't see how —"

"Shhh." Francesca raised the violin. "Just close your eyes and relax."

I clenched my eyelids shut. As Francesca began playing, I tried to erase my thoughts, but my mind swam through a dizzying swirl of primary colors, oversized violins, and dark chasms. The sight of Daryl's terrified face shattered the swirl and smoldered in my memory like a sizzling hot brand.

Francesca's tune shifted to the first measures of Brahms' Lullaby, the same piece my real mother had used to settle my mind on so many nights. She hummed along, adding words to her soothing voice, now deepening into my mother's lovely contralto. "Nathan, my darling, you are brave and worthy. You are a valiant warrior, and you have fought with all your might, but now you need to rest. Shut out the failures, for they are in the past and cannot be changed. Let the worries of the next battle slip away, for it is in the misty future, a time unknown."

The sound of Kelly's heavy breathing blended in with the lovely tones and Mom's gentle voice.

"Go now to be with Kelly. She waits for you in the land of dreams. Take her hand and travel to that world. Your wounds will not suffer at her touch, and the journey of rest will make you strong."

Francesca's voice faded. The swirling colors again appeared. They slowed and took shape, creating the form of Kelly reaching for me. I extended a hand. She grabbed it and pulled. I fell toward the colors, splashed into the painting, and blended in with the artwork.

I sat upright, Kelly at my side with her arms wrapped around her knees. Sitting across from us, Scarlet took the same pose, her bare toes touching my shoes. The mirrored walls of the supplicant's dome reflected our seated forms.

Scarlet smiled. "Welcome, my love. You were wise to visit me in this manner."

CHAPTER SEVENTEEN

I MET SCARLET'S WIDE-EYED gaze. "Are you and the other supplicants keeping the stalkers busy?"

"Yes. Cerulean, Amber, and I have engaged them in a more direct battle than usual. Even though they know they are really asleep, they will not soon back down from the challenges we have delivered. When it comes to dream stalking, they are a proud people."

I set a finger on the terrazzo floor. "So, if you're in a battle, how are you here?"

"It is part of the strategy. The stalkers lost three of their warriors, so I excused myself to make it a balanced fight, a battle of song taking place in another part of this realm. I hoped all along you would join me, so it works out perfectly." She rose to her knees, laid her hands on my shoulders, and kissed me on the cheek. "I know what you have done. Repairing the cosmic fabric is a violent affair, and you took great risks. If not for the ongoing battle in the land of dreams, a cadre of stalkers would have awakened to join the three guards, and they would have killed you all."

She settled back to a seated position. "I also know what you have lost. We realize that the suffering of the few is often necessary to end the suffering of the many, but that does little to ease your pain. Even as I heard Kelly's cries from the heart of Sarah's Womb, I felt remorse for asking my beloved to rescue me."

"Your beloved?" Kelly said. "You mean, Nathan?"

She gazed at Kelly, compassion in her eyes. "Yes, he is my beloved, because I have become his supplicant, his prayer mistress, the one who would give her life for him if need be. Yet, you, Kelly Clark, might well see my words as romantic advances, mere flirtations or tokens of superficial lust. If I have caused you any emotional turmoil, I beg your forgiveness. There is no such intention in my mind."

Lowering her head, Kelly whispered, "I forgive you."

Scarlet scooted closer and leaned her head against Kelly's. "Thank you. And now I apologize for another error on my part. I am called to be a rescuer, but I have begged for rescue and have thereby heightened my beloved's danger. Instead of seeking deliverance at his peril, I should rather be content to suffer at his hands."

I glanced at my blood-smeared palms. "Suffer at my hands? Why?" Even as I spoke, Patar's words drifted back to mind. *Slay the supplicants. Cast their bodies into Sarah's Womb, and harmony will be restored.* Did Scarlet know?

She pulled back from Kelly and returned her gaze to me. "You have healed many wounds today, Nathan, but until the breach is completely sealed, the stalkers will be able to continue their assault with their machine." Her countenance turned grim. "I take it that you have not seen Lucifer yet."

"I heard about it. What does it do?"

Scarlet's brow turned downward. "Lucifer transforms energy into a force that degrades the dark matter in the cosmos and tears apart the fabric that separates the worlds. The stalkers use me and my fellow supplicants to transform our harmonic prayers into dissonance, dark energy that will feed their destructive machine."

"How long has this been going on?" Kelly asked.

"Mictar has been feeding and testing Lucifer for centuries, always looking for a breach in the barrier between this world and the three earths. When the scientists in your world learned about the weaknesses between the worlds and tried to exploit them, Mictar was able to penetrate a small rift and began seeking ways to complete his plan."

Kelly's cheeks turned pale. "Why hasn't he used the machine already?"

"He needs a catalyst, the purest of energies, the gift of light and life."

As memories of Mictar's electrified hand returned, I shuddered. "People's eyes?"

"Not the eyes themselves. They are but a spiritual channel to the soul. He absorbs the essence of light and life through the eyes, but the process destroys them. When he returns to this realm, he will feed Lucifer with the stolen energy, but he needs a special catalyst to create the final chain reaction that could very well complete the process we call Interfinity."

"But he had a chance to steal my mother's life essence, and he didn't. He kept her alive to learn the secret of Quattro."

A loving smile blossomed on Scarlet's face. "A demonstration of his one weakness—hunger for power. He knows the mirror has a mysterious power that has thwarted his efforts, and he wants that power."

"Is that why he captured you?"

Scarlet shook her head. "He doesn't know that I give you aid through the mirror, only that I help you somehow, so he hoped to sweep me out of the way. It hasn't occurred to him that the supplicants would aid people with no thought of reward. He has no concept of a selfless act, so he likely believes the mirror you have been carrying has power in and of itself." She tapped her chin with a finger. "Still, I wonder if he yet has a plan for your mother. With his lust for life energy, I cannot understand how he resisted taking such a powerful force as hers."

"What would happen if he got hold of one of the mirrors?" Kelly asked.

Scarlet's smile wilted. "If he were to handle one of the mirrors a gifted one has used, he would be able to see a supplicant through it and learn the power behind Quattro. If Nathan of Earth Red was the last to use it, the mirror would maintain an energy channel directly to me. Mictar would be able to use his own power to reach into it and kill me. I would not be able to defend myself."

"If he wanted to kill you," I said, "why hasn't he already? You're just sitting here under this dome. Couldn't he reach you whenever he wanted?"

She shook her head. "When Mictar captured me, I was in a weakened state after using so much energy to save you and several others from the falling airplane. I assume he brought me here to do away with me, but he hesitated, because he wanted to contemplate how best to use me. While he paused, the other stalkers put me in this prison."

"To keep you from escaping?"

Scarlet gave me a sly wink. "To protect themselves."

I lifted my brow. "To protect themselves?"

"Yes, my love. Listen and learn." Scarlet shifted her gaze toward the ceiling and hummed. As her hum grew louder, she formed soft words that blended into her tune as perfectly as a fragrance in a gentle breeze.

> To supplicate, meditate, ruminate,
> 'Tis a cut by knife, a lonely life, filled with strife.
> I can never be a mother; I can never be a wife.
> I can only be a servant whose heart with love is rife.
> But in my supplications, in songs for precious few,
> I bare Shekhinah glory, and pass it on to you.

Radiance flashed. Scarlet's body brightened, the purest white light pouring from her skin, eyes, and hair. As she raised her hands, the light spread throughout the dome and covered me with tickling sparkles.

Scarlet continued her song, beginning the tune again.

> To activate, animate, initiate,
> A kingly heir, the faith you wear, a life of prayer,
> You must never fear the darkness,
> You must never breed despair.
> You must lift your hand toward heaven
> And give up all your care.
> And in your supplications
> To the king in whom you trust,

You take this glory in your hands
And rise up from the dust.

As the radiance scattered and fell to the floor in a flood of sparks, Scarlet's song reverted to humming with a few soft words sprinkled in.

"Never doubt … Never fear … Never give in … I am always near."

Scarlet's lips formed a gentle smile. "The stalkers know that we are more powerful than they, so they used deception to lure Cerulean and Amber into a trap. The dome contains our energy and prevents us from harming them and them from harming us. But if Mictar learns about the mirror's path to my heart, he can absorb my power and kill me."

"And feed Lucifer," I said.

"That is a purpose we must stop at all costs. As I said before, the suffering of the few is often necessary to stop the suffering of the many, so it would be better for all if you were to kill us and end the madness of the stalkers. Yet, if Mictar is the one who takes my heart, he will gain enough energy to become unstoppable."

"Your heart? What do you mean?"

She unfastened the top button on the front of her dress. "Here. Let me show you."

"Wait." I held up a hand. "Don't do that. I don't need to see—"

"See what, Nathan?" She moved her fingers to the second button but left it fastened. "Surely you don't think I am making romantic advances, do you?"

"Well … I'm not sure what I was thinking. It's just that I shouldn't look at—"

"My heart?" Sadness wilted her expression. "Nathan, if you are to defeat the stalkers, you must recognize that you are in a prison of your own making. Just as surely as I sit in a dome of glass, you have constructed walls round about you. You think you are heeding God's will, yet you are following edicts chiseled in stone rather than the love written on his heart. If you will defeat the stalkers, you must learn this soon, for a time will come when you will face a far more daunting obstacle than your sense of propriety regarding what lies behind my buttons, and you will need my heart to overcome it."

She pulled her lapels apart, popping the buttons loose. Underneath, a void appeared—no skin, bones, or arteries, just a red heart floating in the midst of darkness, throbbing at a rapid pace. "You see, Nathan, there is nothing impure in my actions, for a heart of love is all I really am."

As if powered by her inner light, a red glow pulsed from her skin with every beat of her heart. "I am called to die, Nathan. I should never have tempted you to think otherwise."

I could barely breathe. My own heart beat exactly in time with hers, and so hard it seemed to be pushing up into my throat. I glanced at Kelly. She stared with her mouth agape.

After forcing in some air, I managed to talk without squeaking. "There has to be a way to save the world and you with it."

"There is." She pulled my hand into the void. "Take hold of my heart, Nathan, for it is the only way to absorb the energy you will need."

I gasped. My entire body shaking, I spat out, "You mean ... grab it?"

She kept a firm grip on my wrist. "Yes, Nathan. Feel the rhythm that drives the music within and fuels the eternal song that lifts psalms of deliverance for your sake and for the sake of those you love."

As I wrapped my trembling fingers around her heart, hot flashes stormed through my body. While the warm organ throbbed in my grip, music flowed as well. Hundreds of songs permeated my mind, arias with words I couldn't understand, yet so lovely they brought tears to my eyes.

Still keeping her hand on my wrist, Scarlet drew to within inches of my face and whispered, "This is only a dream, but you will remember this touch forever. When we finally meet in reality, you will know what to do." She touched her lips to mine and exhaled her sweet-smelling breath into my lungs.

An electric jolt threw me back. Kelly caught me in her arms and set me upright. Panting, I looked again at Scarlet. Within the void, her heart, now imprinted with blood from my hand, slowed its beating until it stopped. Then, with her head bowed as she rebuttoned her dress, her eyes shifted toward me, a gentle smile again emerging. "You have no reason to fear, for this is only a dream, and my real heart has not stopped beating."

I looked at my bloody palm, still tingling from the electrified touch. "Why did you do that?"

"To ensure that you remember that my heart is available should you need it." Scarlet looked up at her low ceiling as if trying to pierce the mirrors with her gaze. "I sense great danger, like a fleeting shadow that disappears when you look for its source. Although you have not seen him recently, Mictar has not rested. I fear that he has prepared an evil surprise for you, and you may well apply what you have learned sooner than you wish."

I, too, looked at our reflections above. "Have you figured out why Mictar wants to destroy the cosmos?"

"I have a theory. If the worlds combine, only one world will remain. I have no idea which one. Any survivors would be at Mictar's mercy, slaves most likely."

I whispered, "He would rule the universe."

"What is left of it."

"What should we do now?" Kelly asked.

"Cerulean, Amber, and I will keep the stalkers occupied long enough for you to escape. Daryl Blue left the portal open to the Earth Blue observatory, and you will find that passage at the point where you arrived earlier." Scarlet's voice dropped to a whisper. "But use it with care. If the observatory is empty, then it is safe to pass through. Otherwise, you must seek another route."

I drew a mental image of the observatory. With Daryl Blue gone, no one would be there to watch for intruders. "I guess you know Daryl Blue fell into Sarah's Womb. What happened to her? Where is she now?"

Scarlet shook her head. "If I knew, I would tell you, but her travels are beyond my vision."

I sighed. If Scarlet didn't really know where Daryl Blue was, what hope did we have of finding her?

"Once you awaken," Scarlet continued, "you must hurry. You have slowed Interfinity's approach, but when the stalkers awaken, they will be sure to redouble their tortures in the dreams of mankind and use the supplicants to once again scourge the interstitial fabric. Although they fear Sarah's Womb, they will likely station guards there to abort any new attempt to play the birthing song."

"All right, but once we escape, what do we do next?"

"You will have to return here with a plan that will conquer the stalkers."

"So we can rescue you?"

"In a manner of speaking." She touched her chest, now covered by her buttoned dress. "You know what must be done."

"You mean ... throw you and the other supplicants into Sarah's Womb?"

She nodded. "It is the only way."

"But why? How will that stop Mictar?"

"Cerulean, Amber, and I represent the music of the cosmos. If we perish in the womb, our power will radiate into the universe and heal the fractures, just as the great violin was designed to do."

I shook my head hard. "It makes no sense. Death to save lives?"

"Nathan, death and life have long been comingled. A seed corrupts before it sprouts. Plants feed in the compost of expired organisms. And the Son of God died to bring life to all who follow in his footsteps." She laid a hand on her chest. "If I am cast into Sarah's Womb, I will become a seed, and Sarah will not only repair the cosmos, she will give birth to new life, including more supplicants like me, that is, the species called the Sanctae. Dressed in garments of red, they will return to Earth from heaven and give aid to those whom God chooses."

"You mean, dead people will come back to life?"

"Not exactly. They will be like visiting angels much like myself." As her eyes misted, her voice cracked. "So you see, Nathan, it is to your world's advantage that I go to this death to save the universe and to multiply my species."

Her breaking heart seemed to tear a hole in my own. She had accepted a cruel fate, wanting to stay alive while knowing that death was her sacred duty.

I clenched a fist in spite of the pain. "If I can't figure out how to save the three of you and the universe at the same time, maybe this universe really isn't worth saving."

Scarlet's eyebrows lifted. "Is that so? We are merely supplicants who live to serve others. Would you risk the universe to save three insignificant souls?"

She returned her gaze to the ceiling. The mirror above now showed a launch pad and a space shuttle blasting off in an explosion of fire and plumes of vapor.

The familiar scene sucked my breath away. Although I had watched it a dozen times on various documentaries, I couldn't break free from its hold. Kelly gripped my arm, her nails digging in.

The shuttle turned slowly, arcing upward and leaving behind a trail of vapor that resembled frozen cotton. As the sun reflected off its pristine white shell, the hypersonic craft soared across a blue canopy, carrying seven intrepid souls into the great beyond. Then, in an enormous billowing cloud of white, the craft blew into pieces. The smoke trail split into twin columns, and dozens of white streamers rained toward the earth.

I lowered my head and closed my eyes. Dr. Simon had failed. Even with all his intelligence and planning, he couldn't prevent the tragedy.

Kelly massaged my arm, soothing the slight abrasions she had inflicted, but they were nothing compared to the lacerations in my heart. I glared at Scarlet. Anger scalded my senses, but I couldn't speak the rage simmering in my gut. It wasn't hers to bear. It was mine alone. I was the one who decided to forsake the seven souls in an attempt to save the universe.

I exhaled heavily. "I see your point."

Scarlet gazed at me, a tear streaming down her cheek. "If you still want me to watch over you, you will have to retrieve one of the mirrors." Her body seemed to slowly vaporize. Brahms' Lullaby filtered in. "My dearest one, my beloved, I desire always to be at your side." Her body slowly faded. "But that is up to you."

I reached out, but my hand passed through hers. "Yes. Stay beside me. Always."

Alarm blazed on her transparent face. "He is coming! Wake up!" She disappeared, and everything turned black.

Something touched my head. As I blinked, the violin grew louder.

"When will they wake up?" someone asked—a female voice, anxious and familiar. The violin stopped. "I hear something. We'd better get going."

As the distant sounds of stalkers' songs seeped into my consciousness, I opened my eyes. Daryl knelt over me, a worried look on her face. I looked at her collar — pink at the top of her reddish shirt. "How'd you get here?" I asked.

"Film at eleven." She grabbed my elbow and hoisted me to my feet, while Francesca helped Kelly to hers.

Daryl held a mirror in her free hand. It had to be the one I wasn't able to find on the seat of the van. Why had she taken it without asking? I shook my head to toss the cobwebs away. That question could wait.

"We'd better scoot before the paparazzi show up," Daryl said.

When we turned toward the mist that shrouded the exit door, I looked back at Scarlet's dome. She stood at the glass and gazed at me, her eyes wide. Cerulean, now on his feet, watched from the edge of his dome. Amber, too, had awakened. With blonde hair draping her arms, she pressed her palms on the glass and stared.

As if drawn by an irresistible force, I turned and crept to within a single step of Scarlet's dome.

When I stopped, she mouthed, "I love you." She touched the top button of her dress but left it fastened and drew as close to the glass as the curved dome would allow. She pressed her hand against her chest in the same place I had seen her beating heart.

I laid my hand on the glass, then removed it, leaving a red imprint. She was the real Scarlet, the physical Scarlet, not a phantasm in a dream. Tears welled as I whispered, "I love you, too."

"Nathan," Kelly hissed. "Someone's coming."

As the chaotic songs drew closer, I backed away slowly. Scarlet, too, backed away, sliding her feet toward the center of her prison.

"Nathan!"

After a final nod to Scarlet, I whirled around and grabbed Kelly's hand. "Let's go."

CHAPTER EIGHTEEN

W E PLUNGED INTO the mist, too thick to see beyond a couple of steps. I bent and stared at the floor, allowing the now-familiar patterns in the terrazzo to guide me toward the exit. When we burst into the clear, we sprinted down the glassy walkway, Kelly and me in front, Daryl Red and Francesca Yellow behind, Francesca still carrying the violin and bow.

"Can you tell where we came in?" Kelly asked, puffing as she ran.

"If Daryl Blue left the portal open like Scarlet said, maybe it'll be obvious."

Something tugged my shirt from behind. "Daryl Blue was here?"

I slowed to a halt and turned around. Daryl Red's curious gaze demanded an answer. "She was here. Didn't Francesca tell you?"

"No."

Francesca lowered her head. "I apologize. I just couldn't."

"Where is she now?" Daryl asked.

I looked over her shoulder. No one was coming. I took a deep breath before answering. "She fell into the void. She's gone."

Daryl covered her mouth. Her face twisted, and she leaned her forehead on my chest. "No, no, no! It can't be! Now everyone we know on Earth Blue is dead!" She wailed something unintelligible, then wept.

I set a hand on the back of her head. With all the tragedies, what could I say that might bring comfort? "Clara Blue's still alive."

As Daryl cried harder, her voice squeaked. "She's dead, too. Mictar showed up at the Earth Blue observatory. That must be why Daryl Blue came here. She had to escape Mictar."

Kelly took Daryl's hand. "How did you find out?"

Daryl sniffed, wiped her nose with her sleeve, and forced a steady voice. "When Dr. Simon and I got back to the mirror at Interfinity Labs, we called up Earth Red first. Dr. Gordon had seen the attack and told us that Daryl Blue escaped. But she couldn't stop Mictar from killing Clara."

I shook my head. Too much death. Way too much. And no time to cry. "Were you able to save your uncle?"

She nodded. "He dreamed about the crash, so it was easy to convince him to alter his plans. He went through the motions of getting ready to fly so the Enforcer wouldn't stalk his dreams, but in the end, he just shouted into the sky and dared the Enforcer to try it."

"Good for him," Kelly said. "Let's hope he gets through the night okay."

"He did. I spent three Earth Yellow days with him. He's fine. I guess a small plane crash wasn't a big enough disaster for Mictar to monitor."

I nodded toward the mirror. "Why did you take that?"

She held it up. "Dr. Simon wanted to harness the power of Quattro, remember? I never had to use it, so he was disappointed, but since I was willing to save my uncle, and he felt so bad about Clara, he helped me come here."

"I left another mirror in the van. Did you see it?"

Daryl nodded. "I saw it when I got back. Dr. Simon said he would return it to your Earth Blue bedroom. It was too dangerous to leave it lying around."

I looked at my face in the mirror—dirty and worn out. But this was no time to rest. We had to find the portal and get moving before the stalkers figured out where we went. Scarlet probably couldn't hold them off for long.

I marched forward. "Let's go. It can't be much farther." When I reached a point where the mist cleared on one side, I pointed at the exposed chasm. "This must be it."

Kelly lowered herself to her hands and knees. "I can see the observatory floor. No sign of Mictar."

I took her hand and hoisted her up. Her keen eyesight in this world had helped once again. "I guess that means it's safe."

"So what do we do?" Daryl asked, setting her toes on the edge. "Jump in?"

"Right. Just like before."

She looked at me. "Like before?"

"Don't worry. It was painless, remember? We—" I shook my head. That was Daryl Blue before. Of course this Daryl wouldn't remember, and she wouldn't be afraid of heights either. I let out a silent sigh. The thought of Daryl Blue's sacrifice again tore at my heart. It was at this very spot that I had given her a hard time for being scared, and what had she given me in exchange? Her life.

Swallowing my grief, I embraced Daryl and kissed her on the cheek. She returned the hug, rubbing my back, then scratching it gently. When I pulled away, she tilted her head, her green eyes sparkling with tears. "Not that I didn't get a kick out of the hug, but what was it for?"

Again I could barely speak. "Because you're just like Daryl Blue."

Francesca turned toward the chamber of domes. "I hear something. A stalker's song. Coming this way."

I waved for everyone to gather together. "Let's do it."

Without another word, we joined hands, lined up at the edge of the walkway, and leaped into the void. Blackness engulfed our bodies, yet only a slight breeze wafted upward as we fell, far gentler than a normal plunge would have caused.

Seconds later, we landed softly on our feet. A single desk lamp provided light. Only shadows lay in view. "See anything, Kelly?"

"This is Earth Blue," she replied. "I'm half blind."

I walked toward the computer desk. Again the competing goals tugged at my mind — rescuing my parents, saving the supplicants, and sending Francesca home. Only one seemed relatively easy to accomplish. We could get it done and move on to something else. "C'mon, Daryl. First things first."

Her voice trailed behind me. "What's first?"

"Contact Gunther. We have to send Francesca back. He can pick up her and the van at the observatory."

"You mean if the van's still there. It was when I hopped from there to the stalker world, but who knows how much time has passed since then?" Daryl sat at the desk and pecked at the laptop keyboard, speaking as she typed. "Hey, Tony, it's Daryl. How're those biceps doing? Listen, if Gunther hasn't already dreamed what I'm typing, tell him to get his butt to the observatory. His van might still be there." She looked up at me. "Anything else?"

I reached into my pocket and jingled the keys. "We'll send the keys with Francesca."

Daryl typed the final words and clicked the send button. Almost instantly a new message popped into her inbox.

While Kelly and Francesca gathered around, I leaned over Daryl's shoulder and read out loud. "This is Gunther at Tony's place. No worries about the keys. I have an extra set and already picked up my van. Now I'll head toward the observatory again. I have been in touch with Dr. Simon, so I learned more about the Interfinity crisis.

"It's strange, though, ever since the Challenger disaster, the dream problem has pretty much ended, so life is starting to get back to normal. Now everyone's arguing about why a space shuttle explosion could make a difference. No need to write back. I'll probably be an hour down the road by the time you finish reading this. I'll pick up Dr. Malenkov on the way. He misses Francesca terribly.

"By the way, Tony's already engaged to Kelly's mother, so that's worth celebrating. Now we just have to get Francesca and Solomon together. I tracked him down at Tony's college and had lunch with him. What a cool guy! But he's so smart, I feel like a jackass around him. See you soon, I hope."

"So," Francesca said, leaning closer to read the text. "You're uprooting me from this great adventure and sending me to marry a man I have never met?" She pointed at herself. "Don't forget. I lost two years in Earth Yellow time. I'm not old enough to get married."

"What are you now?" I asked. "Sixteen?"

"Last I checked, but when you miss so many months, birthdays get tough to figure out."

I looked up at the mirrored ceiling. It showed only blackness. "My parents' wedding was in December of nineteen-eighty-six. That's probably not very far in Earth Yellow's future."

She poked my side with the violin bow. "Listen, I want to work this out as much as you do, but I'm not getting married at sixteen years old."

"Shades of *Fiddler on the Roof*!" Daryl brushed the bow away as she rose from her chair. "Whatcha gonna do, Mr. Matchmaker?"

Kelly, her eyes now glassy again, reached for Francesca and patted her arm until her hand rested on her shoulder. "Come with me."

I let my gaze follow the two girls into the darkness. What did Kelly want to tell her? I turned to Daryl. With her bright eyes and wide smile, her face beamed, as usual, but her slightly older visage gave her an air of wisdom. "Don't worry, Nathan, dear. You can trust Kelly."

"Yeah. I know. I'm just curious, I guess."

"Just be patient. She'll spill it eventually." Daryl swung the chair around to the computer. "I'm going to check with Dr. Gordon real quick—see if there's a bad-guy forecast. You know, partly cloudy with a chance of Mictar floating over the horizon."

"Can you bring them up on the ceiling? We should close the portal so the stalkers can't find us. Besides, I'd like to see Clara." I scanned the room again. If Mictar killed

Clara Blue, her body was probably around somewhere. It wouldn't be like him to drag it along. "I'll look for Clara Blue's body while you switch the telescope settings."

"Coming right up." As Daryl reached for the laptop, a deep voice boomed from above.

"Don't touch that setting," a man hissed, "or my prisoner will die."

Daryl jerked her hand back and looked up. "Uh-oh."

I squinted at the dark scene above. Near the apex of the curved ceiling, Mictar stood at the edge of the misty world walkway, distant but easy to recognize.

"If you seek your tutor, Nathan Shepherd, you will find what's left of her in the elevator." Mictar made a slurping sound, then laughed. "Her life energy was a bit old but invigorating nonetheless."

My cheeks ablaze, I shook a fist. "Coward! You attack old ladies and sneak up on your victims from behind." I pointed at the floor, spewing my words. "Why don't you jump down here and face me man to man?"

"Your bravado is quite humorous when you are surrounded by three protective females." A chuckle drifted down. "The rooster crows while the hens shelter him under their wings."

I clenched my teeth. A dozen retorts stormed through my brain, but they all seemed like the rants of a child. As I stared at Mictar, something new came into focus. He clutched a handful of black strings. Was it hair? Was he dragging a body, the prisoner he mentioned?

I whispered to Daryl, "Is there a way to magnify him?"

"Yep." She eased her hand toward the touch pad. "Here goes."

I glanced at Kelly and Francesca standing hand in hand near the telescope, their heads angled upward and their eyes wide.

Above, Mictar's image zoomed closer until his body nearly filled the curved ceiling. A woman hung from a tangle of black hair in his tight fist, her face suspended a few inches off the walkway surface while her body lay prone behind him.

"Mom!" I shook my fist again, spitting as I screamed. "What are you doing with her? Give her back to me or I'll …" I let my voice trail off. I had no idea what to say.

"Or you'll what?" Mictar's evil grin spread across the top of the dome. "If you see fit to match your actions with your bold words, go back to where you found your mother earlier. Follow the sounds of my choir, and you will eventually find me. If you hand over the Quattro mirror, I will restore your mother to you alive."

Mictar walked away, dragging Mom's limp body behind him.

Still clenching my pain-racked fist, I spun to Daryl. "Get Dr. Gordon!"

"Coming right up." Daryl tapped on the keyboard and made the adjustments—switching the settings on the radio telescope, playing the music to arrest the chaotic sounds, and opening the audio channel to Earth Red. Within seconds, a mirror image of the observatory floor appeared on the ceiling showing Dr. Gordon Red and Clara Red looking up at us.

Clara spoke first. "Nathan, you look upset. What happened?"

"Mictar has my mother. I don't know exactly where, but he dared me to come and try to rescue her."

"What are you going to do?"

"Not much choice." I looked at the mirror on the desk where Daryl sat. "I have to save my mother."

Kelly and Francesca walked to the desk. "We'd better send Francesca to Earth Yellow first."

"Too early to ship her now." Daryl pointed at the laptop screen. "I'm watching the clock. It's been two hours and seven minutes, Gunther Standard Time, since his email. He has a ways to go."

"Then Kelly and I'll go and chase Mictar now," I said. "You and Francesca can get Dr. Gordon and Clara up to speed while you're waiting for Gunther to get to the Earth Yellow observatory."

"But I don't know the whole story," Daryl said. "I walked in on the show when the credits started rolling."

"Okay. Here's the super short version." After taking a deep breath, I told the story rapid-fire, giving all the details I thought important. Dr. Gordon and Clara listened in silence, Gordon pacing with a hand on his chin and Clara staring from her chair.

When I finished, I spread out my hands. "That's it. Kelly and I had better run."

"I agree," Dr. Gordon said, now looking up at me. "Since Earths Yellow and Red have stabilized because of your healing actions, travel should be safer than before, but that stability might not last long."

I picked up the mirror and gave it to Kelly. "Will you hold it while I play?"

"Wait," Francesca said. "I have something to tell you." She drew close to me, almost toe to toe. "Kelly convinced me. I'll do what I have to do, even if it means getting married so young." Raising hesitant fingers to my cheek, she whispered. "Earth Yellow needs its version of Nathan Shepherd as soon as possible."

As Francesca handed me the violin and bow, my insides quaked. I replied in a matching whisper. "That's an amazing sacrifice. I think it'll all work out."

She kissed my cheek. "If your father is anything like you, I'm sure it will."

Again flushing hot, I gazed into her gleaming eyes. "I … I don't know what to say."

"Just be sure to tell Kelly why Nathan Shepherd is who he is." She touched the violin bow. "Remember, your talents are a gift, not a birthright."

I watched her finger rub the bow's polished wood. "I'll remember."

She backed away. I couldn't keep eye contact, at least not without breaking down. Forcing a smile, I turned to Daryl. "Are you going back to Earth Red after you send Francesca home?"

She shook her head. "You guys can keep world hopping if you want, but someone needs to run the Earth Blue observatory."

"What about Mictar?" Kelly asked. "If he shows up here again, he won't hesitate to kill you."

Daryl grinned. "I dealt with Tony nearly every day for over two years. I have a sixth sense now about when tall, bug-eyed guys who want to suck my life energy are coming."

"Let's get serious," I said. "It's really dangerous. You shouldn't stay."

"Well, if it isn't Mr. Dangerous himself telling me what to do." She gave me a light punch on the arm. "Go get 'em, tiger. I'll be a phone call away if you need me."

I shook her hand, interlocking our thumbs. "I couldn't do it without you."

She pulled her hand away and stared at her blood-smeared palm. "Then take my advice. You wash up and let Kelly-kins change her bandage. Otherwise you'll leave a trail even a hound with a sinus infection could follow."

CHAPTER NINETEEN

A FTER CHANGING HER bandage, Kelly walked into the telescope's shadow with the mirror square in both hands. She pointed the reflective surface at me as I stood ready to play the violin. Now clean, my wounds burned like fire. Still, my hands felt nimble enough to manage a tune.

Above, Clara and Dr. Gordon watched from their upside-down perspective while Daryl looked on from the Earth Blue computer desk.

Once again playing Foundation's Key, I kept an eye on the dark reflection. Although my fingers and palms ached, I pushed through the performance. As before, the mirror showed the Earth Red graveyard, but the rift in the dark sky was much smaller.

I stopped playing, reached to the floor, and picked up a small flashlight I had found in the desk. Pointing it at the mirror, I nodded at Kelly. "Here we go."

When I flicked it on, the beam bounced off the glass, enhancing the light with supercharged energy. Static pounded from the speakers in the observatory wall. Spinning darkness enveloped us in an ebony cocoon, slowly decelerating until it came to a stop.

I reached out a hand. The inky blackness felt solid, a thin fibrous netting like black spider webs, yet not sticky. The noise died away. Pressing my feet down, I tested the dark surface — solid, not a hint of crumbling, no chance of plunging into the realm of dreams.

"Kelly," I whispered, "are you here?"

She tugged on my shirt. "Right behind you."

I turned toward her, but only blackness met my eyes. Her gentle breaths caressed my cheek, letting me know that she stood close. "Good. Stay close." I tucked the violin under my arm and aimed the flashlight into the darkness. It was time to push ahead and find the hideous monster that dared to drag my mother around like a discarded mannequin.

The beam washed over a fibrous mass, a stringy substance that looked like the thickest cobwebs in the cosmos. Although the flashlight beam started out strong, when it struck the webbing, the light energy poured down the strands. As it trickled toward the floor, the material emitted a crackling noise, and the liquid light thinned the net as if burning it away.

I clicked off the flashlight. Better save the batteries. Although cutting the strings might help, the process was way too slow.

"I hear something," Kelly said. "It sounds like stalkers doing their shrieking circle around Scarlet's dome."

"That's what we're looking for. Mictar must be nearby."

She turned me ninety degrees to the right. "The sound's coming from that way. I'll correct as we go."

I pushed a mass of webbing to the side and walked forward. With every touch, the strands popped and crackled, emanating tiny multi-colored sparks that sprang up and died away. With thick outcrops of tangled netting obstructing the path, we high-stepped, sometimes planting our feet in soft, crackling piles. As we pressed down, the surface felt like spongy moss but looked like glittering obsidian.

I halted. The popping sounds continued for a moment, then stopped. Could the extra noise have been an echo? Not likely.

"What is it?" Kelly asked.

"Shhh." I touched her arm. "Hear anything?"

"Besides the horrible singing?" She paused for a second. "No."

I lifted a foot and pressed down again, raising another shower of crackling sparks. "I mean that noise. When I stop walking, I hear it again."

"The singing pretty much drowns everything out for me."

I strained my ears. Only Kelly's breaths interrupted the dead silence. "Can you translate their song?"

"Some of it." She drummed her fingers on my arm. "They're going on and on about a final merging of the three earths, something about a great sacrifice that will turn on the Lucifer machine."

"That can't be good."

"Now they're saying only one Earth will survive, and they will inhabit it once the rodents are eliminated."

"Their pet name for humans." When I pressed on, the extra popping resumed. Whoever was following always waited for us to start moving again before taking his own steps. Yet, Kelly didn't hear it, so maybe it was just my imagination.

After a minute or so, Kelly turned me a few degrees to the left. I paused and craned my neck to listen. Dissonant song finally reached my ears, warped and far away. The stalkers were out there somewhere.

I turned and listened for our follower again, but the shrieks allowed for no other sounds. Even if we were being stalked, what could I do? Just wait around for an ambush? I lowered my head and trudged on.

Kelly grabbed the back of my shirt. "Slow down. If we're getting close to those white-haired freaks, I'm sticking to you like glue."

As we struggled forward, the song grew louder. "If you hear anything important," I whispered, "let me know. Otherwise, we'd better keep quiet."

"Will do."

After a minute or two, I reached a thick wall of webbing, too thick to swipe away. I turned on the flashlight and set the beam on the black barrier. The light poured down the surface, sizzling all the way to the floor.

I flicked the light off again and felt the spot with my fingers. Although the beam had left a dent, it wasn't more than a centimeter deep. It might take hours to burn through the stuff.

I set the flashlight, violin, and bow down, and tried to tear at the wall with both hands, but my nails couldn't penetrate.

After a few seconds of futile scratching, I picked up my items and whispered, "The wall's too tough. Maybe we can find a way around it, but I might need both hands."

I slid the flashlight into my pocket and pushed the violin into Kelly's grasp.

"I heard it," she said.

"Heard what?"

"The popping noise behind us. Someone's back there."

"If Mictar was going to attack, I think he'd have done it by now."

"Maybe not. He could be waiting for a more convenient place. It feels kind of stupid to march right into his lair."

"I know. But I don't think we have much choice." Laying a hand on the wall at my side, I pushed forward through thick webbing, trying to forge a path parallel to the barrier. Still clutching my shirt, Kelly followed.

The foul vowels continued to emanate from beyond the wall. As I trudged, it seemed that the wall curved, as if it were a circular shield protecting whatever was inside. I halted and slid my hand upward on the barrier, standing on tiptoes to reach as high as I could. The shield curved slightly away. The barrier was a dome, a much bigger, darker dome than the prisons that held Scarlet and the other supplicants.

I knelt and pushed my fingertips into the intersection between the shield and the floor. The wall bent inward, allowing my fingers to slide through. With a quiet grunt, I lifted until the thick cottony material budged.

Now able to curl my fingers up on the other side, I pulled harder. The material spilled slowly around my hands, like viscous gelatin warmed by my touch. When I lifted the curtain a foot or so off the floor, cacophonous vowels poured through the gap, now much louder than before.

I lowered the wall and rose to my feet. "It's heavy, but I'm sure you can handle it. If you hold it up, I'll squeeze through. Then I'll hold it up for you from the inside."

She pulled harder on my shirt. "I don't want us to be separated, not even for a second. The minute you get inside, who knows what might happen? Mictar might grab one of us, or you might fall into someone's nightmare."

"Do you have another idea?"

"Remember what your father said?" She pulled my wrist and dragged my knuckles over the mirror's surface. "When you get in trouble, look at the mirror. I'd say being stuck in a cosmic spider web with that creep lugging your mother around fits the definition of trouble."

"If I aim the flashlight at it, we might get transported again."

"Don't use the flashlight."

"But I can't see the mirror."

"Scarlet has a light of her own. I think she'll shine it for you, but you probably have to ask." Kelly pressed my palm flat on the glass. "Just talk to her and see what happens."

I stared at the spot where my hand met the mirror. The image of Scarlet came to mind, her pleading eyes as she leaned close, my fingers wrapped around her pulsing heart, and, as I drew my hand away, the bloody imprint emblazoned on the heart's surface.

"Scarlet?" I whispered. "I could use some help here. Can you give us a little light?"

Warmth surged through my fingers. My chest tightened, squeezing out a gasp. Light seeped around my hand, outlining it in red. The glow spread over Kelly's face, her expression solemn yet filled with wonder.

I pulled my hand back. As if sketched on the surface by an animated light pen, Scarlet's image appeared in the reflection, the same pose she had struck when I saw her in the dream, her dress open, her heart pulsing bright red. Crimson light burst forth in a broad ray that rocketed past me and melted strands of black webbing.

I took the mirror, now warm at the edges, and pointed it at the dome wall. The red light sizzled against the barrier and streamed down to the floor, like blood flowing from a wounded beast. The beam narrowed into a slender shaft and cut into the thick material. Reddish sparks erupted and arced to the floor where they jumped around in a frenzied dance before dying in a puff of smoke.

Moving the mirror in a tight circle, I burned a swath, cutting deeper and deeper as I edged toward the wall. Several seconds later, the light made a narrow breach all the way through.

The horrible song exploded from within. The mirror's light dimmed, and its cutting power diminished. The dripping red sparks solidified and dropped to the ground as black beads that rolled across the floor.

I swept the beads away with my shoe. The foul vowels were neutralizing Scarlet's light, somehow transforming it into dark energy. I stepped closer and stood within a few inches of the wall as I continued cutting. The breach grew. The soft, pliable material thinned to the point that anyone could slide through the barrier.

I gave Kelly a nod. "Go. I'll be right behind you."

The red glow covering her frame in its bloody mask, she pushed the dripping curtain to the side and stepped into the dome, the violin tucked close. The moment I squeezed through, Kelly grabbed my arm. Her shivering body sent tremors into my own. "It's so cold in here."

The stalkers' wails pounded my eardrums. "And loud."

Still holding the violin, she pressed a hand over an ear. "They're cheering. Like someone scored a touchdown."

"That can't be good." Using the mirror's waning beam, I scanned the area. Emanating from the center of the room, dozens of dark streams passed horizontally through the red light toward the surrounding wall. As one of the streams brushed my cheek, a burst of song blasted into my ears, and a cold chill plunged through my skin. The cloud of black splattered against the wall, combining with other streams to seal the breach Scarlet had cut.

"Looks like the door closed behind us," Kelly said. "No going back now."

"Right. Let's find where those black streams are coming from."

I angled the still-glowing mirror toward the source of the streams and crept forward. In the absence of black webbing, Kelly and I moved easily across the dark floor, though the flowing air grew colder, and the horrendous singing heightened.

After a few seconds, we reached a dark hole in the floor, an eight-foot-wide circle from which cold, song-soaked air poured forth, gusting and spewing new black streams with every dissonant phrase.

Now shivering harder, Kelly hugged me with her free arm as her teeth chattered. "Any ... any idea where we are?"

I gazed into the hole. "Right over the three supplicants' prisons, I think. This must be where the stalkers create dark energy with their songs. I guess the energy absorbs light and heat and solidifies in the wall and that tangled web around us."

Kelly pointed toward a spot above the hole in the floor. "What's that?"

A dark form hovered several feet higher than our heads, almost invisible in the crimson-coated dimness. I aimed the mirror at the vague shape. The residual glow swept across the form — a woman suspended in midair. As the song ebbed and flowed, her long dress flapped around her legs. She rode the current, rising and falling with the sounds, but her dangling feet stayed out of reach.

Kelly whispered, "I think it's your mother."

"I think you're right." I pressed my hand against the mirror. "Scarlet, can I have a little more light?"

A gasping reply wheezed from the surface. "Nathan ... the stalkers are weakening me ... but I will do what I can."

As the red glow strengthened and illuminated the area, the woman's face clarified. Long dark locks brushed across her face and flew above her head as the cold breeze buffeted her body. Her skin seemed polished, reflective, almost like a Barbie doll's plastic coating.

I shivered. "It *is* my mother."

"Nathan!" Kelly shouted. "Behind you!"

I spun in place. A tall specter lunged toward me, a long black arm reaching out. I ducked, dropped to the ground, and swept a leg under the attacker. My foot struck something solid. The shadow lurched forward and toppled over me. Still clutching the mirror, I rolled out of the way, leaped up, and rushed to Kelly in the wash of red light.

As the shadow climbed to its feet, Kelly and I ran to the opposite side of the hole in the floor.

Kelly's teeth chattered as she shouted above the screeching din. "Mictar?"

"It's got to be." My own chill heightened. I slid close to Kelly and pointed the mirror at the slowly approaching phantom.

The tall shadow stalked into the red glow. With a smirk on his pale, narrow face, Mictar stopped at the hole's edge, holding something in his hand that was too dark to identify. "I must admit, I didn't think you would come. Playing house with your harlot is too much fun."

Fighting off the shivers, I squared my shoulders, though I stayed quiet. His taunt cut me once again, but why let him know?

Mictar took two long strides around the hole. Kelly and I matched his movements, keeping him directly opposite us. He pointed a long, bony finger. "Give me the mirror, and I will let you, your mother, and the harlot leave in peace. This place is beyond your understanding."

The song died down. A dim, pale blue light shone from an invisible source within the hole. The cold wind eased, and Mom floated down to eye level. With her skin white and her body stiff, she seemed more like an embalmed corpse than a living human. Still, light glimmered in her eyes, a sign that she was alive.

I reached for her, but her hand dangled a few inches too far away. Should I jump? If I caught hold of her, would we fall into the hole?

I looked at the mirror, the reason he wanted me to come to this place. He wanted it badly. I held it high. "Give her to me first."

"Oh, I see. You lack trust." Mictar gazed at Mom, his eyes wide as if admiring his prisoner. "If you look closely, you can see that I have kept her alive. She would be of no use to me dead. That's why I never took her eyes when I had the opportunity. I needed at least one gifted human to finish my work."

"So," I said, "you want the mirror, and I want my mother. We're at a stalemate."

"Not necessarily." Mictar pointed into the surrounding darkness. "Leave the mirror wherever you wish and walk away from it. While I go to retrieve it, you are welcome to collect your mother and leave."

A whisper drifted into my ear. "My beloved, I see where you are now. You are inside the Lucifer machine. According to the stalkers' songs, Mictar has taken all of the life energy he has stolen and poured it into your mother. He plans to use her as a catalyst to activate the energy and spread it throughout the machine. I am sure disaster will result."

I glanced at the mirror. A hint of Scarlet's troubled eyes appeared in the reflection. I couldn't just hand her over to that monster. There had to be another way. A bluff, maybe?

Retreating from the hole a few steps, I pulled Kelly along. "Suppose we decide to keep the mirror and leave my mother with you, would you let Kelly and me go?"

Mictar raised the object in his hand into the light—a jet-black violin. "Since I have Francesca, I have no use for you, and I likely will not be able to capture you in an expeditious manner and take the mirror. When I am done here, you will die, so it matters little to me what you do now." He lifted a white bow to the strings. "If, however, you wish to stay, by all means do so. You might learn a thing or two from a real violinist."

As Mictar's thin hands gripped the violin and bow like a seasoned master, the words he spoke at the hospital returned to mind. *Your base use of that instrument proves that you have no respect for its true power.* At the time, the statement seemed little more than a verbal slap, but now it echoed as a dark prophecy. The sight of the black violin and white bow made me ill. Something terrible was about to happen.

Mictar stroked a string, then adjusted its tension. As he continued tuning, Kelly whispered, "I have a bad feeling about this."

"No kidding. It's like waiting for your own funeral to begin. Got any ideas?"

"Dissonance creates the dark energy." She extended the violin toward me. "Here's your weapon to counter it. Go to war."

"Shouldn't I use the mirror? Won't Scarlet be able to help?"

"Maybe. You hold the violin." She took the mirror and pushed the violin into my hands. "I'll hold Scarlet."

I scanned the dark floor. "Where's my bow?"

"I don't know." Kelly pointed at a spot near Mictar's feet and whispered, "There it is."

The bow lay two steps to the stalker's right at the hole's ten o'clock position, ourselves at six o'clock, Mictar at high noon.

He began playing. The notes, although perfectly rendered, gave no hint of structure or form. Light flashed from his hands and arced along the bow and over the strings. The same sparkling light that had sucked the life out of so many victims now made the black violin seem to blaze as it poured out measure after measure of dissonance. He shouted into the hole "Sing, my people! Let every earth hear the sounds that will finally bring them together!"

The voices burst into song again, this time louder and fouler than ever. Cold air blasted from the hole, pushing Mom higher in the blue light. The dark streams collided with her body and bounced off, seemingly energized and animated as they rushed away.

I raised the violin and looked at the mirror. It still glowed but only enough to illuminate Kelly as she held the square with both hands. Plucking the strings, I played the opening measure of Beethoven's Moonlight Sonata, but with one of the strings missing, I had to figure out new fingering with my raw, bleeding hands. How could I possibly win a battle of violins?

As I played, the notes seemed feeble against the onslaught of the stalkers' song and Mictar's resonating instrument. He glared at me and played more vigorously. Black vapor poured from his violin and streamed toward the feminine body floating above our heads. As if echoing the notes, sparks of white sizzled through the streams and covered her with an electrostatic aura. Her body twitched, shocked by every twinkling light that surged between her and Mictar.

"Louder, Nathan," Kelly said. "I feel the mirror getting warmer. Give it all you've got."

I pulled the strings harder. A rush of white light rose from each one, but as it lifted into the air, one of the dark streams zipped by and swept the light away, like a crow snatching a morsel.

As I moved my hand up and down the fingerboard, I played on. More light erupted from the violin. More dark clouds gobbled up the sounds. The mirror's glow strengthened. Scarlet's eyes grew brighter. Red light washed over my violin. As the next flash of light erupted from the strings, the dark streams veered away as if forced out of their flight by the new fountain of red.

Pain surging through my fingers, I kept an eye on the bow and continued the sonata. Kelly and I stepped toward the edge. The blast of frigid air pummeled us, but as Scarlet's light strengthened, warmth from the mirror radiated across our bodies and pushed the cold back. Mom floated lower in the column of air. Her face stayed quiet and expressionless as the stalker's electrified onslaught continued.

Scowling, Mictar eased around the circle. Kelly and I again shuffled in the same direction to match the stalker's movements. Only a few more steps and we would be within reach of the bow.

Mictar shouted into the hole. "We are almost there, my people! This fool with a fiddle is no match for us!"

The cold gale freshened, amplifying the noise and lifting Mom higher. Her body convulsed. Black streams shot out of her hands and feet and zoomed into the far reaches of the Lucifer machine.

A loud crack sounded from below. I looked into the pale blue light. Were the glass walls that displayed the earths cracking? Shuffling to stay on the opposite side of the hole from Mictar, I located my bow again, still not quite within reach. I could make a leap for it, but what should I play that would counteract this apocalyptic noise?

I refocused on the strings and continued the pizzicato performance, adding as much vibrato as I could. My hands ached more horribly than ever, but I couldn't give up. I had to fight harder—pour more energy into the music, fill it with the passion I felt for Mom. I had to battle this monster and rescue her and the entire universe. Yet, I had only a violin and a plucking finger. How could that possibly be enough to overcome the flood of dissonance?

A voice drifted from the mirror, soft and indistinct. Scarlet's face clarified in the reflection, somber and glowing with crimson light. As her lips moved, her song energized, and the lyrics formed in red clusters of radiance, each cluster reflecting the character of the words in power, resilience, and emotion.

> The strength of pure evil, the darkness, desire,
> The greedy, the grabber, the lustful, the liar,
> The music of takers can never withstand
> The song of the giver, the bloody red hand.

I snatched up the bow and began playing Scarlet's tune. Although the notes were foreign, somehow they came to me just in time to move from mind, to my crippled hands, to the strings of the violin.

He plays for his maker, his mother, his bride;
He takes no account of his pain or his pride.
His weapon, his music that calls for a song,
The lyrics of old that bring right to a wrong.

As I played, Mictar locked his stare on me. The black vapors from his violin collided with the white that rose from mine, meeting in a striped swirl around Mom's body. Pain scorched my hands. Blood oozed over the bow, but, as Scarlet's song strengthened, I played on.

With fingers of scarlet he reaches for life;
Through boundaries forbidden he plunges a knife.
The heart I laid bare is the flesh on the cross;
The kiss is the wine that sets flames to the dross.

The mirror's clusters of crimson light expanded, ate through the dark streams, and joined in the battle of black and white vapors swirling around Mom. A splash of sparks burned away the blackness in the cyclone, leaving only a spin of red and white. The blue light from the hole faded. As the wind died down, Mom sank toward the hole.

Again Mictar screamed into the void. "It is time! Sing the death march, and I will activate Lucifer's fist!"

A new song rose from below—frenzied, chaotic, screeching. Mictar stroked his black violin furiously, lifting the thickest black clouds yet into the air. The dark streams curved and encircled the hole in dozens of orbits, ranging from lightning-fast rivers of black near the center to slower, more distinct streams as the orbits fanned out over our heads toward the dome's outer walls.

The streams congealed into a single thick cloud of black that spun around Mom and sucked away the red and white swirl. The new cloud sparkled with purple light and illuminated the chamber with a violet hue. The force of the orbits burst open the surrounding wall, and the cloud spread out into the webbing. Like a swarm of locusts, the sparks buzzed through the strands, eating through them with ease.

A male voice sang far in the distance, well beyond where the former wall had stood. Beautiful and somber, it sounded like a father calling his children home. A helper? I hoped so. We needed one.

More cracking noises erupted from beneath our feet. The channels between the earths had to be multiplying. I played harder, louder. We were losing the battle, but what choice did I have? The cosmic fabric was being eaten away by the swarm of dark energy, and the universe lay in my hands—my aching, bleeding hands.

Now crying as Mom spun slowly in the swirling wind, I swayed in time with Scarlet's song, a new song, a louder and more plaintive cry.

O light of dawn! O sound of spring!
O freedom bells! Arise and sing!
Without your voice, without your song,
All light is dark, all right is wrong.

Reveal your aid, your shepherd's staff
That kept my life from being chaff,
That stayed the stalkers' bleeding verse,
That eased my supplicating curse.

As Scarlet's voice faded, a new song rose in the swirling wind, the familiar vowel sounds of the stalkers, yet carrying a strangely beautiful melody.

Near where the black-webbed walls once stood, a tall figure emerged from the torn strands, leaning into the tornadic flow of dark streams as she sang.

"Abodah," Mictar shouted as he continued playing his violin. "Leave, you traitor. You have no business here."

Still fighting the wind, she staggered to the edge of the circle and scowled. With a series of short notes, she sang her answer.

"I am not your slave," Kelly translated, her shouts beaten back by the cyclone. "Nor am I a traitor. I have come to set these captives free."

Mictar sneered, but he seemed out of breath as his fingers continued to fly up and down the violin's neck. "It is too late. Lucifer has the catalyst in its grip, and the dark energy is ripping apart the barriers. It would take much more than a singing supplicant and a boy playing a three-stringed fiddle to stop me now."

Abodah set a hand on my shoulder and sang a soft tune.

"Stop playing," Kelly said. "You are only delaying the inevitable, and you must be strong enough to follow my counsel."

I lowered the violin and shook my stinging hand. "What do I do?"

A deep crease spread across Abodah's forehead as she sang again.

Kelly leaned close to me as she translated. "Sacrifice. When we stop this machine, the supplicants will be the only way for him to create dark energy." She pointed at the hole. "For the sake of billions on the three earths, you must go down there and kill Scarlet, Amber, and Cerulean."

CHAPTER TWENTY

A S THE WIND blasted my face, I looked at Mom, now spinning faster and faster. Just pausing to listen to Abodah's advice had already accelerated Lucifer's destructive force. "What about my mother?"

"Leave her where she is," Kelly said, still translating for Abodah. "If you are going to accomplish your mission, she will be a hindrance to you. You cannot drag her with you and still carry out this plan."

"How do I get into the supplicants' domes?"

Abodah pressed her lips close to my ear and sang seven high notes. When she straightened, she continued her song, and Kelly gave it words. "That is the key to Scarlet's dome. Lower each note by one octave to open Cerulean's, then another octave to open Amber's."

Abodah shifted her gaze toward Mictar and sang a final few notes.

"Go now," Kelly translated. "This stalker of souls is mine."

As Abodah walked around the circle, Mictar stayed put, his face defiant as he continued playing his violin. Still, a hint of concern crept across his eyes. With her head erect and her stare fixed, Abodah closed in, raising her hands, palms out, as if creating a shield in front of her.

I backed away from the edge of the hole, shivering in the blistering torrent of cold. Kelly did the same. She tucked the mirror and grasped my wrist, again shouting to compete with the riotous noise. "Are you really going to do what she said?"

"I'm not sure yet, but I know one thing I'm going to do."

"What?"

"I'm going to rescue my mother." Taking a deep breath, I nodded toward the hole. "When I get to the bottom, I'll try to signal if it's safe." I pulled free and ran toward the hole. When I reached the edge, I leaped toward Mom's spinning body while still clutching the violin and bow. When I collided with her, I wrapped my arms around her shoulders and my legs around her waist.

Now spinning with her, I sank slowly ... too slowly. With every revolution, Mictar and Abodah flashed across my vision on one side and Kelly on the other. The two stalkers fought hand to hand, while Kelly dashed toward the hole's edge. When I spun to the other side, a sudden weight thumped against my back, and a slender arm joined mine around Mom's shoulders. Soft lips and a whisper tickled my ear. "Not for one minute, Nathan Shepherd, will I let you leave my side."

With her cheek pressed against mine, we descended, now much more quickly. The spinning slowed, allowing a better view of Mictar and Abodah as they wrestled on the floor. With Mictar no longer playing the violin, the cyclone slowed as well, but the wind from below continued blasting cold air upward through the bluish light.

As we descended below the top of the hole, Kelly's shivering arms sent tremors through my body. The edge of the mirror bit into my side, but the pain was worth it. Scarlet had come along for the ride. Yet, the touch seemed cold. Had she used all her energy? Would she be able to help us once we arrived?

The blue glow faded to purple, then to black. After a few more seconds, faint light emanated from far below, a circle of white that grew rapidly as our rate of descent increased. Soon, the three domes appeared. A group of stalkers encircling Scarlet's dome continued singing their horrible verses, apparently not yet noticing the three bodies floating into their domain.

Below, Scarlet lay motionless on the floor under the center of her dome. Cerulean looked on, his hands pressed against the wall of his prison. Amber, too, stood near her wall, her eyes fixed on Kelly, Mom, and me.

The three earths came into view on the surrounding matrix of glass squares. Hundreds of deep channels now etched paths between the planets, each channel with mist of blended colors running through it. The mist collected in blankets of clouds hovering over the channels' end points at the surfaces of the earths.

As we came within twenty feet of the floor, a male voice rose with the upward draft, a lovely tenor, sweet and pure. An alto blended in, as clear as carillon bells. Cerulean and Amber lifted their heads and sang the most beautiful vowel song I had ever heard, filled with passion, yet flowing with peace.

One of the stalkers pointed at Cerulean and shrieked four loud notes. The others stopped singing. Some hurried to the boy's dome while the others ran toward Amber's. The stalkers shouted heated notes at each other, as if arguing about which supplicant to surround with their dissonant song.

The wind eased, further increasing our rate of descent. At this speed, we would have to hit feet first and roll while hoping the two supplicants kept the stalkers occupied. I couldn't possibly fight that many, especially if they wielded sonic paralyzers.

As we descended toward the door to Sarah's Womb, I slid down Mom's body. At the last minute, I swung all three of us away from the door, touched down with one foot, and propelled us into a roll while holding the violin and bow aloft.

When we came to a stop, I jumped to my feet, helped Kelly to hers, and straddled Mom as I raised the violin to my chin. Kelly pressed the mirror against her stomach and rolled her free hand into a fist. With new blood streaming down the front of her sweatshirt, she looked like a warrior ready for battle.

As I played the notes Abodah had whispered, one of the female stalkers turned and shrieked three vowels. Several others spun toward us. Two of the males withdrew sonic rods and marched our way.

When I played the final note, Scarlet's dome let out a loud hum. The two stalkers halted and exchanged glances. Fear widened their eyes. I played the code again at a lower octave. Cerulean's dome hummed a note, one step up from Scarlet's. Then, after I played another seven notes at the next octave down, Amber's dome joined the other two in a harmonic trio of resonating hums.

The two stalkers holding paralyzers retreated and joined the others, then they all backed toward the door that led to the glassy walkway.

Scarlet's dome evaporated, leaving only a circular swatch of faded terrazzo. I gave the violin and bow to Kelly, picked up Mom, and staggered to the circle. Scarlet lay curled in a fetal position, her arms crossed and her body shaking.

After setting Mom down, I dropped to my knees next to the quivering supplicant.

"Scarlet?" I laid a hand on her sweat-drenched red hair. "Can you hear me?"

Her eyes fluttered. She turned her head and blinked at me. With barely a whisper, she said, "My beloved?"

Kelly knelt beside me and handed me the mirror, but Scarlet brushed it to the side. "There is no need for that," she said, her voice fragile. "We have seen each other through glass, mirrors, and dreams, but now, at last, face-to-face." She raised a hand and laid it on my cheek. "And touching you is my dream come true."

Her fingers, warm and soft, seemed to reach into my heart and wring it out like an old sponge. Tears crawled down my cheeks. My throat clamped so tight, I could barely squeak. "Are you … going to live?"

Cerulean and Amber lowered themselves to their knees, completing a circle around the fallen supplicant. "It depends," Scarlet whispered. She unfastened her dress's uppermost button, exposing the top of the void. "Will you take my life and give it to another?"

"To another?" I looked at Mom. With her skin pale and slick, she hardly resembled the vibrant woman I once knew — the warm, loving Francesca Shepherd. She lay cold and stiff, staring upward with unblinking eyes.

Kelly laid a palm on Mom's chest. "I'm not getting much. Maybe a flutter. I don't think she'll last long."

I clutched Scarlet's hand. "Isn't there another way? Can I take your place? I would die for my mother if I could."

"Not you, my love, for you are not a supplicant. Nor Cerulean, for he can die only for an Earth Blue soul. And Amber's life is reserved for someone on Earth Yellow. Only I can do this, but you must transfer my life to hers. The power is in your hands." Scarlet pulled apart her lapels, popping open three buttons. "You know what you have to do. You must slay this supplicant."

I lifted a hand and stared at my wounded palm. Blood still oozed from the lacerations. I shifted my gaze to the hole in Scarlet's chest and the heart floating in the midst, beating erratically as she labored to breathe. I had touched her only in a dream, a grip on her heart that never happened and a caress of lips that was a mere thought. Now she begged me to steal her life.

I turned toward Kelly. As I gazed into her eyes, I silently begged for help. She would understand my turmoil, interpret my cry. I needed her to speak the words that would release me from my self-imposed dome.

Kelly laid a hand on my cheek. "It's the only way, Nathan. You have to do it. You can't die for your mother yourself."

As Kelly pulled her hand back, a sob erupted from the pit of my stomach. Weeping, I reached into Scarlet's body and wrapped my fingers around her heart.

She grasped my wrist and heaved in a breath. Then, letting it out slowly, she smiled and whispered, her voice little more than a sigh. "I give my life energy to you now, my beloved. Taste the freshness of a life reborn, drink the nectar of love renewed, feel my presence in your soul. Then, when the fullness of my power embraces you, use it to awaken your mother." She clutched my shirt and pulled me close. As her lips brushed my ear, her voice spiked with urgency. "But don't ever … *ever* forget me."

Feeling her heart throbbing in my hand, I gasped shallow breaths. "I'll never forget you. Never."

Scarlet's smile widened. She blinked rapidly. Then, she heaved in another breath and sang in a whisper, each word labored and failing.

> To give! To give! My spirit cries out.
> I have no gift but life.
> Into thy hand I pour it out
> And finally end my strife.

Her lips trembled. "Now, Nathan. Take my kiss of new life."

I touched my quivering lips to hers. Her chest expanded once more, and she let out a long sigh. Her hot breath poured in and filtered into my lungs, fresh and soothing.

When I lifted away, her head lolled to the side. A weak smile graced her lips, and her eyes closed. Her heart fluttered once, then fell still.

I released her heart and pulled back my hand, my skin now hot and throbbing. Had I really absorbed her life energy? Trembling, I fastened her lowest button and reached for the next.

"Nathan," Kelly said. "I'll do that. Go to your mother."

With tears dripping onto Scarlet's dress, I shook my head. "I have to do it. Don't ask me why. I just have to." Yet, I knew why. Scarlet had given everything she had to me, even life itself. I had to be the one to seal her shroud.

As my aching fingers fumbled with the buttons, the aroma of roses freshened my nostrils, and a bittersweet film coated my tongue. A sense of cool wetness slaked my parched throat and eased the constricting muscles.

When I fastened the top button, I shifted on my knees toward Mom and looked at Cerulean and Amber in turn. "What do I do?"

Amber, her lips straight and somber, grasped my wrist and moved my hand over Mom's mouth. "Lay your anointed palm here and call upon the interpreter to push on her chest three times. Have her say, 'In the name of the Father, the Son, and the Holy Ghost, restore the breath of life and renew the spirit within this fragile shell.'"

I laid my bloody palm over Mom's lips, spread my fingers across her cheeks and nose, and nodded at Kelly. "Go ahead and push."

Placing the heels of both hands on Mom's sternum, Kelly pressed down. "In the name of the Father ..."

Dry air cooled my palm. When Kelly lifted her weight, suction from Mom's nose and mouth pulled my hand closer and made my skin tingle.

Kelly pressed down again. "The Son ..."

The air blowing out felt drier and colder.

She lifted her weight. Suction again pulled my hand. Stinging pain crawled across my skin and radiated up my arm.

Kelly pushed down once more. "And the Holy Ghost, restore the breath of life and renew the spirit within this fragile shell."

Air poured from Mom's mouth, blistering cold. Icy currents injected my bones with numbing pain. My arms and legs stiffened. My knees and elbows locked, and my fingers felt as rigid as icicles over her mouth.

When Kelly pulled back and knelt at my side, the rush of cold air reversed and rushed into Mom's lungs.

Like lava rising from a volcano, heat boiled deep within my chest and spread out into my limbs, loosening my joints. As warmth pushed into my cheeks, the smell of roses again brushed my senses, and bittersweetness coated my tongue.

The volcano erupted. A flood of superheated energy surged through my arm and gushed into my hand. Red light flashed from my fingers and coated Mom's face with a scarlet glow. As sheer agony ripped through my brain, I lifted my head and let out a guttural scream, a high piercing note that shook the floor.

Mom's body jerked. She coughed, then sneezed. As her eyes blinked open, I pulled back my scalded hand, peeling away loose, melted skin that had adhered to her face.

Her brow arched, and her eyes darted. "Nathan?" Her voice sounded like a tinkling bell, quiet and clear. "Are we in heaven?"

"Mom!" I threw my arms around her and pulled her against my chest, rocking her back and forth. Sobs choked my words. "No ... we're not in heaven. But ... but you're alive. That's all that matters."

She hugged me with loose, weak arms. "Oh, my son, my son! It is paradise to see you again!"

Kelly's voice quaked. "Hello, Mrs. Shepherd. I'm Kelly Clark."

As I pushed away, Mom smiled. "Yes, Kelly. I met your counterpart on Earth Blue. You ... I mean, she saved my life there."

"She did? How?"

"I hope to tell you the story later." Mom glanced around the room until her eyes locked on Scarlet's body. "Your supplicant? Is she ..."

I nodded. "She died to resurrect you, but that's *my* long story."

Mom brushed a tear from her eye and continued scanning. "We're in the stalkers' lair. Where are they?"

"Gone. At least for now." I rose and reached out the less bloody of my two hands. "Can you stand?"

"I think so."

I hoisted her up and nodded toward the two living supplicants. "This is Cerulean and Amber, the supplicants for Earths Blue and Yellow."

Cerulean bowed, shaking his stark blue hair, while Amber spread out her yellow dress and dipped into a formal curtsy. Cerulean gazed at Mom with his stunning eyes. "I am not of your world, but I am at your service."

Amber stepped forward and touched my hand. "Your bow hand is in need of repair. You will not be able to play your instrument."

I looked at the torn, melted skin. Puffy redness swelled my fingers. "True. At least for now. But Francesca Shepherd is here. She can take over." I looped my elbow around Mom's. "Do you know where Dad is? Did he ever come back to that place where I found you?"

She shook her head. "Soon after you and the others fell into the void, the floors around me became solid. When I tried to search for your father, Mictar ambushed me and put me in his machine. Since he enjoys boasting about his accomplishments, I picked up some clues about the structure of the realms. We need to get back to the Earth Blue mirrors and look for your father there."

"I hear something," Kelly said. "Sounds like the stalkers, but I don't see them."

I pulled Cerulean closer. "I got the impression that the stalkers are afraid of you and Amber."

The slightest of grins bent the young man's face. "Of that you can be sure, yet I do not know if Amber and I can repel them all. Scarlet was our leader, and her courage and wisdom exceeded ours."

A deafening crack rifled through the room. At the Earth Red side of the chamber, two huge rifts shot out from the surface of the mist-shrouded planet and slowly crawled across the wall toward the other two earths. Glass squares exploded in their paths and rained sparkling shards to the floor. Earth Red itself expanded, pulsing and throbbing as if ready to burst. At the rate the cracks were moving, they would reach the other earths in mere moments.

Kelly whispered, "What does it mean?"

"The end of the worlds." I looked at Scarlet's motionless body, still lovely, even in death. Although I knew what to do with her, the thought made me sick to my stomach. "Can you open the door to Sarah's Womb?" I asked Cerulean.

"Yes, though I weep at the reason for your request."

"Thank you. And keep the stalkers at bay." I stooped and slid my hands under Scarlet. "I'll be back as soon as I can."

Kelly picked up the violin and the mirror. "I'm coming with you."

With a grunt, I straightened, lifting Scarlet's limp body. "Of course you are."

"And I, as well," Mom said. "You will need a violinist to open the lower door."

As I shuffled toward the floor panel, I nodded. "Let's hurry."

Cerulean strode ahead, his slender body seeming to glide as he approached the door. He knelt at the side of the glass panel and sang. Rapid-fire notes burst forth from low to high on the musical scale as if someone had run a finger along piano keys. The lights in the panel flashed in response. Cerulean took a breath and sang two more series of notes to unlock the door.

He looked up at me. "It is open, my friend. Do what you must."

I looked back at Earth Red. It still throbbed like a heart. More glass squares popped as twin jagged tentacles reached toward the other worlds. I set one foot in the door's viscous liquid and sidestepped down the stairs.

As I descended, Cerulean and Amber turned their backs and stood hand in hand, guarding the entry. A few white-haired stalkers appeared in the misty distance, but they ventured no closer.

Without a word, Mom and Kelly followed, Mom carrying the violin. I walked into darkness, but having traveled this path a few times, I had no trouble navigating the rocky steps. Still, sidestepping with a dead girl in my arms made for slow going down the steep stairway. I hoped to avoid scraping her on the walls. Even in death, every hair on her head was sacred.

"Mom," I called. "We'll be at the next door in a few seconds. Did you hear Cerulean's notes?"

"Yes, Son. A string on the violin is missing, but I can manage with three."

I slowed my pace. Although the dark corridor revealed nothing, I sensed the door's looming presence. "We're here. Go ahead and play it."

She squeezed past me. Seconds later, seven notes lilted in the darkness, then repeated twice to complete the key. As before, a glow appeared around the rectangular doorway and ate away at the edges. Soon, light from the chasm shone into the corridor and washed over Mom, still poised in playing position, the same pose her younger twin had taken not long ago.

Rumbling thunder erupted from the void, making our corridor shake. As I leaned against one of the walls to keep my balance, Mom hummed a tune. "I hear a song. It is as if Sarah is singing to us in the midst of her groanings."

I leaned out. As another rumble sounded, a dim red glow rose from the yawning chasm, mixing with the varied light rays emanating from the outer walls. When I pictured myself throwing Scarlet in and watching her helpless body plunge into darkness, nausea churned in my stomach.

Kelly drew close and whispered. "You need to hear what Sarah has to say." She cleared her throat and sang, her words flowing in a rhythmic cadence, strong and clear.

> The womb of Sarah sings a prayer;
> She begs for children in her care.

For now 'tis time to pay the price,
A daughter born to sacrifice.

Beloved son of gifted birth,
A scarlet child of scarlet earth,
You hold her body in your grasp,
Another dome, another clasp.

O man of sorrows, gallant knight,
Whose heart doth quake at such a plight;
Release this child of sorrows nigh,
Then "free at last" will be her cry.

When she finished, she sniffed and wiped her nose, and spoke no more. Mom, too, stayed silent. In the wash of Sarah's glow, they looked at me with sad expressions.

The red light rained over Scarlet's lovely face and painted her lips and cheeks with a crimson blush. Even in death she emanated youthful innocence, pure love, and the radiance that only the passion of sacrifice can generate.

Sarah's Womb rumbled once again. I kissed Scarlet's cheek, then, after rocking her body back once, threw her into the chasm.

I dropped to my knees and watched. As her tiny form shrank, her arms and legs flew about, and her dress flapped in the upwelling breeze. Her hand brushed one of the violin strings as she plummeted past. A loud note thrummed in response. As Scarlet's body melded with the red glow and disappeared, the note deepened and grew louder.

The corridor shook once again. I lost my balance and teetered over the ledge. Mom and Kelly each grabbed an arm and pulled me to safety.

The trembling stopped. The tension in the air eased. Still on my knees, I took a deep breath. "Let's get out of here."

I climbed to my feet and walked backwards up the steps, trying to catch the vestiges of Scarlet's radiant presence. The ladies followed. Their tired bodies struggled up the stairs as the faint red glow framed their faces in scarlet. I turned and walked forward. Even the color brought pain. For the rest of my life the color red would remind me of this tragic day.

As the string's thrumming note continued, Kelly interpreted, trying to keep the rhythm in spite of her heavy breathing.

> I'm free at last! Let all rejoice!
> O raise your head! O lift your voice!
> Let angels sing, let earth agree,
> Imprisoned billions now set free!

The ground trembled again but this time as if settling rather than breaking apart. I maintained a slow pace, not wanting the song to end too soon.

Kelly continued.

> Beloved Nathan, son of song,
> You broke my chains, made right the wrong.
> I asked for rescue, begged for air.
> You saved my soul from Mictar's lair.
>
> So now I leave a gift sublime,
> The poet's flair for words and rhyme;
> A smell, a taste, you'll know I'm near;
> Unbidden words will soon appear.

Kelly's voice weakened. I turned and signaled a rest. She nodded, leaned against the side wall, and sang on, her voice stronger again.

And then another gift I'll bring
To add to hymns your heart will sing;
For songs of love deserve reply,
A dance that lasts until you die.

A day will come when love mature
Will take the hand of one made pure
In everlasting song and dance,
A knight, a lady, sweet romance.

Kelly smiled. Gazing at me, she reached out a hand. I took it and drew close, listening carefully as her voice waned and fractured.

What once was scarlet now is white,
A dove redeemed, her plumage bright,
With feathers spotless, fresh, renewed,
Restored, untouched, no stain imbued.

Tears flowing, Kelly closed her eyes as the dying tone of the strummed violin breezed past. Her voice warped, and she sang like a wounded songbird, faltering at almost every word.

A day will come … my love, my life
As you caress … your lovely wife
To let her love … and lasting bliss

She opened her eyes and looked at me again. Pure love flowed from her beautiful blue orbs as she finished.

Erase your Scarlet's dying kiss.

I drew her into my arms and held her close. As she wept against my chest, the aroma of fresh roses caressed my senses. A thousand words sprang to mind, a song that begged to be sung, but it would have to wait for the right time, the right place.

Mom crossed her arms and gazed at me with a warm smile. She already loved Kelly.

Kelly drew back and brushed away tears. "The other two supplicants are waiting."

We trudged the rest of the way up the stairs. When we reached the top, we crouched together under the glass door. Mom played the seven notes three times. I pushed through the glass and stepped up into the misty world. Hand in hand Mom and Kelly walked through the doorway. Kelly's face, though flushed and tear-streaked, beamed like the sun itself.

Cerulean twisted in our direction, still in a guardian stance with Amber. "The stalkers are assembling deep within the mist. I suspect that they are preparing for an attack."

CHAPTER TWENTY-ONE

W ITH CERULEAN AND Amber following, I led Mom and Kelly out of the floor panel area and toward the exit to the misty hall. "Think we can sneak past them and make it to the exit?" I asked.

Cerulean peered through the mist. "It is not likely. They are adept at—"

Something thumped behind us. Mictar shuffled across the circle where Scarlet's dome once stood, dragging Abodah by her hair. Dozens of deep scratches gouged his face, and blood dripped from his chin down to his shirt.

Mictar jerked Abodah's body forward and slid her toward us. She came to a stop next to Amber's bare feet, her loose limbs flopping like a rag doll's. Gasping, he extended a rigid finger at me. "I will not be beaten so easily, fiddle boy. You have merely delayed the inevitable. Interfinity will come."

Cerulean pointed at the glass squares behind Scarlet's circle. "You are already beaten, you fool. One of the worlds you wanted to enslave has been set free."

I looked at the wall. As if slung away by a catapult, the image of Earth Red shrank, now the size of a baseball and getting smaller. The jagged channels leading from the other two earths had shriveled and were receding.

"Who is the fool?" Mictar said. "You have pronounced your own death sentence. Now these Earth Red refugees know that the deaths of the supplicants will free the other earths."

Cerulean ripped open his shirt, revealing a pulsing heart within a dark void. With every beat, a blue glow radiated from his chest. "I am ready to die. Are you?"

When Amber began unbuttoning her dress, Mictar waved a hand. "Oh, stop the theatrics. You supplicants always think you're actors on a stage."

Amber refastened her top button and took Cerulean's hand. "We project the reality within us," she said, "without shadow, without shield. There is no guile in our words."

"While you," Cerulean added, "brew deception in every word you speak. My offer to die is unmixed truth, and I make no apologies for my dramatic flair."

Mictar nodded toward the image of Earth Blue, now covered with clouds of green haze and bombarded with channels streaking across from Earth Yellow. "For whom will you die? The gifted ones on your planet are all dead. What gifted hand will draw out your healing energy and transfer it to a new host?"

Cerulean glanced at Amber, then at me and the others. He seemed unable to reply.

As I flexed my aching hand in and out of a fist, no response came to my mind either. Yet, words erupted unbidden, taking on a sharp tone. "The abode of the lambs is not for the wolves to know. We will keep our own counsel." I closed my mouth. Where did those words come from? Inhaling, I again detected Scarlet's presence. The girl with the rose-petal scent had risen to speak in my stead.

"Bah!" Mictar waved a hand. "You don't fool me for a second. You have no idea how to save the other two worlds." He nodded toward the exit. "Or yourselves."

A white-haired singer stood at each side of the door. With sonic paralyzers drawn, they locked their stares straight ahead. At least fifteen others marched out of the mist and spread into a horizontal line as they approached, each with a paralyzer in hand.

When they came within twenty feet, they formed a semicircle that blocked our escape. Once in place, they stopped and held out their rods, like soldiers waiting for a command. Although their erect bodies seemed disciplined and ready, fear streaked their faces as their gazes locked on the two surviving supplicants.

"Now," Mictar said, "we shall see who is ready to die."

As if turned on by a single switch, the sonic paralyzers flashed light from their ends, some red, some yellow, some blue. A squealing note erupted from each, loud and piercing.

I slapped my hands over my ears. Agony throttled my brain. Dropping to her knees, Kelly did the same, arching her body over the mirror square, now on the floor. Mom bent at the waist and groaned.

Cerulean and Amber spread out their arms. Cerulean took in a deep breath and sang a long, low note. Amber added an alto note that drilled into the musical battle. The supplicants' music seemed to repel the paralyzing noise, but how long could they keep it up?

The stalkers' line fractured. At least five backed away a step. Some held their rods with jittery arms while others placed a hand over one ear.

"Cowards!" Mictar screamed. "Two supplicants cannot overcome all of you!" Yet Mictar came no closer. As he circled me, he kept plenty of space between himself and the supplicants. Shouting to overcome the battling tones, he pointed at me. "We are at an impasse again, son of Solomon. Your father would be proud. If you could find him, I'm sure he would tell you so."

I lowered my arms and clenched a fist in spite of the pain. "What do you want now? Scarlet's dead."

"I want the mirror." He shifted his finger toward the spot where Scarlet once sat imprisoned. "And now that she is gone, I will be able to use it without restriction."

Kelly rose to her feet and handed me the mirror. "Does it still have power?" she whispered.

"I don't know. I'm not sure if he knows, either."

"He's no fool," Kelly said. "We shouldn't let him have it."

"If you give it to me," Mictar continued, "I will not only tell you where your father is, I will release all of you, including the two supplicants. Your father is alive, but he won't be for long." He waved a hand at the stalkers. They turned off their sonic rods and drew back a few paces.

Cerulean and Amber stopped singing, both breathless. Amber coughed, while Cerulean clutched his chest, still keeping an eye on Mictar.

As silence descended on the room, Mictar eased closer to me. "What do you say? Will you accept freedom and full restoration of your family, all for the price of a square of glass?"

I looked at the mirror. The surface reflected nothing. Perfectly transparent, it showed blackness tinged with a vague red glow. I searched Mom's eyes for an answer. "Any advice?"

She compressed my shoulder. "If we could be sure he is telling the truth, we could give him what he wants. Regaining your father is worth far more than losing the mirror."

"Mictar telling the truth?" I laughed under my breath. "The lambs should never trust the wolf when he speaks. Yet the wolf is often unaware of the trap that lies in plain sight." I closed my mouth. Where did that come from? I hadn't even thought it. Was Scarlet helping me decide? Had she set a trap for Mictar?

Watching him out of the corner of my eye, I turned to Kelly. "If I can clear the way to the exit door, do you think you can get Mom and the supplicants to Earth Blue?"

She nodded. "But I told you, I'm not leaving your side, not for a minute."

I lowered my voice to a whisper. "Kelly, you have to. We're all making sacrifices, right?"

Sighing, she returned a shallow nod.

"Then trust me. If this works, it might take quite a bit more than a minute."

"I trust you," she said, looking me straight in the eye. "More than ever."

"Okay, then." With the mirror tucked under my arm, I walked toward Mictar. "Tell us where my father is, and let them go. And you have to let them take Abodah's body, too. I'll stay here with the mirror as a pledge until they're safely on their way."

Mictar stared at me for a moment, raising an eyebrow. "You make a solemn promise to give me the mirror?"

"I do."

Mictar laughed. "It is so easy dealing with humans who choose to bind themselves with codes of honor. They are fools to give up the arsenal of deception."

"Stop babbling, Mictar." I lifted the mirror high. "Are you going to take my offer, or not?"

"I accept. You will find your father in the dreamlands of Earth Yellow. Amber knows how to get there."

I turned to Amber. "Is that true?"

She knitted her brow. "I do know how to get there, and I am sure I could locate him eventually, but we would have to go there physically to make a bridge of escape."

"And can you do that?"

She gave me a firm nod. "I can."

I looked at Cerulean. "Can you take us to the dreamlands of Earth Blue?"

He blinked his radiant blue eyes. "Certainly. Why do you ask?"

"A friend of mine named Jack is there. We have to rescue him, too."

"I will help you search for him."

"Thank you." I withdrew my phone, set the timer for five minutes, and gave it to him, whispering, "Now lead everyone to the portal. If I'm not there when this alarm goes off, take everyone to Earth Blue without me."

"I understand." Cerulean slid the phone into a pocket, scooped up Abodah's body, and led Kelly, Amber, and Mom toward the door. The stalkers parted down the middle, giving them plenty of room to pass as they hurried through the exit at a fast trot.

I closed the gap between Mictar and me, extending the mirror. "Here it is. I'm keeping my word."

"Of course you are." As soon as Mictar jerked the glass from my grip, he nodded toward the stalkers. They closed ranks and blocked the path toward the exit. Mictar laughed, making his ponytail sway behind his head. "You're a bigger fool than I ever imagined."

I backed away. "I'll use your own question. Who is the fool? The one who sacrifices all he has for the ones he loves, or the power-greedy monster who craves mysteries beyond his understanding?" I nodded at the square. "Go ahead and try to use the mirror. I want to be here to see what happens."

Two stalkers grabbed my arms, one at each side. I struggled, but when one showed me his sonic paralyzer, I settled down. "What's the matter?" I shouted. "Scared of a kid who's smarter than you?"

Mictar waved a hand. "Release him. He is not a threat." Narrowing his eyes, he took a step closer to me. "Is this a battle of wits, son of Solomon? Are you baiting me to use the mirror because you think it will bring me harm, or are you bluffing, hoping that I will now be fearful and not use it?"

"Like I said …" I folded my arms in front. "We will soon learn who the fool is."

"I see." Mictar set the mirror on the floor and backed away, matching my distance from its edge. "Let the battle begin."

As Mictar glared at me, I hid a nervous swallow. Since I had no idea what the mirror would do, I wasn't bluffing. I just trusted that the plan came to mind because of Scarlet's influence. Yet, she was dead and gone. My ploy might be nothing but vain hope in a phantom.

I cleared my throat and summoned an icy stare. "What are the rules?"

"Very simple. I believe the mirror is a window that is energized by spiritual power, and the catalyst is music. The dark energy I can create will make the mirror into a portal through which I can reach and gather all the life energy I want. I will feed on hundreds of souls and rebuild the Lucifer machine without the need of transforming the supplicants' energy or even traveling to your worlds.

"It is now clear to me that the power called Quattro was actually Scarlet using her sorcery through that cross-world corridor." He pointed at the mirror. "The danger is that if Scarlet's spirit still resides within, and I cannot reach her body, her power would likely kill me. But if I choose to shatter the mirror, I will destroy her soul and lose a powerful device for my future plans.

"Now, the choice is up to you. If you pick it up, my people will attack you. If Scarlet is in the mirror, she will come to your defense, and you can easily defeat them and escape. If she is not there, my people will kill you, and the mirror will be mine. On the other hand, if you leave the mirror with me, I will let you walk out of here to join your friends. If Scarlet is not within, I will kill hundreds, perhaps thousands of people with it. If she is, then she will destroy me, my brother will help you heal the wounds, and all your problems will be over."

I stared at the mirror. Every option seemed terrible, and the five minutes I gave Cerulean was probably ready to expire. If I wanted to join the others, I had to decide right away. "Let me get this straight. You're saying I can do whatever I want with the mirror, right?"

"Correct. Make your choice now. I don't wish to endure any dawdling."

I walked straight to the mirror, picked it up, and charged toward Mictar. I reared back and swung it at his face as hard as I could. The edge caught him square in the cheek, cut through his nose, and came out the other side. With a return swing, I bashed him in the head with the flat of the mirror, smashing the glass into hundreds of sparkling shards. Bleeding profusely, Mictar toppled and landed face first on the floor.

I kicked some of the shards at him. "How's that for a battle of wits?"

The ear-crushing sound of sonic paralyzers filled the air. I cringed, doubled over. A stream of words ran through my mind, song lyrics. Then a shout punctuated the final line. *Run!* I sprinted toward the line of stalkers. I opened my mouth to sing the lyrics, but Scarlet's voice burst from my throat.

> Begone you stalkers of the night!
> And flee the wrath that gives you flight.

The white-haired soldiers scattered, some dropping their rods as they retreated into the room's mist. I zoomed out the exit door, cut through the cloudbank, and burst into the open on the glassy walkway between rising columns of mist.

Well ahead, four human shapes appeared in the vapor-rich air — Cerulean with Abodah draped over his arms and Mom and Kelly standing next to him.

Just as I arrived, the phone beeped in Cerulean's pocket. I withdrew it and slid it into my own pocket. "Sorry I took so long," I said, trying to catch my breath.

"Did you give him the mirror?" Mom asked.

"In a way." I tried to smile, but my lips wouldn't turn. "I shattered it on his head. I don't think he'll be bothering us anytime soon."

Cerulean shifted Abodah higher. "What do we do with our blessed ally?"

"Is she dead?" I asked.

He nodded. "A traitor to her people, yet a savior for worlds she has never seen."

"I will take her," someone said.

The voice came from behind the mist in the direction opposite the stalkers' chamber. A tall white-haired man strode out from the cloud—Patar, his face grimmer than usual. As he approached, he extended his arms, making a cradle. "I can see my brother's handiwork," he said, his eyes fiery red. "Yet it seems that you have escaped his wrath."

As Cerulean passed Abodah's body to Patar, a dozen conflicting thoughts rushed through my mind—anger, sadness, revenge, bitterness, sympathy—all pushing through to be spoken, but, even though this was the same man who insisted that I kill Scarlet, I couldn't bear to say anything harsh. I just breathed out a quiet, "Where have you been?"

"I apologize for my late arrival. I was in the midst of the celestial fabric countering the Lucifer engine. If not for my song, the cosmos would have shattered."

"Yeah, I think I heard you." As the scent of roses again flowed, I nodded at him. "You have lost a mate. I have lost a beloved friend. I pray that their sacrifices will never be forgotten by the worlds they died to rescue."

"Well spoken, son of Solomon." A hint of wetness glinted in Patar's eyes. "You likely have little time to spare. Since the portal window is not set to a specific destination, you will need to be anointed. Then, you must go at once."

Cerulean leaned over the edge of the walkway on the opposite side of the portal chasm and scooped mist into his cupped hands. He straightened and extended his arms toward me. "This will mark you for travel to Earth Blue."

I dipped a finger into the mist and dabbed my forehead with the wetness. When everyone had been anointed, I grasped Mom's hand, then Kelly's, ignoring the pain. Turning back to Patar, I said, "Will I see you again?"

"It depends. You have seen for yourself the healing results of my counsel. You know what I expect you to do."

I looked at the two remaining supplicants. Amber, every bit as lovely and mysterious as Scarlet, caught my gaze. She folded her hands in front of her waist and gave me a smile that could melt the coldest heart. Cerulean's sapphire eyes sparkled. Somehow they revealed his spirit—as deep as Sarah's Womb, as honest as Scarlet's songs, and as selfless as Abodah's life-giving sacrifice.

Turning back to Patar, I gave him a nod. "I know what you expect. But I'm going to do everything I can to find another way."

"Then you will likely see me again." Without another word, Patar turned and walked away in the direction he had come.

As the stalker blended into the mist, a gentle pull turned me toward Mom. She raised my hand to her lips.

Then, with a soft kiss, she bathed my knuckles with her warm, moist breath. "There is a new song in your heart. I'm looking forward to seeing it lived out in our next journey."

Holding a crippled violin and a bow with several hairs flying loose, she gazed at me, her raven locks a frizzy mop, her skin pale and smudged, and her eyes sparkling with love. She no longer looked like the greatest violinist in the world. For now, the virtuoso performer had left the stage, and my loving mother had joined me in the audience.

I shifted my gaze to Kelly. With blood staining most of the front of her sweatshirt, obscuring the fierce cardinal logo across her chest, she was the image of the ultimate sacrificial lamb, and at the same time, a lion with a ferocious bite. Yet she was even more than that. In the beauty of undying, unquestioned love, she was like Scarlet in so many ways. Even better.

Now trembling, I edged toward the precipice, still holding Mom's and Kelly's hands. "Let's go."

The five of us leaped into the void. Darkness swallowed the light, but soon a blue path formed, a glowing ribbon that guided our fall. It split into hundreds of colors and painted a familiar scene, my Earth Blue bedroom, still strewn with mattress padding and pieces of the broken desk. Mom and Kelly materialized at my sides, then Cerulean and Amber.

Cerulean's body carried a thin, blue aura, as though he were coated with phosphorescent paint. Amber's complexion seemed normal for a fair-skinned blonde, though her hair and eyes glowed as if bathed in golden sunlight.

The matrix of mirrors still covered the wall, reflecting everyone in the room. Kelly shuffled toward it. Her injured shoulder drooped as she blinked at the images of three weary travelers and two radiant supplicants. "What now?" she asked.

I looked at Amber. "How do we get to the Earth Yellow dreamlands?"

The petite girl glided forward. Her smooth steps carried her body as if she were a princess, though her simple garments labeled her a pauper. "We must locate a portal viewer there, one that belongs to the Earth Yellow realm."

"A portal viewer?" Kelly repeated.

Amber touched one of the mirror squares on the wall. "The device you call a Quattro mirror. When we obtain the correct square, I will tell you what we must do, but we will have to find the gifted one born on Earth Yellow. The one for whom I supplicate is accustomed to exploring dreams, so she is ready and able to help us."

"Do you mean Francesca?" I asked.

Amber glided to Mom and caressed her cheek. "Yes, my beloved Francesca, the Earth Yellow counterpart of this beautiful lady, is the gifted one."

I smiled. "We spent quite a bit of time with her, Mom. I didn't know you had so much spunk when you were younger."

"Spunk?" She laughed. "Maybe I've grown old too fast. I think I need to show my son a little more of my old self." She delivered a mock punch to my cheek. "If it's spunk you want, it's spunk you'll get, especially since we might have to move heaven and two or three earths to find my husband."

I winked and withdrew Nathan Blue's cell phone. "We'd better get going."

"Calling Daryl?" Kelly asked.

"If she's still there." I read the display. The phone had service, but just barely.

I pushed a speed dial and waited. After two rings, a stressed-out voice punched through the earpiece. "Nathan! Where have you been? Do you have any idea what's going on here?"

"Not really. But we managed to save the world."

"Not this one, honey. It's snowing in the Congo, a hurricane struck Antarctica, and the Mississippi River is jammed with ice from Minneapolis to New Orleans. We might be getting Earth Yellow's weather, but we're getting it in all the wrong places. And Tony says Earth Yellow is in chaos, too. He—"

"Tell me later. Listen, are you still in touch with Earth Red?"

Daryl groaned. "That's another problem. We have radio telescope contact, but no visual. The frequency has been changing, but it was slow enough for Dr. Gordon and me to keep up with it. Everything's peachy now on Earth Red, but I think we're drifting apart."

"Is it still possible to get home? Earth Yellow is our first stop, but we have to be sure we can make the jump when we get done there."

Daryl's voice crackled over the fading connection. "Maybe, but we might need to click Dorothy's ruby slippers together to make it work. Dr. Gordon and I will experiment. We'll try to come up with something by the time you get here."

"Well, you don't have to worry about Mictar for a while. Scarlet and I kicked his butt back in the misty world, so you should have clear sailing. At least you can be glad of that."

"Glad? Great. Now you're Pollyanna high on testosterone. If you could beam up Mr. Spock instead, I'd appreciate it."

I grinned. "We don't need a Vulcan to solve the problem. If anyone can figure it out, you can."

"Thanks, Captain Kirk, but now I'd better change out of this red shirt. And don't forget your buddies back home."

"You should hear from us soon. Everything happens so fast on Earth Yellow, maybe it'll only be a few minutes for you. Talk to you later."

I terminated the call and looked at my traveling companions. Light from the window shrouded all four in the failing glow of sunset. Mom sat on the mattress with Kelly, stretching back her sweatshirt and peeling away her blood-soaked bandage. Cerulean and Amber whispered to one another, their eyes shining brighter than ever.

Kelly looked up at me, smiling and wincing at the same time. With her hair in disarray, a gash still marking her brow, and blood splattered from her chin down to her hands, she was a mess … a beautiful mess.

My lips trembled, but I managed to return her smile. The scent of roses again washed over my senses. I leaned close to Kelly, close enough to hear her pain-filled, shallow breaths.

I whisper-sang Scarlet's prophetic good-bye.

A day will come when love mature
Will take the hand of one made pure
In everlasting song and dance,
A knight, a lady, sweet romance.

When I finished, I touched her bloodstained cheek, still whispering. "How long can your lonely heart wait?"

Kelly laid her hand over mine, tears sparkling in her glazed eyes. "As long as it takes, Nathan Shepherd. As long as it takes."